Waterline

By the same author

God's Own Country

Waterline

ROSS RAISIN

HarperCollins*Publishers*Ltd

Published by HarperCollins Publishers Ltd

Originally published in the United Kingdom by Viking,
an imprint of Penguin Books: 2011
First published in Canada by HarperCollins Publishers Ltd.
in this original trade paperback edition: 2012

HarperCollins Publishers Ltd
2 Bloor Street East, 20th Floor
Toronto, Ontario, Canada
M4W 1A8

www.harpercollins.ca

Library and Archives Canada Cataloguing in Publication
Raisin, Ross
Waterline / Ross Raisin.

ISBN 978-1-44340-899-8

I. Title.
PR6118.A38W38 2012   823'.92   C2011-905789-1

Author photo: Anne Tipton
Typeset by Jouve (UK), Milton Keynes
Printed and bound in the United States
RRD 9 8 7 6 5 4 3 2 1

I

One here, a soft fog of flowers painted on the front.

There's plenty more like that, plus as well the wild flower kinds. Meadows. Bustling hedgerows. A woodland clearing mobbed with bluebells. Hard to imagine there's this many types of card in the supermarket. A churchyard, quiet and peaceful with brown leaves blowing about. A teddy bear. And another here that's for some reason a cat gazing out the window at a sea view.

It's Robbie that wanted to put the cards up. He wasn't much wanting to do it himself, but Robbie had dug the heels in. What else are you going to do with them? Stick them in a drawer? Leave them lying on the counter with the funeral programmes and the electric bills? So now the pair of them are in the corridor, fixing them up to the red ribbon that Robbie's fished out from the Christmas cardboard box. The light dimming in the front door. Dull laughter from the living room, where the rest of them are sat watching the television.

'You know all these people, Da?'

'No really, being honest. There were some the day even, I don't know who they were. A few would've been from the department store. And then the family, course.' He nods at the living room wall. 'I preferred no to ask.'

Robbie is reading inside a card. 'They could've introduced themselves,' he says, closing the card and pegging it with a red plastic Christmas tree. It's normally the wife does this, getting up the greetings cards. This same red ribbon drooping off the pictures about the living room; pinned-up spruce as launch bunting around a ship, dutifully awaiting the chop from whichever of the wee begrudging women of the royalty have been sent up.

There's going to be too many cards will fit in the lobby and corridor. Robbie asks will they get up the rest in the living room when Alan and Lynn are away to their bed. No, he tells him. He isn't having

I

these cards all about the room when Robbie and Craig are sleeping in there. No that it makes a great deal of sense but. When everything else in the room is some kind of reminder. Fact is, if you start taking down all the things in the place that are fingered with memories, then that's the whole house emptied.

Dear Mick,

Words don't say enough. If there's anything we can do, please let us know. All our thoughts are with you the now.

Love from Derek and Jean and all the family

One thing you can be sure, it's the women that have written them. Nay chance any of this coming from the husbands. All our thoughts are with you the now. No that it should be but, no that it should be. It was the same story earlier: the women all hats and hands and kind words while the husbands stood in beside them, cloyed up. He would've been the same but. No denying it. Silent, listening politely while Cathy said everything that was needed. These were men like him, guys he'd worked with, easier with steel sparks showering on top their head and their mate pattering bullshit in their ear. You can't blame them. As natural to them, a funeral, as redundancy. And the response aye the same: straight to the bar, boys.

'I was talking to Claire,' Robbie says. 'You know, was with Maw at the store?'

'I mind her, aye.'

'She was saying how bad they all took it when they heard. Says the place hasn't been the same the last year.' He looks round at the living room door and says in a quieter voice, 'She couldn't understand Lynn's stupid finger food either. Serious, what was all that about?'

'I missed out on it.' He takes a peg from the box and looks up at Robbie. 'They're trying to help, Rob, that's all.'

'Come off it, Da. Mozzarella fucking parcels? In the Empress? Fuck off. There was a whole black bag left afterwards at their end of the table.'

True enough. He'd actually watched Desmond clearing it out

afterwards, when everyone had went. A quick sniff and a nibble of Lynn's various parcels, weighing up the resale possibilities, before dumping them in the bag.

Mick had kept himself in with the main group, huckled together at one end of the spread by the sausage rolls and the cheese sandwiches, Robbie and his wife either side of him like a pair of minders. Craig keeping to himself, away in a corner. Truth be told, he wouldn't've objected trying one of Lynn's mozzarella parcels, but it would have meant going over the other side of the table, where Alan and Lynn were holding court with the rest of Cathy's family. Most of they lot he hadn't even seen since the wedding; so you're talking thirty-five years ago. And that's the ones that came. Some of these he'd probably never clapped eyes on in his life. He'd gave a bye to the idea of going over. Leave that lot to themselves, he thought.

It was only the weans, scooting about the place, who moved between the two groups. And the brother-in-law, of course. Man of the people Alan there, he didn't miss his opportunity to introduce himself. Heartfelt greetings to the ones he knew – quite a few of them from back in the day in the yards – never mind it was him who'd bloody laid them off. Christsake. Smiling away there. No hard feelings, eh? We didn't want to do it but see that was the times, there was no choice.

Mick had made sure to keep his distance. Took himself away for a pee when it looked one moment Alan was coming over to speak to him. When he'd closed the lavvy door behind, he saw that Desmond had gave a proper clean in there. There were toilet rolls stacked in the windowsill, and he'd moved the rotten rolled carpet that used to be outside the window. The blockages cleared from the urinals. A few extra pineapple-soap chunks. Strange how it goes but that was probably the only moment all day when he was close to greeting, when he saw that. He stood there a moment after he'd finished peeing and for a few seconds just, something got hold of him and it was an effort to stop the tears coming on. This pure strong feeling that you could only describe as utter gratefulness toward the guy because he'd cleaned out his toilets.

When he came back out, the brother-in-law had moved away, his big broad shape over on the other side of the room, doing the rounds. He was like a politician. Getting into the group at the bar, shaking hands, making sure everybody knew it was him had paid for it all.

Robbie is looking at him. 'It wasn't on either' – he jerks his head at the wall – 'that speech of his.'

Mick doesn't respond. He pegs up another card, overlapping them as they get near the end of the corridor.

'He barely mentioned you. Craig and me, sure, but anybody could've listened to that and thought you and Maw had never met – that she'd lived her whole life up in the Highlands with the sons of fucking lairds chasing after her. She'd have skelped him, if she'd heard it.'

He goes in the box for one of the last tree pegs. He isn't getting into this the now. No with the guy sat there in the next room. He keeps quiet, and the two of them get on with the job in silence a while.

'Sorry, Da, I don't mean it like that. It's just, mean, he's a bloody blowhard.'

'Robbie.'

'I know, sorry.'

They have done along both sides of the corridor. There is a small stretch just, by the living room door, left to fill.

'I'll put these up in the kitchen somewhere,' Robbie says, holding up his last handful. He walks off, and Mick stands a few seconds looking down the two lines of cards. The sound of the television gets louder, fades away again. There are two cards next to each other, he notices, identical. Foggy flowers in a vase. Intrigued a moment, he steps forward to get a look who they're from.

Pete and Mary; Don and Sheila. He must have opened these cards himself sometime over the last few days, but he hadn't took full notice of the names. Both couples were there the day. There hadn't been much chance to talk but it was good to see them. Familiar faces. The men bloodshot and bald the now but aye familiar. He sees Pete now and then because they stay no that far away still, but Don, he couldn't have seen him in twenty years. Twenty-one, in fact. He can mind fine well actually the last time he saw him: they were in the Empress, the same stools they'd been stuck to for months, fuck this, fuck that, fuck the brother-in-law, fuck Thatcher, fuck the dunny money, bastards. But they'd took their dunny money and by then they'd drunk most of it, and the last he saw of Don he was steamboats and drawling how him and the wife were moving out of the city. They were back the now, they told him. Found themselves a nice done-up flat in a tenement in Drumoyne, where the landlord wasn't quite the robber their last one was.

The wives must have read about Cathy in the *Southside News*. Went to the Co and plumped for the same card. He imagines Mary and Sheila going in for it, putting it on the counter with a paper, pack of fags, Lotto ticket.

He gives Pete and Mary's card a read:

Mick,

We were so very sorry to hear about Cathy. She was such a wee gem. I still mind fine well the launch days and the pair of us dressed up in our finest, and you and Pete three sheets to the wind! Pete is working on the crane at the old John Brown yard at the moment, of all places. I know the last year must have been very hard on you and the family, Mick. If there's anything at all we can do,

All our best,
Pete and Mary

He smiles. She does go on, Mary. He puts the card back up on the ribbon. He's heard about the crane. Turned into a visitor centre. He's seen it lit up pink and red at night a couple of times when he's been over near Clydebank. The last he knew, they were talking about putting a restaurant in the jib and making it revolve. He'd read that in the paper. It was part of a project to represent the industrial heritage of the area. A revolving pink restaurant. You've got to wonder how they dream these things up. And see the view? That's one thing for starters they'll have to change. All very well getting the full panorama but if all you're looking out on is a puddled wasteland every direction – gangs of weans playing football and smoking, pigeons roosting and crapping over the rusted fabrication sheds – it isn't going to make your mozzarella parcels taste much the better, is it?

In the kitchen Robbie has put up the cards on top of the micro-wave. He takes the last lot out of Mick's hand and arranges them in with the others. Through the wall, next door's baby is wailing. Mick leans against the counter and looks out the window at the back garden, the tubs of flowers that have gone thin and yellow, overgrown.

'Don't feel ye've got to stay, Robbie,' he says.

'We'll stay as long as we can, it's no bother. Anyway, Christ, we've come that far, there's no point us leaving yet.'

'I know that. But Jenna will want to get back soon. It's no right spending too long away when they're that age.'

'He's fine at his grannie's. Knowing Jenna's maw, she's probably teaching him how to make homebrew or go tracking through the bush.' He balances the last card on top of the microwave. 'Anyway, we're not leaving you on your own with the Highlanders.' He is grinning. 'How long do they plan stopping, you know?'

He's about to tell him he isn't sure, they haven't said, but just then the sound of the television comes loudly from the corridor. There are footsteps, which pause a moment, then continue toward the kitchen. Craig comes in the room without speaking or looking at either of them, and opens the fridge. He crouches, looking inside the door, but he obvious can't find what he wants and starts moving aside the packs of sausages on the bottom shelf.

'After a beer, son?'

He doesn't reply. Keeps looking, next shelf up.

'They're in the carrier on the side here, if ye are.'

He gets up, giving a quick look at the cards on the microwave. Then he goes for a can out of the bag over by where Robbie is standing.

'Thanks,' he says, snapping the can open as he leaves the room.

He wakes and looks out the window at the dark. A few wee lights on in a few distant multis. It's awful warm but. He considers a moment getting out of the bed to open a window, and stays a while trying to work up the energy to go do it, but in the end he gives it a miss and stays put where he is. Ye buried the wife today. She died, and ye buried her. Somehow it's no registering. He repeats it to himself a few times, but it's as though the words don't make sense, he can't get understanding them. What he feels instead is the same as he felt the day last week the hospital telephoned to say she'd passed away. Relief, is what it is. It is a relief the funeral's over, that it's went off okay; Craig didn't put the mix in; he doesn't have to talk to Alan about arrangements any more. He doesn't have to imagine her in another bed somewhere while he's lying here. Course there's other things he could be imagining but they're so far off seeming real they're out in fucking hyperspace. He turns over, sticky, heavy and sticky. It was hot the day too. Obvious enough they were all sweaty and tickling in their hats and their suits, but what can you do – it's a funeral.

He kept off saying it earlier, but he's really hoping Robbie and Jenna will stay a while longer before they disappear back to Australia. That he won't be left alone with these more testy elements of the household. Although surely the Highlanders won't be here much longer. There's nothing for them to do now that the funeral is over, and there's nay danger Lynn is wanting to stop around enjoying the luxuries. Craig – that's another story. And not one that he's too keen sharing, that's clear enough. He's here the now because Robbie's told him he has to be here, and probably he'll be away as soon as Robbie's gone. No that Yoker is the other side of the world, but the way he's acting it's fine well possible that it'll be Robbie that's back here again first. He needs to talk with him. Go for a drink. Find out what's going on in that brainbox of his. They both of them need to do that. And if they do, maybe best for his own part swerving the fact he's no greeted once since she died; that all he can think is: it's a relief, and when are all of these lot going to get out of the house.

2

The multis stand solid in a row like a picket line, looking down over the red tenement streets filing toward the Clyde. From up on the seventeenth storey, the view's a beauty. You can see the glimmering glass roof of the Botanical Gardens north of the river. Kelvingrove Park. The Exhibition Centre's silver armadillo. And further on, the skyline of the Campsie Fells, keeping the city in. Joe doesn't much look out at these things though. If he's looking out, it'll be at Ibrox. The ground's a few minutes' walk from the multi just. On match days, he can see the supporters coming in from all around, crowds growing on the pavements outside the pubs, pouring in through the streets.

This morning but he's having a see out the window as the sun comes up. Watching the dismal light peter in through the streets that run straight lines toward the river, bending only where they have to go around the stadium, or broken where they've took out the tenements and no got round to replacing them. By the river, there's the twinkling new apartment blocks at Glasgow Harbour, the dry ski centre, and down the water, the shipyards, what's left of them. Govan, this near side; Scotstoun, across the water. From where he is, he can just make out the top of HMS *Defender*, sat at her berth at Govan. She looks from up here like an Airfix model, with her miniature gun and helicopter pad on the flight deck. That's where Joe is headed, the light nearly up now and him away out the flat, clicking shut the front door to go pick up Suggie.

It is six o'clock. There's never anybody about in the building now except for one queer old ticket he sees on the stair sometimes, who gets up to give his dog a walk. It isn't so bad, this time in the morning. He's tired, but it's fine. The back shift is the one that kills him. He presses the button and the lift doors are straight open. They cleaned it out a week or two ago, so it's no bogging like it was, but it's been wrote on already. CUNT, one wall says, nice and simple. He gets out on the ninth floor and goes toward Suggie's.

He chaps the door. There's a light on underneath. A good sign. He's tired enough himself this time the morning, but he's pure sparkling compared to Suggie. There's times he'll be banging five minutes before there's any answer, and a couple of mornings he's resorted to giving it a wee clang with the fire extinguisher off the wall fixing. The door's looked better, in truth. Today though Suggie opens it on the second knock. He's in his pants still, but he's up.

'Come in, mate.'

Joe follows him in and sits on the settee while Suggie goes in the bedroom to get dressed. The television is on and he looks at it without paying much attention. There's a fair number of empty cans about, on the table, over the floor. Suggie must've had some mates round. No the less, he's dressed quick enough, appearing at the bedroom door in a couple of minutes, red eyes, grinning, his yellow helmet in his hand.

'Right, we off, well?'

Once onto the street the two apprentices get making their way briskly through the crisp cool morning toward the yard. They go over Saturday's match again, a couple of times, but most of the way they walk without talking. The roads are near deserted. A few cars. The old boy from their block, coming back with his dog. They give him a nod.

It wasn't always like this, course. Their fathers and their grandfathers have shown them enough photographs – photographs there's plenty of in the grand crumbling library they are walking past now – how it used to be. These same streets a hundred years ago, sixty, forty even, mobbed with hundreds of workers starting out for the day shift. Tired and quiet, like this pair, getting moving. The noise of boots on the road, the hooter about to sound up the way and signal the start of work. The occasional wife in a tenement window in her nightdress, watching her man off, and him finding his way into his own team, grouping up as they move on – riveters, caulkers, blacksmiths, the welders clear visible in their spotted hats and their leathers, boilermakers, platers – the whole black squad marching on up the road. And at the back, the apprentices, pishing about.

A different story the now. Two lads in blue overalls walking through the empty streets like a pair of convicts who've just survived the end of the world; passing by the primary school, the park, the red-stone tenements, and the terraces of grey pebble-dash houses with their wee patches of front garden.

One of these, the grass growing longer than its neighbours, has a great flash Saab parked bold as day out the front. Inside, Mick is listening to the brother-in-law snoring loudly through the wall. He's put them in the boys' old room, so they will be lying there asleep across the way from each other, the two beds having been pushed years ago as far apart as possible. The sound he's making, Alan must be on this side closest to himself. If there'd been anywhere else to put them, he'd have put them there, but there wasn't, simple as that. So they'll have to put up with it just, staying in a weans' room. Nothing has changed in there since Robbie was eighteen and he moved to Australia – it'd hardly changed in fact for a long time before that – the opposing walls still covered with football stickers and Blu-Tack scabs, a great worn circle of carpet between the two beds, faded from years of board games and fighting.

He turns over, toward the window. The snoring unrelenting. Christsake. The man can't keep quiet even when he's asleep.

Down the stair in the living room, Robbie will be slumbering on the floor with an arm curled around the wife. They are on a pile of stale brown blankets Robbie found from somewhere. No that they two mind. They don't. They're fine. On the other side of the room the older brother lying there in his sleeping bag and his legs poking out from the end of the settee. Thinking his thoughts. Thinking his thoughts and keeping the lot of them to himself.

The truth is, it is good of the Highlanders to have come. They could have drove down for the funeral and then been away back to their lochside and their mighty brick stronghold and that would've been that, never to be seen again. They don't have to be here. It is Alan's choice that they are. That's obvious enough, the way she pin-pricks around the house. The peeved squeezed eyeballs every time she gets inspecting a piece of cutlery or a glass out the cupboard. Go on, well, Lynn, what is it ye think, eh? Because ye're no making it quite clear enough with the subtle facial movements there. Ye think it's a dump, eh? Well go on, then, and get to fuck why don't ye?

The snoring has stopped. For a few minutes, the house is peaceful. A thin shaft of light is through the curtains, falling on the carpet at the bottom of the bed. After a while though, the snoring starts up again, quiet at first, then gaining force. See another way you could look at it: he's retired a long while the now, so an event like this isn't exactly getting in the way of things for them. They can make space for times like this. Births, deaths, the graduation of the miraculous son, no able sadly to make it yesterday because he's over in America, making his millions, how lovely for him.

As well, their summer holiday is by. A trip to France this year, cycling round the vineyards and taking photos of each other in food markets examining the local sausagemeats. He shouldn't be so hard on them. It can't be easy of course for the brother-in-law either, let's no forget, the responsibility he's got to shoulder. The responsibility he's aye got to shoulder.

Mick gets out of bed. It's early still and everyone else will be asleep, but he goes in the bathroom to wash his face, puts on a short-sleeve shirt and trousers, and steps down to the kitchen. He checks in the cupboard to see if there's any bread left, but it's been finished, so he closes the cupboard door and sits down at the table, looking out the window, where a wee disappointed sparrow is hopping about the grass wondering how there's nay food put out for him these days.

So this is grief, well. Sat at the kitchen table with all your joys and your miseries sleeping and snoring about you and you sat there wondering what to do for your breakfast. Maybe it's by, maybe that's it, he's gone through ten months already and the moment when she's dead actually marks the end of it because she's gone now, she's no laid there dying in front of him one day to the next. It's over. He'd greeted back then, alright, when they'd been told. On his own, or the pair of them together sat clutching to each other at this same table. That day the doctor phoned them up and asked could they both please come in to see him. The X-ray results were returned. It wasn't her back. Pleural mesothelioma. A total white-out of her left lung. A year, maybe, at the most. He closes the eyes and tries picturing her, her face, before that, while she looked healthy still. It's a blank but, the brain doesn't want to go there, so he sits with the eyes closed just. A moment of peace. You keep on. What else can you do? You keep on.

Down on the floor by the bin he notices a box of cereal. He picks it up, gets himself a bowl and shakes out the last flakes and the sawdust from the bag inside. The Highlanders are going the messages later, they announced last night, so there will be plenty enough food for them all soon enough, even the wee chap outside, given up and flown off the now. It'll be organic, course, but such is life, eh. Him and the sparrow aren't complaining.

Above his head, somebody is walking about. He puts the box back by the bin and gets the kettle on, returns to his seat at the table. And again, the same thought that keeps coming back: he is alive. He's the picture of bloody health sat at the kitchen table. The floor creaks again above his head. And no just him as well, still alive.

That evening they all sit in the living room with the television on, eating the spaghetti Bolognese that Lynn has made. Everybody agrees it is good and tasty, except for Lynn, who says it should have garlic and it should have tomato purée and it should have whatever else in it. She hadn't thought to get these things when she was in the supermarket. If she'd known there was none in the house she would have bought them. She isn't acting it there; they've bought no end of other unnecessary stuff. Parmesan, wine vinegar, three different kinds of bread. It must have cost a fortune. When they arrived back and got everybody outside helping unload the dozens of carriers from the boot, he and Robbie gave each other a look over the top of the car, the meaning of which was clear enough. How long do they think they're staying? They then proceeded to organize the putting away of the messages, cheerily deciding what was to go where, chucking out whatever dregs or no-good-enoughs were already on the shelves, as if by buying in all this better class of groceries, the kitchen was now theirs to do with as they wished.

The news is on. They sit watching and eating in quiet. It is the fifth night now Robbie and Jenna have brought through the chairs from the kitchen so they can all be in here, and they are in the habit already of keeping to the same seats. Alan and Lynn take the settee and, opposite, Mick sits between Robbie and his wife, the three of them sat close together like a row of naughty schoolweans sent to the headmaster's office. Craig is over in the armchair by the window, the head down, concentrating on his plate.

'It's some place now, the shopping centre at Braehead,' says Alan, setting his empty plate on the carpet in front of him. 'All new stores since we were last down there.'

The three of them look up and agree.

'I suppose it will be,' Mick says. 'I never go.'

'It's a great M&S,' says Lynn. 'Two levels, and a decent café. We stopped in for a sandwich when we'd done. And there's a dry ski slope down there now, I couldn't believe it. You should go over there and take a look, Mick.'

The weather comes on. It has been record temperatures for August, the guy says, and September is going to continue the same. Mick minds the time Cathy went down to the M&S, and what she'd thought about it, coming home with a single carrier of potatoes and mince. She wasn't impressed. It's too bloody expensive, was the verdict.

'You've seen the new apartments at Glasgow Harbour as well, have you?' Robbie says after a while, looking at Lynn.

'Yes. You pointed them out, didn't you, Alan? Very modern. About time they made more use out of all those dead areas along the river.'

'You think?' Robbie says, putting in a mouthful of Bolognese.

'I do,' Jenna breaks in, likely sensing Robbie's mood. 'Better developing than leaving it a wasteland.'

'There you are, then, Da. You should get one. You could have a wee balcony to sit on and look out over the water.'

Jenna gives Robbie a look, which because they are sat so close is right in Mick's face.

'There's no point leaving it to decay like it has been. Those cranes, and the berths all crumbling. It's not safe, for one thing. You're just being a mule, Robbie, you know it.'

He is feeling uncomfortable, these two starting to argue around him. He gets off his seat. Plus he needs to go up and check how much is in his wallet, to give toward the messages. As he leaves, he starts picking up the empty plates from the floor. Jenna is immediately helping him, reaching down for the Highlanders' plates before he has the chance. Maybe it isn't on purpose, but you never know. She's sensitive to things, Jenna; she knows the score.

In the kitchen they stack the plates by the sink. They're about to turn and go out when she presses her hand gently on top of his on the counter.

'You're pretty quiet today, Mick. How are you?'

'Coping on, I suppose.'

She smiles. 'It can't be easy, not when there's' – she raises the eyebrows a little – 'a houseful.'

He feels awkward, their hands touching there like that. Guilty, somehow, daft as it is.

'You shouldn't feel afraid to talk to these boys, you know. Even Craig. He's grieving, that's why he's being like he is.'

He tries to smile. She's a good girl, Jenna. Cathy was aye fond of her. She's down the line, is what it is. Honest. She's like Robbie that way, only less of the argle-bargle tendencies.

'It isnae that simple. He blames me.'

'He shouldn't. He's being selfish.'

'Aye, well. Maybe.' He looks away down the corridor. 'He keeps it inside himself. It was his maw he talked to.'

'Bulldust. You're here. And Robbie. He can talk to you.'

She takes her hand away.

'Come on,' she says, 'let's see how the party's going.'

'Okay. I'll be through in a moment, I'm going the toilet just.'

He goes upstairs to the bedroom. A ten-pound note, plus a bit of smash, it's all he's got on his tail. He can't offer that. If he gets up early again in the morning, maybe, he can nick out to the cash machine before any the rest of them are up. See what's in the account, then give Alan his share when he gets back. He'll tell him later the night that's what he's doing.

It's no exactly cheery, the mood in the living room. They're all sat there in the same positions, the television noisily on in the corner. It's like walking into a hospital waiting room, a bunch of edgy strangers pretending they're interested in the telly adverts – see maybe what he should do is bring in some old magazines for them to have a rummle through, distract themselves with the horoscopes and out-of-date TV listings.

He takes his seat. Looks around the room. Jesus. How long is this going to go on?

Jenna speaks. 'When are you back at the garage, Craig?'

They all turn to look at him. He keeps his eyes on the television. 'Don't know yet. Couple days. Depends how much is booked in.'

'Will you stay here or go back to your flat?'

'Go back. Too far to travel in from here.'

She doesn't push him. That's clear enough all he's going to say on the subject, and the room is silent again as they get back to their television watching. A quiz show. Two families in Englandshire competing one against the other for the incredible cash prize. A bald proud uncle with the spotlight on him now, chosen as the family expert on geography matters. A bit of patter with the show host as the countdown appears in the corner of the screen. Are you feeling confident? he gets asked. He is. It's his favourite category on the *Trivial Pursuits* at Christmas. Wee smiles along the family row.

It is the television that has become the centre of their movements. Up until yesterday it was Cathy. Her bed on the ward, when it had just been Robbie and Jenna here in the house, and then when she went, the arrival of the Highlanders and all the funeral arrangements to be sorted: undertakers, cemetery, wake spread; GP, register office, council. Now that it's all finished though, there's nothing for them to do but stick the TV on. Fact is, if it was to stop working they would be royally fucked. Or go home, maybe. He gives a keek over at Craig. He's sat with the arms folded, no expression, just staring. Don't come near me, is what he's saying. Don't come near me or I'll stiffen ye. He needs to get a moment to speak to him, Jenna is right about that. He'll be away without a word otherwise and then Christ knows what happens after that. Silence, probably.

He has brought it on himself but, he knows it fine well. No like he's made such a big effort to talk to the boy; ever, actually. All they years of sitting in the living room when Craig's come round to visit, leaving him and his maw to have their patter in the kitchen. It adds up sooner than you'd think, all that time. You start no to see that she's the one holding it together, and that without her, what kind of a relationship is there between you? Plus as well the boy as good as thinks that he killed her, which could prove a wee conversational stumbling block.

Alan gets up, asking if anybody is wanting anything from the kitchen. He goes out the room, quietly shutting the door behind him. In a moment – during which the bald uncle gets the spotlight took off him having pure disgraced himself as the family expert on geography matters – Mick follows him. He steps in the lobby just as Lynn is reminding everybody that she had known two of the answers.

Alan is bent inside the fridge. Mick comes in the room and he glances up at him as he pulls out a bottle of wine and sticks it on the counter.

'Would you like a glass, Mick?'

'I'm okay, thanks. No much of a wine drinker.' He stays by the counter, shuffling the great dump of post into more of a tidy pile.

Alan fetches himself a glass from the cupboard, pulls open a drawer for the corkscrew and gets opening his wine. Mick loiters over in the corner. He feels like a bloody houseguest. Alan takes a sip of wine and puts the bottle back in the fridge.

'You get to many Rangers games these days, Mick?'

'No much. Cathy being ill, it's –'

'No, sorry, I don't imagine you have.'

He has another drink of his wine. Mick fingers the envelopes. In truth, it's almost ten years, after Robbie left, since he was going to the games. And as well the season ticket increases. He slots the post in by the mini television. That's another thing will need seeing to before long. Brown envelopes. Some of these are from the same senders. Council. Housing Association. Her name is still on most of them. What happens about that, well? Is it the register office that wires it to all the relevant parties? Your computer tells my computer that such and such is to be wiped from the account. See the way it is with these bastards though, you more likely have to tell them yourself. Ten minutes waiting on the line to tell some poor bored hen in a call centre in East Kilbride that you want to advise a change in circumstances: I'm just ringing up to inform ye that my wife's died. Duly noted, Mr Little, I'll log it in the system for you.

Alan is staring away into the dark outside the window, drinking his wine. Then he turns round to him.

'How's work these days?'

There's a genuine unexpected topic of conversation between the two of them.

'It's a while since I've been driving, actually.'

'When do you think you might go back?'

'Well, I don't know. Soon enough. They said take as long as I want.'

'That's good of them.'

'Well. See they're no too busy.'

He should have said about the money earlier. Quick and simple.

'You know, Mick, you mustn't think that Cathy's family aren't here for you. They are. It's been hard for everybody.'

'I'm sure it has.'

'It's a really tough blow.' He makes it sound like a post office closure. 'You know any time you want to come up and stay at ours you're more than welcome. Have some dinner. Go out on the boat.'

'Right, thanks.'

Alan is stroking the stem of his wine glass. He turns again to look out at the small crap garden.

'Look, all this shopping,' Mick begins. 'Will ye let me give you something for it?'

Alan turns toward him. 'No, Mick, you don't need to.'

'No, I will. I won't have us not paying our way.' He glances up the corridor to the living room door, as though he's been sent to represent the others, the family shop steward.

'I won't take it. It came to a lot, anyway. I wouldn't want you to.'

'Wait here a moment just, will ye?' He leaves Alan fingering his wine glass while he goes from the room.

When he returns, Alan is stood where he was.

'Here.' He holds out the crumpled tenner. 'I'm going the cash machine in the morning, but here's this for now.'

The brother-in-law looks at the note a moment. 'Okay, then, Mick.' With a slow movement, he takes it from him. 'Thank you.'

He puts his glass down on the side and takes his wallet out the trouser pocket. As he flips it open, slipping the note in the back, there's an identity card, the top of his head poking out of one of the slots. A company card. How's he still carrying one of those? He's retired more than five years now. They must have kept him on, well – a consultant or something. An adviser. What I advise you is this: we've no enough orders for new ships and the yard isn't making enough profit, so get out the dunny money packets and lay the buggers off.

He is picking up his glass, and walks by Mick to the door. 'There's beers in the fridge if you want one,' he says over the shoulder.

Mick watches him away, the cards down the corridor flapping in the draught as his great back moves past them.

He stays in the kitchen a while, staring down toward the lobby. Then he opens the fridge and gets out a can. He drinks half of it in a single drain. Puts it down and wipes his lips.

Wanker.

3

It is hot and he can't sleep. The alarm clock across the way getting on for three o'clock. It's been pure stifling like this the last few nights and by now the heat is gathered in the upstairs rooms, no wind to blow it out. Earlier, Robbie and Jenna had went for a bit of air before bed, and came back saying it's near as muggy outside as it is in. Then Craig went out too, on his own, as he'd done the other nights. To the pub; you could smell it on him when he got back in. Mick had waited up after the others were away to their beds, but Craig was later back than usual, and in the end he decided it felt the wrong moment and he gave it a swerve.

He gets up and opens the other window. No difference. He leaves it open anyway and climbs back in the bed. She wouldn't've let him have it open. Breeze or no breeze. She hated a chill that much, grumbling on next to him with the covers pulled up to her chin, cauled tight around her. A soft familiar lump there in the bed. He stares at the alarm clock, waiting for the minute to switch over. This room, it's no like the other rooms. She has a say here still: the mirror with its collection of receipts and holiday competition cuttings wedged in the frame; the clutter of magazines by the wall; the electric heater on the other side of the bed with its broken outer bars.

He gets up again and goes out the room, needing the toilet. Afterwards, he goes down into the kitchen, where he turns the mini television on quiet, sits down at the table. Another quiz show. A young girl hosting it. She's got on this lunatic smile as she picks up the phone, waiting for the caller to guess the blank. The first word is *Iron*. The guy on the line seems pretty sure he's got it. '*Statue*,' he says. The girl turns to look at the giant screen behind her in mock excitement. 'Let's see if it's there . . . No!' She slaps her thigh. 'Not this time, Terry.'

It's fair obvious the people ringing up to do this at half three in the morning are either blootered or they're no the full ticket. The next one, a shrill woman called Christie, could be either way. 'Is it *board*?' she asks. It isn't. 'Unlucky, Christie. Better luck next time.' There is what looks like a flicker of desperation on the girl's face. I hope they pay ye well for this, hen. He turns it off and gets up to go back to bed.

3.54. The alarm clock, that's her as well. She'd got it years ago with his saved-up petrol coupons from the cab. He knocked it on the floor a couple of days ago when he was tidying up the things on her table, and the plug came out. Setting the time and date again proved a complete impossibility – he's never all these years figured out how the thing works – and so for the past two nights the alarm has come on at some point in the early hours. Both times, it took him bloody ages working out which button shuts it up, and then he spent what was left of last night finally fixing it out: time, date, bastard thing. No that he was that put out, in truth. He was awake anyway.

He moves himself over the other side of the bed. He may as well have stayed put in the kitchen. Given a call in to the show. *Iron Age. Iron Lady.* A look of pure relief on the girl that she's no the only sane person up the night. Down there in the kitchen, the living room too, the things are things just, she isn't present in them. Hard to say how that is when it's her that bought most of it but that's how it feels, unlike up here in this room. He's surrounded by her here, but he isn't a part of it himself. It is strange, the other side of the bed. Unknown lumps and bumps of wiring poking up at the mattress. He's got a queer awareness of what it would have felt like for her, on her side. He lies a while longer, staring at the alarm clock, until, at the back of five, he gets out of bed and lays down on the floor next to it, pulling the covers down over him.

There is a toilet roll under the bed. A pair of broken sunglasses. He should give a clean under there, he gets thinking as finally he starts to drift off. Add that to the list.

4

A cemetery worker is busy sweeping along a flagstone path, collecting up the dirt into a wheelbarrow. He has seen the man there by his wife's grave each of the last few days: he comes in the morning and stands there a long time, staring down at the ground. Obvious that he's having a hard time of it, and so he makes sure to keep his distance now as he gets about clearing the path and tidying the area around a plot he's to measure and mark later the morning.

He has seen the rest of the family here as well. They come all at different times; even before the service, he knows from his manager that there'd been some difficulties with the arrangements. A guy that it seems is the brother of the deceased comes with his wife, and they stay a short time rearranging the flowers; the son with the queer accent, he gets here after lunch and stays holding his partner's hand; and then the older son comes after the others have gone. He's always the one that stays the longest. Yesterday, he was sat on the grass next to the grave almost the whole afternoon, getting a book out at one point and just staying there reading.

He pushes the wheelbarrow off down the lawn to the store room, where he puts it away with the broom and the shovel. He fills a bucket with water and takes a stiff brush, a pair of black rubber gloves and a container of solvent from a shelf, then he goes out of the store and down toward the road. The cemetery wall has been defaced again – K.A.H., it reads, sprayed in large black lettering over the concrete – and he kneels down on the pavement to get scrubbing at it with the thick creamy solvent. From where he is, he can just about see the grey head of the man, grieving beside his wife's grave. Poor guy. There had been kind of an awkward atmosphere after the service, and it's a fair guess the family relationship's no the best. Always politics somewhere. He was in the yards, this one, according to his manager. That whole length of path is lined with the names of yardmen, copped their whack before their time.

A whole shop floor under that lawn, he'd heard the registrar say a while back, and it would be true enough, except that so many of them are the wives and weans. He keeps on scouring the wall a few more minutes – it doesn't get rid of it, but it's the best he can do, the solvent and then the sun beating down on it between now and when it gets painted over at the end of the summer. When he's done, he picks up the bucket and container and walks back through the cemetery, passing the man, who is stood now by the black iron palings on the other side of the grave, gazing down.

Mick is reading the tags on the flower bouquets. There's a new big bunch from the Highlanders that they must have got in the Marks and Spencer. A smaller one from Pete and Mary. He puts the tags back as they were, and gets ready to leave. The first few times he's come here, he's stayed almost an hour, looking down at the mound of not yet sunken earth. He tries to imagine her. It's no easy but. Each time, he ends up standing there just, trying to feel that she's there, trying to see her face, but it's no happening, is the truth – he may as well be stood staring at a car engine for all the closeness he's getting.

Maybe when the headstone is up, it will feel different. Although even that hadn't been without its difficulties. It was him that gave the inscription for it; Alan had paid. The only thing they'd went halves on was the coffin. When they were in the funeral director's, Mick had called for a modest and simple box, saying that it was what she would have wanted, although of course he knew fine well that if she had any say in it she would have gone for the most expensive one in the shop. He turns to leave, looking down at the space next to her as he moves off, lush and well tended, the stalks of the flower bunches resting down over it, like she's saving a seat for him on the bus.

The Highlanders are in the kitchen when he gets back, one of them carefully monitoring the grill and the other holding a saucepan.

'Craig about?' he asks, his head through the doorway. Sausage and beans, it looks like.

'In the bathroom, I think,' says Lynn. 'You ready for some breakfast?'

'Aye, thanks,' he says, eyeing the sausages as she gets turning them over. 'I'll be through in a minute.'

He goes up and waits just inside the bedroom, hoping to catch Craig as he comes past. But when the bathroom door clicks and he makes his move, it is Robbie that is stepping out. They stop there a moment on the stairhead.

'Been the grave?'

'Aye, I'm just back.'

'You okay?'

'I'm fine, Rob, thanks.'

In the kitchen, he and Robbie get themselves a plate of breakfast from the dishes on the table and go through to the living room, where the others are already eating.

Robbie and Jenna have booked their flights, they say. Monday morning. There's a stop-off in Hong Kong, and they could've arranged to stay a night, but they're wanting to get back to the baby. At the mention of this, Lynn gets telling the story of their own trip to India a couple of years ago: how the flight was a nightmare and the locals pack into the trains like pilchards, and there's cows in the road but if you hire a driver he won't even pamp the horn at them. Mick's not much interested in another of Lynn's stories; he's thinking instead how he's going to manage taking Craig aside. His best bet, he knows, is when the house is quieter, that's obvious enough, while the Highlanders are off on one of their visits to the Botanic Gardens or the Tenement House. He'll have to wait just, bide his time. Chin him before he goes visiting the grave.

But the Highlanders have for some reason decided against an excursion. They stay in the house fussing on all morning, and it means the right moment doesn't come; and so by early afternoon, when Robbie and Jenna return from the grave, Craig is out the door. Like the other days, he's away a long while, not getting in until the back of six, when the house is busy and the Highlanders are preparing food again. It isn't until after tea and the evening of television watching, when Craig is about to get up and leave, that he has an opportunity.

Craig is after excusing himself from the room, away to the lobby to put on his jacket. Mick gets off his seat and follows him.

He is by the front door, the jacket on, searching his pockets.

'I might come join ye for a nightcap, if that's alright,' Mick says, reaching for his own brown jacket off the hook. He can feel the eyes looking at him.

'Aye, if ye want.'

They keep on quick along the pavement. The blue light of televisions flickering through windows as they go down the street; heads, lager cans, weans lying on their fronts. Craig is walking at a fair crack. They stay side by side, and he has a job keeping up.

'Ye go the Empress, is it?'

'Usually. It's quiet in there.'

'Aye, well, nothing changes, eh?' He falls back to let Craig pass a lamppost, and hurries on after. 'There many in there ye know?'

'No really. Only Desmond.'

He chuckles. 'See that's what I mean. Nothing changes.'

Desmond. A fine familiar and reassuring figure. Comb-over wrinkling under the gantry lights; the big potato hands lining up whisky tumblers along the drip trays to catch each last drop from the lager taps. He should thank him again for the wake, he gets thinking, as they turn onto the high street. It's busy the night, smokers stood outside the Brazier and a queue out the door of the chip shop. Rangers were away the day but there's still plenty of Bluenoses about the place. The two of them march on through. Keen to get on and be sat down with a drink.

It's not Des behind the bar though. There's a woman he doesn't recognize as he goes up for their drinks and Craig sits down at a table in the corner. The tumblers are there on the drip trays though, so he's about somewhere. Probably in the back, reading his detective novels. Glass of Grouse. Fag plugged in the ashtray. Disturb me at your peril, hen, disturb me at your fucking peril.

She holds the glass under the tap and allows the froth to slurp over the rim, slowly pooling in the tumbler underneath. Mick turns to keek over at Craig, where he is sat by the window staring up at the football highlights. Why is it they're here, again? He's no too sure any more. What was he expecting – a nice wee chat? A pure certainty that isn't going to happen, and yet here they are; he's pushed himself on the boy to come out for a drink but now they're here he knows fine well it can only end in a fight. What choice has he got but? Nay choice. They need to have some kind of a conversation, whatever else happens. It isn't his fault the boy sits there like a cauldron and you can't get near him. Not totally his fault, anyway, no the full share.

He pays for the drinks. As he picks them up off the counter he catches sight, through the bar, of a recognizable shape sat in the parlour, hunched over a Guinness.

'Pat,' he calls through. No response, so Mick puts the pints down a moment to go round and say a quick hello.

'Pat.'

He looks up.

'Mick. How ye getting on?'

'Fine. Keeping a lid on it, ye know.'

Pat looks through to the main bar, past the two lagers sat on the far counter. 'Ye have the family with you, eh?'

'I do. All of them.'

'It was Tuesday, they said.'

'It was, aye.'

Pat nods. 'Ye have my condolences, Mick.'

With that, he turns back to his drink, and the matter is at a close. Condolences dispensed. They say goodbye.

Round the other side, Mick picks up the lagers and regards Pat a moment sipping his Guinness. He's certain a worse state than whenever last he saw him. The nose is badly gone the now, sore and swollen, delicately fractured with blood vessels. What do you expect? The guy's been coming in here for decades. He's in with the bricks. He was sat right there almost thirty years ago when him and Cathy moved back from Australia, his grumbling presence even then moiled into the sight and smell of the place, as crucial a part of it as the framed battleships along the walls or the great dark stain on the ceiling. There was a brief period just, after the smoking ban came in, when he stopped coming. Desmond had told him, the big hands braced on the counter, that he'd no choice but towing the line. He wasn't risking the fine. Pat had simply got up off his stool and walked out. 'That's fine, well. I will take my custom elsewhere.' And he'd went round the bar and left, simple as that, closing the door quietly behind him. That's me, pal. I'm off. Ye have my condolences. He was back within the month though. Climbed onto his seat at the bar and ordered his Guinness as if nothing had ever happened. No word was spoke again about the incident, and you'd never know that Pat gave it another thought except that now, whenever he goes for a smoke outside, he lights up his fag as he's walking through the bar, and takes that first draw while he's still in the lobby, getting open the door.

'Here we are, son.' Mick places the pints on the small table and sits in opposite.

'Cheers.' Craig takes a drink of his lager and looks back up at the television. Mick joins his gaze. Hibs and Aberdeen. No the most compelling TV viewing. The commentator is the main noise in the room, which is pretty empty. A few tables across there is a man silently out with his wife; by the toilets, the occasional whine and clobber of the fruit machine, a young lad going away at it.

'The Rangers game been on yet?' Mick asks.

'No yet. They won though.'

Through the bar, past Pat, there's two old boys on the faded red wall seat that goes around the parlour, pattering away together. He takes a long sup, observing Craig over the top of his glass.

'When did ye last get down?'

'Eh?'

'I say when was it ye last got down?'

'How ye mean? Down where?'

'Ibrox.'

'Oh, right. Years ago. With you, probably.'

'Christ, long time ago, that. Motherwell, was it, two–nil? I can mind that, I think.'

'It was Hearts.'

'Aw, aye, that's right, it was.'

They go quiet again. Get watching the football. The Celtic match comes on and the man and his wife turn to have a look at the screen. They've played at home and he doesn't recognize who they're against, but whoever it is, it looks like Celtic have cuffed them. Is this what he's been doing? he thinks with sudden pity. Sat here watching this keech on his own. Is it that bad he'd rather this than stay in the house? Obviously it is. What can he do about it but?

26

There's nothing he can say that's going to put everything right, no now, it's too built up, and the boy's obvious no in the mood to listen either so anything he says is just going to dig him up the worse. Being honest, the best thing is for him to get back across town to his flat. Go back to work. See his mates. He's no doing himself any good maundering away here, and the truth is, say what you want about it, but it will be a relief tomorrow when he's gone. There. He admits it. The bastard father, spilling the beans. Celtic's match is still on – three–nil, four–nil, more maybe – but Mick's gaze drops away from the screen and he starts staring at the wall underneath the television mount, at the brown pitted wallpaper like moulding orange peel, and at the pictures hanging unevenly in rows. Ships and footballers, mixed together: the *Bloodhound*, HMS *Valiant*, Davie Meiklejohn, HMS *Indomitable*, Willie Johnston, RMS *Empress of Japan*, Alan 'The Wee Society Man' Morton. Clydebuilt, each every one, crafted and revered all down the water, talked about over people's teatimes, sold off to England. Some of the players probably worked on these ships. They probably did; that's how it was. They would have served their apprenticeships on the yards, black squad, up early for a day's work, and then away for a quick shower and a bite to eat and they'd be down the training pitches. There was one guy he'd went to school with, Andy Loy, was in the juniors at Rangers: a great young player, fast, skilful, but he didn't make the cut. Close, but no quite. He'd stayed on at John Brown's instead, and become the yard's ratcatcher. A terrible job in truth but the daftie bugger had loved it. This wee stinking hut that he'd worked out of – the shelves piled with poisons and explosives and rusted weaponry – but the swarming hordes all about the place never getting any less because Andy wasn't going to risk losing his job so he only ever killed the male ones.

The fruit machine is ringing and a spew of coins clatters into the collect tray. The lad has struck it lucky. You can see by his face how pleased he is, the money falling out from the machine for quite a long while. Good for you, pal. Mick gives him a grin as he comes past on his way to the bar with the coins cupped in his hands, a wee smile from Craig too, glancing down a moment from the television. It's his own face, if anything, not his mother's. They've similar features. It gets more noticeable the older he is. Even a few grey hairs showing already. That'll be another thing he can hold against him.

He stays looking at the boy for a moment before turning back to the wall. Rats. That was one thing that never changed. As a wean, his da would take him into the yard sometimes when a ship was due for its trials, and they'd stand together in a big crowd of boys and yardmen as the ship got fumigated, waiting for the moment when hundreds of rats started pouring down the mooring ropes, and then the popcorn-popping sound as everyone got batting them with their shovels.

Desmond is walking over.

He stands over the table, a great bear blocking out the television.

'Mick. It's good to see you.'

'And yourself, Desmond. How's it going?'

'No bad, aye, no bad. Quiet, like, but what can ye do, eh?' He claps a giant hand onto Craig's shoulder. 'Robbie still here as well, is he?'

'He is. And the Highlanders. They're off the morrow but, any luck.'

'Aye, well, good of them to stay this long, I suppose. Alan been putting the mix in?'

'No, he's been fine, to be fair. Lynn's been cooking for us all, so there's no complaints really. Look, Des, I wanted to say thanks again for the other day. It –'

'Aw, Mick, serious, it's no a problem. Ye're very welcome. And it's no like I'm mobbed with custom, know?' He looks round toward the bar. 'I'm sure Pat coped with himself for a few hours.' He chuckles, taking the hand off Craig's shoulder, and looks down at the table. 'Another drink, boys?'

Craig shakes his head.

'No, we're alright, thanks,' Mick says.

'Okay, well, yous two take care. I'd best go see what state this bar's in.'

His massive arse is moving away to the bar. They look up to the television as the Rangers game comes on. There's an early goal. He doesn't recognize the scorer. Maybe he should try and persuade Craig to stay for another drink. Force something out of him, at least. How's he getting on up in Yoker, for one thing; is the job working out? Apart from the bits and pieces that Robbie's told him, he honestly wouldn't know. Does he have a girlfriend even? The thought of asking him something like that. Excuse me, son, but I was wondering just if ye're seeing anybody the now, and how does she get on with these thundery mood swings of yours? Probably he wouldn't be like that with her though. See she would understand him; she would make time and listen to him.

Desmond is talking to the new barmaid, showing her something at the till. After a moment they move along the bar and he pulls down a couple of whisky bottles from the gantry, unscrews the pourer off the fuller one and starts marrying them together, shaking out the last few drops from the empty. Then back onto the rack. He leaves her to get doing the rest of the bottles while he goes over by the till, carefully patting the comb-over, and observes her. The thought occurs to him then, minding the hand on Craig's shoulder, that possibly Desmond knows more what's going on with him than he does. If this is his hideout, where he comes to get away from the house, from him, he might well have talked a little to Des. Even if no how he's feeling, then maybe at least some of the other stuff, like how's his flat and his job, and is his boss a bastard and all that type of thing.

'I'm off home, Da.'

Craig stands up, pulling his jacket on.

'Okay, son, I'll come with ye.'

It is dark, walking back. The streetlamps are on, and there aren't as many people about as earlier, though there's still a queue in the chip shop. They turn off the high street, through an alleyway, and past a group of bevvied-up young lads playing football in the dim light of a back court. It could have gone worse, he tells himself. They got through it without any explosions, at least. That's something. Give it time, is the best thing. Let him be alone with himself for a while, no having to deal with people in his face the whole day. He's a solitary kind of a person, anyway, so he'll figure himself out if he's left to it. They come past the bus stop at the end of the road and as they get near the house he can see the lights are off downstairs, so Robbie and Jenna must be away to bed.

Even as he opens the front door, it doesn't really hit him that she isn't going to be there. There's no thudding realization whacking him over the head or anything like that, it's more a feeling like she's out, like it's bingo night or something. He goes into the kitchen and gets himself a glass of water while Craig goes up to the bathroom. The Highlanders have tidied away all the cans and the bottles into separate carriers, he notices. He drinks his water and waits until he can hear Craig coming down the stair. They pass in the corridor.

'Night,' Craig says, going into the living room.

'Night, son. See you in the morning.'

He hasn't slept in the bed any of these last nights. All the bedding is now pulled onto the floor, against the wall, with Robbie's old camping mat underneath for him to lie on. He's been sleeping better there. No perfect, but it's better. It still takes a few hours each night, trying to block out the sound of Fred fucking Flintstone through the wall, until he gets drifting off. And when he does, he sleeps in short, deep spurts, waking often, and usually from the most pure vivid dreams. She is there in most of these, even if it's just for a walk-on: crossing the road as he's waiting in a car stopped at the lights, or sat near to him at the bus stop eating a sausage roll. More often though, the dreams are about her, or the two of them together. He had one, she was in the kitchen getting tea ready, some keech on the mini TV in the background, and she's chatting away to herself as he comes in and gets himself a beer out the fridge. Then when she sees him she starts straight away apologizing, saying she's no had time to fix out a proper tea and so it's ham and eggs and he's genuine bemused, laughing, because what's wrong with ham and eggs – that's a great bloody tea.

It is colder the night and he's got the windows closed. Still the odd noise from outside: a front door shutting; a car speeding toward the river. He pulls the covers in close over him, and starts to feel quite snug there on the floor, and maybe it's the beer he drank but it isn't long before he has started gradually, comfortably, to drop off.

He is in the bed and she's lying next to him, facing away, snoring. He can't sleep, it's that loud. The noise increases steadily to a peak, and stops with a jolt; a moment of peace and silence as she lies there breathing heavily, and then it begins again. He props himself up on his elbow and looks over at her. The flesh of her neck bunched against her chin. He gives her a shunt with his elbow and lies quickly down again. Silence. A few moments' respite, and then it gets up again. He gives another nudge and she grunts to a stop. He closes his eyes and pretends he's asleep. She mumbles some nonsense a few seconds and goes quiet. After a while he feels himself starting to fall to sleep, the eyes slowly closing, but then she's at it again. He gives a real shunt this time, and turns quick over onto his other side. There is a chuckle. 'I know what ye're up to. Pack it in, eh.' He kids on he's asleep, but he can't keep it up and soon he's chuckling too.

He turns over toward her, but she's gone – he sees her suddenly over by the wardrobe, getting dressed. 'Come on, you, get a move on. They'll be closing soon.' He gets up and changes and they go down the staircase, but when they get to the bottom they are on the lower deck of a bus, taking a seat at the back over the engine, because she is cold. She keeps chuffing her hands together to warm them up. They are about to get off, and the driver calls to them to come over. When they get to the glass side of the cab he looks in and it is the barmaid from the Empress. She's got all these photos stuck up around the cab. This one of her weans, two wee girls, playing in a paddling pool. She looks annoyed about something. 'Go on, get off, then,' she says, so they do and they step out into the car park of the Co. He fetches a trolley and they go inside, where it's very busy, and hard to move around. He jostles the trolley up an aisle, with the wife in beside him reeling off a list of things they are needing: carrots, tatties, bog roll, flowers. She sends him off to the freezers for a chicken, but when he's got it he can't find her again, the place is too hoaching with shoppers. He tries going down the central aisle to look both sides and he is up and down twice before he sees her – she's at the checkout, sat in a booth. When he gets on the approach he can see that she's wearing a blue shirt and a Co badge with her name on it. He gets unloading the trolley and she passes each of the items over the scanner, her head down. He notices then that she is greeting. 'What is it, hen?' he says, but she doesn't answer, she keeps scanning the shopping. 'It's okay,' and he tries to take her hand as she scans the bog roll. 'We can go now,' he says. He can't see her face but he knows she's smiling, and she stands up to leave the booth, but the door is locked and it won't open. She shakes it, and he gets helping her but it won't budge and he can hear her sobbing again. 'Climb over it, hen. Come on, try, will ye? We can go now, look, I've got all the shopping – I got the tatties, see?'

He's said these last words out loud, he realizes, sitting up from the mat with a plaster-peeling sound. He stays a moment with his arms folded on top of his knees, getting his bearings, looking out the window to get a fix on what is real. The brainbox in a muddle still. He stares out as, slowly, it clears. There's something of a moon the night. You can see it above the dark blocks of the multis. Five or six black shapes with only a few windows lit, and the yellow spines of the stairwell lights – one of them flickering, up near the top.

5

Craig is the first to leave. His bag is packed up and ready by the door when the rest of them have finished their breakfast.

'What time will you start work tomorrow?' Lynn asks him as they gather in the lobby, watching him put on his jacket.

'I'm in early. I'll talk with my boss and see what's what.'

He gives her a stiff hug, and the rest of them line up along the corridor to see him off.

'Don't be a stranger, now,' Alan says to him. The kind of thing you say to people who are strangers.

'Okay,' Craig replies, and it is actually rare comic – the look on his face – it's that obvious he'd rather top himself. Mick looks over at Robbie, wondering if he's thought the same. Robbie's looking pretty serious but. He's next up, and he gives his brother a tight squeeze. There's a look between them that's hard to read. Understanding, maybe. Disagreement.

When it gets his turn it is in the end quite easy. With all the rest of them stood watching there's no question of a wee private chat, so they stick to the formalities just. A brief hold. A pat on the back.

'Come over for your tea sometime soon, eh?'

'Okay, I will.'

And he's away. Off to wait at the bus stop and get moving across town.

The Highlanders are next. A drawn-out carry-on of hugs and promises shortly after *Cash in the Attic*. Poor Lynn hardly able to bring herself to get leaving, she's that torn up about it.

They decide the three of them to go for a walk in the afternoon. The sun's come out again after the cloudy spell of the last couple of days, and they go up the park for a bit of a wander. It's enjoyable. Being able to relax and have a bit of patter finally, and no be wary the whole time of treading on eggshells. It's a shame there's only this day left. Robbie and Jenna's flight goes early in the morning. They've got their taxi to the airport booked already, and Jenna has tidied up their stuff from the living room. For now, walking through the middle of the park, past a fringe of small planted flowers, Jenna is asking him what his plans are for the next couple of days, after they've gone. He'll give a call into work, he says, see when they need him. Get the house cleaned up. Finish off the parmesan. He grins, but the pair of them have got their concerned faces on. Obvious enough what they're thinking: how will he get on, on his own? Will he manage? Will he hit the drink?

'How was it last night, with Craig?' Robbie asks.

'Yeh, it was fine.'

'Really? The two of you get to talk?'

'Aye, well, kind of. Mean, it isnae easy. But there was no bust-up at least. How, has he said anything to you?'

'No. Not much, anyway.' They slow up a moment as a young boy chases across the path after a football. 'See I was just wondering last night if he might talk to you about compensation and that.'

'No, he didnae. He has to you, then?'

'Not directly. I know it's on his mind though. He brought it up the other day, how more cases are being brought, and there's been some big victories and that. There was one last month, apparently, don't know if you saw, a hundred and fifty grand, he says.'

'It's no a victory, Robbie.'

'I know, Christ. That's not how Craig sees it either, you know. He's angry, Da. He's just angry. He needs to blame somebody. And they're as good as anybody, aren't they – the employers, the insurance companies – he's right about that, isn't he?'

They come past a battered play area with a swing and a mangled see-saw. The seat on the swing is come unfixed from the chain on one side, and juts down like a broken bone.

'Da?'

'I don't know, Rob. I don't know what I think.' He looks ahead up the path. 'You agree with him, then? You think we should put in a claim?'

'I'm not sure. It's your decision, Da.' He glances across at Jenna.

'We're obviously not going to be around through it all, so it's not for me to say.'

'Of course it bloody is. She was your maw too. You've as much right as Craig or anybody else.'

Robbie goes quiet as they walk on. He notices, further on, Jenna take his hand as the path widens and they come toward the far side of the park.

'Now's no the time to be thinking about it, anyway,' Mick says after a while. 'Come on.' And they leave the park with the sun still going brightly over the tenements, starting back to the house.

They get a carry-out from the curry shop for their tea, a bit of cargo from the offie. Robbie insists paying for it. Says he's hardly put his hand in his pocket the whole while he's been here. Fine. It's no like you can argue with him anyway. They watch a film after they've eaten – a good one, Australian, as it happens, even though it's just what's on the television. It's about this guy who's a notorious hardcase, robs drug dealers and cuts their toes off kind of thing, but who doesn't let a long stretch in the clink stop him from keeping up with his psychie tendencies: stabbing, torturing, and then writing a book and becoming a celebrity – true story, apparently. Robbie and Jenna tell him the guy's well known over there as a writer and a lunatic. When the film's finished, they stay up and finish the beers. Chatting. No about anything much, just chatting. It's good; he enjoys their company. It is the back of midnight by the time they're done, so when their taxi comes at six the next morning to pick them up, the pair of them are a wee bit groggy-looking as he comes down the stair to say goodbye.

He gets a good long hug off them both.

'Like I said, Da, I'll come over again soon. That's a promise.'

'Ye don't have to promise me, Rob. I know the score. It's okay.'

After the taxi has left he comes back inside and carries upstairs the pile of bedding that Jenna has left neatly folded by the settee. When it's all put away he comes back down and makes himself a cup of tea.

He gets a window open in the living room. Let the place breathe a bit, lessen the aroma of farting sons. Poor Jenna, serious. She for one must be looking forward to being in her own bed again, that's a banker. Getting back to the baby. It's been a long time away for them, new parents that they are, and he's genuine grateful they stayed this long. Robbie might well say that he'll be over again soon but it's a daft promise to make, which is how he wasn't entertaining it, no even for a moment. Maybe if they leave it a while, then next time Damien might be old enough they can bring him too. Get him introduced. It's one of the things he's had a struggle with, Robbie, that his maw never met the baby. He knows that, because Jenna told him. Robbie didn't want to say anything about it himself because he thinks it's too close the knuckle and he doesn't want to make things any the harder for his father. Which is daft, obviously. It's something he wouldn't've minded talking to him about. But that's Robbie: always this sense – whether it's the Highlanders, or it's Craig, or it's the compensation – that he's trying to protect him. Keep things from getting any the worse. That he doesn't completely trust him to cope with things on his own, without him, without Cathy.

He goes into the kitchen and opens a drawer. From under magazines and cookbooks he takes out a card, then goes to sit down at the table and read again the letter that is tucked inside it.

Mick,

I am so sorry for your loss. I wouldn't for a moment tell you I know what you're going through because it's different for all of us, but I know nothing can prepare you for when it happens. And when it does you need to know your friends are there for you, like you and Cathy were for me when John went.

It's not my place to say it Mick but you can't blame yourself. We didn't know in those days. How could we? There wasn't all the studies like there are now. I know it's a difficult situation for you because of Alan being in the management and now's not the time for it either, but if you want I can tell you the people to go to if you're thinking about going down the justice and compensation route. Like I say, I know you probably don't want to think about any of this yet but they knew, Mick. Even back then. They should have done checks. For Christ's sake, John used to come home in his overalls white as a baker and I'd shout at him for getting the dust in my

carpets. It's not about the money. It's about justice. If you want to talk
then please do give me a call. I'm on the same number. God knows, it
might do me good myself. Take your time.

All the best
Alice

After a moment, he slips the letter back inside the card and returns it to the drawer. The idea of it – justice – seems pure absurd. Alice is gone down that route and fair enough, that's her decision, but the thought of it – how many thousands have died and still you've to tear yourself inside out dragging through the courts before any of these bastards will admit for a moment it's their fault. And it's no even him dead. Him that played snowballs with the stuff and came home with it stored in the turn-ups of his trousers. Justice is a word for it maybe, getting the payout, but it doesn't feel sitting here like the right one, no the right one at all.

He goes back through and flicks the tellybox on, settles himself into the cushions, and it isn't long before he is away to sleep.

She is there in his dreams again. They are that real – that's what's hard to get the head round. The two of them are washing and drying up. They're eating chips. They're arguing in the garden. Short dreams that come and go but don't finish, carrying on one to the next but connected somehow, linked up, like a chain of islands each with their different goings on but the same backdrop all around, the same light, the same weather following through the dreams so that if in one of them the wind is blustering at her washing while she hangs it out, in the next she'll be there in the crowd at a ship launch with everybody holding on top of their hats.

The sun is on his face, and he spots the postie turning in through the gate. He gets sat up. The body feels heavy, solid. He listens to the footsteps on the concrete and the clank of the letterbox. He is awake, that's obvious enough, but he has this sense of being detached from things. As if all these goings on around him – the sunshine, Phillip Schofield grinning on the television, the post tummelling onto the mat – they are all part of some other life, one that he can see, but he's not involved in. Mental, really. But that's what it's like. And even though he knows fine well that she isn't going to come down the stair and collect the post – open the door, chat with the postie – he can't shake the feeling that she will; that she is part of this other life, this real one, which he is outside of.

He will need to give work a call later, tell them when he'll be back. They've said he can have as long as he wants, but obviously there's the money to think about, and anyway there's no use really him rotting about the house doing nothing.

He gets up and goes over to look at the photo of Damien on top of the television. He's a cutie, that's for sure. Nay wonder they're keen to get back to him, the wee sausage-fingers. He is grinning away under a massive floppy white sunhat, sat on a rug on a crowded beach, all these brown bodies, baggy shorts, bikinis in the background. His own fat little body though is whiter even than the sand, which you know will be his maw protecting him from the sun, no doubt wary of the wee man's Scottish ancestry. You can see clear enough but that he's an Australian. Even at six months, that's clear enough. It's the eyes, the same as his mother's, big and happy, and no to mention the baggy shorts he's got on already. He's easy-oasy, you can tell. Not like Craig was. Jesus. Craig was never an Australian baby, that's for certain, never mind he was born there. Even as a tiny wean, he was Scottish as thistles, that boy. Greeting or sulking the whole time, and these great red skin rashes he got at even the slightest bit of heat. It was as if he knew already he was a Weegie even before they moved back.

No that the two of them had coped that much the better, being honest. He can mind well enough, even looking at this beautiful beach here, how it had been; how they'd become more unhappy the longer they stayed out there. Port Melbourne. It had seemed like a dream at first, Cathy stood queuing on the dock in her new dress, a whole shop's worth of creams in her handbag. After '72 and then the final ship completion at John Brown's, all the closures and the lay-offs everywhere, here was something to feel hopeful about at last. Free passage. Settling-in allowance. Secure job. Hallefuckinglullah. And it was a decent life too – sixty dollars a week, and no freezing your balls off like on the yards at home – although, that said, it did get sometimes too much the other way, and you'd be there in the plating shed thinking you were going to die of the heat. Stable work but. Strong unions. The wife got a job as a shorthand typist for a shipping firm and for a few years they were happy, they really were. There was the card schools on Fridays and the trips to the beach for the women – a giggling procession of them wrapped up like nuns, they were that feart of the sun. A whole clan of Weegies down there eventually, all staying together within a few streets. The Tartan Terrace. It was bloody true. Didn't last but, didn't last. After Robbie was born, and Cathy pure homesick to get back, biting his ear the whole time to tell him Alan had another job lined up for him, at Govan, where he was a manager the now. The funny thing as well: it probably made it the worse having all they Glaswegians around. That just made her long for the place even more, made it all the more obvious that this wasn't home, however much she tried to re-create it. Plus the heat. They never could quite get used to the heat.

Robbie has managed though. He's adapted much better than they ever did. Strange to think about it now, all the fights they'd had about him moving out there – he was only eighteen, what was he going to do? How was he going to live? – but he's proved them all wrong, that's for sure. He picks up the photograph and puts it on the small table by the settee. Tomorrow, after he's gave work a call, he'll go up the high street and get a wee frame for it. A good plan; that's definitely what he'll do. He is just sitting down again when the sparrow flies right up to the window, perches there, looking in. Here ye are, fat arse. He hops about a moment, and flies off. Poor wee guy, he's been waiting for something to eat round the other side, but he's been forgot about again. A feeling of guilt comes on him, and it's enough to make him get up and go through the kitchen to find the poor bird something to eat.

He empties the last of the bread onto the grass and stays there a moment, waiting for the sparrow. He doesn't come, of course. He's waiting himself, for Mick to clear off back inside, so after a minute Mick turns and gets leaving. He glances over the fence at next door's washing on the line, a baby-sized Rangers kit inamongst the socks and pants. Without even thinking about it he is looking in their garden, and he sees a cot and then the woman next door sat outside her kitchen with her Bristols out. Christ. He ducks down and turns straight around to look the other direction toward the houses on the other side. Fucksake – did she see him? If she did she's going to think he was spying on her, and how's that going to look? The wife's dead less than a fortnight and he's got his tit-goggles on already. He wonders then if in fact she knows about Cathy, if any of the neighbours do. Maybe they don't. But what does that matter – it doesn't – it's no like they spent much time with any of them all these years that they've stayed here. There's no noise of her moving about on the other side of the fence, luckily. He starts walking, slowly, stooped, back into the house.

Bloody hell. Still, you've got to laugh. He opens the fridge, but it's almost empty. Some sausages left though, so he pulls them out and gets a fryer going on the hob. Cathy would knot herself at that story, guaranteed. It's pretty funny, really. The sparrow is there out the window now, and he minds that's the last of the bread, so a sandwich is out the question. When the sausages are ready, he puts them straight onto a plate with a dollop of tommy sauce. He's no that hungry anyway.

He brings the bedding down and sleeps that night on the settee. It's pretty comfortable. More so for him than it would have been for Craig, clearly, himself being a good few inches the shorter. He stays there into the next morning, the sheets pulled over him most of the time because he's getting the occasional shivers, even though the sun is streaming through the gap in the curtains. He lays there and tries willing himself to phone in to work. He should tell them he'll be back by the end of the week. Crazy but he feels genuine nervous about it, even picking up the phone. Like he's a teenager who's met a lassie at the dancing, and he feels all jookery-pokery about ringing her. He minds that first time he called Cathy. Nervous as hell waiting for next door to finish on the line. All they prompts of jokes and conversation ideas written on the back of the *Record*, and his maw eavesdropping through the curtain of their room and kitchen.

'Hello, Muir's Private Hire.'

'Oh, hello, Lynsey? It's Mick Little.'

'Mick, how are ye?'

'Fine. I'm fine. See I'm just calling to say when I'll be back.'

'Aw, right.' There is the noise of the dispatch radio in the background. 'Look, Mick, don't worry about that. It's no problem. We don't need you.'

'No, really, it's nay bother. I can be in Thursday – actually, the morrow, I could come in the morrow.'

A storm of static on the radio and then a voice he doesn't recognize.

'Mick, do ye want to speak to Malc? He's just come in the door.'

'Naw, it's alright.'

'Okay. How are ye anyway? The family are there staying, I heard.'

'Aye.'

'That's good. Must be a comfort eh?'

'It is.'

'Look, Mick, take care of yourself, and take as much time as ye need, alright? We don't need you in, really we don't.'

'Right, okay. I'll see you, well.'

'See you, Mick.'

That's that done, then. His heart is beating quite hard as he puts the phone down and leaves the lobby into the living room. There he is again, the bloody sparrow. He for one knows what Mick's been up to, lazing on the couch, even if nobody else does. Come on well, ye greedy wee bugger, come on.

There's an unopened box of thin toast biscuits in the cupboard, something the Highlanders must've got in. He takes it outside, keeping crouched down, and breaks up the toasts, emptying the whole of one plastic packet onto the grass. He shakes out the crumbs, then he unsnibs the shed lock for one of the fold-out chairs and puts it up against the back of the kitchen. Better sat out here than sweating indoors. He opens another packet and eats a toast. Quite nice. He eats a couple more. There is the sound of a chair scraping on the other side of the fence. A moment later, and there's another. Impossible to know exactly why he does it but he slowly lifts his chair a touch closer, quietly, until he can see a tiny sliver through a crack between the fence slats. Part of her arm is visible. A bit of magazine. It's no that he's being a pervert, that's no it at all, it's – he doesn't know what it is – but he goes in a little closer so the angle widens and there, again, is her breasts. One of them, anyway.

Christsake, man, what are ye doing? But he stays looking, transfixed, with a kind of wonder, no really even aware of himself doing it, as if him and the breast are existing in two different worlds and somehow it's not actually happening.

A breast. It's pure jolted him. When was the last time he'd touched one? Actually touched one, except to sponge underneath? He hasn't thought of sex, he realizes, in a very long while. Not really. Not in a real way. The illness ate away at his own desire for it the same as it ate away at everything else. After a certain point, as she got worse, the need to get her comfortable, to stop her being in pain, it started overpowering all the rest. Even just the physical desire to be touching each other – not just the sexual ways, and let's be honest it's no like they'd been jumping all over each other exactly for quite a long time – but even just needing to be touched, you lose it. You forget. He turns away from the fence. No that it was like that at first though. He'd felt it keenly enough then. The fear of losing all that, their physical needs for each other, as it started becoming visible, even a couple of months in, that the disease was taking hold. She wouldn't let him see her. She started getting changed in the bathroom, and wore his trackie bottoms to bed. When once, near the beginning, he tried to touch her, she had turned away from him, sobbing, and after that he didn't try again for fear of upsetting her.

So that tit in the fence, it's a surprise. He gets up from the chair, looking the other direction – a man two gardens down the way sat with his giant white belly out, drinking a can – and goes back in the house.

There's a jumble of post on the mat. He gives a flick through it. A couple of flyers for a new pizza carry-out; more browns; what looks like a few extra condolence cards. He leaves the lot where it is on the mat and goes back through to the living room. Still this leaden feeling about him, lying in his stomach like a brick. The sausages? No. That was yesterday, and he'd only ate one of them. In fact he should get eating something, and that's maybe it even – the lack of eating anything – because he hasn't ate a full meal since Robbie and Jenna left. He's no hungry but, that's the problem. He'll think about it soon, he resolves, but for now he stays on the settee. Coming inside has made him feel a bit of a chill, so he gathers the covers over him and tries getting warm and comfortable. There's this sense he's got as though he's waiting for something to happen. Everything is dulled, even his hunger. He really is not hungry. Which is a new one. Normally he's a genuine trougher.

He wakes, taking a moment to understand by the light outside and by a dim calculation of the TV schedule what time it is. About six, he guesses. Hungry or not hungry, that means all he's ate in two days is a sausage and a couple of toast biscuits, which is a pure nonsense, clearly.

Fridge: empty, apart from the parmesan. Cupboards: a few bottles of things, a tin of tomatoes and the toast biscuits. He eats all of one packet, chewing drily, and leaves the last couple for emergencies and the sparrow. That'll do as a starter, he decides, looking out at the garden, and the gloaming coming on, the shed door no shut properly. There is the new pizza carry-out, he minds, but straight away gives the idea a bye: he hasn't enough cash on his tail, and as well the thought of going out, of walking on the high street and queuing up in the place with its new bright neons and the brand spanking plastic no yet covered in scratches and stuck with chinex. The effort even of thinking about doing that bears on him like a weight. But just at that moment he has a brainwave. The freezer. He's forgot about it until now and, getting open the door for a look in, it's easy to see how – it being something of a no-go area, the seal covered all around with a huge furry moulding of ice, like frozen moss. Still, there's things in here. There's all kinds of bags and boxes, although you can't see what any of it is because it's all glazed over with a thin dust of ice like a postie's frost, so he puts his hand in and gets brushing it off. Waffles, choc ices, boil-in-the-bag fish in sauce – no thank you very much – peas, the wife's crispy pancakes, which it's more than his life is worth stealing from her –

There is a sudden tug at his stomach, a recoil, like the instant of a fall before the insides catch up. His hands are shaking. A dizzy confused sick sensation and he has to grip the side of the fridge-freezer to steady himself.

Crispy pancakes. Bingo tea.

There are peas gone over the floor, but he stays pressed against the fridge without moving. His stomach is aching, and he feels sick.

And then he is – a dry, coughed-up retch of thin, clinging dribble. Jesus Christ. He didn't see this coming; he'd've been the better going down the new pizza take-out, all things considered, and he starts to chuckle, his forehead juddering against the freezer. See maybe he would've been done in there too, how could you know? They wouldn't have known how to deal with it if he had, that's for sure, looking confused at each other in their smart new caps and uniforms – this wouldn't be in the training.

The box is soft and battered the now, almost a year old. It needs chucking out but as soon as he has the thought he gets the dry boak in his throat again. Bingo tea: crispy pancakes, beans, tinned potatoes, tommy sauce. Her sat eating it and the strange chemically smell of those terrible fucking tatties, then off to the bus and a kiss for him and the boys. Now ye'll no let these two stay up the night, eh? I want them in their beds when I'm back. And always the wee grin between them as she leaves, because she knows well enough there'll be a pair of bahookies scootling up the stair when she comes in. He can see her, clear as anything. Her face, beaming, drunk. Mick, I've bloody gone and won – footering in her bag for the money – I've only bloody gone and won, see, and she pulls it out with a great daft smile like a magician's assistant. His eyeballs feel cold; he closes them. She won two hundred quid once. They spent a few days in Wemyss Bay and bought a mini television for the kitchen. He can't mind her winning that much any other time. Just little wins, tiddlies – ten or twenty pound – and she'd never share it, that money, it was hers, she'd declare with glee, and she'd buy herself tights and Barbara Taylor Bradfords.

He minds abruptly the woman next door; him spying on her through the fence. His stomach starts racing. What was he doing? He feels pure scunnered at himself, and he screws the eyes closed but the thought of it won't let up, the sense, somehow, that she knows.

He realizes then that his forehead is stuck to the freezer.

He tries to pull away but it's joined fast, and the skin stings when he tugs at it. Bollocks, he cries out loud, and draws back again, slowly this time, but no joy, he's too long frozen to it with sweat or tears or however it's happened, it doesn't matter – he's glued on the freezer, is all that counts. Bloody eejit. He is laughing, and it jerks on the skin. Leave him alone two minutes and look what happens.

44

He tries a new approach, damping a finger with warm spit and rubbing at the join, repeating the action over and over, hoping he might be able to peel away by fractions, but still it doesn't seem to be working, the skin feeling scorched now and him beginning to panic. What a way to go: we found him starved in the kitchen with his head stuck to the fridge-freezer. Suddenly geeing himself up, he places his hands either side and rips himself away. He yelps at the sharp burning sensation. Then, stupidly, as it dies to an achy tingle, he checks if there's any skin left on the ice. There isn't. He shakes his head. What a fucking haddock, serious, and he turns to bathe the head with some warm water from the tap.

Falling, again the sensation of falling. He rests his head, carefully, sideways on the kitchen table but he can't get rid of the falling sensation even when he shuts his eyes, so he just stays there motionless, listening to his belly underneath the table away on a merry dance. He can't see her now. Can't picture her face. The various parts of her are there still when he tries imagining her – the hair, the jimmeny teeth – but he can't pull back and get a sense of her, what she looks like, her face.

Ingredients: cooked chicken (2%), sweetcorn (1%), bacon (1%), coconut fat, smoke flavouring, sodium ascorbate, sodium nitrate . . . Jesus. If it hadn't been the asbestos killed her, it would've been the crispy pancakes. He turns the box over to read the other end, handling it carefully, like an old photograph. Fifteen minutes under the grill, simple as that.

There isn't any tinned tatties, or beans, so he grills up the waffles instead, and arranges them on a plate with the pancakes and a few thumps of tommy sauce. He sits a while looking at it. A familiar smell, and a good one, no like they potatoes. But it's a smell just. And it doesn't make him want to eat it. His stomach is bad still and he knows the second he puts a bite of this down, it'll be coming straight back up. So he sits, staring, toying at it with his fork, pulling open a pancake and pressing out some of the shiny cream gloop. Wondering what in hell he's doing. What, was he going to try and imagine that it's her or something, stupit, fucking stupit, and he feels instantly sick at the thought of what he's doing. He pushes the plate aside and stumbles over to the sink.

6

He cannot sleep properly. Each of the next few nights he wakes in the dark, sweating, the settee hot and clammy against his skin. Staring at the display clock on the video player, waiting for it to be morning. When the dawn does come, and all the familiar shapes in the room start becoming visible, he is up quickly, a restless energy about him. He moves back and forth between the living room and the kitchen, getting the kettle on, both TVs, opening cupboards, then no minding what he's looking for, shutting them again.

By the afternoons, he's tired out. No hungry still either. When it gets dark outside again he forces himself to grill up a waffle, but otherwise he doesn't eat. He stays in front of the television in the living room, not so much looking at the programmes as at the set itself, how familiar it is: the dusty top of the video player; the wee carpet troughs just in front of the broken rollers where it used to stand years ago, before Robbie spilled a Coke bottle over the whole area.

One morning, he gets up off the settee and goes straight upstairs. He strips the walls in the boys' room of the few dog-eared photos stuck above the beds. Then into the bathroom for the framed one above the lavvy; the staircase; the lobby; the photo packets in the kitchen drawer.

He begins piling them in rows on the floor in front of the television, like an audience.

After half an hour, the collection has spread to the settee – a crowd of Cathys laughing and posing, the head always turned a touch the left of the camera. Himself in a lot of them too, stiffly smiling next to her. There are more still with the boys in as he selects through the packets: quite a few from when they were schoolweans, trips to the theme park, the pair of them tired and wet in their macs, or chasing about in their first Rangers kits. One of these, he takes out and puts on the floor with the others. It's of the four of them all together, sat on a bench eating open bags of chips, Craig squeezed in next to Cathy, clung to her like a little demon. He can mind the day still. The first time they'd let the boys on the rides, Robbie biting his ear the whole afternoon for a handful of smash to go on the arcades, and some poor wee lassie boaking up on the rollercoaster, these long tendrils of vomit flying past their faces.

He can't get a fix on her. Even if he stares for minutes at each one, trying to mind what the occasion was, what she'd been saying as the picture was took, it's no use. And anyway, all this, it's just confusing matters, because these photographs cover years, decades, and she looks different from each one to the next. They are all *of* her, clearly – the pretty, smiling teenager, or here with the gelled fringe and blonde bubble perm – but when does the picture stop changing so that he might get a final hold on who she is? Not at the thin, sagging shape that she'd become, no danger. Even if he could pick out an image and say, aye, that's her, that is *her*, it wouldn't fucking be that one.

There aren't any photos of her like that though. The collection stops a few years back, when the camera seized up. The last one is Robbie's wedding. Himself, Cathy and Craig stood in their best, sweating in the sun under this giant tree and looking pure uncomfortable, done up hot and greasy as fish suppers.

It's no doing any good, this. He should leave it by. Plus he needs to get something to eat. The stomach is spitting tacks, and he's got to get something down him. Hard to move but. To get out the room and stop staring at all these pictures laid out on the floor. Each time he thinks he's going to get leaving a new photo will catch his eye and he'll crouch down in front of it trying to remember, trying to be inside it. One here that normally hangs in the lobby near where the coat hooks are. Port Melbourne. Cathy is knelt in her shorts battling on at the garden, her forearms stained up to the elbows in dark, red soil. She never could make anything grow. It was too hot and dry for all the wee shrubs and flowers that she fussed and footered over. In seven years, the only thing he can mind growing in that small, square garden was a single yellow dahlia. The rest the time it was full of balding lilac bushes and brown dead things. She is smiling but, in the photo, ever hopeful. Smooth plump arms. The tan line on her chest as she arches over, going at the ground with a trowel.

Was it already in her then? Dormant. Waiting. How could you know? You couldn't. She looks the picture of health here, that's what anybody would think, and Craig's babby toys are there in one corner of the garden so this is past thirty years ago, but it's possible it was in her even then. Probably it was. They're saying now it can be forty years, the incubation period, hidden away inside the body, inactive, until the moment it decides to crawl out and stiffen you. He peers in closer, even though he knows there is nothing to look for. And even if they had known, even then, would it have been any the better? Would the doctors have been able to stop it? Would they hell. Once it was in, it was in, like Thatcher. The end inevitable, no matter how long and hard the struggle. Better never knowing, is the truth. Better sudden and final.

Stupit, but he studies the other photos, looking for signs, anything. Something they should have spotted at the time. Obviously there's nothing but. Nothing. Only her getting older: smile creases around the eyes; the body a wee helping heavier; grey seams developing in the hair, until for a whole packet it's brown again, and then she lets it have its way and the grey returns.

Enough of this. He needs something to eat.

He goes in the kitchen and keeks warily at the fridge-freezer, and he is about to go toward it, but instead he starts scanning round the shelves and the cupboard tops. He opens a drawer and takes out the cookbooks and then the messy pile of gossip magazines, putting the lot in a pile on the counter. Then he's into the cupboards, taking out a mug, the biscuit tin, a handful of teacloths from another drawer, even a fish magnet from the fridge together with the faded offie coupon underneath. He brings it all through into the living room. He works quickly, too quickly to get thinking about what he's doing and stop himself for being a complete fucking eejit. He goes up the stair to the bathroom. There are things in here too. Her books: she kept the Barbaras in here for some reason he'd never been able to fathom, stacked by the door next to the wash basket, the covers curling over at the corners from damp. He picks up an armful and hurries them down the stair.

As he comes out of the living room again he sees the front door mat and pulls it out from under the post. He stares at it a moment.

Then he puts it in the living room with the rest, and goes back up for her lotions and potions – all of it still there untouched – shower cap, lady razor, her bloody toothbrush even, dried out now as a thistle.

He stands by the television and looks out over what he's done. The settee covered with all this stuff, a wet patch on the arm under the shower cap. Nothing. It looks like a bloody jumble sale.

He needs suddenly to be out of there, out of the house. The heart is going like the clappers and he can feel panic taking a grip of him, this sense that somebody's going to come in any moment and see what he's done.

There is nobody about. Only the sound of his own feet on the pavement, as if the city is emptied from around him. A fine day but. A beauty. The highest windows of the multis glinting in the sun. He carries on along the road and he is going toward the cemetery, simple as that, it's no a decision that he's made, it's just what's happening. When was the last time he spoke to anybody? There's a question. Robbie. No. Lynsey. The thought of it now, talking to somebody – a conversation – he can't imagine it. What would they talk about?

Still but it's good to be out the house. And the sun, a bit of sun on the face, it does you good. He is feeling relaxed. When he gets there he might have a bit of a sit down – there are these benches that he's seen, these old wooden ones that don't exactly look the height of comfort, with three slats for the arse and another three for the back, but so what, who's counting? See if there's one in the sun. A sit down. Maybe a wee snoozle.

It is quiet in the cemetery. The grass has been newly mowed. The smell of it is in the air, and there's shreddings on the path as he walks through past the large older headstones, ruined and leaning like teeth. When he gets to her plot he stands there a while, looking down. The mound has sunk a little, he notices. An odd thing, the peace of it. It's no as if she is here with him, he doesn't believe that – a presence of her beside him – and no that he believes the other either, that she is gone with the Big Man. See if they'd both believed in that, then she's more likely to be in the Bad Fire the now, the way they'd spoke about Him over the years. Anyway about it though, there is genuine a peace here, a slowing down of things, and it is making him calmer. He closes his eyes. Imagines the coffin, lowering slowly into the hole, the steady white-knuckle concentration of the pall bearers guiding it down like cargo. Until that point, there'd been nothing to associate her with this place. They never came here. She's never stood here folding up washing, or eating her tea, or going through him for this that the other that he'd done. Maybe it's because this is the only place she isn't missing from, maybe that's the peace of it.

He sees then the flowers, white ones with egg-yolk centres in a wee pot plant placed where the headstone will be. They are new. The old ones actually have been cleared away, so somebody's obviously come and spruced it up a bit. Craig. It must be. He's been in before work then, or his lunch break – no, he's too far away to get here and back that quick, so it must be after work that he's come, that he's coming. Keeping up his vigil and swerving on the idea of a visit to his da, who's no been the grave himself even once since Craig left last week, as Craig is no doubt aware.

He leaves down the path and out the cemetery, away down the street until he reaches the park. It is quiet here too, nobody about as he goes in through the entrance gate. It's always quiet in here, that's the best thing about it, and how they used to come in from time to time. No the worst park in the world. No the worst. No the best either but, don't kid yourself. All you find in here is the occasional old guy on a bench, or a group of schoolweans having a smoke, or sometimes a scaffer or two smashed up on the superlager, pishing up a tree.

There are plenty of decent-looking flowers in here. They are planted around some of the paths and the trees, and they're no that dry and wilted either, even with the weather like it's been. There is a bed of these nice red ones on the outside of a path that rings a chipped dribbling fountain. Just the job. He follows the path until he gets to the flowers, and he's about to bend down to pick a few when, a short way ahead through the trees, he keeks the parkie, pushing his wheelbarrow of weeds and dirt. Mick carries on along the path. When he comes back round to the same point, the parkie is turned the other way picking something up off the ground, but it's still too much a risk, so he keeps going round. The bastard's probably trying to trick him. Pretending he's fiddling at a plant when in actual fact what he's up to is putting the surveillance on your man here, who to be honest must look like some kind of nutcase, now on his third lap of the fountain. Probably he looks the part too. He's not shaved since the funeral, and also it's fair to say he could maybe do with a wash and a fresh change of clothes but such is life, eh.

The guy is still poking about up the way, so he moves right out of the parkie's line of sight, hiding himself behind a good thick tree. He stays there, waiting, each now and then sticking the head out to check the lay of the land. The parkie's got army shorts on, and a yellow high-vis bib, so it isn't a problem keeping track of him. He waits. Before long the parkie gets moving on, going toward a wee brick outhouse type thing, and Mick takes his chance, stepping out from the tree and quickly across to the fountain.

He kneels down, and starts nipping off the stems of the flowers. The blood is going, he can feel it throbbing in his ears. A grin coming on. Pretty daft, really, the way this has turned out.

'Hey! No, hey, you can't do that!'

He's been clocked. Sounds like an East Europe. He stands up and runs for it.

The guy is still shouting behind him, but Mick doesn't turn round, he makes for the entrance, the stomach cramping and his breath all over the place. Stupit, stupit, pure fucking ridiculous, but all the same there's something of a thrill about having done it and as he gets to the road he holds the flowers aloft, punching them in the air like a baton. He starts laughing. Ye great bloody bampot, serious. He slows to a jog along the pavement and looks round over the palings, where the parkie is standing some distance off, watching him, probably confused at why some headbanger has just nicked his flowers.

He lays the flowers down on the grave, a little way off from the others, and leaves.

When he reaches the turn into his street, he is still breathing quite heavily. In fact that is probably the first exercise he's had in years. Plus as well no having eaten. Nay wonder he's a mess. He is turned into the street and it is quiet, but as he walks on he sees, further up the pavement, one of the drivers from Muir's. Steve. Impossible to know if he's spotted him yet, but there's no turning around the now, it'll be too obvious if he does. Panic starts immediately to tighten through him. He lowers the head and speeds up, staring down at the street, his feet scuffing the tarmac, dog-ends floating beneath the grates of each stank he comes past. The heart is off again, beating wildly – look at the feet, look at the feet – but course that's just going to make him look the more pitiful, isn't it, but so what, so what, if it stops him getting noticed just, stops the possibility of a conversation, of being forced into the world of other people. He should have passed by now. Mick looks up, slowly, angling his head gradually to take in more of the pavement ahead. They've missed each other. He's not been spotted. Relief pours through him, and he glances round to see Steve, a fair way past and crossed onto the other side the road, away with his carriers.

The house. The front door. It opens with a wee stiff shove and there the lobby and the corridor, dark and cool after coming in from the sunshine. The silence of it. Where to put yourself. He comes in and goes through to the kitchen. Gets the kettle going. Mugs clinking out of the cupboard. What a bloody morning. Christsake.

He has made two mugs. No point dwelling on it though. He tips one down the sink and takes hold of the other in both hands, letting it warm through the fingers. Something of a queer smell – probably the milk isn't the freshest. It's fine but, fine, he'll drink it. And then the question again, where to put yourself? What to do now?

What is it that retired folk do with theyselves? All that time they have. Feeding the sparrows, the tellybox on, the park, wee familiar walks down the water, stopping and sitting to chat about this and that. All the patter you can have about characters from the past and how things were before the yards were closed, and what do ye think the now of these high and mighty new flats going up across the way there? The Iron Ladies, as ye used to call them.

There it all is still in the living room. The jumble sale on the settee and the photos still scattered over the floor. It seems even more ridiculous the now than it did before, but he leaves everything where it is and goes to sit in the armchair and finish his tea. He scans out over the photographs, and notices that a couple of them are gone partly under the settee. He gets up and pulls them out. Black and whites, good ones, he'd no paid them much attention earlier. One of them doesn't have Cathy in, he's put it out by mistake: it's himself just, he looks about nine or ten, so it can't be long after his da died, and he's stood in the back court outside him and his maw's tenement, grinning for the camera.

The other one is even better. He can mind it exactly. Twentieth of September, 1967. Launch day of the QE2. You don't forget a day like that. He picks up the photo and takes it over to the armchair. Even though it's faded you can still see what a sunny day it was, the yard mobbed with a great crowd, more than 30,000 there. Cathy had fussed on that much when he'd gone to pick her up, getting her clothes right and her flask and her oatcakes ready, that by the time they arrived the yard was that busy it took over half an hour for them to find Pete and Mary. In the photo, the four of them are stood in a line with their arms around each other's shoulders. He can mind even who it was had took it for them: this wee doddery man in a suit with his hair greased down, parted in a side-shed, who'd gave them his walking stick to look after while he fiddled on trying to get understanding the camera buttons. Cathy and Mary, in their bonniest dresses, holding hands. Himself and Pete blootered. Pete is holding the old boy's stick, leaning down on it, and the rest of them laughing at him.

He stares at the picture. He knows the face as well as if he was seventeen still. But it's just a picture. It doesn't tell you who she is. It's just a picture of a young girl on the edge of a photograph, giggling next to her best pal. Mary. He recognizes that face keen enough too. Cathy standing just off to the side, like she always would, no that Mary was any the prettier, nay chance, it was a question of confidence just, that's all it ever was, and Cathy a wee touch the rounder maybe but so what? At the very beginning it was Mary that him and Pete both had their eyes on. And it had dug his insides up at the time when it was Pete lumbered her first at the dancing, and even then that was only because Pete was further on with the refreshments that night.

Cathy knew all this. She'd told the story that many times herself. Still but. Mary had been first choice; see you could joke about it all you like but that was how it had happened. There's no changing it.

Easy to forget with all the time that's passed. For him, anyway, easy for him to forget. But then you start to wonder: does something like that ever genuine go away? Even after the yard folded and the four of them drifted apart – Cathy and him away to Australia, Pete and Mary to one of the New Towns on the outskirts of the city – did she ever think about it?

He and Cathy would only have been seeing each other a couple of months when this photo was took. Probably he was still beeling at Pete. No that you can tell here, the two of them staggering about holding on to each other, fresh from another visit to the friendly old hen in the pinafore apron handing out the specially blended *QE2* whisky. Yous two again, well? Go on, then, give me your cups, ye pair of troublemakers. Near to her, there'd been the bookie taking bets what the name would be: Churchill at three to one, and him and Pete had the John F. Kennedy at five to one, and he can't mind what odds *QE2* had been but certain nobody had guessed it would be that. Except for auld Aberconway, that is, John Brown's chairman, stood up on deck, Princess Margaret in her white wool coat stood in next to him. And then the Queen herself, of course, she knew; even a wee smile from her as she cuts the ribbon and presses the release button, the crowd starting up with the chants when the ship doesn't budge off her blocks. 'We shall not be moved,' they'd sung. Pete shouting out, 'Give her a shove!' and the girls trying to get him to shut his mouth. Then a moment later she starts to shift and there's a great cheer goes up as she slides down into the water and seven hundred tons of drag chain scutter down the slipway after her.

In an instant he is up and grabbing an armful of all this stuff from the settee, bundling it against his chest and away out the room, up the stair.

A shove of the bedroom door and he goes quickly inside, no hanging about as he drops the things onto the bed, the sheets bare and wrinkled, a slant of light hitting where the pillows would be.

He doesn't bother with putting the photos in their proper places, he piles them all together and gets them taken up to the bedroom with the rest, a sweat coming on as he hurries up and down the stair. He can picture Mary well enough. He can see what she looks like – the exact image of her face less than a fortnight ago at the funeral talking to him and giving him her consolations. He can see Mary; but he can't see the wife. In fact he can see just about anybody he puts his mind to apart from her, he can picture Phillip fucking Schofield the better than he can Cathy – the squeezy-arsed grin and the silver hair and the all-of-a-sudden serious hands clasped together leaning forward – there he is, fucking Phillip Schofield.

He collects the cookbooks, magazines, the Barbaras, the lot, all of it dumped into the bedroom, a dribble of sweat running down his temple now as he comes back in the living room for more. All this stuff, he needs shut of it. It's not helping him remember her – no in the right way, it isn't, no the right way at all – it's just reminding him she's dead. And that applies to all of it, the whole fucking lot: tapes, tape player, plant pots, salt cellar, vacuum cleaner, all of it, it can all fucking go.

He stands there, looking around him. Dark outside the window. The room is almost bare: just the settee, the armchair and the television, rooted, in defiance, to their usual positions. He sits down and puts the TV on. The carpet could do with a clean: collections of dust and dirt lined in squares and circles over the floor. The vacuum is away though, buried in the bedroom under a ton of other stuff; and anyway he doesn't care that it's dirty, what does it matter, there's no point being in there even, and he gets up suddenly to go to the kitchen. His mouth is parched. He gets himself a glass of water, drinks it down next to the sink and is about to sit down at the table, only he can't shake this feeling that he needs to keep moving – keep doing something – and if he doesn't he will sit down and never be able to get back up again. Probably sensible, actually. See if he sits and does nothing then that just means he's going to think about it all, and if there's anything he has learnt the day, it's that thinking is an unwise idea; thinking only tires you out, makes you act like a lunatic.

7

'See me over the remote, will ye, hen.'

'Here. Mind there's my programme on soon but.'

'I know.'

He flicks the channel over and hands her back the remote, careful he doesn't overbalance his tray, and carries on eating. It's a good tea. A chilli. She's put something in it, he's no too sure what it is, but it's got a wee bit different of a flavour about it, which he's liking.

'The appointment go okay the day?' he says.

'Fine, aye. The doctor gave her a new prescription. Says it might help her sleep better.'

'Seems to be working, eh?' He smiles, glancing up to the ceiling, and keeps on with his tea. It's quite loud, the TV, he realizes, and he stretches over for the remote to turn it down.

'I saw Mick Little the day, ye know, one of the drivers at Muir's.' She nods.

'I no tell you his wife died?'

'No, Christ, that's awful.'

'Cancer, I think, mesothelioma.'

'That's awful. Poor man.'

'I know. He looked bad as well, broken, ye know?'

'What do ye expect? His wife died. How ye think he's gonnae look?'

'I know. I know.'

He scrapes up the last forkful of chilli and puts the plate by. She's checking her watch, he notices, no wanting to miss her programme. It's not on for a few minutes yet though, so they keep watching what's on, something with a guy on a boat talking into the camera.

'Ye speak to him?'

'Mick? No. It wasnae the right situation. I was coming back with the messages, I passed him on the street.'

'How ye no speak to him, well?'

'Naw it wasnae the right timing. What am I gonnae say, serious? It's best no intruding. She only died a few weeks ago, I think.'

She finishes eating and puts her tray on the floor.

'He coming back to work?'

'Maybe, I'm no sure. Possibly not actually, what with how quiet things are the now. Might be he's near retirement anyway, I don't know.'

'Ye could give him a knock, maybe, in a few weeks, see if he wants to go for a drink.'

'Maybe, aye.'

'You and Bertie and all them. Give him a while and then call in on him. He'd probably like that, if he's no going back to work.'

'Come on but, what am I going to do, call in at his house? It's no like I know the guy that well. I don't want to go nebbing in on him.'

'Ye've been drinking with him before.'

'Aye, I know, but that's different, that's at work. It wouldnae be normal, chapping his door, ringing him. The guy doesnae want to feel like a fucking charity case, does he?'

'He got family?'

'He's a son, aye, up in Yoker, far as I mind. Guy doesnae want people chapping his door every five minutes does he?'

'I don't know. I don't know the man. It's awfy sad but.'

'It is.'

She picks up the remote and turns the channel, pushing back into her seat as he collects the trays and takes them out the room.

8

The waffles ran out a couple of days ago and he is actually feeling hungry for once. No wanting to leave the house but. No wanting to be in it either, so it's no the ideal situation: moving from one room to the other, unable to settle anywhere until eventually he does sit down at the kitchen table and he stays there for quite a long time, not thinking, waiting just for the hunger to get the better of him and force him out the front door.

There's McDowell's, and that would be the obvious choice, the familiar place, but what he's after is a bit of peace as he's eating his bacon roll and so he goes a bit further down the high street to the other one, the Millennium Star. The same recognizable sounds and smells but: bacon hissing on the fryer, the half-tuned radio, the week's pile of newspapers next to the tea urn. There's a raggedy old ticket near the door, bent over the day's paper. He's probably been in all morning, squinnying at the racing odds. Mick gets himself sat in the corner, away from the old guy and the only other table: three roadworkers silently beasting into chicken dinners with peas and gravy and roast tatties. The girl comes over and he orders himself a roll and a tea. She gives him the once-over before she walks away, but there you go, he's no exactly looking his best, what can you expect?

They're East Europes, these three. Big, quiet baldy crusts – a sure banker there's a whole coachload of them sleeping shifts in a tenement single-end somewhere, and so what, good on them, see if it's no them doing the work then who else is going to do it? These young lads you see loundering about the streets and the schemes complaining there's no work for them? Nay chance. And if all the yards were still standing, you know fine well it would be these boys working on them, building the ships. Hot, hard, dangerous work, no for the lounderers of this world. There'd be no complaint from these but; a bedroom of bogging feet but there goes another paycheque straight on the plane and have you got any more shifts for me, gaffer?

The salty smack of the bacon tastes good. He eats slowly, in stages, making sure it goes down nice and easy. She's still got her eye on him, the waitress, drying cutlery into a tray. Worried he might do a run-out. Maybe he should get out some bits of smash onto the table. She's no half so suspicious of the old ticket by the door but, that's clear enough, the way she's trotting over for a wee patter and a top-up of his tea mug. Canny old scaffer. He's got it sussed. He probably comes in every day. Then on the panel, claiming for all his afflictions, the money never seeing further than the fifty-yard stretch from here past the bookie's to the offie. No that you can blame him but. If they want to top up his tea for free then it's no like he's going to stop them, is he? This is his patch; they know him here, and he is tolerated and fed titbits like a stray cat. How wouldn't you keep coming back?

Bread and eggs and biscuits and all this stuff they do their own brand of in the Co. Plus a bottle of whisky, for good measure. He's got himself a trolley, although he isn't intending filling it, see even if he wanted to he doesn't have enough cash on his tail. He last went to the cash machine just before Robbie and Jenna left, and he saw then that the account is pretty low getting. Which is how there's no choice but to phone in to work again when he gets back, and tell them he's coming in to sort out renting a car. Nay excuses this time.

It is quiet, this time of day. There's a calm atmosphere in the place, full of the steady sounds of overhead lights and fridges and a wee forklift chirring past with boxes of butter packs. Further down his aisle, there's a woman battling on with the messages as she tries to get her weans under control, pulling them out of freezers and fishing out rogue items from the trolley, crisps and cans of ginger and all these things that have found their way in there.

He stands watching his shopping move along the belt. It would have been an idea getting a vegetable or two. A bag of peas, or a nice big cabbage. Too late the now but. Next time maybe.

'Mick.'

He turns round. It is Mary. Pete is behind her.

She makes as if she's going to come toward him, but his trolley is in the way.

'How's it going?' Pete says.

'Okay, Pete, thanks.' The whisky bottle teeters as the belt jerks forward. He reaches for the divider, and his hand is shaking a little as he puts it behind his shopping. He keeps it held down a moment. 'Good time the day to come, this, eh?'

They are both looking at him.

'It is, aye,' Pete says. 'Quiet.'

The cashier is finished scanning his things. She's waiting for him to move forward, his items strewn now over the bagging area.

Mary is watching him. The cashier is watching him. They're bloody all watching him. His amount is showing on the screen, and it's more than he was expecting. He gets out the wallet, his hands still jittery and the whole thing turned by now into a self-conscious show of himself; nothing he can say or do that doesn't some way point at it, the dead wife. What's he doing for money now he's no been working? Is he gone on the broo? Or is he gone on the whisky, look?

There is enough money, and he pays. He gets bagging up as Pete and Mary's shopping starts coming down the belt. Chicken pieces, a *Still Game* DVD, a curry pack, wood varnish. That's the weekend lined up, well, chugging along. Suddenly a squeeze on his arm, and he looks into Mary's face, smiling at him. Here it comes, then.

'Mick, it's good to see you. We've no been thinking about anything else.'

Pete is looking on with a small pinched smile.

She takes her hand away. 'Call on us, please, Mick. Any time eh?'

'Thanks, Mary. I will.'

He picks up his bag and he sees that the cashier is at it now as well. All three of them smiling pityingly at him as he's about to leave; they look like relatives stood around a hospital bed.

He gets the kettle on, watching the sparrow outside pecking at bits of bread, and goes upstairs to wash his face. There'll be no more horrifying of waitresses in cafés, he has resolved. Then he comes down to drink the tea and watch a bit of television.

It is too hot in the house, so he gets up to open the windows – the one in the living room and then the kitchen back door. Let a bit of air pass through. And after that, a whisky? Why no? The afternoon's getting on now, and a couple of biscuits and a whisky could be just the thing. Calm the nerves. Get relaxed. Then when he's settled he can pick up the phone and ring in to work. No use sat about here all the time doing nothing, he's the better getting moving and keeping the brain occupied, and as well the whole social aspect, a bit of patter with the passengers; the other drivers. He gives a wee laugh. A bit of patter? And what about? Did ye see the game at the weekend, what a cracker, eh, and we were out after and ye'll never guess what happened, wait til ye hear this yin. Life goes on, Mick. What is it ye expect, eh, ye want us to stand about in silence because of what's happened, and it's no that we don't sympathize because we do, it's just life goes on, our lives they go on. Suddenly a loud bang jumps him, and a jet of whisky hits him in the face. He wheels round to look at the doorway, understanding: the draught, it must be. His hands are started going as he puts his glass down to go and fix it out.

It is. It's the draught. He closes up all the doors and windows and goes back to sit down and calm himself. Straight away it's hot again, but he'll have to live with it just, better that than a fucking heart attack.

Lynsey will have left the office by now; somebody else on the dispatch. Somehow, the thought of talking to her again, it unsettles him. Implications. All these bloody implications that there's no way around. Lynsey and the wee giggle they could always have, a flirt, you might call it even, but it's fine, it's fine because you get to an age and you're married and sex isn't in the equation when women are talking to you. You're no a threat, so you can have a laugh and a giggle because nobody's on the lookout for your physical needs and your desires – but now – see now those are all busted into the open and people are wary of you because that's exactly what they're looking out for.

He calls the office line. It keeps ringing, and he gets ready for what he's going to say on the answering machine, but mid-ring it gets picked up.

'Hello.'

He considers putting the phone down.

'Hello?'

'It's Mick. That you, Malc?'

'Aw, Mick, hi. How are ye? Ye're calling late, eh?'

'I didnae think ye'd be there still.'

'No, I got stuck here. I had paperwork to fix out and then the phone wouldnae stop.'

There is a pause.

'I'd like to come back in, that's how I'm ringing.'

He can hear Malcolm breathing on the other end.

'Thing is, Mick, we're no too busy the now. Mean, if ye want to take some more time, see the family, ye know, that'll be fine, it's no a problem.'

'No. I'd like to come in.'

He can smell the whisky returning off the receiver.

'Okay, well, that's fine. Ye sold the car, didn't ye?'

'I did.'

'Right, so we'll get ye one to rent again. Come in whenever and we'll find some shifts, okay?'

'Okay.'

'I'd best get leaving, Mick. We'll see you, then.'

'See you.'

He sits down, closing his eyes, trying to compose himself. It's done. Task completed. Now relax. But just then it occurs to him he hasn't checked the phone messages in a long while and there might have been a call. He goes back in the lobby to the phone. There's three new ones.

'Hello, Mick, it's Alan here, just to say we'll be with you late afternoon, it looks like. Depends how the traffic is. I imagine you might not have a lot in, food-wise, so we'll pick up some supplies on the way. See you in a short while, hopefully.'

What was that about no having a heart attack? Jesus. It takes him half the message before he realizes it's an old one and the Highlanders are not in fact about to arrive any moment. He replays it for the date anyway, just to be sure. Delete.

The next message is Robbie.

'Hi, Da, just calling to say we're back, and to see you're okay. Flight was a fucking nightmare in the end – not enough ground staff or something in Hong Kong so we were held up five hours, so we're both kinda whacked now. Jenna's asleep upstairs with Damien. Anyway, hopefully the Highlanders didn't hang around too long and you're doing okay. I'll speak to you soon, alright. Take care.'

The last is Robbie again.

'Hi, Da, I guess you might be working. Anyway, I'm just after seeing how you're getting on, is all. I'm back at work myself this last week, which has been good, you know, takes your mind off things a bit – Jenna's asking to tell you hi, Da, she sends her love – so, yeah, give me a call. Any time is fine, and I can ring you straight back. Okay, take care, speak soon, bye.'

End of messages.

Dark outside. He switches off the television. Pulls the bed covers and the pillow out from beside the settee, then goes upstairs and finds the camping mat. He drags everything together to the kitchen back door, and goes out into the garden.

It is cool outside, but pleasant enough, no wind, no noise either. He walks up to the shed and goes inside. There are boxes and a hammer on the floor, which he picks up and puts onto the cracked plastic table against the back wall. Then he takes the chairs and the rusted mower out to the back of the kitchen and returns to the shed with the bed covers, laying out the mat, the pillow, the blankets onto the floor. There is just enough space for it. A final check out the door that there's nobody spying over the fence, and he closes it behind him.

9

It is cold. There is a wind got up, and he lies with the covers pulled close, no able to sleep, listening to the glass clacking loosely in the window frame. He should have gave it a bit more thought, brought some blankets out. Good job he minded the whisky, well. He takes another mouthful, gulps, and feels it burning down his throat.

He turns over. Can't fucking sleep, man. Nay chance him going back in the house though. He'd rather go cold than stay the night in there: all the rooms, despite the clearout, still hoaching with nudgewinks, making him think about everything. No that he's faring the best out here either, in truth. We've no been thinking about anything else. We've no been thinking about anything else. Really, Mary? Ye sure about that? You've been thinking about what DVDs to watch and that your fence needs a varnish, but no, no, see what we've really been thinking about is Cathy and this terrible situation here. That's what's been on our minds the whole time. And have ye gave much thought, Mary, how it's Cathy copped her whack and it's no you? That's the question. Pete was in the yards the same amount of time – to the very day, in fact; they started the very same day – and you've shook the overalls out and washed them and vacuumed the carpets exactly the same as Cathy has. And why no Pete, for that matter? Or himself. Always the same question, coming back at him. How is it no himself? Him that was working with the stuff every day, brushing against the laggers and their buckets of monkey dung, walking under scaffold planks with great showers of it floating down like snowstorms. And the best question of all – ye ready for this, Big Man – how isn't it the brother-in-law? See if there's anybody deserves to cop their whack then it's him, surely, it's him and all the rest of they lying bastards, because they knew, they knew long before anybody else did what the dangers were, but they did nothing. Nothing. All the reports they must've had telling about the risks, and all of it sided off for the more important business of trying to keep up with the Japanese and the French and the Germans. How not the brother-in-law? But he was shut away, wasn't he, the door snibbed closed, pouring whisky down the throats of shipowners and insurance men. We've upheld our responsibilities and don't think we haven't. We've put the signs up – telling about ventilation and masks and dust checks and all these things that were never bothered with and nobody ever thought to ask for because you couldn't read the bloody sign even, it was that covered in fucking dust.

He presses himself into the crack between the ground and the wall, trying to stop the wind getting a run on him as it races through. The whole of him is aching. Hardly a surprise. It's pure ancient, this camping mat, worn down almost to nothing and if it wasn't already then it will be soon, all this tossing and turning he's doing. Another gulp of whisky. And another. Liars. Fucking liars – see what about all they poor bastards up at the asbestos factory actually making the stuff, hadn't they been lied to worse than anyone? You'd see them coming out with it pasted wet over them from head to toe from hosing the machines down. Each holding a newspaper to stick under the bahookie when they sat on the bus, trying no to piss the driver off. They'd been told it was only dangerous when it was dry. So they took it home, and then what happened – what do ye think bloody happened? – it dried again, didn't it, but that was fine, far as the powers that be were concerned, that wasn't a danger. Fucking lies, all of it. They deserved everything that was coming to them. And if it was him dying, then maybe he would go down that route. Secure a future for Cathy. But it wasn't; it was him brought the stuff in the house. And he should have known. Even if no at first, way back, then he certain could have done later on, when there was the warnings and the newspaper reports and he could have seen through all these lies and no been so blind to it. He'd even worked with somebody who thought they'd took a bad back. Actually known somebody die who'd thought that at first, but then when it was Cathy in the doctor's he didn't think to say anything about it, he fucking forgot.

Could ye have put it out at any time, anything ye can mind? Well, the vacuuming, maybe. See I had a wee twinge doing under the kitchen table no long back. And that was that. Decided. She'd took a bad back. All ye can do is rest it up a few weeks and do nothing – let the man of the house get acquainted with the vacuum for a while, eh? They'd all had a chuckle at that. And he did do as well: vacuuming, cleaning, ironing, with her sat laughing at him the whole month until they went back in when she couldn't stop coughing.

He can't shut the thoughts out now. He presses his forehead hard against the wood, as if to fight against them, but it's no use, it doesn't help. And see if he did put a claim in then the reminders would be there the whole time – for months, years, however long it took – and even that is still ignoring the main thing: why should *he* get a windfall? Him that brought it into the house and handed her the overalls to wash and here's two hundred grand, pal, take it, it's yours – you deserve it.

10

The head is crawling. Stupit. He looks over at the bottle and not only has he wrecked his head, he's also wasted half the whisky rations. No very wise, but there you go, it's no the end of the world; which, in fact, isn't looking too bad this morning: the sun streaming in onto his legs through the small grubby window. He lies there awake a time, listening to the sound of things outside. Birds. A door closing. A distant radio. And all the while playing his toe around something soothingly cool and damp that it's probably no wise investigating what it is.

Anyway, up and at it. He goes to the kitchen, where he takes off his shirt and trousers and gives himself a wash from the sink. He dries himself with the one remaining teacloth, puts the clothes back on, and makes himself a pair of boiled eggs and a slice of toast for cutting into soldiers. Nothing like a boiled egg for a hangover. Except when he lops the heads off he finds he's done them too long and they are gone solid, so he scrapes them out with a teaspoon instead. He needs to go into work the day, get some shifts. It's unavoidable. The longer he leaves it the less they'll want him, and anyway he needs the money.

He stays sat in the kitchen a long time trying to force himself up. But he can't do it; he isn't ready. It feels too much – anyway he looks at it, it feels too much, even bloody getting there, christsake, even the prospect of that is bringing him out in a sweat. The morrow. He'll go the morrow. Rain or shine.

The nights are getting colder. He goes in the house and up the stair one afternoon for more blankets, a fresh shirt and trousers and a jumper, an action that proves a pure effort of will in itself even, just drumming up the balls to go into the bedroom. And the whisky is long finished too, which doesn't help matters.

After three stops, he starts to relax a little. Nobody is noticing him. They're on a different planet, these people, with their earphones plugged in, or just staring out the window. Even when Bertie the workshop mechanic gets on, it's fine, because he's stood in a spot near the back of the bus from where Bertie can't see him, two dozen armpits and raw razored faces in the way between. It's pure illogical but. He's going to have to see him soon enough, he knows. And Bertie's alright, anyway. He's a rare auld ticket in fact, always in there with a joke or a wee story to keep everybody amused. Mick watches him through the armpits. Even Bertie is away with the fairies this morning, it seems, dreaming up something or other, a funny tale to tell the drivers.

He lets Bertie get a way up the street ahead of him, and follows on behind. The stomach is something jittery getting when he turns onto the lane, but there's nobody about and so he goes straight in the office, a shabby small space set into one corner of the workshop, with a plywood divider on one side, and a computer desk and Lynsey in her headset on the other. She's typing something and doesn't notice him when he comes in. Her face concentrated on the screen, clabbered with make-up.

'Mick,' she says, looking up.

'Hello, Lynsey, how's it going?'

'Fine, Mick, fine.' She is uncomfortable seeing him, it is obvious enough. Doesn't know what to say. That makes two of them, well.

'I spoke to Malcolm. He said to come in.'

'Did he? He's no told me anything.' She looks at her screen a moment, then back at him. 'He's gone out just now, I don't know when he's due back. Will I give him a call on his mobile?'

'No, no, that's fine, Lynsey. I'll wait for him a while just, if that's okay?'

'Aye, if ye like.' She smiles, and he tightens up, ready for it, but then she says, 'There's Bertie about somewhere, and a couple of the drivers. Go have a wander. I'm sure they'd like to see you.'

He looks at the divider. The sound of an engine from in the shop.

'If it's alright I'll stay here for now, if I'm no disturbing you.'

'Naw, it's fine. Don't worry. Ye sure ye don't want me to give him a call but? See I don't know when he'll be back and he might be a while.'

'It's okay, thanks.'

There is a chair on the other side of the office, and he goes over to sit on it. He stays there a moment, looking around, noticing the gap beside the divider that looks into the shop. He gets up again, Lynsey glancing at him from her desk, and he walks over to a metal cabinet, on top of which is a paper. He stands reading it, or looking at it anyway. The corkboard on the wall beside him is pretty empty. Normally there would be a long list of accounts and pre-bookeds on there, but there's only a few names scribbled on, under the yellowing page-three girl who's been pinned on that board for over a decade.

'I might nick to the shops a moment actually, Lynsey, while I'm waiting.'

She keeps her eyes on the screen a few seconds before turning round.

'Whatever ye like, Mick, that's fine. I'll tell Malc ye've been by, will I?'

'Do, please, Lynsey. I'll be back in a wee while just.'

He leaves the office, giving a keek into the workshop as he turns toward the lane, where he can see Bertie, chatting with Steve and a young-looking guy that he can't see the face of.

Crapbag. He's a genuine crapbag and no other word for it.

He is in a bar near to work. He came in because it looked quiet through the window, and he was just wandering about, no sure where to take himself. Crapbag. These are his friends, christsake; well, if no exactly friends then his co-workers at least and that's something, sure that means something. Even now, it does. And no like they don't have their own problems to deal with. Steve, with the wee daughter's illness; Bertie, and his troublesome relations with the drink. Sure Bertie would be good for a patter; if there's one thing he's got still, it's his patter, even if he's lost the rest. Amazing to think now, how he used to be. The figure he was forty years back almost, during the work-in. A five-foot queerie with jug ears – no way anybody would ever have thought he could hold a crowd the way he did – but when he was stood up on his brazier with a hundred black squad around him, he'd have the whole yard in his spell. The high wheedling voice, beeling at the government, two hundred clatty ears hanging on his every word. The guy could go on for hours. It was the likes of Bertie that kept them going: even when the redundancies were announced, they stayed put inside the yard, kept building, didn't let the liquidators or any other of these bastards past the gateman; and all through that winter and into the next spring Bertie and the other shop stewards would still be there to hand them their wages. The campaign fund keeping strong; the wives and girlfriends bringing them their food parcels. Cathy and her piles of ham rolls wrapped in newspaper, passing them to him over the barrier.

Hard to believe, looking at it now – at Bertie, old and trembling – that they'd won.

He gets up and goes to the bar for a final drink.

'Half and a half,' he tells the barman, watching as he reaches up to the gantry for his whisky. Christ but the drink makes him maunderly. These will definitely be his last. A maunderly old crapbag, is what he is, and he grins to himself, the guy coming over with his beer and his whisky. He's a great beardie young fella, with small sore-looking eyes like a pair of arseholes, and an oversized T-shirt that says VAGITARIAN – one of they ones you only ever seem to see extra-large guys wearing. He puts the drinks on the bar top and Mick pays and goes back to his seat in the empty room. A cruel bastard, ye can be, Mr Little. A cruel auld bastard and ye know it. Aye, I do, I do, but see that's the drink to blame again, if the truth be told.

An unexpected turn of events: he has found himself in an electrics megastore. How he's ended up here it's hard to say, and given that the stumbliness of the drink is taking effect and that he isn't actually needing a new iPod the now, it probably isn't the most sensible destination. It's woke up the security guard though.

Nay chance he's going back into work now. That is obvious enough. No with the length of time he's been out for, and the smell of alcohol on him. He walks around at random, half aware of the guy watching him. There's golf on the televisions all down this aisle he's in, dozens of them all showing the same event: one of these sponsor's tournaments with a few pros playing round with rich men and celebrities – retired footballers and elderly film actors, that type of nonsense. Alan would love it. He's probably watching it the now even. Christ he's probably playing.

There is laughter somewhere. It's hard to tell where it's coming from, how far away it is, but it is a man and a woman. He has grown to recognize the voices from hearing them talking together sometimes if it's a warm day outside. They were arguing earlier the afternoon but now the sound is clearly of laughter, finding its way in under the door and through the cracks in the window frame.

He is cold. He has lain there with the covers pulled up all morning and there's nay chance he's tweaking the door open so he'll have to live with the smell just – the clinging stink of a fish supper he brought back a few days ago. A while later but he is too thirsty, and he does get up, leaving the shed to go for a drink of water from the kitchen. He is turning the tap when the phone starts ringing in the lobby. It startles him. He stays there, frozen, with the tap still running and his arm beginning to shake. It rings a long time. He waits for it to finish and he turns the tap off, putting the mug on the counter, and leaves straight out the house by the front door.

Maybe he'll take a walk down the water. Keep moving; he needs to keep moving.

He isn't too sure the time, or even what time is safest to come these days and what's best left alone, it's that long since he's been down. So he comes slowly up the path, scanning up the way ahead. There is a young couple he comes past, with their two tiny weans. One of them is in a pram, and the other running about, scampering between the headstones and her da trying to coax her back. She's got the right idea but. Why no run about the place, instead of teetering around the graves? They're dead, christsake, they're no bloody sleeping.

There's new flowers again. The ones Mick left himself are there next to them, gone dry and brown by now. He picks them off the plot and gets them slung over the palings. Strange Craig's left them there, although – no, see even that is probably done on purpose, as a reminder, a marker of the da's last visit. That's exactly the kind of thing he would do, in fact.

It's started drizzling, so he walks over by the palings and stands under a bit of tree. See what makes it the worse is it's hard no to pity the boy. The same useless fucking pity that everybody's so keen to stick on him, he's doing it too, when he imagines him up there in Yoker alone and angry, naybody to talk to. Or maybe he does. Who knows? There had been a girl he was seeing, Tina, was she called, but there's no way of telling if they're together still. Maybe not, in fact. It had seemed like something of a loose kind of arrangement, from what Cathy had said. He should ask him. He gives a short laugh at the idea. He's only once before been up to see him, and that was a few years ago. Into the dingy flat boufing with dirty plates and filled-up ashtrays, but no his place to say anything, so he didn't; and neither did Cathy even because, as she says, it's his life to do as he wants and see if he wants to make mistakes then he'll make mistakes, and he'll learn from them, same as the rest of us.

The family are on their way, ahead of him as he leaves along the path. The wee girl holding her father's hand, and him leaning over and giving the wife a kiss on the side of the head. You don't think, when you're that age, about all this that might happen – that is going to happen, actually, a pure certainty it is going to happen. You're too busy with getting the food on the table and clothes on the weans' backs and feeding the wife's bingo habit to start thinking about what like it might be when one of you is gone. And too right. Jesus. Too right. What a thing to think about.

There is a man outside the house. Mick has turned the corner into the street and is coming up the pavement when he sees him, standing at the front door. Mick turns straight around. Keeps moving. Gets back down the end of the street to the bus stop and spies through the glass. He's still there, just stood, waiting. From here, he can't see properly who it is, but he's sure he doesn't recognize him. He fights to get the breathing under control. Maybe it isn't his house, and he's mistaken, it's actually next door. It isn't but. It's definitely his house. The man is peering in the window now, cupping his hands around his face. He chaps the door. Now what? Wait, just wait. The man turns and starts inspecting the grass at his feet, as if he's looking for something, and then he's up to the window again, spying in. For a second, a strange hopeful thought hits him that maybe it's a robber, but just then the man turns and goes out the gate and he can see his face. It's nobody he recognizes, a big guy in a shirt and tie, who is getting now into a dark red car parked on the street outside. It's a while before he leaves but. The car stays there another few minutes before it starts pulling out from the kerb and swings round, moving off in the direction away from the bus stop.

Mick waits a moment longer, watching carefully. As he gets up and starts toward the house, there is laughter, and he spins around to see two teenage boys knotting themselves looking at him from one corner of the bus stop. He walks away quickly, checking around him, and gets in the gate and then the house, hurrying through it and out into the garden, snibbing the latch of the shed as he comes inside.

II

The cold. It is setting in. Keep the whisky flowing, my man, keep it flowing. He unscrews the cap and takes another bolt – a bottle he'd minded was in the kitchen, unopened, laid out on top of the cupboards. A present from Alan last Christmas. The usual gift from him, but no complaints, he's bloody grateful, serious. The bottle carefully chosen, you can tell: decent enough it's obvious he's spent some money, but never a single malt, never something that the average man, in the brother-in-law's opinion, should be drinking. But fine. Fuck it. Fine. Cheers then to the brother-in-law and to his charming wife, who haven't as it happens been down once to visit the grave since they left. Which tells you everything, really, everything. Still but you can't have it all ways, eh, and the better that he doesn't have to see them; plus as well of course, how does he know for sure that they haven't been? Maybe they have, see, maybe they have. No way. They haven't. There would be some display of flowers or something. They have not been. See if they come at all, they'll come when it suits them. When there's a film they want to see, or they need a new computer.

A stifty wind in under the door. He pulls the blankets close. Jesus, he's hungry. He drags the emptied tool box from under the table and feels about inside it for the end of a packet of biscuits, then gets eating a couple. It's nearly finished, the food store. A battle plan needed. Another problem for another day.

He has had a pure stroke of luck. He'd been one afternoon rummling about in the back of the shed for anything useful there might be, and he found the wee battery radio they used to put outside sometimes when they were sat or she was at the gardening. It's still working. A miracle. And it's good too, having it on, no bother that the reception is pretty fuzzy, it's better than nothing, especially these nights he's laid there just, with the brainbox going, no able to sleep.

He listens to the quiet voice of the nightwatchradioman. He's talking about this TV programme that he watched the day about assisted suicides and people going away for them, the legalities and all that. Mick's no hearing it all, but it's relaxing, the sound of the guy's voice. There is a call-in after, but they don't stick to the topic. People can ring in saying whatever's on their minds. What do ye think will be the score Saturday? Barry in Pollokshields predicts a thumping away victory for the Gers, and a hat-trick for the new boy. Here's hoping, Barry, here's hoping.

The food store is gone. It's fine but, it's okay; no like it has come out the blue. He's been intending the last few days to go the messages for one or two items. Bread. Biscuits. Cheap things that don't need going in the fridge and he can keep out here. Another bottle of whisky would be much appreciated too, but he's got to be careful watching the pennies, got to start thinking where's the money going to come from. He closes his eyes. Got to do this, got to mind to do that. It's too much to think about. Easier to shut the eyes just and go to sleep, no have to deal with anything just now.

12

Des is standing on the pavement out front of the Empress when he spots the distant figure of Mick approaching down the street. He drops his cigarette to the ground, picks up the broom that is propped against the wall, and gets sweeping the lunchtime dog-ends into the road. No that there's a great many. There'd only been a few in: the small group of staff from the recruitment agency round the corner, a couple of shopping-centre workers, and Pat, who is the only person left in the bar now, quietly drinking his Guinness over the racing odds.

He finishes clearing the pavement, and waits to say a hello to Mick if he isn't stopping in for a drink. Halfway down the street though, Mick crosses over and goes into the closemouth of a tenement on the other side, a blue carrier bag in his hand, and disappears. Des goes inside. He pours a refill for Pat, a Grouse for himself, then goes into the back for a sit down.

Maybe it had been someone else. Looked like Mick but. He sits back and lights a fag, keeping an eye through the bar to the lobby entrance. The family must have all gone by now: it's well over a month since Craig was coming by those nights, so he's obviously back up in Yoker. They might be on with a claim by now, from what Craig had been saying then. Awful fucking sad, what had happened. She was a great woman, Cathy, a cracker. Always had been. Back in the day, he used to have something of a crush on her. When he was a young guy first working the bar for his father, he'd look forward to her coming in with the other women during the work-in. There will be no bevvying, the shop stewards had told their men, so they were doing it for them, they'd joked. Just awful bloody sad. It could've been any of those women – still could be. The whole area is a timebomb. It could well be him next, or Pat, or any of the men that he'd stood and listened to from behind the bar, right from when there first started to be the rumblings, talking about it like it was something far off and no to do with them, even though they were sat there with the dust caked in their ears and their arseholes. A customer is coming into the lobby entrance. Des gets up, reluctantly wedges his fag in the ashtray, and goes through to the bar.

Mick comes back into the shed with a wee feeling of triumph and puts the items into the food store: bread and biscuits, a packet of cheese, tinned apricots and luncheon meat; even a paper for something to read and while away the hours. See all that stupit carry-on and then in the end it was fine. He's probably only been gone twenty minutes. He gave the Co a swerve, so all he did was get to the cash machine on the high street, draw out a note and ignore the fact the account is gone overdrawn, then dot in the minimarket on his way back for all these bits and pieces. Easy-oasy.

Now that it's done he steps out of the shed again and sets his sights on the house. He may as well get everything done in one go, collect more plates, a knife and a fork, and fill up the watering can with fresh water. Then he'll be set.

He stands outside the shed and looks down the line of back gardens, all empty; wet leaves and rubbish strewn about. Five minutes and he'll be done. Put the blinkers on, get in and get out. He starts toward the house. Grey pebble-dash; green back door. Strange but he doesn't recognize it, it's that unfamiliar somehow. If he'd been in the shed and he'd tried thinking what colour is the back door, what colour is the front door even, he wouldn't have been able to say, serious, he wouldn't. All they details: doors, carpets, furniture, they all merge into a general feeling you have, a habit, of being in the house. A place you return to at the end of the day after your toils, and relax. The familiar routines – putting your keys on the counter, sticking the kettle on, getting sat in your chair – it's natural just, you don't even think about it. All of it so far past the now. Gone. None of it fits.

The bulb is out in the kitchen. He goes to the cupboard for plates, working by the dim light coming in through the rain-smeared window. Grey shadows on the counter from the kettle and the toaster. He gets a cup, a knife, fork, then he rinses out the watering can; gets filling it with clean water. What would be a good idea as well is pulling the covers off Robbie's bed: the nights are too cold getting, even with the extra blankets he's brought out. He goes out of the kitchen and it's the speed of things, the combination of them all happening together, that undoes him. The light no turning on. The tide of envelopes by the door. A noise upstairs – a bump. It all happens in a second, before he can get registering any of it, and his heart banjos right up his fucking throat and he has to shove against the banister, pressing his back to it and craning to look up the stair. His breathing is heavy and snatched, he can't control it. It is gone silent up there. But then there's another bump somewhere above his head; he makes a dart for the living room door beside him. Quiet as he can, he crouches down behind the settee and gets lying in the narrow gap between it and the wall.

His leg is murdering underneath him, but he doesn't budge. Still nothing from up the stair. The blood in his ears is making it hard to listen, but he strains to hear, ready for any sound in the ceiling above him. Stupit. He is trapped, and whoever it is that's up there is just waiting, because they know it, or they've went, or they weren't even bloody there in the first place, Christ knows. So he stays put, the leg aching and his knees pressed into the back of the settee. From where he's lying, he can see part of the video player under the television, but the display clock is blank so he can't tell how long he's been there, maybe only a few minutes, or maybe hours, who knows?

Quietly, stiffly, he gets himself out from the settee. His ears are pure bursting, he's listening that hard as he edges out from the room and into the corridor, quickening his pace, coming into the kitchen and grabbing the things before getting out the back door. He clicks it softly shut behind him. A quick look at the upstairs window before he reaches the shed, but there's nothing.

He is sat in the straight-backed hospital chair with the plastic peeling off it and the foam poking out, while she stares out of the window. The white curtain is pulled shut in a horseshoe around them, and there's the peaceful hum of a dozen sleeping, snoring, dying women in the room outside. Through in the corridor, the faint hurrying patter of nurses' feet. And beyond the window, where she's staring, a gardener, whistling himself a tune as his pink head tots in and out of sight behind a hedge. After a while he comes round the near side of it, and he's got his shirt-sleeves rolled up, it's that sunny a day. The windows are open, and it's awful welcome, the freshness of the air outside coming in with his wee tune, pouring into the stale room. All of a sudden there is a fart somewhere outside the curtain – a loud, long, trumpety job – which causes him to chuckle and look at her, but she hasn't noticed it, she's still fixed on the gardener. She has been asleep all morning and she's lying restfully the now as he sits quietly watching her.

A nurse pops her head through the curtain at one point, gives him a smile and disappears again. She didn't signal she was coming in, it occurs to him when she's gone. But then what would be the point? She is the one that's changing her clothes, helping her go to the toilet. There's no need being discreet any more; it's past that. Maybe if he'd been sat there himself in the bare scuddy, his balls sticking to the seat, then maybe she'd start giving the signal. He grins. Aye, probably.

There is the gentle hushed sound of a relative talking. Outside, the gardener is lopping the heads off a line of finished flowers at the bottom of the hedge. Still the bright, tireless whistle. He looks at her. Is she listening? Can she hear it? He realizes then that he doesn't know if she can or not – if she's listening, if she can see him, or if she's just staring out at nothing. And that is when he understands. It's the precise moment, in fact. Maybe she can hear it, maybe she can't, but either way it doesn't make any difference because it's only time now, only time that is in the way. He stands up from the chair to move toward her, and her eyes shift to take him in. He smiles, and brushes the headscarf back to give her a wee kiss on the forehead; then he leaves out of the cubicle to go and get a coffee from the machine down the corridor.

13

The biscuits are gone stale. There is the dull snap of wet fibreboard about them now, and the cheese has broke out in green spots and a white frilly moss. He opens the door a nook, pushing against the sludge of wet leaves gathered against it, and slings out what's left for the birds. No use it going to waste.

The shed isn't best equipped for this rainy period that's come on. It gets in under the walls and the door, and drips down off the window. The blankets are pretty damp getting by now. Probably he'll come down with some horrendous illness and go the way of the cheese. The sparrows the first to find him, to notice he's copped his whack when they start pecking inside on the lookout for food.

Enough of that. Talk about maunderly. Jesus.

He is running out of shit pits. There's nay chance he's going back in the house, with its strange atmosphere and its lack of lights and its mysterious bumping noises up the stairs, so that just leaves the bucket at the back of the shed. He did consider using it before, when he stopped using the house toilet, until he came to his senses and realized that would be mental. Instead, he'd took a corner of the garden, the border on one side where Cathy used to plant her flowers, and used a trowel to dig a line of small pits, each with the mound of soil next to it to cover over after he's took a crap. But now the line is almost filled. And as well, he needs to get some toilet roll. All he's got left to use is torn out half-pages of the *Southside News*. A delicate operation, serious, though it doesn't make much difference how gently he does it – the backside is getting sorer, and blacker, pasted each day with new articles about tenement regenerations and Roma beatings.

There is a noise coming from outside. A faint, distant, rolling sound. He thinks at first it might be the wind, which is piping cold pea-shooters at his feet from under the door, but he understands after a while that it's Ibrox. There is a match on. He tunes in the radio, but the commentary isn't the clearest so he gives that up and listens outside just, waiting for the wind to blow him a favour. It does, and a few times he hears a muffled roar going up. Maybe the new boy is on form. Taken the league by storm this past couple of weeks and making mincemeat of opposition defences. Whatever the score is, it seems like they're winning, and the result is confirmed for him later, because there's car horns pamping in the night, together with what sounds like a brawl away on the high street.

Here they come, the wee chaps. He listens, enjoying the sound of it, as they begin skittering on the concrete outside the shed door. Something aye comforting about the noise of them pecking the ground, tapping, the odd time, on the side of the shed.

Until recently there'd just been the one – probably the same patient guy that's been coming all the while – but he's obvious gone and let dab to all his mates that they can come and eat here, and now there's a whole mob of them. Good for him, no keeping it all to himself. Obviously no an English bird. A genuine Southsider, that sparrow. It's mostly just bread he's buying now, each few days when he works himself up to leaving the shed, and he keeps a couple of slices from each loaf aside to put out for them. Sometimes, when he hears them arrive and gets open the door latch, he lays a short trail of crumbs from the outside, into the shed, to see if he can get any of them to come in. There's one time, he managed it. This tiny head, poking in the door and then following the line, unaware, or otherwise unbothered by the great hulking creature that was keeping still and watching him from the darkness under the table. Sometimes as well he tries to sneak a look outside at them, but each time he does they all fly off, and he has to wait a few minutes until the noise starts again: that small fluttery sound of them out there, getting beasted into their breakfast.

15

A dark red car is turning off the high street. It comes past the park and the cemetery, slowing a moment for a pair of old women to cross the road, then continues on until it pulls into a residential street, and a few seconds later parks up against the kerb. A short bald man gets out, followed by a larger, younger man in a pullover. They come through the gate to Mick's house and stop by the front door. The older man knocks firmly, while the other peers into the living room window. There is no response from inside the house so the older man hunkers down and looks through the letterbox. In a moment he stands up and pushes an envelope through the flap. Then the two men, without speaking, go back through the gate, get into the car and leave.

On the other side of the house, in the shed, Mick is sitting up close to the radio. It is almost out again, the sound distorting quietly like voices inside a hull. He needs batteries – all the ones that were in the house are used up; more bread as well; cash. For now he clicks the radio off and gets the few remaining pages of the paper over for another read, nothing else to occupy his mind now that the morning is by and the sparrows have finished their breakfast and left.

**FIRST TENANTS MOVE IN TO NEW
HOUSING ASSOCIATION
DEVELOPMENT**

**SLOVAK ROMA COMMUNITY
GIVES A HAND TO SOUTHSIDE
CLEAN-UP**

**LOCAL LOLLIPOP MAN HAS REAL
STAYING POWER**

He gives a read of that one:

Britain's top football juggler broke the record for keepy-uppies on Tuesday, when he kept a ball aloft for six hours at Debenhams in the St Enoch's city-centre shopping mall.

Sadly, his effort was declared unofficial because there was no representative from the *Guinness Book of World Records* present at the event, although Graeme, 45, has still raised thousands for charity.

Afterwards he said: 'I could have kept going but I had to stop because the store was closing.'

Mick gives a wee smile. Good on ye, pal. The thought of him there in the Debenhams, a crowd of skiving weans and confused old hens gathering round. 42,500 keepy-uppies. Fucksake. That's just mental. Interesting but, these stories that you hear. This other one he minds – about a restaurant owner with a rat problem: they're eating into his food stores and frightening the customers. See but these rats are too canny for the traps, and when they do eat the poison it isn't strong enough to kill them, so the guy decides he's going to leave his cat there the night in the hope the rats will start crapping it and scarper. So he locks the cat in the restaurant, and when he comes in the next morning he finds it out the back court, on top of the beer crates, devoured, only the poor creature's carcass left, and even then some of the bones are away.

Where'd he heard that story? Robbie, was it? Aye, it was – he'd been telling them while they were watching the TV, Lynn shifting about on the settee with a look on her like she'd just sat on a dod of crap, and Jenna elbowing at Robbie telling him it's no an appropriate story to be saying; but him carrying on anyway, nay doubt enjoying putting the mix in.

Probably he's been calling, Robbie. Likely he will have gave Craig a call too, asking him what's the story with the da.

He doesn't want to think about any of it though. It's more than he's up to the now; what he needs to concentrate on is this immediate situation in front of him. First things first, he needs cash, and that means bulling up to go into the bank to see about an overdraft.

He walks quickly, taking the back ways where he can until he has to come out onto the high street. He goes a short cut before the Empress, through a tenement close. There's nobody about. The door to a garbage cage is flapped open and the wheelie bins strewn all at angles inside it from the binmen coming collecting the morning. He comes down a side street and stops at the entrance to the high street, eyeing left and right. It's hoaching. It must be lunchtime: schoolweans outside the chip shop; traffic hurtling – and then, just his bloody luck, he keeks the woman from next door, pushing a pram on the far pavement. He retreats back into the side street, head down, observing the feet. Maybe she wouldn't recognize him even. There is some sort of oil smear down the one trouser leg, he notices, starting above the knee and staining all the way down to his shoes. Perfect. See there's him trying to keep the head down and remain unnoticed, but just look at the state of him – he's bloody bogging – he may as well be wheeling her along after him with a flashing light on top the coffin.

He looks up and watches the neighbour away down the pavement; the messages done, off back now to get on with the business of looking after the snapper, the husband no about, seemingly. And where is the husband? How come you never see him about? Easy to think the worst sometimes but maybe it's just that he's off on the rigs or something, you never know. Cathy would have known, sure enough, but otherwise you never know. There is a lull in the traffic and pedestrians, and he steps out onto the pavement.

When he gets there, the bank is queued out. He decides that he's best waiting until after lunch, and turns the other way down the street.

Which is how he finds himself in the library. It isn't what he intended, but he'd no been intending anything, and it looked quiet inside, so in he went.

She's very helpful, the girl at the desk. He can't have made himself awful clear when he came in, stood there staring just, not knowing if he needed a ticket or anything to go in.

'Can I help ye there?'

'No. Aye, well, see I'm just hoping to have a look round at the books.'

'Ye been here before?'

'No.'

'Come on well and I'll get ye up and running.'

She lifts the desk counter and he follows her as she gets showing him all the different sections while he shuffles behind picking books out at random, trying to seem like he's interested in them and he isn't just in there because he's too feart of everybloodywhere else. And it's good too, somebody being kindly that he doesn't know, who doesn't know him, who isn't sticking the whole pity routine on him. By the time she leaves him at it, he has a whole pile of books that he hasn't a clue what they are. He sits down and opens one of them, all the time looking about to see if anybody is watching him. No danger of that but. It's pretty empty in here. There is a guy that looks like he's a scaffer asleep with a newspaper spread out under his forehead, and three old hens at a table in the corner, each with a copy of the same book. Quite an animated conversation they're having.

'. . . he's clever, I think, he just doesnae get the credit, ye know. All these people that used to come on the show, and he could talk with any of them.'

'Aye, and he's awfy handsome too, say what ye want, but he is. Especially when ye look at the wife there next to him, she's that weary-looking.'

'Aw, come on, of course she's weary-looking – the man's a balloon!'

The three of them start chuckling.

'He is, Helen, he's a bloody balloon.'

The scaffer is woken up. He's got a pen and he's started ringing the classifieds, working down the column, putting a circle around every one. Fair play to him. I admire your confidence, my man. See really that's what he should be doing himself, having a look what jobs are going. If he can't deal with going into Muir's, then he'll have to think of something else, because he can't exactly live off nothing. What money they had, they used up while she was ill, and an overdraft is only going to last so long. A new job. Maybe move somewhere else. A different town. He turns the idea over for a moment. A wee flat somewhere he doesn't know anybody, with only a few simple things he needs in it – TV, kettle, heater – new, replaceable things.

The thought of Muir's, and seeing Lynsey again after he'd done the run-out last time. What they must be saying about him. His chest starts to tighten and he has to concentrate on his breathing, try to control the panic. Across the way, the guy is still going through the columns, ringing the lot, and he wonders if maybe he's some kind of headbanger. But then maybe he's just in here for the same reason he's in here himself. This is his place of refuge, where people leave him in peace and he doesn't have to worry about the outside and all the rub-ye-ups. That's him the now too. Another headbanger in the library. He stands up abruptly to leave, making sure to thank the lassie on the desk and picking up a copy of the *Southside News* as he goes out.

It is quiet in the bank, only a few people queuing up and two clerks on. Nobody he recognizes. He has to collect himself, get it done with, get it over, go back to the shed. The recorded voice calls him to a window. There is a young guy behind the glass. His neck is pinched and red, bulging out from his collar.

'I'm wanting to see about an overdraft.'

'Okay. Pass me your bankcard please.'

He takes it out of his pocket and drops it in the drawer. Across from him there is a dithering old guy stood at the next window – 'Ma what?' – and then the voice through the glass: 'Your statement, sir, I need to see the statement.'

'The account is in debit.' The clerk is looking at him.

'I know. That's how I'm wanting to see about an overdraft.'

He goes back to his screen, tapping away at the keyboard.

'See, I'm afraid there isn't the option of an overdraft on this type of account.'

'Okay, right.'

That's that well. He looks round and the old guy is still rummling shakily in his mac pocket for his statement, pulling out streams of tissue, coins, bus tickets. When he turns back to the window, the clerk is tapping at his keyboard still.

'It might be best, in your circumstances, looking into if you can get a new type of account. I could give you some information.'

So there it is, then, even the bank knows – it's there on his screen.

'I'll leave it the now, thanks.'

Hunger. No surprise there. He lays in the dark looking up out the window at the moon, big and bright the night. The food store is empty. Him and the sparrows finished the last of it for breakfast so now he's pure starving, and you'd think he would be feeling some kind of urgency about the situation but he's not – no a great deal anyway – it's in fact more a kind of relief now that he's no money left. Strange. Figure that one out. No money, no food, and no chance he's going cap in hand to anybody. The idea of that knots him up – obviously it isn't an option – but he allows himself for a moment to imagine it, some kind of odd pleasure from kicking his own head in. Going to Pete for a lend of some money. Anything we can do to help, Mick. Anything we can do. Except fucking for that, Jesus Christ, are ye cracked?

But of course the brother-in-law, that's a different story: he'd be pure delighted, guaranteed. A great song and dance over it, the ceremonious fetching of the chequebook, the smug showy putting on of the wee reading glasses. How much would you like, Mick? Really, it's not a problem. How much? And going on the broo is out the question too. The thought of that is almost as bad as the thought of going to those other two. Queuing up with the wine-moppers, filling out forms and forms and killing her over and over with each one. The same as it would be with the compensation. Deceased. Deceased. Deceased.

He'll be fine. He'll find a way. No like it's the first time he's found himself without any money, that's what he's got to mind, and this time as well it's just him, there isn't a whole family to support. Nothing could be as bad as the last time, when the job Alan had got him after Australia eventually fell to pieces. All they weeks and months of will theys, won't theys, and then the first wave of redundancies starting. Dozens of meetings with the shop stewards and the union men, and all that talk of refusing to give them an inch, don't forget the spirit of '72 and all that, but in the end it came to nothing. That's exactly what they got. Nothing. Alan and the Bowler Hats making their arrangements for theyselves, and all the rest of them left out to dry. See that was a worrying time. The severance cheque didn't solve anything, and the wife's job obvious wasn't going to keep the four of them for long. The arguments they had. So ye won't even consider it, well? It's the damned pride, is what it is, Mr Little. Ye know Don Paton is gone on the broo, so Sheila tells me, and no drama. I'm no saying it's easy, I'm no daft, see I'm only saying this frequenting of the Empress every afternoon and sitting about the house like a pound of mince isnae helping anybody.

She was right, obviously. And her taking on more hours at the store, it was hardly fair, plus on top of that having to come home knackered after work to him there on the settee, grumbling and drunk. Again. After she'd went through all this with him fifteen years before. Her working and him on the bevvy. Desmond the only person who was doing any the better out of it, his bar mobbed with black squad the whole time, drinking and shouting and scheming their plans of attack, convincing themselves that things could be got back how they were. That they knew what they stood for. I am a shipbuilder. That right, eh? So what are ye now that the shipyard has copped its whack and the job is away? I am a shipbuilder. Once a shipbuilder, always a shipbuilder, and all that tollie they'd told they-selves. No just the jobs that went, but the life. Ordinary life, it was gone; it had to be admitted. Himself a culprit. One of the worst. He wouldn't let go. Couldn't cope with the idea that things had changed.

He turns over stiffly and pulls the blankets up to his chin. The nights are too cold now to sleep all the way through. A rain is start-ing, pattering above his head. He needs to figure something out. He will but. He's managed before, and he'll manage again. Before he eventually got in with the private-hire driving he'd had to leave town to do it, disembark to Newcastle, the short-term contract at Swan Hunter. You battle on just. That's what he'd done then, even if he did spend most of that time lonely and drunk, and it had been against her wishes in the first place. She'd not wanted to be left on her own, looking after the weans, but he'd done it anyway, the same as he always did, the same as when they went to Australia – had that been a joint decision? Had it hell. He'd told her that was what they were doing and so they did it. The moon there out the window. A full one. The great yellowy cunt, bright as a bare arse. Always his idea. Pack your things, hen, leave your job, your friends, your home – we're off! That's how it had been. His idea.

'Ye have the item with you?'

'Aye, it's just here.'

'Can ye put it in the tray for me please?'

He takes off his watch and places it in. She inspects it a moment, turning it about in her fingers. She's pure laggered in jewellery: her fingers and thumbs, a gold necklace, and these wee pearly bullets in her ears. Must be she gets a discount.

'Give me a moment please.'

She swivels out from her chair and goes through a back door, and he stands waiting in the empty shop. It isn't like he expected. What was he expecting? Christ knows. Not this, anyway. There's nothing antiquey about the place, that's for sure, all bright lights and a blaze of yellow in the display windows. Sour red carpeting and security notices on the walls. It's like a bank. Actually, no, it's even worse than a bank. He goes over to the window to look at the pieces. Hundreds of rings and bracelets, each of them their own sorry story. In fact, see why don't ye just go and slit the wrists in the corner here – ye may as well if ye're in the mood, ye maunderly auld bastard, christsake. There is a dull chap on the security window as the woman returns.

'Twenty pound.'

'Serious?'

'It's quite worn.'

'No, mean, it's more than I thought.'

She smiles. 'Want it back, well?'

'No, no, it's okay, thanks.'

She is still smiling as she takes out the money and puts it in the tray.

A grey, dreich day outside, the tops of the multis merging into the clouds and the sound of car tyres hissing up water as they come past. Twenty quid. He should probably feel pleased but he's too bloody starving, on the approach now to a minimarket for a sandwich.

The watch was a fiftieth birthday present from the other drivers at Muir's. It must have been pretty expensive if he was getting twenty for it now. That birthday – him, Cathy and the boys, they'd went to a restaurant in the centre. He tries to picture her, but he can't. It was just before Robbie left for Australia because Craig was digging him up the whole time – gonnae send Kylie my love and all this – he wouldn't leave it alone. They'd sat at a table in the corner and she'd been next to him, the place full and noisy, the waitresses with these old-fashioned aprons on and Robbie awful cheeky getting with them, to Craig's annoyance. He can't see her though. He knows she's there sat right next to him but she's the only part of it that's a blank.

He gets his sandwich, and he walks over to the cemetery to go sit down on one of the benches and eat it.

Still a blank. The familiar tightening of his body coming on and he has to relax. He has to relax. Normally he can do that in here, that's aye how he comes, but he's no helping things rubbing himself up like this; he should just calm it down, eat his sandwich. Craig. Craig is here. He's going up the footpath. The first instinct is to duck the head. He's walked right past him, and now he's away up the path toward the grave. Did he see him? Impossible to know, he might've, he might, how could he not've – he's come right beside him. The heart going mental. His body rooted to the spot, but nothing he can do: he can't get up because that will obvious draw attention to himself so all he can do is stay put and hope he doesn't turn round. He gives a keek up. The back of Craig's jacket, a way up the footpath now. He watches as the boy passes through a line of trees to the next lawn and stops when he reaches the grave. He's got his work clothes on, by the look of it, although it's hard to tell from this distance. He's just standing there, looking down. Me and you, Maw, it's me and you against all the rest of them. He stands there a minute or two before he starts to bend and crouch down, and as he does so he turns his head. He is looking straight toward him. It's a bare instant just, a single second, then he turns back to the grave.

He flicks the light switch out of habit but of course it doesn't come on, but so what, he doesn't need to see any of it, the less he can see in fact, the better. As it is, he can still make things out in the half-dark. The mound of post at his feet; the bare, ripped ribbon dangling off the wall. This needs to be done quickly, or if not he's going to collapse in a heap no able to get up and that'll be that, never to be seen again. Except by the man up the stair, of course, that bastard – he needs to be calm, concentrate – no think about a man up the stair. He keeps it all blanked out as he goes through the kitchen, fetching a carrier, and then gets up the steps to the bedroom. He moves quickly inside. Ignores the dark heap on the bed. He pulls open her drawer and grabs a handful of jewellery, dropping it into the bag. His breath is snatching now, coming in jolts, but he's managing it, he's coping, taking another couple of handfuls to empty the drawer, and the truth is it feels good – there – so fucking what? What difference does it make anyway? She's dead. She's not going to wear it.

He'd be pure raging if he knew. But he doesn't, and he can get to fuck if he thinks he's got any more right to her than anybody else. He goes out of the room and back downstairs, where he gets his jacket and the small battered holdall from the lobby, and starts putting things into it: the carrier of jewellery, then out to the shed for his change of clothes and the newspaper. Then he's away. Gone. Goodfuckingbye.

'Ye back, then?'

'I've brought some more things.'

'Go on, well, let's see.'

He empties the carrier into the tray. She gives him a look but he ignores it, and he stares away toward the window while she inspects through it.

'Is it for loan or sale, this?'

'Sale.'

'Okay, well we buy gold and silver by the gram, so I'll need a wee while to price this lot up, that alright?'

'That's fine. I'll wait.'

She gives him £250 for all of it. It's worth a lot more, he knows, but no like he has much of a choice. There's a ring in there that used to be her grandmaw's, which must be worth a couple of hundred on its own, plus a few other things that were handed down to her when she was a wean in a big house in the Highlands and she hadn't yet disgraced and ruined herself with the dirty plater husband.

It's pishing it down when he gets outside. He could get on the subway, all this cash he's got on his tail now, but he needs to be careful saving it so he waits for a bus instead, standing a long time with the wind blowing in and water dripping off his nose. He gets the next one into the centre and gets off at the coach station. There is only a short queue at the ticket desk.

'When's the next coach to London?' he asks the guy.

There is a bronze statue by where the man waits. A life-size young couple greet each other, a bag on the floor beside them, and he is lifting her up, their lips about to meet, one hand sliding down over her bottom. The man smiles, looking at it. A couple of girls come past and notice the statue; they start giggling. His own bag is not much bigger than the bronze man's. In it, his few clothes, his work boots, a plastic wallet with his valuables and a little food for the journey. Already there is a large group waiting by the glass doors for the London coach, but he sits further off, on a plastic orange seat by the statue.

He goes inside his coat for his phone and makes a call.

'Yes?'

'Yes, my name is Juraj. I am arriving in London tonight.'

'Got an address?'

'Yes.'

'Passport?'

'Yes,' he lies.

'Right. You'll find details where to come in the morning. There will be a van waiting. Bring the passport, and the driver will need your expenses up front. He'll take you straight to the site.'

'Okay. Okay. The flat is not shared? My wife and son come here soon. The other man said it is not shared.'

'No, not shared. Polish?'

'No. I am from Slovakia.'

'Right, well. Plenty of Polish there. Slovak too probably. You come at six tomorrow. Details are in the flat.'

He puts the phone back in his coat and continues to wait for the coach. Things will not be easy once he arrives; he is not stupid. When the agency in Slovakia arranged for him to come to Glasgow, they told him the same thing. You will have your own room. It will be comfortable for your wife and child when they join you. And on the outside, the red brick building did look beautiful, if you ignored the – 'Govanhell' . . . 'Fuck off gypos' . . . 'Scum' – local poetry. He could not bring them to a place like this. Five cramped streets: no privacy, no heating, no landlord. White and Asian gangs. In London, at least, they will be hidden – Roma, Polish, Pakistani – nobody will care.

An old woman is standing in front of the statue. She looks at it for a moment, then moves away to where a line is forming in front of the glass doors. Back home, it is getting more dangerous: last month, his wife's brother was badly beaten and left in the tip next to where they live. There is no choice now but for them to come here; it is the right decision. The driver is opening the doors and climbing onto the coach. He stands, picks up his bag and goes to join the queue.

There are no empty pairs of seats left on the coach, so he sits down next to a man who is staring out of the window with his hands on top of his bag, clasping it to his lap. Past the man's head, he can still see the statue through the glass wall of the station, and he continues looking at it until the engine starts up and the coach rolls off. He grins. When my wife arrives here, he thinks, this is how I will touch her bottom.

A young guy with a shaved head is come and sat in next to him. It's okay but. He doesn't look like the type that's going to be chinning him all the way down for a conversation. Which is good, because it's a long-enough journey. More than nine hours. Arriving in London in the wee hours, when the pubs are shut and the cafes aren't yet open. He could've planned it better, serious. He could have planned it at all, in fact.

By the time they get leaving the city and the sudden leap of green at the end of the schemes, the gloaming is come on outside the window and he is falling asleep. When he wakes up the lights are turned off and it takes him a moment to mind that he's on a coach, people snoring around him, a dim strip of lighting along the aisle floor, fallen crisps and a crisp packet and legs stretched out. He looks out of the window into the rushing darkness. He doesn't feel jittery. He feels okay. He doesn't feel anything.

A while later and the neighbour is awake. Mick can hear him shuffling forward and unzipping a bag down by his feet. The sound of paper, or plastic, tearing. Then the smell of food, a sausage roll, which he brings up to his mouth and starts eating. Okay, well, a plan. The first thing when the coach gets in is to eat: probably he'll have to find a petrol station or a 24-hour minimarket and wait in the coach station until everywhere else starts opening up. Then onto the job hunt. For starters, this one he's seen in the *Southside News*.

The guy is looking across at him.

'You know where is King's Cross?' he asks, as if they've been pattering away all this time.

'I've no idea, pal, sorry. I've no been to London before.'

The man nods and carries on eating his sausage roll, then after a while he gets out his mobile phone and starts thumbing away. It's a pretty decent point – does it matter that he's never been there before? No, it doesn't. That's the best bloody thing about it. He needs to keep things simple. Keep away from any reminders. Go see about this job advertised in the paper and get on top of himself, fix things out. Englandshire. Nobody will guess that one. He's only been twice before: the six months in Newcastle was the last time, and way before that, when they weren't long married, a visit to Cathy's cousin and the husband in Northampton. Fucking terrible. There were a few of her relatives set up in England, and they'd spent a miserable week with these, himself going about the place trying no to spill and break things and none of her lot speaking with him unless it was to ask him stupit questions about the yards, that same way people use when they ask a wean how school is going. They didn't come to the funeral, that pair, as far as he can mind.

It is raining. He sits back and looks at the giant windscreen wipers going back and forth on the front window. Thinking about England. Newcastle. How he'd felt going down this very motorway, moving further away from home; the argument that him and Cathy had got into the night before he left, both of them shouting, Thatcher on the television in the background, bringing the poll tax to Scotland. See in truth he'd been lucky getting a job at all, because Swans had went the same way as everywhere else – privatized, shrunk – but he hadn't felt lucky; he'd felt fucking terrible. He'd rented a room in a house with quite a few Swans workers, young lads mainly, and a guy his own age from Southampton, he can't mind his name. They'd all go out together to the bars, come back and get the landlady raging. But the clearer memory is of the nights he'd spent alone in his room, drinking, wondering what in hell he was doing in this place. Sat there on his days off, the TV on, until it got too much and he'd go the long walk to the phone box a few streets away.

The neighbour is snoring. Mick turns toward the window, trying to shake the mood that has come over him. Remind himself it wasn't all bad. Because it wasn't. They were good men, for one thing. Mad for their football, anyway. There were always games down by the jetty after lunch; races up the bank by the young lads at the end of a shift; nicknames – Big Yin, they'd called him right from day one, because they knew Billy Connolly had worked on the yards. He never really felt part of it though. He couldn't, no with Cathy and the boys up in Glasgow. And it wasn't his yard; his river. He didn't belong there. Didn't get the same feeling from it: that sense of the river always being there, around him, inside him. The sheer thrill of a ship on its stocks, grown from just a few small pieces of metal, walking toward it each morning and seeing that it was bigger, looking like it was parked there at the end of the street, looming over the end tenement. He can mind exactly the feeling of it. The sound of the hooter. The gates opening and the mass of workers teeming through. Getting into the yard and seeing that the graffiti on the hull had been added to – jokes, patter, Proddy slogans – so that when the ship was near completion you'd look at her and the whole of her side would be a mess of chalk scrawlings. Comic pictures of the managers. Competitions of who could write the highest. Two-year-long conversations. And then, when she was built, it would all be painted over and there'd be no clue as to what was written underneath; except if you looked hard enough, the tiny scribbling along the waterline where the painters had wrote their nicknames.

The driver is pamping the horn to get everybody awake. Mick stands groggily, and presses into the line slowly moving down the aisle. As he steps off the coach, away into the terminal, it is the first chance he's had to see the other passengers. There's a fair number of East Europe types amongst them, it looks like. Something about the quiet way they get on with things, filing off to the exit and seeming to know exactly where it is they're headed – even the neighbour, striding off with his bag over his shoulder, King's Cross here I come.

There is a snack machine in the arrivals terminal and he gets himself a Mars bar, then sits down on one of the backless plastic seats, pulling his jacket tightly about him, and tries to get the brainbox working.

Somebody standing over him. A big fella with a meaty face.

'You okay there, mate?'

A sliver of belly poking out beneath the shirt.

'Do you know where you are?'

Mick chuckles. 'I've no got a clue, pal.' He notices then there's the half-eaten Mars in his lap.

'You can't stay here, I'm afraid.'

'It's fine, see I must've fallen asleep for a minute just. I'm looking for a cafe that's open, if ye know somewhere.'

'I do actually. There's one just round the corner, as it happens.'

He points Mick what direction it is and waits for him to get up and leave.

When he gets there it is open, like the man said. The pleasurable sound of chairs and plates and low conversation as he steps in and gets himself a table, reading the breakfasts off coloured sheets of card above the kitchen. A few coach-driver types drinking coffees. A street cleaner in a high-vis jacket, and he minds suddenly the incident with the parkie and the stolen flowers, but he shuts it out straight away as the guy comes over for his order. Bacon and eggs, and a tea. He's pretty friendly, the time of morning it is, humming himself a wee tune. Turkish, if the poster above the kitchen is anything to go by. Things have started well. A hot breakfast about to arrive, in a little wink-wink of a place that he's found, when instead he could easily be pounding about the streets right now for a petrol station.

When he's finished, he goes up the counter and asks the guy if he knows anywhere nearby he might get a room for what's left of the night.

'Hostel? B&B?'

'B&B, aye.'

He reaches for his order pad and pulls a pen from his trouser pocket, but then hesitates, deciding against it. He points an arm to his left.

'You see this street? You go down, you go left under the bridge, and there – there are many places. Ten minutes.'

Mick thanks him and picks up his bag to leave. No bad, eh, this London. No bad.

He can see the bridge up the way. It is a railway bridge, he can make out as he gets closer, walking alongside the high sooty walls that follow the road beneath. There is a narrow street just before the bridge and he turns onto it, past a builders' merchants and an MOT garage under the arches. A few minutes down and he spots a cracked white plastic sign: BED AND BREAKFAST: SINGLE £25, DOUBLE £40, FAMILIES £60. Fine. It will do. He just needs a bed for the night, it's no like he's choosy. He goes up the steps and there's no obvious buzzer so he tries the door, and it's open. He treads into a dimly lit corridor with a worn red carpet and the ribs of the floorboards showing underneath. Yellow, chappit wallpaper. At the end there is a sign – RECEPTION – and an arrow pointing up the staircase.

He goes up to the first stairhead, where there is a door with a crumpled plastic file pinned on it. A piece of paper inside. *Back in 10 minutes.* It doesn't look likely. Probably it's too late the now to get somewhere, but just then a man appears on the stairs behind him, another Turk, by the looks of him.

'Have you lost your key?'

'No, I just, mean, I was hoping to get a room.'

The man leads him up the next flight of steps, fishing a bunch of keys from his pocket, and unsnibs a door.

'Single room?'

He nods.

'Single room is £25.' He stands there scrunching the keys down by his side. Ye reckon he wants the money up front, well? Mick gets out his wallet.

'Whereabouts is breakfast served?'

'No breakfast.'

'Eh? No breakfast? It says "Bed and Breakfast" on the sign outside.'

'No breakfast.' He takes his money and leaves.

No breakfast, then. Mick stands at the door and takes in his room. Poky, a stale clinging smell, the same peeling wallpaper as the corridors, and what looks like a giant shite-mark on the carpet. It's better than a shed though, so nay point complaining. There's no curtains, instead a grey veil pinned over the window with an orange glow coming in one side of it. He climbs onto the bed, which seems clean, and is that tightly tucked it looks vacuum-packed. He lies on top of the covers. He should be doing a stock-take of the situation, he knows, but his head is aching and it's hard to think clearly, so he lies there just, the eyes closed, vaguely aware of a streetlight buzzing outside, and at one point the rumble of a train going over the bridge.

Later the night he has to pee, the need for it building and building until it's too uncomfortable, and he gets up. He waits at the door a while, listening to make sure there's nobody about, then he comes out, and up the next flight of steps to a door marked BATHROOM. No that he wouldn't have telt it by the smell: sharp, sour, mixed in with bleach, the bottle of which is left out, sat on a ledge under the sink. When he's done he comes back in his room and snibs the lock.

Morning. He lies there a long time. His stomach is uneasy, and the whole of his body is aching like he's just come off a back shift. The streetlamp is turned off and daylight sifts dirtily through the window veil, exposing the room. That scunnery brown streak on the carpet, he can see now that it's a scorch mark. Christ. Ye dread to think.

A noise outside the door makes him jump. Somebody pounding down the staircase. Quietening down the next flight, quieter, then silence. His heart is racing at the suddenness of it. Just a noise. It was just a noise. Somebody running down the stair, it's nothing out the ordinary. But he is panicking and it's a struggle to get control of it as he presses the side of his head into the pillow, hearing the thump of blood in his ear. That's just the problem but – it *is* out the ordinary. No like he hasn't heard people running down stairs before, but no *here*, no in this place he hasn't.

Just a noise, just a noise.

But he's got nowhere to put it. A fucking noise, man – they've gone by now – but it's bouncing around inside him, unable to come to rest because everything else is jumbled up and bouncing around together, and he can't act or think normally because what *is* fucking normal? Answer that one. What is normal? There isn't a normal. He swings his legs over the bed and sits up. Everything racing and rushing. He is sucking for breath but it's no good, sitting up is making him feel boaky, so he lies back down again and gives up trying to stop it. Thoughts hurtling in, he can't keep them out. She is normal. That is what normal is. There, he's said it. But now everything is birling around and it's all to fuck because that's the thing he's been trying to steer clear of, thinking about the wife, and now he's let it in and there's no controlling it. *She* is ordinary life – she's as much a part of him as his legs or his stomach – and without her all the rest has lost the plot. The stomach fucking especially.

Cry, man. Just bloody cry. Nobody's watching. But he can't let himself – it's there, he can feel it in his throat like a furball, retching and stuck, but he's too feart to let himself. It'll just make him the worse. And then he definitely won't be able to stop, he'll be here the whole day bloody greeting.

There are voices in the room below. So what? He's staying in a Bed and Breakfast – well, a Bed – what do you expect, he'll have to deal with it just. He can't hear what they're saying but it sounds like there's a few of them, a family, because there's a baby shrieking or crying or making some kind of a racket. He gets up off the bed and pulls the table that's under the window over to wedge against the door. Then he gets back on the bed. No television, so no easy way to ward off the brain, except for sleep, closing the eyes and sleeping, he could sleep all day, he could sleep forever.

Later he goes down and gives another £25 to No Breakfast, who counts the money carefully and slides it in his pocket.

That night he sleeps fitfully, in and out, a lot of it just staring at the orange glow through the window.

The people down the stair are arguing. A woman shouting. It goes on for quite a long time and then there's a door shutting and it goes quiet. He needs to get some food. No easy thing going out into the day but. What he needs to do is just blank everything out, kid on that he isn't actually existing and do the zombie walk to wherever the shop is. Nobody knows him anyway. That's what he has to tell himself. Nobody knows him.

He finds a Costcutter after the bridge. There is a radio playing but he can't hear the words. He gets a damp pasty in a packet from the fridge, a couple of lager cans and a sandwich for later. He doesn't look up at the man as he pays. Another guy by the door as he goes out, sat behind a kiosk like some silent gremlin, selling phonecards.

The next few days he slips into a routine. Out to the shop in the morning, and forcing the food down when he gets back. Then sleeping and drinking and keeping the brain quiet until he has to go down and give No Breakfast his money. The wee patter between them: how's it going, pal? Oh, not too bad, thanks, business pretty steady at the moment thanks to you and as well the family downstairs. Good, good, I'm pleased. Clutching for a normal. It is some kind of an ordinary, however crap.

18

He opens the *Southside News* and gets to the page:

> Major hotel chain, UK airports: Glasgow, Birmingham, Manchester, London Heathrow. Staff wanted, all departments: Housekeepers, Food and Beverage Assistants, Breakfast Chefs, Kitchen Porters, Reservations Assistants. Live-in positions.

Work. Work is what he's came down here for, and work is what's going to get him back onto his feet. Spend too long without employment and what else are you going to do but occupy the whole time alone with yourself until the brain is turned to mince? That's another reason he'd never go on the broo. Work is busyness at least. So he needs to get off his bahookie and get some, get on the keel and give Robbie a call, because this keeping him in the dark cannot go on. And so what if he's never been a kitchen porter before? He can do it, he can lie if he has to, and it's perfect, really: something different from what he's done before, no reminders. Plus as well the money situation: he's running out.

He washes himself, or tries to anyway, with what little water he can bleed out of the shower head. Afterwards, a good examination of the face in the mirror. He could fine well do with a shave, but he doesn't have a razor. Still, it's long enough now that he has a decent beard on. A respectable beardie man, a Sean Connery type, that's the way he should look at it. Although being honest, respectable is probably up in the air when they get to looking at his clothes. He's got on the shirt and trousers that he had in his bag, but the problem is that both of them are crumpled as a toad's foreskin. See what he should do, he should probably give a phone down to room service and ask No Breakfast for a lend of the iron. He forces a smile at the idea of it. He feels okay. He feels fine. He is going to get on.

He packs his bag and leaves away into the street. What he needs is a good shovel of food, to keep him going the rest of the day, and where better to get it than at your man's down the way, the cheery Turk.

After eating, he gets negotiating the subway. Finding it is easy enough, although the actual thing itself is genuine a bit more complicated; a Rubik's Cube of colour-coded trickery compared to the one he's used to. He manages but. He is managing.

There is a young guy on the line of seats opposite him. He's got on a pair of tight blue trousers and pointed white shoes, his legs crossed over like a woman's. The pointy foot joggling in the air with the bumps of the track. He's reading a magazine with a cartoon drawing of two men on the front with comic stretched faces. He's about ages with Robbie and Craig. What would they make of him? Just then but the train comes to a halt and he has to concentrate to get hearing the driver, and he is able to stop the thought before it can develop. He needs to keep focused. The brain is a genuine minefield of all these thoughts that he's got to keep himself from thinking, for the moment at least, just for the moment, until he's got himself back on his feet. Then he can see where he's at.

The hotel is one of a fair number along a drag that he has to cross a great tangle of carriageways and multi-storey car parks to get to. It's huge – they're all huge – and ugly. A block of grey, stained concrete; the only colour is the massive lettering of the hotel's name above the doors. The woman that he speaks to on reception is friendly enough but.

'The operations manager is in a meeting until three,' she tells him after she's put in a call. 'Do you mind waiting?'

'No problem.'

The operations manager, it turns out, after he's waited a long while on a seat fixed to the table in an empty restaurant, surrounded by plastic plants, is a woman. She doesn't shake his hand. 'You're a kitchen porter,' she says, going behind the bar to make herself a coffee. 'You're not agency though?'

'No.'

'Do you have a CV?'

'No.' Great start. Bloody haddock. 'See, I was in the shipyards, and then my last job I was a cab driver. But when I was younger I used to work in kitchens. Hotels and that.' A pretty obvious lie. She is behind the bar still, looking at him as she stirs a sugar into her cup. It isn't the face of an impressed person.

'I saw the job advertised in a paper.'

She frowns. 'When?'

'A while back, actually.'

She comes out from the bar. 'Well, it's up to the chef anyway. Come this way.'

He follows her round a corner into a passageway where the carpet stops, and there is a pair of swing doors with small porthole windows. Blinding bright inside, mobbed with men in white jackets. She goes in and he waits outside, a tight feeling in his chest. Relax. Just relax. She is stood just inside the kitchen, and a tall man is coming over toward her. Behind him, at a gas range, one of the chefs is pouring a packet of something into a pan. The tall man keeks at him through the porthole.

'. . . is him,' he hears her say as the doors swing open. She walks off without looking round and the man is stood in front of him.

'You've not done KP before, then?' He is Irish. He's got baggy red and white checked trousers.

'No, mean, not for a while.'

'Scottish?'

'Aye, Glasgow.'

He folds his arms, narrowing the eyes and smiling.

'Here's the million-dollar question, then – Bhoy or Bluenose?'

Mick smiles. 'Bluenose.'

The chef gives himself a comic slap on the forehead. 'Fucking typical.' He grins. 'No, it's fine, it's fine, I don't give a shite. And you're the right colour anyway.'

He goes in the swing doors and Mick follows, keeping the head down and avoiding looking up at the other chefs. He reaches for a pen on top of a whiteboard by the door.

'What's your name?'

'Mick.'

He writes it down next to BREAKFAST: MICK WASH I.

'You've timed it well in fact – we had a guy left yesterday.'

They walk through the kitchen. He is staying calm. Heat, young men with shaved heads, the sound of a radio. They go past a heap of crates, and the kitchen throats into another room, smaller, dimmer than the main one. A very black man in dark green overalls is clattering a pile of frying pans into a sink.

'Eric, take this fella down to the staff rooms.' He turns to Mick. 'Take whatever one is free and get yourself settled in for today. Breakfast starts at six so get here just before and I'll sort you out some overalls,' he says, and leaves.

The black guy hasn't looked up from the sink, and Mick wonders a moment if he has understood. In a minute though he stretches off his rubber gloves and goes out through a fire door, the tap left running.

He follows behind him as they go down steps and through corridors, and it's becoming clear enough that your man here isn't going to speak, walking slowly ahead, the bare back of his neck shining under the fluorescent strips. At one point a stretch of tubing is out, and they walk on in near complete darkness until the next lit corridor, then down more steps, right into the bowels.

'Here,' the black man says, and goes back the way they came.

He is left in a long corridor with doors both sides. One of them is open, and he sees inside that it is a bathroom. He goes down the line of doors. Low music coming from one; snoring, another. Otherwise the place is silent. He stands there, wondering what is his next move. This is mental. Unreal. It's that far removed from reality in fact that it's hard to believe there's not some kind of chicanery going on, the auld brainbox playing tricks. But to these people it's just ordinary; he is ordinary even, that's the strangest thing. All of them – the manager, the chef, the kitchen porter – it's like they expected to see him here. He hasn't caused the barest ripple of an interruption. Go downstairs and go in your room and you're working at six the morrow, and everything just carries on as it was.

Somebody is coming out of a door down the way. A girl. She's in her pyjamas and barie feet. He stands there rooted as she comes toward him, and he's about to have to say something when she turns into the bathroom. She didn't seem to notice him even. What, are they on drugs, these people? He feels like he's totally lost his bearings, the quiet sounds of snoring and music and humming strip lights around him, a girl in her pyjamas, and he's losing track already if it's day or if it's night. The toilet is flushing. She comes out and starts walking back to her room.

'Excuse me,' he calls out. She doesn't hear him.

'Excuse me.'

She looks back blankly.

'Can ye tell me which of these is free, please?' He can see now that she's been asleep, the eyes half closed.

She shrugs her shoulders. 'I think maybe this one.' She points to a door by the bathroom, and pads off.

He pushes the door open slowly and the shapes inside become clearer as the light from the corridor filters through. The room is empty, the bed made. He finds the switch and the bulb takes a moment stammering on. It is like a compartment in a storage warehouse, threadbare and windowless; tiled drop ceiling. There is a sink and a chipped white Formica wardrobe, a waste bucket, a chair and a small table with an alarm clock, the hands pointing just the back of four. Unreality has hold of him now, carrying him numbly on as he arranges his few clothes in the wardrobe, takes off his shoes, puts them under the table and gets lying down on the bed. Careful. He needs to be careful. Too easy to get maunderly and think about things – the lack of daylight, for one, Christ – but actually what he should be thinking is good positive thoughts. He has found himself a job. He is on his feet. He has got himself what he was looking for. What was that, well? It was an anonymous room in a place with no reminders and no bastards to pity him or stick the boot on. The image of Craig in the cemetery comes suddenly to him, but he knows he has to shut it away, shut it right away. He looks about him. See if he gives the room a bit of a spruce up it might not be so bad. A mini television. Plants. Maybe he could knock a couple of plastic ones out the restaurant even – there ye go, now you're talking man, now you're bloody talking.

There is noise outside the door just before five: foreign voices, shouts, a woman laughing. Then it goes silent for half an hour, until all at once the noise returns and there's a few minutes of activity before it quiets down again. After that, there's just the occasional sound: doors shutting, a voice coming past, the flush of the toilet through the wall behind his head. Later the evening he leaves the room and finds his way eventually out of the hotel, making his way over to the terminal, where he gets a jacket tattie and a pint.

He doesn't sleep the best, so the early start isn't a problem. He is up at the kitchen for quarter to six, waiting in the potwash. Through in the cooking area he can hear the Irish chef instructing his shaven-headed team to get set up. After a few minutes he comes into the potwash holding a fryer smoking with bacon fat, and sees Mick standing by the machine.

'Shite, yes.'

He goes off a moment and returns with a pair of overalls. 'He'll show you, but it's easy enough. Wash 1 means you stand at this sink and scrub most of the crap off everything, then you stack it in these trays for him to put through the machine. And you clean the kitchen stuff.' He points at the bacon pan hissing in the sink.

There is nowhere to get changed so he puts the overalls on in there, on top of his clothes. And that is the first thing he learns: not to wear anything underneath. Within half an hour he is pure sweltering from his exertions and the heat of the machine. Wash 2 is fine but. He's got the right idea – just the bare black skin visible under his overalls whenever he bends down to stack something – he's genuine fine and breezy. No that he's said as much: he's hardly spoke a word since he came in. It isn't the same one as yesterday – he's taller, this guy, and he's fucking fast. It's hard work keeping up putting the plates and cups in the trays before he grabs and trammels them along the runners into the machine – the hoosh of steam as he pulls it down and sets it running. Thirty seconds and they come out dry, it seems, because he piles the lot straight up and takes it over to the racks. When he does speak, it's to tell Mick that he's doing it wrong – 'No. No' – and he'll stand in front of him and start stacking the trays himself. It's doable but. He is doing it. He is managing. First day on the job and he's on top of it.

It is a separate world but, the potwash. He'd've thought it would be different to this – all noise and shouting and Gordon Ramsay, waiters running about with their arses on fire – but it isn't. It's oddly quiet in there, cut off, just him and Wash 2 scrubbing and stacking, scrubbing and stacking. There is the clanging and jouncing of ovens and grills from in the kitchen, and each while a chef coming through, shouting, 'Hot pan,' but even through there, there's no noise, no patter. Strange. It's fine but. It suits him. Ye keep the head down, ye do your job. Scrub, stack; scrub, stack. The faces of waiters appearing at the hatch above the sink to dump the dirties on the ledge. You new, pal? What's your name? Good to meet you, how's it going? They don't speak. They don't see him even. Fine. That's fine. And there's something quite satisfying about the work as well – no exactly stimulating but it's mechanical, you get into a rhythm, repeating the actions, challenging yourself to get the pile down. The empty ledge. A wee pat-the-back moment of job satisfaction. See that, Wash 2? First shift but no messing, eh, no fucking messing about, look.

Of course but he's jumped the gun. There he is thinking he's such a big man for keeping his piles down, while there must be hardly anybody in the restaurant. It doesn't start coming properly until an hour in. Plate piles begin growing on the ledge, tall teetering columns of bowls and cups; the cutlery bucket swelling like a haemorrhoid; and the waiters finding their tongues at last, beefing that they've no space to put the dirties. He's not keeping up and he's soon enough sweating all over the place in a panic, desperate to get it down before the Paddy chef comes through and sees.

Wash 2 is fair agity getting with him by now, butting over to get the piles and stack them himself. And then, just when it's coming on the busiest, the baldies start barging in with all their pots and pans, fat-fryer baskets, chopping boards, long metal trays lined with burnt knickers of egg. His heart is racing. He gets rushing about, losing his scourer, piles increasing all around him. He trips on a heap of pans by his feet and near goes on his neck. Bracing his hands on the sink, he takes a couple of deep breaths, the black guy glaring over at him. Get beasted in just. Get the piles down before the chef sees, finish this shift – then he can put down a marker, then he'll know where he's at. He leans toward the machine, ignoring Wash 2, pulls over an empty tray and gets loading.

Toward the end of the service, as he's thinking it's started to quiet down, they begin coming with great long dishes and glass bowls in from the restaurant. He gets scraping them out, chucking leftover sausages and grapefruit segments into the bin, until one of the waiters starts going through him, saying he has to wait until they've cleared all the food themselves. It must get reused, he realizes. All of it, too, they clear the lot. Even the eggs, man, Christ.

By the time it's over he is pure wheezing, blowing for tugs. And that was breakfast – Christ knows what like the lunch service is, or dinner. Or if he has to work them all, either, that's another thing he's still in the dark about. Still but he got through it. His standards were up in the air quick enough, but he got through it – congealed crockery going straight in the tray and the scrub, stack of earlier turned into a dump, dump, dump. Fair unlikely that it was coming out the other side clean, but Wash 2 didn't seem too bothered, he just wanted to keep it moving through, the piles kept down, the waiters shut up. To keep their faces away from the hatch.

Wash 2 takes off his gloves and motions Mick to follow as he goes into the kitchen. The baldies are bent and kneeling, scrubbing inside the ovens. Wash 2 writes his hours on the board and hands him the pen when he's done.

'Dia, is it? Hello.' He holds out his hand. 'My name's Mick.'

It doesn't feel quite the right thing, a handshake, but the guy takes it, with a small nod of the head. 'Breakfast now,' he says.

Mick follows him into a bare, bright room with tables put together into two long rows. There is a queue of twenty or so staff getting food from a table in the middle. As soon as they go in he feels exposed, stood there in the bright room for everybody to look at. There is the noise of chairs scraping as people take their places and start eating. Dia is gone ahead into the queue, and Mick joins the end of it, one of the chefs getting in just before him. He stays close behind and shuffles forward. There is a great purple wart on the back of the guy's neck, his skin raw and pink around it where it's been catching his collar. Somebody behind him too now, he can hear him puffing his frustration at the queue. 'Come on, come on.' His eyes on Mick's back, taking him in. Chefs pushing in further up the queue; nobody saying anything.

Here are the eggs, then. By the time Mick gets to the table, eggs is mainly what's left, plus a few sausages, beans, fruit salads. He doesn't care. He just wants to get sat and get eaten, go back to his room.

Dia is on a table of black men, four of them sat together in green overalls. Mick goes to the other row, sitting himself at one end where the seats all around are empty. Further down there is a group of women, all dark haired, foreign-looking. One of them keeks over at him at one point, and he realizes he must be sat where their pals are about to sit. He eats up his breakfast quickly and at random. No that it's a meal you'd want to linger over. One sausage, a slice of bread, and a small clot of beans sharing juices with three pineapple slices. Nay wonder they're all so miserable.

Everyone's in their own group – the baldies at one table, the waiters another, the receptionists – all of them keeping in with themselves. It's like school. And it's so quiet, that's the strangest thing. Hardly anybody talking, just chowing their food down in silence, the only noise in the room the sound of knives and forks hitting plates. Most of them look foreign, maybe that's part of it, the lack of mixing. Still but, who's he to talk, the cloyed-up Scot there at the end of the row.

He is finishing off when the head chef comes in and walks over to him. He stands stooping opposite him, his hands pressed on the table.

'Go okay today?'

'Fine, aye, once I'd got the hang of it.'

Some of the women are looking over.

'You need to get your speed up, that's all.' He stands straight, looking off toward the door, then back at Mick. 'Next staff food is at five, and your late starts at half past, okay?' He pats once on the table and walks away.

He doesn't go to the next staff food. He holes up in his room, laid on the bed in his pants and his socks, done in, drifting in and out of sleep through the afternoon.

The late shift is longer, relentless, more types of crockery. At least but he is in the bare scuddy underneath the overalls, which is a pure blessed relief compared to earlier. And as well he manages to wrestle a few more words out of Dia, who is on with him again.

'Where are ye from?'

'Ghana.'

He realizes it's coming to a close when the waiters are only leaving tea and coffee cups, and these wee pots skinned with leftover mustard and ketchup.

When the kitchen start bringing all their pots and pans through, Dia gives him a hand scrubbing them clean, and afterward shows him where the mop is to follow where he's already swept. They are about done when one of the baldies comes through with a bottle of beer in his hand, sheer-legging over the wet floor to reach for his knife bag off one of the shelves. A beer. That would be pure fucking heaven right now. He doesn't say anything to Dia though, and they finish up, draining the machine and bringing out the rubbish bags before they leave, away back to the staff quarters.

He gets into his room and tummels onto the bed.

19

The next day is much the same; and the next. His body is feeling like it's took a kicking. By the time his day off comes, he's that exhausted it is all he can do to get out of bed in time for staff food, and he spends most of the rest of it asleep.

The rota is two shifts each day out of breakfast, lunch or dinner, and one day off a week. His mind is occupied, near enough, and then when he's no working he's too tired even to think. He gets kept on Wash 1 for the first week, either with Dia or with Eric. He doesn't try getting any patter out of them so it's aye quiet working, but no that it's frosty or anything, it's fine, it's just work. They two have their own reasons they don't yap on, the same as he does, and so they get on with it just, silently working as a team while the baldies flash in and out with hot pans and the waiters gurn through the hatch.

The afternoons, which are only a couple of hours if he's on a lunch, he rests up in his room, or he goes out the back fire exit to the terminal for a pint, or sometimes, if he can't stomach the idea of returning for the lunatic buffet, a sandwich.

The later staff food is harder going even than the breakfast. Usually there's a tray of mince, without tatties, and a tray of carrot omelette, or onion omelette, or sausage omelette. Then it might be chips, which are away in a second, and hard, chewy rice that gets stuck between your teeth. He sits at the correct table now. Takes his place with his African co-workers and chows away silently next to them. He asks the other two their names. Obi and Vincent. They wear the same green overalls, but they work in a different kitchen, he doesn't know where.

One day after the breakfast shift, the head chef comes in the potwash to tell him he needs to go up and see the operations manager: she has to get his details on the system.

He goes after staff food. Her office is on the same level as the kitchen, through a corridor with the same scuffed carpeting and bare walls as the rest of the staff side, but the occasional plastic plant and a wall clock with the hotel logo on it. A few shabby efforts at perking up the gloom – it's in fact no unlike the walk used to be up to Alan's office – which maybe explains how his stomach is feeling right now. Away, it's Mick! Good to see you. You're a kitchen porter now, I hear. Good for you, that's great.

He's about to chap the door, but he hears voices inside, what sounds like an argument, and he hangs back. Hard to make out what they're saying, but it's two women. Probably he should get leaving. But then there is movement inside, and he presses back against the wall as one of the housekeepers comes out, leaves the door open, and is away muttering down the corridor. The operations manager appears, sees him, scowls.

'I'm here to fix out my details.'

She turns away. 'Wait.'

The door shuts, and a few moments later she shouts him to come in.

She gives him a sheet of paper to fill in and ignores him, busy writing quickly onto a pad. She's rattled, clear enough. He can feel the movement in the desk as she writes. A great black printer between them with Post-it notes stuck on it: *Tronc adjustments. Gerry, Plane Food, 4 p.m.*

Scottish, he puts on the form, and Mick; the rest he makes up. He's filling this out on a need-to-know basis, is how it's going to go, and there's fine well certain things they don't need to know. Provan, he calls himself, after Dave Provan who played for Rangers when he was a wean. As he passes the form to her, he says that he doesn't have a bank account. She doesn't try hiding the scunnered expression that comes on her face, but it seems at least she believes him. They'll pay him in cash, she says, until he's got one. An envelope job. Nay problem. Nay problem at all.

When the first paypacket comes, handed to him by the head chef at the start of one dinner shift, he doesn't have any pockets to put the envelope in, so he tucks it in the top of his pants. When he's signed out and he gets back into his room to take a look, one side of the envelope is clabbered with sweat and it pulls apart easily. There is a wad of twenties. No a great lot of twenties, mind, for the hours he must have worked. He sticks it on the table, under the alarm clock. Next day off, he'll go buy a mini television. Christ knows where but. It isn't like there's shops around; or pubs, minimarkets, offies. The area around the hotel is a demented wasteland of concrete and car parks, carriageways and flyovers. The only place to go is the terminal. From what he can tell, none of the workers much leave the building. They keep to their rooms, or they lounder about the basement amongst their own squad. Mostly, though, they work. There's staff on twenty-four hours, and he's got accustomed by now to the comings and the goings during the night: the banging of doors and shuffling in the corridor; the toilet flushing and the noise of the pipes in the walls as the different groups come on and off shift.

Mainly it is KPs and housekeepers down there in the basement. The doormen as well, and the night porter, whose room is across the way from his and he hears getting in each morning just the back of six. Each squad is divided by continent, it seems, as if these are skills you're born into, the cleaning of saucepans and toilets. The KPs, apart from himself, are African; the housekeepers, South American; most of the chefs and the receptionists, East Europes; and the waiters, fuck knows.

That's what Dia has told him. The KPs are pretty much the only ones that ever talk in English. And they understand better than he'd thought, the times that he's had any conversation with them; which isn't a great lot, to be honest. Eric is still quiet with him while they work, although he has noticed that he's aye similar with the others when they're together. Dia is a wee bit more talkative getting with him though, telling him sometimes which of the waiters and the chefs he dislikes the most.

Outside of the potwash and the lunatic buffet, there aren't many places to go: there is a small staff room, round the dogleg at the bottom of the corridor, with a table and a few chairs, a battered oven, a kettle and a toaster, but Mick never goes in there, so the only place he sees anybody is in the laundry room. He goes in one afternoon, with a carrier of socks and pants, and Dia is at one of the machines taking out his clothes. Before he gets leaving, Mick chins him to ask about their pay. Dia smiles.

'It is not very much.'

'Aye, I've noticed.'

'You write down how many hours but it is always the same.'

'They take some off for the accommodation, then? They must do, eh?'

He grins. 'Oh, yes. They do. And food. We stay in a fine hotel. See?' He looks up and around at the drop ceiling. 'You are not with the agency?'

'No.'

'You are lucky. You are an Englishman. I am with the agency.'

'Careful, pal, I'm Scottish.'

Dia laughs. 'Yes, yes, sorry. Scottish. We are the same, then.'

Mick smiles. 'Aye, well, maybe.'

The next time he is on with Dia, they speak some more. Dia asks him about Scotland and Mick begins telling him about the yards, what like it was working in them. He quietens up soon enough though. Dia is obviously interested, but he doesn't press him. It's surprising, in fact, how much he knows already. He knows all about the big boats that were made on the Clyde, which probably goes to bloody show what dark part some of these ships they made had to play in people like Dia's history. Mick realizes he doesn't know if Ghana has a coastline even. Pretty bloody ignorant, really, but he doesn't ask. Dia tells him about his family. He has a wife and a baby, he says, at home in his country. He's going back soon to work as an accountant. That's what he studied, accountancy, christsake.

He is getting on. He's no maundering up in Glasgow with his head stuck to the freezer or rotting in the shed like a sack of potatoes; he is getting through the days and the already familiar pattern of work, sleep, work, sleep, work, day off, work. Over the next couple of weeks, he goes each few days into the terminal and gets a supply of four-packs for the bargain price of £6 each. One day off soon, he'll get out and onto the subway, buy the mini television, allow himself to think about giving Robbie a call. Even to see outside of the airport, that would be something.

He is dozing in his room one afternoon when he hears some kind of commotion down the corridor. He ignores it at first, but after a few minutes he gets up to have a hingie out the door at what's going on. It is coming from round the dogleg. He walks down the way, and keeks inside the staff room as he goes past. All the housekeepers are in there, it looks like, and as well he notices Dia and Eric inamongst. The women are talking in Spanish, but maybe those two understand anyway; it wouldn't come as a great surprise, in truth. He goes in the laundry for a moment, listening to the babble through the wall, then he leaves away back to his room.

He wakes up, sweating. The jittery sensation of knowing he's awake and the dream is by but the feeling of it staying with him. He sits up with the sheets resting damply on his stomach, the head muddled, the image still there. She is knelt down in front of him and he is looking at her from behind. A great dump of washing in front of her, and she is lifting a pair of overalls out of the pile. He closes his eyes and tries to keep the picture moving, to see the front of her, but his chest and then the whole of his body has started laddering, hardening. The yellow edge of light on top of the door and the dim shapes of the room coming into focus. Wardrobe. Table. Clothes left lying on the floor. He is in the hotel. A potwasher. On again the morning, a matter of hours just.

He gets up and perches on the end of the bed but it's impossible getting a hold on anything, it's all birling about the brainbox. He stands up and moves toward the bundle of clothes by the table, picks up the overalls and gets them under his arm. He claws a fistful of coins from the wardrobe drawer and leaves the room into the ever-lit light of the corridor.

His limbs are stiff as he walks and he's not feeling totally in the present, no at all in fact – he feels half asleep, the dream still pulling, like drag chains, behind him.

The laundry room is empty. He goes in and gets a punnet of powder from the dispenser, and puts the overalls into one of the washers.

He sits on a chair and watches them spin and flump through the glass; shuts his eyes and tries to see her.

The sound of a door opening and footsteps in the corridor. One of the housekeepers is at the doorway with her dressing gown wrapped about her, a pissed-off look on her face. She comes toward him and bends down, putting a hand on his shoulder.

'You should go to bed now, yes?' she says with a small sad smile, then she is away.

20

The butter bucket. Daft but you get fixed on it, studying how full it's getting, sat there on the ledge where the waiters scrape the butter dishes into it; a measure of how busy the service is. And then you start guessing what level it's going to get to, is it going to beat the record and all this. Daft. But it keeps the sanity. The busiest shifts, it's best taking a deep breath and getting stuck in, no a word between the two of you, each in your own worlds, the machine booming, the baldies shouting through for pan collections, and the ping of microwaves in the kitchen going ten the dozen like a sweet shop after school closing.

He gets put on Wash 2 now as well, which is pretty much the same story as Wash 1 except you get pish-wet through to boot. In the quieter moments, he talks to Dia, and a little bit to Eric now, who near knotted himself the morning he came in with his overalls a size snugger from drying them too quickly. 'Staff food is good, hey?' And he'd had a right chuckle at him. 'Must be, aye.'

One thing he's noticed: the lull before service starts, the waiters come past the hatch with a tray of teas and coffees for the kitchen. It's the same story with beers too, when the chefs go into the restaurant at the end of the night for a drink. There's times when he'll be pure murdering for a drink himself after a shift, but the other KPs don't seem bothered. Maybe a religious thing. Or maybe because it's normal just, it's the way it goes and they accept it. One shift he asks Dia about it, how they never get brought a tea in. Dia laughs. He pats the top of the machine.

'The machine does not drink tea,' he says. A strange way of putting it, but he gets the point.

Later the same shift, he tells Dia he saw the meeting in the staff room.

'It is terrible, terrible, they do this. These people' – and he chibs a handful of teaspoons toward the restaurant – 'we must not give them one inch, or they take the mile.' Mick can't help smiling at the phrase, but the head chef comes through that moment and they both quieten up. When he's gone, Dia tells him what the story is, with one eye watchful of the throat into the kitchen.

The housekeepers, he says, are wanting to go on strike because they aren't getting their correct pay. Some dirty chicanery it sounds like too. The hotel has started only clocking their hours for the time they actually spend in the rooms. So if any of the guests decide on a lie in or a lumber before breakfast, and don't vacate when they're supposed to, the housekeepers have to wait without being paid for the time.

'Serious?'

Dia nods slowly.

'How do they know? How they know the cleaners aren't in the rooms?'

'They spy.'

'Aw, that's terrible.' He pulls the machine down and starts a new cycle. 'And ye're joining in yourself, well, if they strike?'

'Yes. If they can do this to them, they will do this to us.'

The whole of the basement staff are in on it, he finds out soon enough. Too bloody right. Dia's no wrong, what he says. Give them an inch and all that. The next meeting is called one morning, wee nods and whispers after staff food, and he goes along to it. It's no exactly organized. The staff room is a fair rabble getting when he arrives, and for quite a long time nobody is looking too sure when it's supposed to start, until a few of them begin shushing their fingers and one of the women stands up on a chair. It's the one he saw in the manager's office. She speaks in Spanish, but he gets the gist. The finger jabbing away. She's good; she holds the room. A certain kind of magic that starts to happen when a person stands up like that and gives a voice to all these disgruntleds listening in.

After a few minutes, she starts saying it in English, 'No pay, no work,' and the KP boys are joined in with the clapping. Obi and Vincent are here as well. He claps with them. It feels good, being part of it. At the same time but, there's a sense of being cut off, all of them, cut off. They're clapping in a basement and there's nobody else here. It's hard no to think how small they are. When the work-in was starting and Bertie was climbing up on his brazier, everybody heard about it. That's how it succeeded. Everybody joining together to support them – the miners, the Dutch, the Beatles – there'd been eighty thousand on the march through Glasgow. Eighty thousand! And, as well, they were actually building something then, they weren't striking, they were actually keeping the work going, how could anybody argue with that? A strange kind of work-in it would be if they tried that here, scrubbing lavvies that haven't been sat on, plates that no food has touched. No the less, no the less. It is good, what they are doing. It is crucial.

He goes to the next meeting as well, a smaller affair with only a handful of the housekeepers and him and Dia. More of it is in English this time. A couple of the women get up and tell how much pay they've had nipped the week, or which rooms hadn't surfaced until the back of eleven. He keeps quiet, listening. Leaves when Dia leaves. When are they going to get doing something about it, is the question he's wanting to ask. If there's going to be a strike, who is behind them?

A day off. The thought of hauling himself up and out of the hotel, buying a mini television, making a phone call. Easier staying in his room, hidden, safe, a few cans left.

Without a window and any shifting of light, it's hard keeping track of the time. There is the alarm, obviously, but that only points what the hours and minutes are, it doesn't give a proper sense of the here and now, passing. It is marking time, but it's not his time that it's marking. A noise in the corridor. Voices coming past, gradually fading. Do terminal patients feel the time in a hospital, laid out on a ward? When the brain and the body are losing their functions, shutting down, sparked and lulled by drugs. Do they know how long they've been there, or do they stop feeling the hours – the long stretches between grapes and colostomy changeover speeding up as the mind slows down?

He gets up and dressed for staff food at five. They sit chewing in quiet. Occasional bits of conversation. He asks Dia and Eric if it's been busy and they tell him no, it's Thursday, always quieter on a Thursday. On the other row of tables, where the receptionists sit, he spots the woman he spoke to the day he arrived. It's the first time he's seen her – probably she only comes down for the lunatic when she's on a double, or maybe she brings her own food in usually, who knows? What does it matter? She is sat pattering with her co-workers. Smiling quite a lot as she talks. Probably that's how she stands out, the smiling, it's no exactly a common feature down here. Dia picks up his plate to get leaving, clapping Mick on the shoulder as he goes.

He stays and finishes his food, half listening to Obi and Vincent talking about an increase in their agency charge – Vincent hadn't noticed it, but Obi is saying he's seen it on his payslip – while across the way, she is the last of her group getting up. He waits for her to move over to the clearing table, and picks up his plate.

'How's it going?' he says, standing in next to her.

'Food could be better,' she laughs, scraping her plate.

'Look, see I was hoping to ask a favour, if it's okay.'

A wee look of surprise, or unease.

'Sure, what is it?'

'It's no a big one' – he tries a smile – 'it's just I'm wanting some paper. Mean, I want to write a letter.'

A look of relief. 'Of course, no problem. Tell you what, if you wait here a minute I'll go fetch some for you now.'

He sits down at a table, watching her go. The heart is clappering, he realizes. Stupit crapbag.

She is back quickly.

'This enough for you?'

He grins: he'd only wanted a couple of sheets but she's brought him the whole caboodle – a full pad of hotel writing paper, a pack of envelopes and a biro.

'Aye, that'll do it. Thank you.'

She gives him a smile. 'No problem. Let me know if you need anything else.'

Back in his room he sits down on the bed with the pad beside him. He tries to think. What is there to say but? There's nothing. There's everything of course but there's no way to put it without saying things he doesn't want to say. Without lying. See if Robbie knew the truth of it he'd be pure beeling. And no just with him either, with the whole family, Craig in particular. And then they'd all be drawn into it. They'd all know.

Dear Robbie,
I hope you and Jenna and Damien are well

is as far as he gets. He puts the pen down and stares about, trying to concentrate. Instead though he starts thinking about the receptionist. He doesn't know her name. He should've asked her. I ought to have written you sooner, I know, or gave you a call, but everything's went that fast I've lost track of how long it's been. Which is kind of true, but it's bullshit still. It isn't what he wants to say. The truth is he just hasn't called. He could have done, but he hasn't, simple as that. Nay excuses. The thought of her again. Being friendly with him, no pitying, friendly. Smiling.

An erection. Christ. He looks at it a while. Ye dirty auld bugger, eh. He pushes the pad aside and sits there staring at his dobber. After a moment he gets up and goes to the door to spy a look into the corridor. A voice, or a radio, sounding quietly down the way, but there is nobody about, all of them working, or asleep, or whatever else it is they do.

He sits on the edge of the bed, cleaning himself off. It is uncomfortable. Sore. He bundles up the toilet roll and drops it into the waste bucket. That's the letter writing by, well. No way he's doing it now. But as he goes to put the pad on top of the table, leaving it there with the pen, a scunnery feeling is started welling inside him. *Dear Robbie, I hope you and Jenna and Damien are well.* That's all he's got to say. And now this carry-on. He needs suddenly to sit down, close the eyes, screw them tight, fight back the waves of disgust that are convulsing in his stomach.

His chest begins heaving, erratic wet dribbles coming out of his nose, and then when he does start to greet it isn't in a great relieving burst like the other one he's just had the now, it is a jerky, tight, drivelling kind of greeting, which doesn't make anything the better because he knows as he's doing it that it isn't for her that he's bubbling; it's for himself. Self fucking pity. The desperate fucking emptiness of needing her there. Needing to tell her that he's sorry, but no for her sake, for his own. Selfishness. He gets off the bed, glancing down, as he goes over to his work clothes, at the stiff little pouch that is sat in the bottom of the waste bucket.

He stays on the chair and watches the machine foaming up. He has stopped greeting and his eyes and his throat feel parched and raw. His dobber, too, a similar sensation. The din of the machine as it starts spinning is reassuring, keeping out the mob of thoughts, but a moment later somebody comes in; he can see their feet out the corner of his eye. They turn around on finding him there and are immediately away. A door closing somewhere down the corridor. Out the blue he starts chuckling: Christ knows what they must say about him when they're all together.

21

She is up early, before the alarm goes off. By half nine, she has washed, dressed and dried her hair, and has a full hour before she needs to set off for the terminal. She switches on her laptop and draws open first the curtain, then the thin veil behind it. On doing so, she wonders if maybe they are better kept shut. It's not exactly the most appealing sight. Car parks upon car parks, an ugly trunk of ring-road, and, more immediately, a view into the corresponding room on the corresponding floor of the next hotel. Their curtains are still drawn, but the light is on. No doubt it looks pretty much the same in there as it does in her own room. The bright, speckled carpet and single chair; the watercolour print in wood-effect frame; the bedside ledge glued to the wall.

She checks in, then opens her inbox. There is a schedule attachment for the next ten days, which she should really have printed out earlier. It would have made life a lot simpler, and God knows what hoops she'd have to jump through to get it printed out in the hotel – it's not exactly the kind of place that has a business lounge – so she gets out a pen and paper to write it out. It's fine anyway. Gives her a chance to make some notes on one or two other things. When she's done as much preparation as she can be fussed with before getting on the plane, she clears her inbox: a few emails from the coordinator and the internal auditor in Zagreb, one from her brother, and an invite to a party that she will be away for. The chambermaid comes in at one point, a couple of quick knocks and then her face sheepishly looking round the door. The girl apologizes – 'sorry, sorry' – and leaves. Closing up the laptop, she stands and goes to switch on the TV.

The trouble with these places, even after you've got over the concrete and the carpets, is always the heating. The windows don't open to the outside so it's inevitably a choice between sweltering, or spending an hour with the baffling control panel and ending up freezing. She decides to swelter. It doesn't really matter; she'll be on her way soon. Certainly she's not going down for breakfast. She saw the restaurant on her way in last night. All plastic plants and unhappy Polish waitresses. Better to brave the airport prices and grab something in departures before she gets on the flight.

In the corridor outside the room, the housekeeper is knocking on another door. There is no sign around the doorknob, so, when no response comes from inside, she opens the door slightly for a look-in. A suitcase covered with clothes is visible on the floor by the wardrobe; she lets the door shut and goes back through the corridor. She has done all the rooms but two, and all but one on the floor above. With nothing else to do but hang about until they are vacated, she pushes the trolley into a lift and goes down to the laundry room. Inside, a few of the housekeepers are sitting and talking; another ironing bedsheets in the steam press. She takes a seat with the others, and waits.

He is lying awake one night when there is a quiet tap on the door. Before he can sit up, Dia pokes his head in.

'Mick, are you awake?'

A remote panic straight away upon him. 'Aye, what is it?'

'Come on. We are doing a raid.' Dia smiles broadly and steps out, letting the door close and the room go back to darkness. He gets up and pulls some clothes on. It occurs to him, amidst his confusion, that Dia knows which is his room.

In the corridor Dia is stood waiting with Eric, Obi and Vincent, all of them grinning and dressed in trackie bottoms. Christ knows what they're up to. He doesn't question it but. Dia puts a finger to his lips and Mick follows with them, away up the corridor toward the hotel. Who cares what it is, it's better than being awake in his room, anyway. He walks behind Eric, who keeps turning around smiling, a small rucksack on his back. He's never seen him so cheery. They are in their baries, all of them. Surprising how pink the soles of their feet are.

'Okay, wait.'

They are at the entrance to the potwash. Dia nudges the door open, looks inside, then turns round and motions for Mick to come in with him. Quickly, without speaking, Eric goes in before them; Obi and Vincent stay guarding the entrance. They've obviously planned it, then; or they've done it before.

It is dark in the potwash, and then in the kitchen, the blue light of the flytrap glinting off the microwaves. Eric waits behind in the throat and he follows Dia, who is taking a key out of his pocket; unsnibbing the padlock to the cold room.

It is big inside, and he feels the chill immediately as he goes in. There are shelves of food all around, cartons and packets everywhere. A whole wall lined with sausage boxes, bloody thousands of the bastards. Giant plastic sacks of chips humped on top of each other like mixing cement, or body bags. Dia clear knows what he's after: he's stood balancing on the chips with his hand feeling inside one of the top-shelf boxes. He looks down at Mick a moment. 'It is okay. The stocktake was yesterday,' he says, pulling out a handful of what looks like steaks, each tightly cauled in plastic.

The two of them are smiling as Dia hands him down five steaks, then gets ransacking another box off to the side. They are surprisingly squishy, the steaks, like tube feed-bags. Dia's got what he's looking for: mashed tatties. Even these are vacuum-packed. Fucksake, they no cook anything theyselves here? Dia gives the signal and they are away, quickly through the potwash and out to Eric and the others, who clock the steaks and start slapping him and Dia on the back.

Genuine a smooth operation. By the time they get back to the basement and go in the staff room, they haven't come across a single person. The door is closed and they start laughing. Eric gives him a no too brilliantly executed high five. And then, as Dia gets the steaks under the grill, Eric pulls out bottles of beer from the rucksack.

'How ye get the keys, Dia?' he asks as they drink.

Dia turns round from poking the mash with a spoon. 'The pastry chef, he is an idiot.'

The steaks are almost black, they're that well fired, and the mash is dry and powdery. Christsake it tastes good but. They eat without talking, like at the lunatic, but this time with satisfied nods and smiles and the sweet pure fucking magic of a stolen beer to go down with it. When they've finished, they clean away meticulously all the evidence and prop the door open as they leave, to clear the smoke. Firm gripped handshakes. Greasy smiles. Bloody genius.

Dear Robbie,

I hope you and Jenna and Damien are well. I'm sorry I haven't called or wrote to you sooner. I was meaning to call but for one reason or another I haven't been able to. It's no excuse, pal, I'm sorry. I'm in London now if you'll believe it. Don't know if I can myself actually. They let me go at Muir's and as well I just needed something different, you know, so when I saw this job advertised and they gave it me I decided I'd come down. I'm working in a hotel, believe it or not, in the kitchen. It's alright. I've got a decent place to stay and it's worked out okay. They are a good lot here, no the bosses of course but what can you expect? I'm getting on fine and I'm well so you don't need to worry. Food's not up to much but!

I didn't tell your brother I was coming down here. It all came about so quick to be honest but I will do when it's the right time, so you're no to put the mix in, okay? He's dealing with things in his own way and he's the better left alone until he's ready, so I'm waiting my time just before I tell him what's what. Same as I was with you, being honest, Robbie, I just needed to wait while I had things fixed out until contacting you. It's just it needs a bit longer with your brother.

I will write again soon, I promise. With where the hotel is, it's probably easier than calling, but when I've got my day off next I will go find a telephone and I'll call you.

Take care, son, love to the family,
Your da

He seals up the envelope and fishes the address out of his wallet. It's a fair pathetic effort but what else can he say? Whatever he puts it doesn't change anything, and as well if he'd been in contact with him sooner and given him the full run-down, Robbie would've been straight onto the plane, knowing what like he is. Nay point telling him it all the now. He is fine, that's all he needs to know. He'd thought about putting in about the stolen steaks or the housekeepers' dispute, but it didn't feel right; plus he wouldn't want him getting the wrong idea why he's got involved helping them.

He goes to the post office at the terminal on his next day off and gets the letter sent off there. Better that than seeing if the hotel's got its own service. You can fine well imagine the crafty bint up the stair, there with her envelope steamer, weeding out the radicals. So, the food's no good, then – that what you think, is it? We'll see about that, Scottie, we'll just have to see about that, won't we?

There is a meeting called for four o'clock one afternoon. By the time he and Eric get there after the lunch shift it is already under way, and they go and join Dia, beckoning them over at the back of the room by the oven. The ringleader is talking in English about a new development. The management, she says, have started putting out more spies on the floors, so what the housekeepers are doing is they've fixed out a system of lookouts, making sure there's always one of them keeping watch at the end of the corridors to signal when a bandit is on the approach. She tells this story that happened: a few days ago two of them are trying one of the doors with no reply, when they get the signal from the lookout and they hurry into the room, presuming it's empty. Inside but, there is a guy in the bare scuddy doing exercises in front of the TV. She does an impression of him, his face black-affronted, hands shooting down to cover himself.

They are all laughing at this story when the operations manager comes in the door.

She stands, looking at them.

'Every person in this room faces instant dismissal.'

She's no beating about the bush, then.

Silence. Confused faces. She's got the heavy team with her, two big fellas stood either side of the door, and another man in a suit beside her.

'Unauthorized meetings and organization of staff without consent is in breach of the terms of your employment, and is an immediately sackable offence.'

She stands there just, the arms folded, triumphant, the Iron fucking Lady there with her mince for brains bodyguards – Haggis 1 and Haggis 2. The terms of your employment? What are they, well? He certain hasn't seen them. Nobody moves. Not even the ringleader. She's still stood on her chair, looking exposed and daft like a schoolwean who's been caught goofing about by the teacher walking in. Everybody's waiting for who's going to do something, and it's clear enough the operations manager isn't in a hurry, the look on her face – she's enjoying it, you can tell. The guy in the suit next to her scanning about the room and marking onto a notepad – their names, obviously, however he knows what they are. Mick stays watching like the rest of them. It hasn't hit him that something real is happening.

There is a loud scurl from up on the chair and the ringleader steps down – she is marching toward the door and the haggismen sidestep together, but then the operations manager moves forward and the two women come at eyeballs.

'It is not a meeting. How do you know it is meeting?'

The arms still folded. Smiling.

'You sack us, then you have no staff.'

She's pishing in the wind but, and the Milk Snatcher there knows it. 'You can let me worry about that.' She motions to the haggismen to unblock the door. 'Those of you who are supposed to be working tonight' – and she looks right at where Mick is stood with the KPs – 'you will not be required to complete your shifts. All of you can remain in the hotel for the night but you will be required to leave the premises in the morning by 9 o'clock.'

And that's that. Show over. They start filing out the room, slow, quiet, automatic, like at the lunatic. The haggismen itching for it to kick off, and the suit guy getting the final names down. There is the sound of the ringleader arguing behind them as they get into the corridor, and then, one by one, they each disappear into their rooms. With the staff room out, there isn't anywhere else to go.

He is laid on the bed and the brain is dreiched over. A chapping on the door. Dia. He comes in, calm as ever; cheery even. He perches on the table as Mick sits up on the edge of the bed.

'Don't suppose there's anything we can do, eh?'

Dia shakes his head slowly, tutting.

'Who's working now?' A stupit question. What does it matter? It doesn't.

'Vincent. Obi is in the café bar, so it is only him.' Dia grins. 'He will have a busy shift. They say they will leave as well but I tell them, no, stay. Why go? They were not at the meeting. Why go? So now they will stay.'

'What about you, Dia? What will you do?'

'I sign again with the agency. They find work easily because they take all the money.' He laughs. 'And the hotel, they go to the agency as well. Maybe they take me again, who knows?'

Mick smiles, and he realizes then this is probably the last he'll see of Dia. Unless he signs with the agency himself, of course, but even the brief thought of that starts curdling the stomach.

'And you? What will you do?'

There's no reason to lie to Dia but he feels instantly on the defensive. He hasn't let himself think about that.

'I'm fine. It's no a problem.' And then: 'There's someone I know telt me he's got a job going if I want it.'

Dia nods. 'That is good.' He stands up and steps forward with his hand held out.

'Good luck.'

'And yourself, Dia, good luck to you too.'

He must've slept a little, because it is morning, almost six, when he wakes up, still dressed. He goes to the wardrobe and gathers up the rest of his clothes into his bag, and that's him, offski. Nobody in the corridor, or up on the next level, as he leaves into the cold dim dawn outside the fire exit. Without much of a thought where he's headed, he goes toward the terminal.

22

'Well, ladies and gents, I'm still waiting for the signal at Hatton Cross. Should be any moment, I'm told, but that's what they said last time so your guess is probably as good as mine. Still time to sit back then, relax, read the paper, do your thing. I'll keep you posted.'

A funnyman, the driver. They're no laughing but. There is a business type sat opposite, shaking his head at the chummy patter that keeps crackling over the tannoy. So what, ye miserable cunts, we're no going anywhere, what difference does it make? See but if he had somewhere himself he was headed, maybe he'd be the same. Genuine a strange feeling. He does not know where he is headed. Unlike all these lot, late for their meetings and that – or maybe they aren't, who knows, maybe your man over there is just acting it, and actually all he's got in that briefcase he's finger-tapping on the now is a packet of sandwiches and a litre bottle of Buckfast.

'Okay, folks, looks like we're on the move, so mind the doors, please, and we'll be off.'

The train starts moving and he tries to think. Where is he going? Out of nowhere he laughs. He can't help it. It's actually funny, the situation. A few scunnery wee looks across the way. Probably they think it's something the driver said – Christ, what kind of headcase must that make him look? Serious but, what is he going to do? A good question, a good one, but still he can't drum up the effort to get thinking about it, and he is falling asleep by the time the train is slowing into the next station, mind the doors doors closing mind the doors please.

It is a decision of sorts, but one it doesn't seem he has made himself. A default. The easiest thing to do with no other brainwaves at the door; because even if No Breakfast is a crabbit bastard – which he is – he's a familiar crabbit bastard, and that feels easier the now than making the effort to think up anything else.

He isn't there though. Nobody is about. The *Back in 10 minutes* notice is up, so he goes back out and to the Costcutter for a sausage roll and a can of lager, and sits on a low wall under the bridge, sheltered from this Baltic wind that has got up.

When he comes back the sign is gone, but on chapping the door it is another man that opens.

'I'm, eh, sorry, I'm wanting a room. I was staying here a couple of months back.'

'Okay, sir, come this way.'

Here's a change, well.

He follows him up to the top floor. There are two rooms either side of the stairhead, and the guy opens one of them and lets him in. There is a television, he notices as he gets handing him the money.

'Okay?' He is younger than No Breakfast. A brother maybe.

'Fine, thanks.'

He must have been fair knackered, because when he wakes up the gloaming has came and went outside the window, and it is getting on for night. Okay, then. Nay use lying there just, composting on top of the bed, he needs to be up and about, decision-making. Better to keep the brain busy chasing after you, than you the one chasing trying to stop it. He gets up and goes over by the window. A plan needed, well. A decent plan. Firstly into the bag for a tenner from the money envelope, then out to the shop for what he needs.

He buys a pen, an A4 pad, a four-pack and a lamb samosa. Also, a free-ads paper, which, it turns out, isn't actually free but then what can you expect, this is London, pal. When he gets back in the room he realizes, seeing his bag, that he in fact already has these things – pen, paper – and the empty, aching sensation that the memory of it brings back causes a setback to proceedings, as he leans back against the wall behind the bed and takes a long drink, trying to quiet it down.

First up, the financials. He gets out the money envelope and counts what he's got, slowly, carefully, the first time, then a couple more times quickly just to be sure, the head of the English queen flashing like a flick book, the expression never changing, fish-lipped and disapproving. £497. Fine. Good. That gives him time. He doesn't have to rush into the first job he finds; he can make sure he gets the right one, a decent employer, no another bandit out to rob him. He opens another can and gets the TV on. Falls asleep in the chair.

The morning, and his back is sore, but he is straight up and about it, pulling open the paper and getting the jobs circled. There are quite a few minicab jobs, which being honest is probably where he should have tried last time, even though most of them are for registered-owner drivers. One or two but, that say they rent a car.

He begins with a place that looks like it's based nearby. He goes out and to a phone box to give the number a call. The familiar nervous feeling as he waits, watching his breath come in fits of mist, before a man answers and tells him to come over right now if he's able.

One thing he's noticed: the bus stops all have these wee maps in them, which makes it pretty easy finding the place. He is there twenty minutes later. There is a sign along the street and a steamed-up window with a light on.

Inside, a man behind the glass.

'Hello, I just spoke to somebody about the job.'

'Oh, right, that you was it?' He eyes him up and down.

'Like I say, I've plenty experience. I've been working private hire in Glasgow more than fifteen years.'

'Right. Do you have a reference?'

'Yes. See, I do, but I've no got it on me.'

'I'll need to have one.' He keeks down at his newspaper.

'What I can do, I can call ye with the number when I get home. I can't mind it off the top my head, is all.'

'Sure, fine. We'll hear from you, then,' and he walks off.

References. That's him screwed, well. Obviously he isn't putting a call in to Malcolm. They don't know he's here, even. That's how he came in the first place, christsake, to get away. Still, he has to crack on. He has to be positive. Not everywhere's going to want a reference – probably there's one or two need a new start straight away and they're okay seeing if he shapes up on the job just.

It is the same story at the next place though. Once he gets over there and he sits in a kind of waiting room – it's a chain place and it's a bit more proper – they give him an application form to fill out. There is nobody else in the room, so after he's tried at one or two of the boxes, he slips away. What's the point handing it in if half the boxes he can't put anything? Address. Telephone number.

References. It is only the back of eleven when he returns, but the day is finished. A quick dot to the shop and he's back in his room, the television on, a Plan B needed.

Plan B gets the swerve for the afternoon. He needs to gather the energies, build himself up to it again. He stays in front of the television; drinks a couple of cans. This programme about these famous people he's never heard of, a group of them going round each other's houses to see who can cook the best meal. Then over to the snooker. The picture is that bad it's near impossible to make out the colours of the balls, but it doesn't matter, he isn't paying too much attention; something comforting about it anyway, the silence, the clock-clunk of the balls and the gravelly patter of the commentators. He's always been quite fond of the snooker. They used to sit and have it on in the background sometimes, him flicking through the *Record* and the wife with her head in one of the Barbaras. Occasionally the both of them chuckling at something one of the commentators has said – double kisses and touching balls and all that – probably the same kind of things she's reading in her book there. The feeling of it is so familiar. He allows it to wash over him, a comfort, a dull, familiar comfort that is eased on by the drink, helping him to drift away just, stop to focus. It isn't the right thing to be doing. He knows that. But he doesn't stop himself, finishing off the cans and coasting further away from the here and now of things until the eyes are starting to close, and he falls asleep.

The one that isn't No Breakfast. He has been banging on the door. He wants his rent money. Mick opens up, rubbing his eyes awake as he goes over to his bag and crouches with his back blocking the guy's view, no wanting him to see as he takes the notes out of the envelope.

He gets onto the bed. The back is hurting. He's got to stop falling asleep in that chair. The television is still on but he leaves it, the volume turned down low as he gets under the sheets, the rest of the night to get through now, knowing he won't sleep.

The man gives him the once-over and says the ad shouldn't have gone in, they've already got somebody hired. A handyman job. There's a fair number of them in the building and trades listings and it's sensible thinking, because it's unlikely any of these places will need a reference and the money is decent, plus it's paid by the day, no the week. He tries the next one on his sheet: *General Handy-person, London W2, 50 hr per week, Mon–Fri, £6.50 per hour, temporary.* When he gets there but the guy asks him where he is living and he can't think quick enough what to say. He starts telling him he's in a B&B the now but he'll be looking for somewhere to stay as soon as he starts working. He gets told the same story: they've took on a guy already but come back next week in case he doesn't work out. He tries one more, who tell him on the phone they don't know about any job, and he decides to call it a day.

The trouble is, even if he does make up an address, probably they'd be able to check up on it these days. Even these yards that are just a mess of scrap metal and titty calendars, they'll still have some way of finding out on a computer if the address matches what you tell them, and then that's you screwed. He switches on the television. Maybe he's looking at all this the wrong way round. What he should be doing is fixing out a place to stay first. But no, that isn't right, he's thought through all this already: he doesn't have enough for the deposit; and even if he did, landlords will aye be wanting references as well. And he doesn't have those, that's for certain. He has to keep going but. Battle on. What is it they say – if ye get chucked in the Clyde, ye swim to the bank and haul yourself out, a fish in the one pocket for lunch, and one in the other for tea.

He isn't going back. That is the one thing he is sure about. Getting the coach up there with his tail between his legs and returning to that dark, silent house he can't even breathe inside, and everyone seeing that he's failed and pitying him. Everyone? Serious? Who's everyone? Nobody even knows that he went. And the house is up in the air by now anyway; someone else moved in, and the housing association after him for rent arrears.

He keeps to his room the next few days. The routine is set in. The shop in the morning, and the rest of the day he watches TV, drinking, dozing, the brain shackled. Zoning out like this, he can control it most of the time, keep his thoughts sluggish enough they can't get any speed up; although the torpor and the drink mean he is sleeping a lot, and that is when he can't control it. She is in his dreams, but out of reach, never clear. One afternoon he drops off and he has this vivid sense that he is in the house, in his chair, half asleep watching the football scores coming in on the vidiprinter. The house is quiet. There is a faint noise of chopping, coming through from the kitchen. He waits for the Rangers result, and when he's seen they've won, he gets himself up from the chair and goes out of the living room. The chopping noise is louder now, and as well the unmistakable sound of boys fighting upstairs. At the entrance to the kitchen he stops and looks at the back of her, chopping, away with herself humming and no noticing that he's stood behind her. Carrots. A stew. The pleasing sound of meat frying away on the hob. He is enjoying watching her – the quick hands scooping up carrot chunks and the smooth movement of her shoulders inside the pullover. 'Ye there?' she says, without turning round. He smiles, walking up to put his arms around her waist. 'Smells good, hen.' He leans forward and now she does turn around but it's no her, it's Mary, kissing him, and he stumbles back trying to grip hold of the counter, carrot tops getting knocked onto the floor, bouncing off the lino.

He wakes up hot and confused. Light outside, but he can't fix out what time of day it is. The racing sensation as his brain tries to make sense of where he is, whether he's awake or not. He is on the bed. Flakes of pastry on the pillow by his face. He flicks them onto the carpet and closes his eyes, everything spinning around.

Worse than these daytime dreams but is being awake the night. The darkness out the window seeming like it's going to go on forever and him hot and stiff on the bed, fragments of memories coming at him out the dark from nowhere. The drink helps. It pulls him under and he sleeps deeply for a few hours, but then always there is that point in the night when he wakes up and it is a long while until morning and he knows he's going to lie there just, a sore feeling behind the eyes, edgy at the slightest sound out the window or through the floorboards.

The daytimes when he is drowsing, he's in and out, on the border of dreams and memories. Not all about her, either; some of them good, wee things from the past. Another dream he has, that isn't so much a dream as a pure lifelike recollection of something that happened once at the yard. It comes into his head from nowhere. Charley Gordon. A great bear of a man, with a thick red neck and the half of his teeth missing out the big daftie smile. This when he was a plater's apprentice at John Brown's and Charley was his journeyman. A Catholic. One of the few, but Charley could handle himself, he aye enjoyed it even, the argle-bargle and the bigotry. All these stories he'd tell Mick of this or that wee nyaff that'd put the mix in and he'd had to sort him out. When he wasn't telling him these stories he was sending him off to the stores for whatever parts it was he needed. Mostly it was something simple and he'd go ask direct from the storewoman – flange nuts and mating screws, all these strange names that the things had – as he shuffled about and looked at his feet, too shy to talk to her. Other times there'd be a whole load of things that Charley would be wanting, and she'd let him in the stores to collect them up himself, up and down the sliding ladders to get them into his sack.

This one time Charley had gave him a long list of parts for a bevelling job he had to do, and Mick knew he'd expect him to be half an hour or so to fetch it all, but, cocky wee imp that he was, he reckoned he knew that store better than anybody, and so the idea comes to him that he'll chance legging it up the road to the pool hall for a quick game, before slaloming around those ladders and getting back in time. Course but when he does get in the store, he can't find half the parts, and by the time he's collected everything it is gone an hour and Charley is spitting teeth, they ones he's still got, anyway. He hardly speaks to him the rest the afternoon and he makes him work like a dog, ordering him everywhere to do all these tasks for him. It takes a few days until Charley's forgave him, and by then it's all a great joke: the tapping on the wrist and the big smile whenever Mick's back rushing in from the stores. So he thinks it's all forgot about, but then later the week Charley sends him off, and he's that wary of making any mistakes it doesn't even occur to him what he's doing as he goes up to the storewoman and asks her if she's got a pair of large red nipples. The slap she gave him, he could still feel it an hour later, stood at the countersinking machine with Charley chuckling away next to him.

Sometimes a memory like that, it appears from nowhere and it sets you wondering about things, like what happened to Charley? He still alive? Did he ever get himself that wee sailing boat and fuck off to the islands like he used to say he would? Who knows? Probably. Aye, probably. He didn't mess about, auld Charley.

No Breakfast is back again. Maunderly as ever. Sometimes it's him, and sometimes it's the friendly one, wanting to chin him for a conversation. He has a sense of floating most of the time now. He's outside of everything, outside of himself, giving the same attention to the world as he would to the TV on in the background – the handing over of his rent; the pamp of a car horn outside on the road; a street cleaner changing a bin, bits of newspaper and a banana skin falling onto the frosted pavement. He watches him absently from the window. A black guy. He's got himself a job, well. How did he do it? Probably he's qualified for something else, like Dia and Eric, washing dishes with a degree in the pocket. They get on with it but. They aren't too proud for any of it because they've got a purpose, is how, they've got a family to provide for and a house to build, so it doesn't matter how many times these English bastard employers stick the boot on, they'll always get back up and get on with it just.

It is night outside. He's not ate in a while but the truth is he can't be arsed dragging himself out to the shop. Hard to believe that no long back he was on the march across town looking for jobs, arranging interviews, speaking to people on the telephone. It takes him a long while getting up the energy to go out, and when he does, it is because he makes a deal with himself that he'll stock up with enough supplies that he can make them last.

He hooks the carriers on the window latch where they can hang outside in the cold. The food he wraps up in another carrier inside the bag, to keep it dry if it rains.

Apart from the rent visits down the stair, and the toilet, he doesn't leave his room for a couple of days at a stretch, each time moving only when he has to nick out for new supplies. The bathroom is on the floor below, and he waits listening through his door until he's sure the coast is clear before he comes out. One morning but, he gets caught out. He's about to go into the bathroom when a door opens to his side and a woman near walks into him.

'You going in there, mate?' She is young, wearing a baggy green sweater and tights.

'Aye, but you go – go on.'

'No, it's alright, I'll wait.'

He sees a sliver into the room as he walks past: clothes on the floor and a man having a hingie out of a window, smoking. Plants, a big poster on the wall. As if they are living there. He takes a pee and feels suddenly conscious that the woman will be coming in there after him. When he's finished, he takes a couple of pieces of toilet roll and wipes away the dark yellow spots that he's dripped on the rim.

The money envelope is getting thinner. As well, the last stores he bought in were badly got by the rain: the sandwiches are eatable, just, but they're too damp to last more than one meal. The cans are nice and cold but. See one thing that's for sure is that as soon as any employers start checking him up in their computers, they'll know straight away from the Employers' Federation or whatever that he's got something of a radical about him – with the work-in and the unions and that. Plus the episode with the hotel now as well, don't think they won't have that logged too, because they will.

There is a programme on. He watches it for a while. It's a good one. Interesting. It's about bears, grizzlies and polars, how global warming is forcing them to live closer together. The Arctic ice cap is melting that much each summer that the polar bears aren't always able to swim north to it like they used to, because it's too far away getting, so instead they're turning south toward the Canadian mainland. Which is where the grizzlies live. The inevitable sectarian battles resulting. But as well what's different is they've started mating with each other. The programme shows this photo of the first cross-breed bear, dead, killed by a hunter. Being honest, it looks to Mick pretty much like a polar bear, but apparently it's got a lot of the grizzly's features. In the photo, the guy that shot it is grinning away like a nutcase. He's got a massive army camouflage coat on, and is knelt down beside the bear with his hands splayed across its back. Stupit bastard. You have to wonder how that meeting went, when the hunter met the biologists: look, I've found you the world's rarest bear, a true wonder of nature, and I blasted it through the neck. The programme doesn't go into that but. Instead it shows all these polar bears loundering the streets of these freezing remote towns, bold as fuck, petrifying the locals outside the minimarket.

He drinks too much that night, finishing all his lager store. It's no a wise move, because instead of taking the edge off things it just makes him the more maunderly, and he lies on the bed unable to stop himself greeting. He is surprised – as if from outside of himself, observing somebody else – how long and loud he cries. The need to be with her coming on him so strongly that he can't stop it, and his whole body becoming tight and strained, searching for the feeling of being with her but no finding it, just a vacuum instead, falling and falling.

He is cold. It looks out the window like no the worst day – sunny, in fact, one of they bright, biting wintry mornings – but No Breakfast is scrimping on the heating and the room feels pure Baltic. He stays inside the bed. Some of the time sleeping, some of it with the eyes open, staring at the ceiling, the brain a blank except for occasional daft wee thoughts, like listening for the announcers between TV shows and counting how many programmes they do before somebody else comes on shift. Wondering what it is they do while the programme is on – do they have to sit there in their booth or whatever preparing for the start of the next show, or can they get up and wander about, get a cup of tea, go the newsagent's for a scratchcard? Daft wee thoughts. Daft wee thoughts that keep at arm's length the more important one of what the fuck is he going to do now that the money is almost run out.

When the time does come, he makes a decision. The twenty that he's got left, he will keep back for food and emergencies. It isn't enough to pay for another night anyway, and the most important thing is that he's got enough to feed himself; plus the emergencies, whatever they might be. Drink, probably, if the way he's craving for one the now is anything to go by. He packs up his things and goes for a wash of his face. Strange, but he has some energy about him now that there is no choice and he is on the move. He switches off the television and leaves the room.

He'd been hoping he wouldn't have to bump into anybody on the way out, but the reception door is open and the younger one sees him coming down. He must think he's paying another night, because he comes to the doorway, only then noticing the bag.

'You are going back to Scotland?'

'No.'

He nods his head. He's an alright type, even if he does stick the nose in too much.

'I'm done with the room but. Thanks.'

23

One thing is for sure: they don't like you sitting down in this city. He's been more than twenty minutes looking for somewhere to park down and eat his sandwich, but he hasn't passed a single bench yet. They don't want you staying put; they want you rushing about, horn-pamping, snatching the free newspaper. There are no people stood outside the pubs smoking. There aren't even any pubs that he's passed, christsake. He keeps on. He doesn't know where he is, and wanders at random, but it must be he does some kind of a loop or something, because after a while he is arrived back at the coach station.

It is hoaching inside, people milling about, queuing, sat waiting in the bays. That's fine but. The more people, the less obvious he feels, and as he walks through he wonders how many others in here are hiding, kidding on they're going somewhere but in fact just keeping out of the cold. He needs to pee. Another problem. A short search and he discovers that it's 30p for the pleasure of using the toilets. The money situation as it is, he'd rather not. See if he was needing a tollie then maybe that would be a proper use of the emergencies fund, but no a pish, nay chance.

There are a couple of carry-out coffee places near the station, but it's a while before he finds a pub. When he does, it is fortunate a busy one, and he has no problem sneaking in the toilet to take a fine long and satisfying widdle. The only problem, once he's done, is that now he's here he could genuine go a pint. No. First he needs to – well, fuck knows what he needs to do first, but definitely it isn't that, so he gets making his way back to the station instead. Finds himself a seat, lodged between a Muslim woman and a Chelsea supporter. There is a voice over the tannoy but he isn't hearing it. He is in the Birmingham bay, is the last thing he notices before he nods off.

When he wakes it is showing 17.44 on the information board. The bay is emptied and he is sat with empty seats all around him. He gets up and goes over to the newsagent's, looks at the price of sandwiches and gives them a bye, deciding on a chocolate bar instead. Then over to the nearest busy bay.

Outside, pulling into the slots a bit further on, the Glasgow coach. He watches uneasily as the passengers start to spill out. How long since he came here? It seems like forever ago but it's only a few months probably. He can't be sure. No the best few months, being honest. Very funny ye sarcastic bugger. The Weegies are started filing past the windows and he looks down. Hardly likely there'll be anybody that knows him, but so what, that doesn't mean it won't happen. It might. In fact it's a racing certainty the way things are going, so he keeps the head down, stares at his feet. His neck starting to strain. Waiting for it – a tap on the shoulder. Someone who recognizes him; someone who'll go back up to Glasgow and say that they've seen him, tell the Highlanders, tell Craig – and just for a split second he allows in the thought that maybe he's been looking for him, maybe actually it's him on the coach coming down on the search for him because how can you know? You can't, and all he does know is he has to get rid of the thought, get hold of it and get fucking shut.

'Hello. Are you okay?'

A young girl, sitting in beside him. He pulls back. Confusion and panic stiffening through him. 'Would you like something to eat?' He sits up and looks about to see if anybody's watching. The girl is sat turned toward him, smiling. She's got a wool cardigan with big wooden buttons; a woolly hat with these two bobble-danglers either side. He doesn't say anything and she starts going in her bag. He stands up. He has to be away. The heart is pounding. He moves down the bay; a man watching him over his newspaper, flicking the eyes back down as he hurries past.

A crawling, scunnery feeling follows him as he moves away down the road. Only one place he's headed the now; screw the rules.

He orders himself a pint. Three pound fifty pence, but no surprises there, he is in London. For some reason. For some reason he is in London. There is a game on the television. A few in watching it, but it's obvious no a football pub because they don't look too interested. The pint is calming him, settling the nerves. He stays and drinks it slowly. Takes his time before swallowing up to leave. Now what? Careful. Best no to think about the big picture right now, because it's just too bloody big, is how, and he's too close up to be able to see it properly. What he has to do is focus on one part at a time, stepping back until he can see the whole thing clearly and figure it out. Wee steps. He is cold, and he is hungry. He does his jacket up to the neck and sets off looking for something to eat.

He finds a kebab shop and goes inside, warmth and grease clinging about him as he joins the line of men at the counter intently giving the guy their sauce and salad directions. He feels comfortable in here. Warm. Unnoticed. The kebab man skilfully shaving strips of meat off the doner like a barber working at a throat. One thing's for sure, he could fine well go a kebab the now. Too expensive but. When it comes his turn he gets himself a bag of chips instead, and goes to sit at a stool in the window, biting them in halves and watching the steam lick out of the soft potato insides.

It is late. He steps out of the shop. This torpor all through him that he can't shake. He starts walking back the way he came; nay other suggestions rolling out the carpet for him. To get warm just. A wee nip of something, just to get warm, it's as far as he can think. Shortly before the pub he notices a side street, dark, too narrow for lampposts. Without much of a thought, he goes down it. It is cobbled, and a couple of cars are parked with the one tyre perched onto a pavement, and at the end there is just a wall, the back of another building. He steps onto a concrete lump and looks over the line of palings into a small rubbish yard at the back of the pub. Weeds and dog-ends and black wheelie bins.

There's only a few customers still in. The television is off, and he sits down at a table underneath it, slowly sipping at his whisky, feeling the warmth of it spread through him. He gets a second, and by the time he's near the end of it the barmaid has the mop out, doing behind the bar counter; she doesn't notice him leaving.

He drops the bag down and clambers messily over the palings, scraping the skin off the back of his leg. There is no lighting out here, but he can make out the push bars on the fire exit and, next to it, a stack of bottle crates. Further in, a large humming box like a generator, with gas cylinders propped against it. He puts his bag down behind the box, the other side from the fire exit, and sits down, hoping it might be giving off some warmth. Nay such luck. Here we are well. No an expected turn of events. He sits blankly for a time, more and more uncomfortable getting with the cold and the hard uneven ground knuckling into his arse through the bag.

After a while he gets up and goes on a search for anything that might improve the situation. And he's in luck, because lodged behind the wheelie bins is a whole load of flattened McCoy's crisps cardboard boxes. Okay. All it needs now is a bottle or two of beer left in one of these crates and he'll be laughing. He checks. There isn't.

The cardboard does improve things, laid out on the ground underneath him, but it's impossible to sleep still, no with this cold knifing at his body. Even with the whisky inside him he's pure frozen. And alert. Listening for the fire exit or anybody coming down the side street, propped rigid against the generator with his bag tucked behind him and the raw skin on the back of his leg stinging against his trousers.

24

He doesn't sleep, hardly at all, a few snatches just. The cold, and his back ridged against the generator, he's stiffened up and he can barely move. All of him is numb. A few times during the night he tells himself he needs to get up, keep moving, go find somewhere covered he can be warmer, but the effort of it is too much. The aching body will not budge. A pain that began in his feet and his hands, tightening over his frame until it has grip of every part of him starts, after a while, to lessen; the outside of him deadened, and the cold then working its way inside, into his nose and his throat, stopping the breath in his lungs and getting inside the brain, forcing it to press, paralysed, against his skull. Noise is increasing. Traffic on the main road. A bus braking. When he does move, he does it very slowly, muscle by muscle. It is dark still but there is a blue gloom to the sky. He gets out from behind the generator; stands up and perches his sore backside against it, looking at the dim yard. Dog-ends outside the fire exit. A cracked glass lampshade leant in a crate. A stack of rusted metal chairs lurching against the wall. He tries to pick up the cardboard and put it back behind the crates, but his fingers won't work so he shunts it behind the generator, then takes a few goes attempting to get his bag and his body to struggle over the palings.

Most the shops are closed. He keeps walking, the autopilot on; cold, still cold. The feet throbbing in his shoes. He finds himself headed for the coach station, as if the body is handling things on its own by now, no trusting enough of him to discuss such matters any more. Fine but. Fine. It's warmer in here, and he sits down in one of the bays. Quieter than yesterday, but it's early yet, and he looks over at the board – 06.53 – the whole day in front of him, unending. He pushes back into his seat with his bag on his lap and falls asleep.

He wakes from an uncomfortable and confusing dream with an immediate sense of alarm that goes twisting right into the stomach. He scans about him. There, again, is the cunt opposite, looking at him over his paper, tapping away with the foot. And there's others too, a whole line of them, watching him, just fucking sat there watching him. He stands up. He can't stay there, all these eyes, and no to mention either the ones in the roof – the cameras – sure they will have clocked him as well, sat two days in a row without getting onto a coach. He goes out of the station and stands by the entrance in a state of near-total unclearness. A man coming up to him jabbing a newspaper in his face and he tries to shake his head but the guy keeps sticking it to him.

'Fuck off.'

The man shrugs his shoulders and goes away, pointing it at a woman coming past.

He walks for a long time. Aimless. Trying just to shake the crawling panic that tenses inside him whenever he gets eyeballed, quickening past them, just keeping going, tired and sore but keeping on the move because he is too feart to stop. He is hungry, so when he comes to a minimarket he goes inside, picks up an egg sandwich and a four-pack and ignores the look on the auld bint's face as she passes it over the scanner.

He is walking and looking for somewhere quiet to sit and eat, when he comes upon the river. And right there on the opposite bank, the genuine shocking sight of a massive red brick power station, long since closed down by the looks of it. There is a bench free and he sits down. No many people about here. A few joggers. A man and a woman both in suits further up the way on another bench eating out of plastic punnets with wee plastic forks. He starts to feel more relaxed. A kind of peacefulness about things here, watching the river and the different boats coming past; the great bulk of the power station and its four giant white chimneys across the water. He snaps open a can. The better keeping out the way of things. Minding his own business and no having to worry about digging up any bastard reading their newspaper or poking it in his face. And if there's nobody about to look at him, then he doesn't have to get considering himself either – and what a fucking affront he is to them, the newspaper-reading types of this world, the young women wanting to foist their sandwiches on him. His bladder is filled up, so he waits until nobody is about and goes a short way down the pavement to pish through the fence.

Later, when the alcohol has took the edge off the cold and the panic, he takes a walk down the water. A good stretch of it, he keeps going for a long time, craps in a Burger King and ends up on a bridge with a beauty of a view over Big Ben, watching lights catch on the water ripples, staring at the strange image of people dancing in silent frenzy inside a boat that comes past.

The pub is closed when he gets back so he won't be paying them any rent the night. The cardboard boxes are where he left them, and he opens a couple out to put around himself like a tube. It is better, but no by much. He's still fucking freezing. He closes his eyes and he can't sleep, instead thinking about his big coat hung up in the lobby, how much warmer he'd be with it on than this jacket. The image of the house briefly staying with him, but fortunately the brain is too dumb with cold to imagine any further.

It is still dark when he leaves over the palings. His only thought: to get the body warm. He lounders along the pavements until the cafes are open, then goes into one for a cup of tea. The man is clear annoyed when he pays up, because he's been sat there that long with just the single mug, but so what, it's no like the place is mobbed with customers, so get to fuck, pal. A walk. The minimarket. Enough on his tail for an egg sandwich, but he gives the drink a bye, because that's the last of his money.

It isn't a bad sandwich in truth, for the price, anyway. No a bad spot by the water either, although as he approaches it now, he can see that somebody else has took it. A fat man in a suit, an empty sandwich case on his lap, just sat there. He walks past and keeps going along the pavement. Just a bench. It doesn't matter. There'll be plenty more down the water. But he can't help looking back, the fat cunt lounging there with his arm stretched over the top of the bench like he thinks he's got the invisible woman nestled in with him. Stupit, being angry about it. Pure ridiculous. But there you go. This guy has messed up his routine. And see as well he's probably got some warm office nearby that he's supposed to be in, with heaters and secretaries and the bloody whisky bottle stashed away in the drawer.

He is stood now, a way off, watching the man, who is fine well aware he's being looked at. He's kidding on he can't see him but. Sat defiant and unmoving, the arm stretched out. Go on, ye cunt, look at me. Think I give a fuck, eh? And now he is getting up, clearly displeased about the whole situation, the poor chap, giving him the ball bearings as he departs, but so what, serious, so what? He's glad. The wee battles you have to win. Good fucking to win one at last. He gets sat down and watches the man away down the pavement, the two great saddlebags shifting above his belt with each step.

A tugboat pulling into a wharf on the other side of the river. WASTE MANAGEMENT, one of the containers says on it. Twelve of them, he counts, full of what – binbags? Chemicals? Household tollies? Where does it all go, that's what you've got to wonder, where does it go to?

A man and a woman are stood in front of him. He has been asleep. The sky is gone darker, car headlights beading over a bridge, and he is hungry. They are talking. Smiling at him. He tries to get sat up, no the strength to move away, warn them off, and they are staying there, giving it this constant gentle patter to him – blankets . . . our Lord . . . sandwich table. He pulls his bag onto his lap. Food. They are talking about food. Cruel, cruel bastards. They know. It's all wired together somehow: the bank and the council and the electricity board and the auld bint in the minimarket. Now these pair. We have been informed as to your penniless situation and so are come the now to stick the boot on. The man is pointing down the road – see the big building there? It's the car park behind it. More smiles from both, and they are away. Nobody else about for miles. Where do they spring from? One minute you're asleep, and the next they've suddenly appeared from out the river and they're offering you sandwiches.

It is colder, and his left leg has got the shakes, a wee trembling that doesn't stop even when he presses down on it. Across the water, the power station is lit up. Something unearthly about it, holding him there, as if in a trance, unable to move, or think, or feel, until the stomach cramps and he is pulled back out of it.

There is a shooting pain in the trembly leg as he walks. He focuses on it, anticipating the short sharp jab each time he steps forward.

A passageway after the building, and through it, a car park. There is a minibus in the centre of it, with a trestle table pushed up against the open back doors. Bodies milling about. He stays in the passageway and watches. There is a group of four or five battered figures huddled on one side of the table. A short way off, a few others, all holding polystyrene cups. His blood is thumping; he steps back, against the wall of the passageway. An urge to bark out laughing moves through him, but it dies in his throat and he presses his palms hard against the wall, forcing them into the firm rough stone. He cannot do this. Better to starve than this, and he turns his face from the car park, starting out of the passageway and onto the street, back toward the river.

He keeps going, following the flow of the water. Now what? A pure aching need for a drink, but obviously that's out the question. The only option is to keep walking, or go back to the pub yard. He is actually that hungry the thought comes to him he could go through the bins. He stops. A car slowing down as it goes past him, coming to a halt at a traffic lights. He needs to eat. He needs to eat – it's that simple.

There are more of them arrived, stood in two groups further into the car park, but he keeps his gaze fixed on the table, steering toward it. He hurries on. A few people stood behind the table in big coats, one of them leaning forwards, smiling. He keeps his head down, doesn't look him in the face. There are cheese sandwiches on a plate, biscuits, crisps, fruit, a bowl of pasta. He clears his throat. 'A sandwich please.' The man puts one on a paper plate, then shakes a few crisps on the side, like a picnic. 'Would you like some soup?' Mick nods. He is handed a cup. 'Thanks,' he says, and moves round the other side of the minibus.

He wolfs the sandwich and crisps, although the soup is too hot to swallow down quickly. Why is he stood there anyway but? He could go. No like he's bloody beholden or anything, but still he stays put, staring into the side of the minibus, trying to get the soup finished and already it's too late, a woman coming round the side, approaching him. He watches her over the top of his cup, his shoulders tensing.

'Hello.' She stands there just, no saying anything, smiling. Obvious it's some kind of a ploy to make him talk. He stays quiet though, the cup held up to his mouth.

'Good soup?'

He nods his head.

'We always try to have a soup on. Especially nights like this.'

The roof of his mouth is scalding. Some noise on the other side of the minibus.

'Do you have somewhere to stay tonight?'

'No,' he says, mainly because he can't be bothered acting it.

She starts going in her coat pockets. 'Here.' Handing him a piece of paper. 'This has the address of one of our winter shelters which is open tonight. It's just off this main road, actually. Not far.' She smiles, and he takes a big gulp of soup, watching as she slips the hand into her pocket again.

'Do you have a faith?'

'No.'

She is unperturbed. 'Well, take one of these anyway. Something to read through, if nothing else.' And she holds out leaflets of what look like Bible scriptures. He doesn't take them, but she has turned round anyway, distracted by whatever's going on past the minibus. Some kind of scuffle is broke out. She starts toward it, and he moves forward as well, by instinct, looking what's going on. Some kind of argle-bargle between the two groups; facing off to each other, lots of shouting and birling about. One of the figures steps forward and there is a surge of excitement in the group behind him – 'Do the soup, do it, do the soup . . . go on, fuck off back to Warsaw' – and a soup cup is thrown, the liquid arching through the air. A melee starting, the Christians softfooting up to it, and he takes his opportunity to go; he puts his plate and cup on the ground and is away.

The cardboard was took out during the day and possibly he is going to die here, sat up against the iceberg generator. Both legs are shaking now, and his face is that frozen the teeth have gave up chattering. Instead, a random spasm of his jaw each few minutes, the two sets of teeth crashing together, so that by this point he's got toothache as well; no part of him wanting to miss out. He is past caring though. Nothing is real any more, even the pain. All that exists is the cold.

The street is dark and empty and he turns back a moment to check the name of it. It's the right one. Why shouldn't it be? What's he expecting: drunken, toothless scaffers spilling about over the road? A giant arrow – down and outs, this way? Further on there is a smaller street off the side, and down it, a church. He goes toward it in a kind of daze, without considering what he is doing; all he knows is that he's definitely way too fucking sober to be doing it. It is the cold that pushes him on, chibbing like a gun between the shoulder blades.

The great wooden door of the church is closed, no sign of anybody about, so he carries on round the side to a single-storey, modern kind of a building. A light through the ribbed glass above the door. He presses on the button, but nobody comes out, so he tries the handle and goes in. A small, dark foyer. Old books on a shelf; a poster on a noticeboard – Sunday service crèche club. Fucksake. What is he doing? Nay turning back now but, because a door is opening; the Hallelujahs are coming.

A tall man with close-shaved hair and glasses is looking at him from round the door.

'Hello. Can we help you?'

'I was told there's a bed.'

'Come in.'

He follows him through into a large hall, the lights turned out, but he can see well enough the humped shapes in bags across the floor. They go into some kind of office, and the man sits down at a table, motioning him to a chair opposite.

'Now, we require very little here by way of paperwork. We provide a place to sleep for the night, a hot evening meal and breakfast. All we ask is that you treat the church and the other guests with respect. That, really' – he smiles, holding up both hands in mock surrender – 'is as complicated as it gets.'

Guests. He serious?

'What is your name?'

He tries to think up something, but he isn't quick enough. 'Mick.'

'Hello, Mick. My name is Yann.' He is smiling again and Mick wonders if maybe this is the hallelujah bit coming. 'Whatever has brought you to us tonight, Mick, nobody here is going to judge you, and anything you tell us will be treated in confidence, as is the case with every one of our guests.'

'I'm no a homeless, just I'm in-between things, is all.'

Yann smiles. He isn't buying that one. 'That's alright.' He starts to get up. 'Let me get you a cup of tea. I'm afraid it's too late now for the evening meal. We don't generally allow admissions after eight, but we do have a space and I know how cold it is tonight.'

'I've already ate, thanks.'

'Good.' He goes to the door. 'Now, I need just to tell you, we don't allow any drugs, alcohol or weapons in here.' He smiles. 'We're pretty relaxed, otherwise.' He goes out the room. Drugs? Weapons? What does he look like to this guy?

A few moments later the Hallelujah comes back in. A small cup tinkling with a spoon and sugar lump on a saucer. He gives it to him and leans down to pick something up outside the doorway. A sleeping bag, and a rolled-up mat. He puts them on the table. 'Finish your tea, then I'll show you through.'

There is a couple dozen bodies. The room honks with feet and drink and urine. Cabbages. He is being shown to a space against the wall in between two humps, and all he can think is – no, he cannot do this. Leave, well. Remove yourself from the place and slam the door firmly shut behind – thank you, oh dear Lord, for no judging me and for the tea but that's me offski the night, goodbloodybye.

'Breakfast is at six thirty,' the voice is whispering, the mat getting laid out for him, 'and all guests are asked to vacate by seven.' Mick sits and takes off his shoes, a pure blessed relief, and even if the brain doesn't want him to be doing it, there's no chance the body is going to listen now as he slides into the warm bag. He will be up and out immediately as he's swallowed down some breakfast. Guests are asked to vacate by seven. What a fucking place. Hotel Hallelujah.

He is facing toward the wall. The bag pulled right over his head. Still but he can't shut out the sounds. Farts and wheezings all around him. Cabbages. He sleeps in fits. His chest cramping each time he wakes and then strains the bag tight about him, but the smell, that smell, it's inside the bag, inside him, right into the windpipe and the lungs, until he is pure desperate for some other smell that he knows, something familiar. But he can't mind any. Impossible to imagine that any other smell exists. It's just this.

A noise wakes him. A shout, somewhere in the room, followed

by a long wail. For a moment there is silence but then it comes again, a loud scurling sound. Like a fox; no something human. He closes his eyes, wanting to shut it out, but he can't, even in the quiet in-betweens, because he is braced, the heart tromboning, waiting for it to come again. He inches the bag down from his face and props up onto his elbow to try and see over the hill of whatever he's next to. There is no movement anywhere. Only the dim shapes of all these others, who don't seem to notice this desperate wailing noise, merging it instead into their own nightmares.

A hand on his shoulder. There is activity in the room, voices, light streaming in through the large, high windows. Somebody stood above him; walking away. He lies there rigid and watches as the cocoon next to him squeezes itself out. No a butterfly, that's for certain. He is old and scarred, the hair clotted, deep trenches in his face. Mick doesn't move, watching from inside his bag – all these hopeless creatures stooping and coughing, gathering up their beds. There is one pair that look young enough they could be school-weans. Blacks too, Asians, the whole circus. Yann is there, chatting with a few of the other Hallelujahs, who bring out long tables and unfold them at one side of the hall. Women start appearing. Broken-looking women, worse gone even than the men. He sits there in a stupor taking it in. He's seen plenty enough scaffers before, in book-ies, the park, on the street, but this is something different, seeing them all together in a room. Yann is coming over.

'How did you sleep, Mick? We have breakfast now, so if you want to queue up, they'll have it out in a moment.' A line is already forming by a table at the other side of the hall. 'Here.' He hunkers down beside him and hands him a leaflet. 'Each of these churches opens for a different night of the week. You can self-refer to any, but you'll need to book your place first.'

He half listens to the rest of Yann's spiel before joining the back of the queue, behind a woman with no socks on, her baries scarlet and bloated. None of it is registering properly. He sits down where there is nobody next to him. Staff food all over again. Except this is a better meal at least: scrambled egg, bacon, beans. Head down, he eats fast, ravenous and wanting to get out. Somebody is pulling in opposite him but. Mick keeks up, then back to his food. A man in a red woolly hat. His giant bawface blistered and shot, a drinker. If he can just get eaten up, leave this place, no talk to any of them. But this guy is staring at him.

'Ye don't always get the beans, know. Serious, ye don't.'

A bloody Weegie. Unfuckingbelievable. Mick doesn't look up. He resolves no to let a word slip out of his mouth.

'See the bacon is always – ye always get the bacon but the beans is hit and miss. Believe that? I'm telling them, get more beans. Beans is cheaper for them and it fills ye up the better.'

Mick nods, picking up his plate and standing.

He puts the plate and cutlery into the buckets on the table. How can somebody like that look at him and think – aye, there's a guy that's on my wavelength? No point dwelling on it but. Probably a headbanger. He goes warily over to his bag and then makes for the door, getting out the building before any other nutter can clamp onto him.

A man in a suit is sitting on a bench. A short way down the towpath, an elderly Mediterranean-looking woman in a huge fur coat is waiting for her small dog to finish shitting beside a tree. The man knows full well that she is not going to clear it up. He knows it, and it is irritating the hell out of him that he knows it, but still he cannot move his eyes away: the dog squeezes out the final pellet, and he watches in silent fury as the woman slowly wanders off in her enormous coat.

The man turns back to his lunch, but that just serves to annoy him further, so he looks up at Battersea Power Station instead – something reassuring about the size and solidity of it. He could kill for a sausage sandwich right now. That was his old routine: after the first couple of weeks last summer when all the new advisers would go together from the Department for Business building to the pub for lunch, he had taken to walking down to the river and buying a sausage sandwich en route. He looks down miserably now at his Boots meal deal: the juice drained in one go, sandwich vanished, colourful delights of the fruit salad still to come. The homeless man is there again. He is sat three benches further up, and there's little chance he could have seen him but even so the memory of yesterday returns, and he experiences for a moment the same sense of panic he had felt as the man had approached him, the crazed look on his face. He seems to be keeping to himself today, ignoring the passers-by and just glaring out at the river in what appears to be the same dirty brown jacket and torn trousers as he had on before.

He attempts the fruit salad. It is dry and soapy; he compresses a piece in his mouth but no moisture comes out. He knows that it is almost time to return to the office, but as soon as he thinks about leaving the bench he starts to become a little nauseous. There is a pre-meet at one to brief the Idiot for his afternoon meetings. No doubt the others will be prepared: they'll have been planning over lunch, devising a briefing strategy. They will have choreographed their spiel; and when, at the end of the brief, the Idiot turns to him and asks if he has any input, he will look every inch the pointless fat fool as he replies that he believes it's all been covered. In his whole time there so far, his single most significant contribution was the moment during a meeting with the Federation of Small Businesses when the Idiot passed him a squiggled note that read: *What is the minimum wage these days?* Remembering the stupid flush of pride that he had experienced on sliding back the answer causes the sick feeling in his stomach to increase now, as he rises from the bench.

A runner comes past in a gold-coloured pair of lycra trousers, his large muscular buttocks seizing as he pounds down the towpath. The man starts back toward Westminster, but immediately as he does so the strange, horrifying image enters his head of himself in the same pair of trousers, entering the building and suddenly everybody looking at him – the security guards suppressing their mirth as he passes through the scanners – and the sight of his fat golden arse repeated all around him in the unending glass and mirrors and polished flooring. Suddenly he stops right there on the towpath, looking round to check nobody is nearby, and, with the fruit salad punnet, he scoops up the four small nuggets of dog shit from beside the tree. He ties up the Boots carrier bag around it, continuing alongside the river, and drops the package into the next dustbin he passes.

Further down the water, Mick is viewing across the way to the power station. One thing that must be admitted: it's bloody big. When did they close it? Who cares, what does it matter? It doesn't. Probably the Milk Snatcher but. We don't want power stations, what we want instead is more apartment buildings – these ones you can see here all along past the bridge, curving swirls of bright blue and green.

He pulls out the leaflet and turns it over. One thing that's obvious, looking at the map: these churches are spread miles apart. And, on top of that, the Monday one is the other side of the map from Tuesday, which does not neighbour Wednesday, and so on, and so on. Obvious it's done on purpose. To make things difficult, for whatever reason. The absurdity of it all. An absurd situation, would ye no agree, Mr Jogger, in your – and let's be honest here – pretty daft leggings? Fucksake, he needs a drink. The pub just a little way down the road but him sat here with no money on his tail. Cruel. Very cruel.

It takes him two hours to walk there, and he arrives while it is still light. Maybe that's how they keep them so far apart. To give the scaffers something to do. Pass the time. The Hallelujah that comes to the door isn't as friendly as the other one. He's in fact quite annoyed that Mick's turned up out the blue without booking his place. He's not supposed to arrive before seven. He should have phoned ahead. A good one, that. See the thing is I was going to call ahead on the mobile phone but then I was that busy on the line with clients and contractors and all that, I forgot. He doesn't bother arguing with the guy. No the energy or the pride, so he keeps quiet and the man agrees to book him in, only he has to go away the now and no come back until seven o'clock. He leaves, walks about, wondering how he's supposed to know when seven o'clock is.

Shepherd's pie and a spoon of boiled vegetables. The set-up is different here – it's a bigger place, and there are small round tables to sit at, but he manages to find one where he's on his own. He recognizes one or two of the faces. The beans guy is here, sat over the way at a full table, laying it off to some poor ancient scaffer about something or other.

The Hallelujahs wait until everybody has got food, then they fix out plates for themselves and sit down inamongst the tramps. Mick stares down at his plate, eating quickly, but nobody comes. Afterwards he gets a sleeping bag and finds a space, then sits against the wall next to it, making sure he doesn't catch eyes with anybody. Some of the scaffers stand together in dirty clusters, talking. Others keep with themselves, avoiding the groups, like he is doing. No. As long as he remains outside of it, eating the food just and accepting the shelter for now, and no talking to any scaffers or any Hallelujahs, then he will stay afloat. Only if he accepts that he is part of this, that he belongs here, will he be done for. Because if he does that, then there'll be no control over it, and he may as well throw in the towel. Game over.

A dribbly day, but no too cold. He takes a free paper from a stall he passes, to lay down on the bench. Irrational, maybe, no the sensible man's choice, but he goes the trek to his usual spot. The night's church is in the other direction but it doesn't matter, better anyway to use up the day by walking. He is sat staring at the power station when a young lad, looks like a student, comes and sits in next to him. It isn't long before he turns and starts talking. Mick keeps quiet, hoping he'll get the message. He doesn't. Incredible sight, he is saying, wet day, and all this. Go bloody sit inside well if it's too wet for you. He has started fiddling about in his rucksack.

'Would you like a muffin?'

Mick ignores him.

'It's okay. It's spare.' He is holding his muffin out to him. 'Well, I'll just leave it here in case you change your mind.'

The boy stays sitting there. He keeps looking over, Mick can see him doing it out the corner of his eye. After a while, he turns toward the lad, the muffin still there on the bench between them.

'I've ate already. I'd take a pound but, get myself a cup of tea.'

The boy obvious isn't too sure about this and he delays a moment, nay doubt thinking – how do I know he isn't going straight the offie with this? Which is exactly where he intends going with it, but the lad is by now getting out his wallet, and he hands him £1.50.

He uses the money smartly. £1.29 buys him a decent-size bottle of Polish lager and he saves the rest to call ahead to the church. It runs out after about five seconds, but the guy rings him back.

The journey is much more pleasurable with a drink inside him. No bevvied, but warmer, more relaxed. In such a state it is easier to ignore all the rub-ye-ups bustling past and eyeballing him along the pavement. Away home to their evenings of curry dinner and telly watching, argle-bargling with the wife. Plenty of scaffers about too: alone in doorways; stood in wee groups; blocking the thorough-fares selling their magazines. He is coming into a more posh area. There are wine drinkers inside a giant café window, flower stalls, well-to-do clothes shops. This one that he passes. A naked manne-quin in the window, bald and bare, with the one hand on her hip. The sudden temptation to run in and steal her. Run off down the street with the baldy woman tucked under the arm. How far would he get? How many yards down the pavement before the heavy mob catch up, huckling him down some back alley to put the boot on?

No that there are many back alleys this part of town. Nay chance. It's all boulevards and butchers round here, they Italian ones with cured meats hanging in the display above the olive oils and the giant cheese wheels.

It is a Catholic church this night, and the space is a side room off the church building itself, the walls above the sleeping mats covered with ornate lanterns and candles, lifelike statues of nuns holding crosses and looking out with serious faces at the scaffers. There are less staying than the previous two nights, but still one or two of the regulars, they ones that know they're onto a good thing and have got themselves in with the bricks. He ignores them, managing to keep to himself. Eats his food. Drinks his tea. There is a prayer session after dinner, but the Hallelujahs don't force it. Quite a few take part though, going through with the Bead Rattler, who has been walking about the place in his robes and his rings, for a wee patter with the Big Man. Hard to know how they're asking him for anything.

He rolls out his mat and his bag and gets lying down. How quick you get used to things. Settle into a rhythm.

In the morning after breakfast, one of the Hallelujahs, a woman, approaches him.

'Sleep okay?'

'Fine, thanks.'

She stands by the tea table while Mick is fixing up his tea and his orange juice. How is it people are always wanting to put the nose in and can't leave him be?

'It's Mick, isn't it? I haven't met you before. My name's Jenny.'

'Pleased to meet ye, Jenny,' and he starts to turn and get leaving back to his place at the table.

'I was wondering – have you had a chance to use the daytime centre at all?'

'I have, aye, thanks.'

'Oh, right. Good. And you know we have caseworkers too, who can help you with accessing services.' The beans guy is arrived at the table making a tea, listening, a wee smile on him.

'Thanks, Jenny, I'll bear it in mind.'

'Right, okay.' She smiles and starts to move off. 'Have a nice day, Mick.'

Oh, aye, it's going to be a belter: away down the boulevard for a new suit, then off to a restaurant with the baldy woman for Guinness and oysters.

'How's it going?' Beans is looking at him, still the wee grin. The red woolly hat pulled right down to his eyes.

'Good.'

'Ye from Glasgow, well?'

No use kidding on now he's been rumbled.

'I am.'

'Whereabout?'

'Clydebank.'

'That where ye were born?'

'Aye, Clydebank.'

He gives a wide smile. One side of his top lip is chappit and bleeding. 'I'm from Paisley.' He holds out a giant purple hand. 'Keith. Ye're no a religious case, eh?'

'No.'

Beans turns his eyes for an instant up to the roofbeams. There is a large dark gouge in the stubble under his chin. 'Thank Christ for that, then. Enough of them about, no think?'

'The Hallelujahs.'

He lets out a loud lunatic laugh, which makes Jenny and the woman she's with look round a moment. 'Aye, the Hallelujahs, you said it, pal, fucking right.'

He is still chuckling with himself as Mick gets leaving.

Where do they go to? There's aye the ones that are sat in the doorways and selling the magazines, but what about the rest of them, where do they go? The women? You never see the women. The nights at the churches, there's been quite a few of them put up. They get a separate room, or if it's one of the smaller places they get a plastic barricade wheeled up in between to keep the men off them. The tollie tugboat is on the approach, docking up with its cargo of shite. He watches it turn around on the water, coiling slowly into the wharf. No great mystery but. It's pretty obvious where most of them go, the men anyway, the male scaffers. They ones that aren't sat next to a carry-out cup, tapping pedestrians for the price of a bottle, are down the broo office signing on. See but how is he any different? Sponging off the Christians for food and orange juice. Fucksake he eats more than anybody there!

He doesn't stop going. He's there each night for his free meal and his free entertainment, listening to the night terrors erupting through the hall. He has a shapeless awareness that he needs to be doing something, but it's getting more difficult to hold the thought and do anything with it. The brain is unable to deal with it. The Hallelujahs aren't but. They keep going on at him about it. Especially the guy Yann. Does he know there's a laundry and showers at the daytime centre? Has he had any thoughts what he's going to do when the shelters close at the end of February? He's going up to Glasgow, he tells him. Going back to see the family. Yann is delighted. That's good, Mick. That's very good.

What will happen to all this lot then? Where will they go? They're that settled into the routine, some of them. Maybe they are actually in fact secret bloody millionaires and when this all packs up they're away in their jets to their lochside mansions, and that's how they're all so unbothered about it, who knows? Because that's what they are. Unbothered. It's true. Rare there is an incident. Sometimes but. Nothing much. The odd squabble a couple of times, arguments over who's took whose sleeping space, but that's usually it. It is a while before he sees anything like a proper fight, and when he does, it's two women. The one of them starts screaming at the other that she's stole her gloves, and when she denies it and starts walking away, the accuser jumps her from behind and gets clawing at her face. The Hallelujahs are straight in there, breaking them up, wheeling out an extra divider the night.

Beans reckons he knows the whole back story. He is sat down at the same dinner table laying it off to him.

'She's had they gloves for years, see. She was gave them as a present by somebody, so ye can see how she's angry. I'd be angry, somebody lifted my hat. I'd be fucking beeling.' Mick sits drinking his tea. 'Know what I think?' Beans continues. 'I think it's no about the gloves. Probably there never was a pair of gloves even. Sometimes it's like that, know what I mean? Christmas is aye the worst. This place is eggshells then. Depends what like is the family situation, course, but most of these lot are biting the carpets.'

Christmas. He's not even noticed that it has came and went. He must have been at the hotel. He tries to mind when it would have been, if there'd been any sign of it, but he can't think; the whole thing is a fog. Plus as well this great bampot right in his face.

'See me, I'm no staying around much longer.' He is looking intently across the table at Mick.

'How's that?'

'Mean, I know this place, close, quite close, beds, kitchens, comfy, ye know, no like this.' He turns and looks about behind him a moment. 'All I want is to go for a crap in peace.'

He is grinning at his joke. Mick notices there are bits of dandruff on the outside of his hat.

'See how I'm telling ye is because you should go there too, we should both of us go there. Ye can't stay here.'

Mick looks away over to where the tables are getting folded back up for the night. The first of the sleeping mats being rolled out onto the floor. He's right, obviously. The memory then of the pub backyard, the cold humming generator. At least this guy has got something going on upstairs, unlike himself. He's thinking, at least. Even the headbangers have the march on him these days.

It rains a couple of days solid. Quiet down by the river during this time, the fast-flowing water foaming and stinking with the downpour. The occasional determined jogger dragging past. It is too wet to stay there. He'll be sat thinking it isn't so bad because the bench is partly covered over by a tree, but then a branch will give up under the gathering weight and dump a bucket onto his head. He goes up the coach station. He sits in the bays, drookit and shivering, frightening the passengers. Pneumonia but, it's good for the handouts. Both days, he taps a pitying face for the price of a can and goes to drink it under the railway bridge, or on the walk over to the night's church.

Beans is sat near the end of a long table, on his own. Mick goes over and sits in opposite him.

'Alright?'

Beans is away with it though, staring down at his untouched chicken and chips.

'What ye said before, mean, I think I might take ye up on the offer.'

Beans looks up slowly. 'Offer.'

'Aye, what ye said, this other place.'

Beans doesn't say anything. He stares off now to the side, at nothing, at the wall. Maybe he's bevvied. He doesn't smell but; no of drink, anyway.

'Well, I thought I'd let ye know, okay.'

He doesn't push it after that, and carries on eating his food while Beans sits there, vacant, until after a while he pushes his chair out and walks off, leaving his food where it is.

Mick watches him, over on the far side of the room, sitting down with his back against the wall. A new one, this. He's never seen him when he hasn't been bouncing off the ceilings and chewing everybody's ear off. He continues staying there, alone, while the tea comes out and then the chairs and tables are cleared away, and he's still there, unmoving, while Mick and the others are getting into their sleeping bags for the night. A Hallelujah goes over to him eventually and he gets up slowly, moving over to his pitch.

The next evening though Beans comes up to him in the car park where Mick is stood waiting for the church doors to open. He does mind the conversation. And no just the first one either, but the no-conversation last night as well.

'So what I thought was Sunday.' There is a scaffer sat smoking on the steps who tilts his head up to listen, and Beans pulls Mick off to the side. 'See the thing is Sunday's a good day to try cause there's always chuck-outs the weekend, after people have been on the batter.'

'I'm no sure, mean it's –'

'Nay worries, I'll sort it, I'll sort it. I know the place, see, I know how to play it.' He grins. 'A bed, man. A fucking bed, eh.'

Hard to know what to think, and hard to think at all anyway, so he doesn't. He sits near Beans at tea and half observes him rattling on ten the dozen to anybody that goes near him. They eat. Go to sleep. Up the next morning and he's out again into the cold, away the long stiff journey to the shelter of the coach station. His feet are pretty swollen getting. The walking, or the temperature, or his socks, which cling now like a second skin. One moment to the next. That is all he can do. One moment to the next. Avoid the Hallelujahs and sit quietly as he gets his ear chewed off by this strange creature that is smiling at him now. 'Come on, then.' Plates getting cleared away. 'Ye ready?'

26

'See, what I'm saying is never let them think that ye've hit the scrape because if they do then that's you screwed, man, terrible, fucking terrible. They'll never leave ye alone. Plus as well they'll give ye the worst of everything – room, bed, fire alarm, giro, the whole bag all to shite.'

Mick looks down at the pavement. It is dark. Cold. Their breath fluming in front of them as they walk. Actually, no – Beans's breath fluming in front of them – because he never shuts up. Since they left the church it's been non-stop: benefits, religion, piles, the population of birds. He needs to rest but he's too tired to think about doing anything but trail along with this guy through the dark streets, stumbling into busyness where the pavements are hoaching at bus stops and crossings; down deserted side roads, past closed shops, pubs, a girl with her arms tightly folded, smoking in a doorway. The problem with birds, he is saying, is that they're all dying because the farmers are greedy arabs and they've torn down all the hedgerows, the same as they tear down the tenements and now there's nothing, everything is bare just. Mick is trying no to listen. This place they are going to was supposed to be close by, but they've been walking Christ knows how long and he doesn't recognize any more where they are. To close the eyes just. Close the eyes. Sleep. No have to think. No have to listen.

'Where d'ye say it is, this place?'

'Naw, don't worry, don't worry. It's near here. I know where it is.'

'Ye've stayed before, well?'

Beans halts abruptly on the spot, jolts his body upright. 'Have I stayed before? *Course* I've stayed before. *Course* I have.' And he starts walking again, chuckling to himself. Has he been bevvying? It's hard to tell. He's a mighty queer ticket, whichever way. There is a period of quiet. They keep on. No a slow pace either – the guy walks with these great loundering strides, the shoulders stooped over and hunching, bunching, as he steps. It had came as a surprise, during the lunatic moment back there, how tall he actually is when he stands straight. A big man, and this large army-type overcoat that he wears, making him look even bigger. Impossible but to tell how old he is. The hair, when he's took off the woolly hat to sleep, is a full coverage – dark, straggling below his ears and greasy as drag-chains. His face though, lined and scarred; purple. Whatever it is he's been doing with himself, it looks like he's been doing it a long while.

He is trying now to hoick his tattered Ikea bag higher onto his shoulder. Mick is conscious of his own faded holdall, smart in comparison, and as well his clothes, which if maybe they aren't the cleanest, they are normal clothes, they are his clothes. He isn't going around in an army greatcoat and a pair of silver running trainers with the soles flapping off them. Beans is hammering away again: the weather, how it's freezing but it isnae wet and that's the important thing because it's blashie weather that's the worst. Jesus, he could do with a drink.

'See, look, this is what I'm telling ye. Here.'

They are outside a grey concrete building at one end of a street. A woman's voice on an intercom by a heavy, unmarked door and they are getting buzzed in. A corridor; straight ahead a staircase and two doors off either side. Bare walls and grey carpet tiles. The strong smell of bleach. Beans doesn't seem too sure where to go and he hesitates a moment, a quick neb in the one door, then back out, and he tries the other one; goes inside. Mick follows him in.

It looks like a doctor's waiting room: plastic chairs backed against the walls and a single battered settee, a small television that is turned off, and a low table sprawled with mangled, thick magazines. An Asian woman is sat at a computer on the other side of a small security hatch. Beans goes straight up and puts his hands onto the counter. They look massive in the stark lighting, veined like cabbages.

'We've booked a place the night. I was in earlier.'

Mick sits down on the settee. Comfort flooding his legs. He could go to sleep right here, close the eyes, go to sleep.

'No, see, I came in Sunday but there was no rooms so I was told come back the day and they told me earlier there was places for us, that's what I'm saying.'

The woman's voice is hushed, barely audible past his huge back. He is arguing with her; the protective shutter above the hatch about to roll down any moment. Beans turns then and comes toward the settee. He dumps down and Mick near slides onto his lap.

'Says we've got to wait for the hostel manager. She's no too sure we're booked in but that's pure crap – I was here the morning and I spoke to the guy, I telt him we were coming. Fucking *indirect* access, ye ask me.' He keeps speaking, but Mick sits in a kind of a daze, wanting to let the brainbox go to rest. Hostel. He is in a hostel. He tries no to think about what is happening; trying no to think about any of it, least of all this blowhard sat here next to him, staring now at the underwear models in a worn-out clothing catalogue. An agitated old black man noses in at one point, his trouser bottoms rolled up unevenly to show dirty yellow walking socks. He glances toward the television a moment, then backs out.

Mick is falling asleep, Beans quietly looking at the magazines, and another man coming in, younger, smarter, a trimmed beard. Beans is stood up, talking to him. The man goes away, through a locked door into the room with the woman; returning with sheets of paper. He gives some to Beans, then he's looking down at Mick, handing him the papers and saying something – he can't hear it properly, it's quiet like a radio with the batteries going – benefits, it is something about benefits. He tries to sit up. The man is talking to Beans again. No visitors. No alcohol. No drugs. He repeats it. Beans nodding his head. Grinning. He looks demented.

The room is small. A cubicle. Three beds with high plastic sides, lined up like cots. He puts his bag down at the foot of one of them and looks out the small window at a brightly lit car park. Lies down on the bed. He can hear Beans outside, laying it off to the man because the room isn't big enough. He stares up at the ceiling. The same smell of bleach; sanitizer. Strange but he is glad of Beans being there. The ceiling is starting to swim. He shuts the eyes. So tired it feels his breathing is about to give out.

A shout wakes him. He sits up. His clothes are on and it is dark apart from some lights outside a window. A hollow racing sensation as he gets his bearings. There is another shout; it is in the corridor – *Go on!*

it sounds like. Then feet pounding and a tremor in the floor as they come past his room. *Go on!* More than one person. Three or four. Men's voices. A moment later it is quiet again, but the tight panicked feeling does not leave him and he lies there rigid, exhausted but no able to get back to sleep.

When he wakes up again it is getting light outside. The room is empty. Tummelled sheets on one of the beds. He is hungry, but he doesn't know if there is a breakfast in this place. He doesn't know what or where the place is either, for another thing. After a while he gets up and listens through the door, and goes out.

The kitchen along the corridor is empty. Plates and pans are heaped in the sink and there are blackened scratchings of food littered on top of an electric hob cooker. Something in the room which is boufing. Doesn't smell much like food but, and he realizes as he gets closer that it is the bin. He moves away from it and toward the fridge. Inside, a bundled-up Tesco carrier and a snipped-open packet of pasta sauce inside the door. That's the lot. A stank of yellowish liquid pooled at the bottom. Second inspections but, and he undoes the carrier to find a plastic tub of cocktail sausages. No like they're going to miss a couple, and no like he's fussy either, so he puts one in his mouth; but there is something wrong about the taste of it, and he gets standing up, shuts the fridge door, awful, fucking awful. Posters on a noticeboard. Needle exchange. Substance-use worker. His stomach lurches and he bends over the sink, about to boak, but he doesn't – he stays there, poised, with the stomach spasming but nothing coming up, just this thin dribble hanging off his lip. He sticks the tap on and swills his mouth. The rush of water splashing against the plates and pans and wetting his front. Where is he? He wants suddenly to laugh. Where in fuck is he? He turns off the tap and goes out, back to the empty room, and into the bed.

Beans is stood at the foot of the bed, looking at him.

'Fancy getting some breakfast eh?'

Mick gets up automatically, without thinking. Starts putting his shoes on. Beans is over by the window, his hands clasped behind his back, calmly gazing out as if it's a loch view.

Once outside, they are straight away on the march. No the worst day. Warm on those parts of the pavement that the sun is shining, although pretty snappy still in the shaded areas, past offices and residential blocks, under a bridge, past a line of parked buses. They go by a small scrub of a square and a mob of scaffers around the benches on one side. Seven or eight of them, women in the mix, sitting and standing about, drinking. Beans slows down, watching them. For a moment Mick is feart he is wanting to go over, but they carry on past, although Beans still has his attention turned to the group. They continue up the way. Truth is, he's glad to be out of the hostel. Away from that room. Probably most of that group back there are staying in the place too. The thought of it, of being in there with them, himself in a room alongside, it doesn't make sense. He can't reckon with it. Better outside in the open, away from it, even if that means being with your man here. They are stopped outside a cafe. A large scratched sticker on the window – a fat chef holding up a steaming forked sausage. Beans is going in, but Mick hesitates outside.

'Ye coming in?'

'Aye.' But he stays where hc is, looking in past the fat chef.

Beans grins. 'It's on me, pal, it's on me, don't worry.'

'No. It's no the game,' but Beans is off inside already, and he follows him in.

They go up the counter and Beans immediately orders two breakfasts and two teas, then they get themselves sat at a table by a wall, away from the busy middle of the room. Pathetic. He knows it is. Somehow but he can't feel it. He's that hungry, and weak – that's what it is, a weakness – that he can't bring himself to say no. The breakfasts come and Beans is beasted right in, mushrooms flying about, ketchup and brown sauce and mustard all mixed together on his plate like a mental sunset. Every bastard in the place probably looking at them. The odd couple in the corner. It's a good breakfast though. A buttery stack of toast, the warm mush of the sausage. Suddenly the thought that maybe Beans doesn't have the money to pay for it either, and he's going to do a run-out. The scunnered faces of the other customers and the cafe owner on the phone to the polis.

He does have the money, it turns out. A ten-pound note comes out the pocket, calm as anything, no chicanery, no hystericals. He walks up the counter just, pays, and they leave.

It is bright out still. They walk for quite a while, Beans talking – they aren't allowed back into the hostel while evening, he is saying – until they arrive, suddenly, at the river. A stretch he doesn't recognize. Beans is saying he wants to show him something, and they go through a gate with a broken padlock – *Permits required to access this property for the purpose of nature conservation or fishing* – into a small wooded, weeded area. Down a sloping thicket and thorns path, long grass and random rubbish – empty cement bags, a broken office chair on its side – to a sprawling bush, which they crawl under, emerging onto a patch of open ground that looks out on the water.

'The veranda,' he declares. They sit down, legs dangling over the banking. He likes to sit here and watch the boats and that come past, he says. And to drink too, judging by all the cans lying about. There is a swan who stays under the scrub off to one side where the banking stops, Beans tells him, only she's no there the now because she's out and about getting her nest together. It's hard to believe him – anything he says – but then Mick sees the nest, lower down, sticking out from under the scrub, all these twigs twined into a great bowl on the wet ground amongst plastic bottles and lager cans. Bold as ye like. He gives a smile at the sight of it. These swans that he minds, who made their nests by the fitting-out berths, their feathers clatty with oil, but who'd come and go like they were boating on Loch Lomond.

At one point during the afternoon Beans goes off for a while, and returns with a couple of four-packs. They sit in the sun drinking, and Mick tells him what type are a couple of the boats that come by, Beans listening as if it's the most fascinating thing he's ever heard.

It is only when it gets evening and they are on the approach to the hostel that it starts to loom over him again. The bare room. Bogging of bleach. Surrounded by homeless. They walk past a bar and he almost asks Beans if he fancies going a pint, but obviously it's impossible because of the money situation. It's bad enough he's tapped him already for his breakfast, plus now the cans. So they go in, Beans away into the reception to chin the staff and leaving Mick to go up on his own.

He is on the stairhead about to turn onto the corridor, but there is noise up the way. Voices. He waits round the corner, the heart going mental already. Hard to hear what they are saying, but it sounds like there's a few of them, and this other noise as well that sounds like somebody thumping rhythmically against the wall. He is that fixed on what's ahead of him, he doesn't notice the group coming up the stair behind.

One of them laughs.

'You alright there, mate?'

He spins round. There are three of them. Young lads. They stand there grinning and leering at him.

'Fine, aye,' and he moves on down the corridor, the others up ahead turning to watch him, and these behind following him, one of them making a tootling noise, like a trumpet. He gets into the room, closes the door and pushes one of the cots up against it.

The sun straining a thin light through the curtain. Beans asleep in his clothes. Noises coming and going outside, keeping him awake, on edge.

It is dark. He has been dreaming. Christmas. Christmases, all jumbled together. The first one he is sat in the living room and the boys and the Highlanders are there sat in their positions, a wee plastic Christmas tree behind the television, Lynn sat on the settee next to Alan with her crabbit face on, like it's the last place in the world she wants to be the now, this craphole, with its stained carpets and cramped corridors, and the wobbling banister as he goes up the stair and into the bedroom. Robbie and Craig sat on the kitchen chairs with plates of Christmas dinner on their laps, looking toward the shape in the bed. Craig cutting up the turkey breast into tiny pieces; quartering the Brussels sprouts.

He is awake. The mind out of its box, spinning, all over the place. A few minutes and he's managed to calm himself a little, lying awake until he is able to sleep again.

Another Christmas. Australia. He is sat at the table waiting for her to come in from the kitchen. The cracker hat clamming to his forehead and the full works there on the plate in front of him – turkey, roast tatties and parsnips, bread pudding, cranberry sauce – and outside, all of the gardens down the road are empty because the whole of the Tartan Terrace is at the same game: the only weekend of the summer nobody's got the barbecue out.

Morning, and he's lying in the bed, the body aching, sticking. Beans suddenly in through the door and frowning. He looks at him a moment. 'Breakfast?'

They sit at the same table, the same positions. The only difference is that Beans isn't as rosy this morning: his back is up from something that's happened in the hostel, and it's making him mutter and scratch fork points through his swirly sauce sunsets.

'See the problem is with these people, they've no respect for a person's privacy, know? Mean, it's no better than the clink, serious, and I'm expecting a bit of privacy myself. That's the least I'm expecting.'

'What happened?'

The eyes widen, far enough to expose the white outsider parts that are normally sheltered under the lids. 'What happened? That bastard the manager, that's what. He says to me, the magazines are supposed to stay in the reception, they're no for taking out. Believe that? He's no even asked me. He's telt me I've got them but he's no even asked me first, that's how I'm beeling about it.'

He cloys up then and they don't talk any more about it. They finish eating and Beans pays.

It is colder, blowier, the day, and after a walkabout they go into a train station, park themselves on some seats by a pasty shop. There is a scaffer hanging about the ticket machines and Beans is watching him, the bristles up, like a dog. The smell of pasties wafting; a rare moment of enjoyment. He thinks for a moment how the shame of leeching like this should be making him the more desperate to get doing something, but it's not, it's the opposite – he doesn't think, doesn't care; he is into the routine. They are walking again. Fine but. Fine. Keeping on the move. A stop at the offie on the way to the veranda, and it is okay once they are sat down because the wind is mainly kept off by the bush all afternoon. As soon as they get leaving though, the familiar feeling starts to kick in, the nerves already on edge.

Fortunately but Beans doesn't go in the reception, he's wiped his hands with them, he says, and there is nobody about as they go up the stair and into the corridor. Open the door and go inside the room.

'Aw, Christ.'

It has been turned over. All the bedding is thrown on the floor and the drawers under the one small table are wrenched open. Their two bags have been taken. He sits down heavily on the bed, his breath constricting. Beans is away out the door. 'Fucksake, man. Fucking hell.' He puts his head down on the mattress. Stares out the window. A wean is kicking a ball against the car park wall. He lies listening to it beat repeatedly on the brick.

'She says there's nothing they can do, we should've locked the door. Bastards. Probably them that did it. Serious. It probably was. Ye okay, pal?' A hand is on his shoulder. 'Look, nay worries. No like we had much anyway eh? First thing we'll do the morning, we'll get out of this place. Okay?' He is hauling one of the cots up against the door. 'The better on our own, serious, nay cunts nebbing about.'

27

The group have been there all morning. At any one time there are between four and eight of them: sometimes a pair will wander off toward the street, or a new arrival will come into the square and for a few minutes the silence is broken as the others get on their feet, talking, shouting. One of the women keeps herself slightly removed, on the end bench. If one of the men approaches where she is, starts saying something to her, she ignores him, and eventually he returns to the others. The air of the group is edgy, quiet, getting worse as the morning goes on. Nothing to drink. She feels cold and nervous, sober, aware of the staring line of people at the bus stop.

Shortly before midday, three men arrive, two of them each holding a heavy plastic bottle of cider. The mood changes straight away. There is laughter and movement, the first of the bottles getting opened and passed around. She stays where she is on the bench, and before long another woman comes and sits next to her, passing her the second bottle. This other woman is grinning, looking at her coat. 'Jesus, Anna, alright for some.'

From the first swallow she is elsewhere. Her fear leaving; warmth spreading from deep inside her; the people at the bus stop disappearing. There is a burst of laughter from the group, one of the men saying something that she cannot hear, and the other woman resting her head now against the arm of her coat, closing her eyes. The woman's hair is thin, and she can see there is a rash on part of her scalp, and on the very top of her head, a large dark blue scab.

A fight has broken out. It came out of nowhere – she didn't see what started it – but two of the men are stalking stiffly around each other, and suddenly one of them crumples to the ground as he is struck by something from behind. In an instant the square is filled with shouting, the others in the group rushing in to join the scuffle.

She lifts the woman's head from her arm, lowers it gently to the bench slats and hurries away.

She breathes thinly as she moves down the street, past a line of parked buses and under a bridge, before slowing, her legs aching and frozen. At least her top half is warm. The coat is expensive and new, with a soft lining, and she pulls it tightly around her, making sure that the top is buttoned up to the neck. She needs to pee, but it is quite a way still to where she's headed, so she takes a detour to a public toilet by the river. When she gets there though, she finds it has been boarded up. Fuckers. She is reminded of the stupid drunk dickheads fighting up at the square and she vows not to return there later in the day, whatever happens.

There is a pub on her way and she goes into it. On entering through the heavy swing doors she is immediately watched by the bar girl, and by the time she has gone down the narrow spiral staircase into a dingy basement corridor, there is a large man in chef trousers standing in front of the toilet entrance. He is slowly shaking his head. She turns, avoiding looking at his face, and goes back up the spiral staircase. She walks through the bar; the girl looking at her from behind the counter. Her limbs are heavy and she thinks for a moment that the swing door is not going to open. She desperately needs to pee. With a painful heave the door pushes open, and she turns her head back as she steps through it.

'Fucking bitch.'

There is at least ten minutes left of the journey and she feels like she is about to piss herself. She comes to a side street leading toward a train station and goes down it, crouching behind one of the cars parked next to a high metal fence. Before she has finished, a man, and then a woman with a young teenage girl, come out of the train station exit and start walking along the pavement on the other side of the street. The woman and the girl are talking and do not see her, but the man crosses the street a short way ahead and must see the urine dribbling into the road, because he looks now through the car window at her and for an instant his mouth opens and he mutters something before hurrying away.

When she arrives at the house her mouth feels dry and her arms and legs are faintly shaking as she reaches for the buzzer. She waits in the doorway, until a moment later a man's voice answers, and there is a click as the door unlocks and she lets herself in.

On the veranda, looking out. A yacht coming past, sails blustering in the wind. A woman's face in a porthole. Away to the Med, says Beans. Champagne and Charlie. Only watch out for the Bay of Biscay or ye'll be boaking it all up into the sea. Anyone's guess how he thinks he knows these things. Maybe he does. The money is finished, he says then, but it's nay worry. He's got a plan. He is kneeling up and lifting the bush to get out. Okay? Okay?

There is a noise up on the pavement. A woman's voice, and, quieter, a man's. He tries to listen, no able to pick out the words, but they are getting closer. A gust of wind or something and suddenly he can hear them coming toward him and he scrapes deep into the bush, lying flat underneath it. He cannot let them see him; he pulls his jacket over his head. But they keep coming – they are onto the path now, and he can see the crabbit face, irritated at all these roots and thorns snarling about her ankles. They spot him then, laid out under the bush. She's pure scunnered at the sight of it, but he has a wee smile on him, unsurprised, keeking down now at the cans by his feet.

It is colder when Beans returns, the river turned black and treacly. He has a dark blue ski-jacket-type overcoat under his arm, and a carrier that he starts pulling things out from: a loaf of bread, an open tin of beans, a stack of beers. He sits down next to him. 'Here,' he says, and lobs the coat over. 'Put this over your jacket. Keep ye warmer.'

They make cold beans pieces out of the first few bread slices, and start on the cans. He has been drinking already, it seems. He isn't out the game, but he's talking loudly, laughing, and he makes them clink cans every couple of minutes – plus, each time, an extra one for the swan. 'Thanks,' Mick says, after one of these toasts, 'the coat and that.'

'Aw, you're welcome.' Beans puts on a panloaf English accent.

'You're very welcome.' He takes a long gulp. 'This fella I know, I called in a favour. He's alright, no a bad guy. He's a cunt, ye know, but he's alright.' They are laughing. A warm enclosed feeling from the beer.

'It because I'm from Glasgow, how ye're helping me out?'

'What!' He sits bolt upright and gets standing stumbling to his feet. 'Ye're from Glasgow? Serious? I'd have gave ye the swerve if I'd known,' and he collapses to the ground again, cackling to himself.

In a moment, Beans kneels up. He gets scrabbling feet first under the bush, thorns pulling at his coat and revealing his back, pale and mealy as a white pudding. His head appears over the top of the bush. 'Come on, I'll show ye.'

They go at an angle from the path, through the weeds and the undergrowth, until Beans stops beside some wire netting. An orange sign on it he can't read in the dark. Some kind of a tunnel underneath the road. Beans peels the wiring back and squeezes himself in behind, the wire springing back to its original position. 'Come on.' He steps forward. An old trainer shoe by his feet.

He gets in behind the wiring and it is dark. A smell of stagnant water. Beans is dragging a piece of matting along the ground. 'Here, lie down.' Bits of rock poking at him, their two backs pressed together, shuffling; warm but, where they are touching. The echoing sound of traffic above their heads and the matting no big enough for both their bodies, part of his leg and his arm sticking out and pressing into stones, rubble. The drink but, it is keeping him outside of it, no fully aware, helping him fall to sleep.

Light. The head pounding. His throat dry, chappit, and his legs and his body senseless, except for a jabbing in the small of his back where Beans's elbow is sticking into him. He tries to go back to sleep, but it is too cold and he can't, so he sits up and looks about him. On one side, through the wire, weeds and trees; a glimpse of the dark straining river. There are bits of wood and breezeblocks in the gloom of the tunnel. Dark water pooled into a stank, a Sprite bottle floating on top. On the other side, more wiring, and past it, a construction site – a great hole in the ground, scaffolding, a mini JCB. Beans is sat up now too. Silent. They stay the both of them like that, sitting, for quite a while, and he wonders if maybe Beans is hungover, that's how he's no talking. But he keeps quiet and to himself into the morning, as they go and sit out on the veranda, cold, shivering, until eventually Beans gets up just, no a word, and leaves.

There is a key ring in one of the coat pockets. *London*, it says on it. A pair of palace guardsmen with their daftie hats on. He turns it about in his fingers. No key. Course not. Why would there be? There must have been once but. Or at least somebody's bought it that had one. A car owner. House owner. Seems unlikely Beans knows a person like that. More likely the coat's been lifted. Nay fucking chance he's taking it off though. He is shaking with the cold now. A bit of a wind and a spray coming off the river. An agity feeling is building, uncertain if Beans is going to bring any drink back this time. He can't bring himself to think about how it will be if he doesn't. A whole day and a night to get through in the cold, time not moving on, clotting around him. He finds a few loose pieces of chinex in the other pocket, puts one in his mouth and chews away.

It is dark when Beans returns. Another half-loaf with him. No beers but. Mick doesn't say anything, and they get eating the bread. He's still in the same mood, Beans, keeping cloyed up, and Mick starts feeling an irritation build inside him that he is behaving like this. He doesn't say anything though. He lets it stay there, choking any words he might get saying, watching Beans chuck the empty loaf packet out onto the water. Sleep is impossible the night. The temperature feels like it's dipped even further. The only warmth, Beans's back sweating against his. He wants to get up and walk away somewhere, just walk, but he can't, he can't move.

Afternoon. The dull anxiety waiting for if there's beer or if there's no beer. There is. A big plastic bottle of superlager. Beans in a good mood too. They get stuck in and numbness starts to flood through him. A distant laugh, which he realizes is Beans. How is he getting it? He'd said the money was gone. He can't be bothered maundering on it but – so what, just drink, just fucking drink it down. He starts laughing. He's like a wee bird. That's what he is. A wee chick, a wee sparrow chick staying put in the nest all day while Beans goes back and forth, getting him food and drink, coming back onto the veranda and regurgitating it up for him. Every day. How many? How many days? Fuck knows, and he is laughing again. He turns round and Beans is laughing too, anybody's guess what at. Strange how the time goes. There it is, stretching out in front of you – only the river, boats, the sound of traffic, and the thought mob raring to stick the boot on.

28

Beans's voice up the path, coming back, talking to himself. The heart starts going, in anticipation, or panic, or habit just, fuck knows. He turns round and looks through the bush, and Beans is there with another man. Panic tightens through him. They are crawling under the bush. 'See here's the guy I'm telling ye about.' The man is nodding at him, sitting himself down on the veranda. He is younger, the hair closely cut, his sweater and his jeans pretty clean-looking. A bottle of superlager is being passed between Beans and the guy, who takes a long pull, gulping twice. Then they pass it to him. The two of them talking. 'They're taking all the old spots, is the problem.' He is English. 'Come over for the building jobs and all that but then they get here and they've already filled all the fucking jobs, so they're out on their arse but they can't afford the fucking fare home.' Beans laughs with him, passing the drink. Then the guy sees the swan and he's off down the banking. A big stick suddenly in his hand and he is laughing, poking it at the nest. The swan is hissing and it's looking like she's going to up and stiffen him any minute, until Beans gets in there first. He jumps on the guy's back and the pair of them start tummelling about in the wet scrub by the nest. Beans on top now, pounding him. Seconds later the guy gets scrabbling up onto the banking and he's away under the bush. 'Fuck are you doing? It's a joke, Jesus, it's a fucking joke.'

He opens his eyes. Daylight. He is outside, and he is freezing. Beans is sat staring out, eating. Mick sits up and he gets handed a sandwich out of a carrier.

He looks at it a moment. 'There's a bite mark in this.'

Beans turns, frowning. 'Aye, so what?'

'Just, mean, there's more teeth marks in it than you've got teeth,' he grins, and Beans creases over, knotting himself.

Later, and Beans is stood above him, giving him these wee kicks in the thigh. 'Come on. We need to go the messages. I told ye.'

Onto the road, the pavements. Odd. Like he's there but he's in fact no there. They are looking at him, but from somewhere else, another consciousness, another world. Like being bevvied. Operating in your own space and everybody else fogging up around the edges of it. No that he's drunk but. The soreness all over his body is sure enough sign of that. 'This is the best time. Ye have to wait the last minute, when the fella's there with his gun, stickering all the stuff up.' True enough, there he is. Fridges. Shopping trolleys. 'Discreet, right. We need to be discreet.' But Mick is started laughing. Discreet! No likely. They look like a pair of cartoon characters, stalking behind tailing the guy as he is going about putting on the stickers. Into the baking aisle. The comforting smell of it. A wean stood staring while his maw chooses between the brown breads. He doesn't know what to make of the pair of them, his mouth in a wee study, slightly open, then he's darting off with his mammy, holding the hand. Beans has a stick of bread, and a piled handful of tinned salmon – *Reduced to clear*.

Outside, in the car park at the back of the building, there is a gap through to where the warehouse bit is. The shutters are closed but up against them there is a stack of red plastic crates. 'Here.' Beans passes him a couple. They are shallow but long and wide, and they have to hold them with arms stretched out, leaving quickly away down the road, taking up half the pavement between them.

'Bread crates,' he says. 'Good mattresses. Plenty of give, see, and they keep ye off the ground.' He's right too. They work well, slotted together with the matting laid out on top, and he is much more comfortable the night, no forgetting as well the bottle of superlager they got from the offie on the way back. He is able to sleep, even though he wakes up often. Each time he does, the tunnel boufing with a rank smell. The sour stankwater – but then there is a hiss of air from behind him, tickling the backs of his legs. The salmon.

Rain. They keep to the tunnel but it is filling up with water, so thank Christ for the bread crates. They stay sat or lying on top of them all night and all day as the blashie weather continues; his body aching, disintegrating, but always auld Beans there, trusty as ever with the bottle. The sun appearing. Beautiful spring sunshine. Daffodils. Bloody daffodils, where they come from? We have received a number of complaints. Sat throwing chuckies into the river, aiming at a can caught up in the yellow foam. Beans is a fair aim. A man of surprises, ye are. Aw, fuck off, pal, I used to play cricket for Scotland, ye know. The pair of them falling about pishing themselves. They are just stood there looking. A few residents have made complaints. Residents? Ye kidding? Who's that, well, the fucking swan? She's fine, man, she knows the score, she's no a bastard like yous. But they aren't finding it so funny, they're just stood there in their high-vis jackets and their fishermen's wading boots. If you don't move, we will have to get the police. Eh, what? Who are yous, then, if you're no the polis? They are laughing again and started throwing the chuckies at these three but the game's over. Up in the air. Suddenly the polis, the protectors of the residents, are arrived and they are being pulled about and corkscrewed up the path – bloody hell, says the one of them, as he keeks the drinks cabinet. They let go of their arms a way up the pavement, and it looks a banker they're about to get slung in the meat wagon, but no – get walking, they are told. The polis following at a short distance behind. Onto the roads and they keep going, miles and miles, turning round one point and the polis are gone, Beans muttering to himself, grumbling, chapping now on a door. After a while an Asian guy opening. No, he says, and he shuts it again.

They are going up a stairwell and his legs give out. He slumps down on the step and Beans is dragging at him until he gets up and labours on. Another door.

'You.'

'Me, aye.'

They are being let in and they follow the backs of a man's legs up a staircase. Who's he? My pal, that's who. A small room and a TV going. He is sitting down on a settee and Beans and the man have went into another room. A plate on the floor with the remains of a jacket tattie, just the well-fired parts of the shell left over. Beans and the man appear in the doorway, grim-faced.

Cans coming out; he gets handed one. The man's eyes are large and swollen, the top lids delicately folded scrotums. The air clung with smoke as he gets through his pack of fags, Beans smoking as well, dog-ends on the floor, a shoe, some bundled sheets. He doesn't say much, your mate, through the smoke. He's fine, he's fine. Darkness, and he wakes, alarmed and shaking. Beans on the settee, one cadaver leg hanging off the edge. He is lying on the floor. The stink of smoke in the carpet. The tattie still there; he crawls over and starts into it, tearing at the boot leather skin.

Always with Beans he's on the march somewhere, some plan or other he's got in his head and he isn't stopping until he gets there. They arrive at a small car park behind a low, flat-roofed building. There is a fence all round with a neat bed of green shoots in front. BUTTERFIELD MEDICAL PRACTICE, on a sign plugged into the soil. Alarm seizes suddenly in his stomach, working up into his throat until he is almost breathless, choking, needing to sit down on the path by the flower bed. Beans slapping him on the back. A pure desperate urge to drink now has hold of him as Beans makes him stand up, and they get walking, away again onto the street.

They come to a park – no a park but more a patch in between a couple of road crossings, with a square of grass and a rubber-matted play area big enough for about three weans a time to go on. A seesaw. A wee elephant slide with a trunk for a chute. There is a bin beside a bench, which Beans has a neb through before going in his pocket and handing Mick a five-pound note. 'Gonnae go the offie while I find us something to eat?'

The man in the offie is a bastard, but what can you do? Mick thumps the two bottles of superlager onto the counter and the guy doesn't say a word, he gives this wee look just, but he's made himself fine well clear enough. I, the seller of refreshments, know that you, the scaffer, are going to get yourself paralytic, and if it so happens that you kill yourself falling into the road, or you kill somebody else falling into the road, then it's no my fault, and I'll stand here with my face to vinegar just to show who is the better out of the two of us. Nay problem. Fine. Just hand over the beer, pal.

29

A woman, coming toward them.

'Excuse me.'

Beans straightening up, the eyes alert suddenly.

'Nay bother, madam. Ye haven't interrupted anything.'

Her hands on her hips.

'You can't drink here. There's kids playing.'

How old is she? Thirty? Forty? Her weans over on the see-saw, and another woman there too, nervous wee looks up the way. Beans is giggling, saying something, impossible to tell what. The woman stood with her arms folded. 'Excuse me.' She is looking at him now. 'Can you understand me?' The weans are stopped playing, lined up on the rubber play area watching. He has a dim sense of wanting her to stay there, a sort of longing, but Beans is acting it still, muttering on, and she is gone, angrily gathering up bags and weans and marching out of the park to go fetch the heavy team, or the polis, or the council – wading boots on, lads, the residents arenae happy.

There is only one bench in the park, so they take turns, a night each, to sleep on it. The nights it isn't their turn they lie out on the grass aside or underneath it. One time but Beans gives a try sleeping on the slide, although it's obvious no big enough, and Mick finds him in the morning crumpled at the bottom of the chute, looking like something the elephant's boaked up during the night.

He wakes. The sour taste of alcohol in his mouth. Against his face is an empty creased bottle that he'd put there as a pillow. The sun is up, and warm already, but he has got the shakes. No just the arms, or the legs, but the whole of him: head, chest, elbows and hips, all the way down to his toes. Shuddering. He caulks the eyes shut but they pinball in the sockets until they are pure throbbing and he can no longer stop this fear that is rising up him, overwhelming him, a genuine terror made all the worse because there is nothing to fix it to, no reason, it is there just. He presses his forehead hard against the slats of the bench, pushing against the ache. Slitting the eyes open. Beans isn't there. The sudden thought but of getting up to look for him – it's impossible, even the thought is impossible and makes his stomach start to heave and his throat retch, even sitting up, even opening his eyes fully, impossible, impossible. Easier to lie there just, shivering and sweating. The sun no helping matters either – sapping him and making him the more nauseous. He hasn't the energy to take off his coat though. The smallest things. Impossible. But through it all he is craving for a drink. An urging of the body; a pure physical need for it, just to stop all this, drive away again the ache and the fear.

It is getting darker and he is cold. Beans has gone for a crap in the bushes beyond the play area. Away on the road, a streetlamp flickering on. Then another. All along the side of the park they are coming on at random intervals, and he realizes that it's the ones in the darkest spots where the smaller trees are coming to leaf which are turning on first. Interesting. The wee things you notice.

Beans is shaking him on the shoulder.
    'Come on, gonnae wake up?'
    'What?'
    'Breakfast.' The familiar grin. His breakfast grin. 'I've been researching.'
    He gets himself up off the ground. It is drizzling and his back is soaked, some of it sweat probably, although he doesn't feel too bad this morning. Their money has ran out, so they haven't drunk the full bucket the last couple of days. They get walking through the rain until a short while later they arrive at a building that looks at first like an office block, but when they go through the glass doors and bare lobby it opens into a large hall, full of scaffers. Bright overhead lights, tables, din. Beans turns to him: 'Ye okay? Check the food, eh. No bad.' He can't see any food. The place is hoaching with scaffers, shuffling about, yapping, staring. 'Ye coming?' Beans is gone ahead and he hurries after him, clinging behind like a wean,

he's that dependent. See what if Beans leaves him? Gets so sick of him laggered onto his back like some diseased lump that he gives him the slip? The possibility of it makes him start to panic as he follows on to a trestle table with large pots of food on it. He waits in behind Beans, copies how he gets his meal and moves to the next area for a tea. They sit down at an empty table and eat hungrily. Toast. Scrambled eggs. 'Pretty good, eh? I should've minded this place earlier. It's one of the best. Only open a couple of hours but, so ye have to be quick.'

A young guy is watching them. He is sat at another table with a couple of others, forking egg into his mouth but clear enough looking over. Beans doesn't seem to notice, or else he's ignoring it. Mick keeks away. He wants to be out of here. Beans has other ideas though: 'Finish this and we'll go the showers, okay?'

In another room there are washing and drying machines, and cardboard boxes full of clothes. Beans is off through a doorway and he is left stood there unsure what to do. An old woman with a name badge hung around her neck comes up and tells him to help himself to some of the clothes, so he rummles through and pulls out a faded black pair of trackie bottoms and a grey shirt with a dark smudge on the collar.

In the next room, through a door marked MEN, there is a queue for showers, and Beans is further up the way already. They aren't communal, thank Christ: there's five or six separate ones, each with a curtain, though a couple of the men at the front are down to their pants already. Fucking terrible, the state of them. Scars and veins and jaundice.

He waits until he is inside a cubicle before he starts to undress. Even removing his coat feels odd. He's no took it off since Beans gave it him. Then he peels off the rest, all of it damp and rotten, clabbered to his skin, and he gets in the shower. It's been that long since he's seen himself in the scuddy that he doesn't recognize himself. As if the body isn't his; it belongs to another time when nakedness was something that had to be dealt with on a daily basis, and now he doesn't own it – he's removed himself from his body like he has from everything else. The only clue that it's there the now: that it hurts. There are bruises on his legs, down his front, his hips, fucking everywhere. His forearm skin is turned loose and chickeny; he pulls on it, the spring gone. The penis down there. Genuine difficult to believe that is his. He puts a hand around it, tries to mind what it means, the having of a penis. Nothing's doing but. His dobber's no sure about it either, and the two of them dither there for a while, waiting for something to happen, a connection. There is none. Or maybe it's just that neither of them are too comfortable about the line of half-naked scaffers queuing outside, which is in fact fair enough, being honest.

He gives himself a good wash, using the soap from the dispenser to rub over his head and his body, and special attention to the feet, which are started looking like a couple of raw beef kidneys. It feels good. The force of the water. Cleaning. Paying attention to all these parts that he's forgot about. The belly button. Armpits. Nipples, christsake.

When he comes out, he goes in the toilets and takes a very satisfying crap. The first time in a long while he's no had to sneak into a pub for one, or go in the park with a stolen toilet roll.

He puts his dirty clothes in a washer. Pretty pleased as well with these new ones. The shirt is a decent fit, and the trousers comfy enough around the waist, even if they are a wee bit on the short side. No the less, see even if his socks are on show, he definitely doesn't look half as daft as Beans does. He clocks him out in the hall and goes toward him, chuckling.

'Jesus. Check you.'

He is wearing a pair of black jeans and a white denim jacket, the both of them a fair few sizes too small for him. Beans grins. 'Gallus, eh?' Then he holds a finger in the air and spins around slowly, showing the back: ATLANTA HAWKS.

'If you say so, pal. If you say so.'

Beans goes back to the clothing room, saying that he forgot to look for another pair of socks, and Mick moves over to the juice table. There are plenty of name-badge people milling about, topping up cups, handing out leaflets, chatting. They don't seem like Hallelujahs. Any case, there isn't anything religious on the walls, only posters everywhere – chiropodist, walk-in clinic, housing advice – things he should be finding out about, probably, but the awareness of it only makes him feel the more sluggish. Through in the clothes room he can see Beans talking to somebody. He is pointing a thumb at his jacket, showing it off, but suddenly a hand shoots out from behind the door frame and grabs him by the collar, pulling him forwards. Beans stumbling, out of sight. There is too much noise in the hall to hear what is going on. He moves quickly toward the room, a few looking in now.

It is the young guy that had been staring. He is stood right up to Beans, putting the face on him.

'Fucking give it me.'

Another guy as well, behind him, eyeballing Beans, who is rocking on his feet, confused. 'Look, see I got it out the box, that's what I –' but he is getting shoved again, the veins on the guy's neck standing out and Beans falling to the floor, straight onto his arse. Mick rushes forward, standing in front of him before the guy can stick the boot on. 'Leave it, come on. What ye doing? Leave it.' The young guy is looking at him, this odd smile, like he knows him.

'The jacket's mine.'

Name-badge men are coming in the door. Beans behind him, getting up. The situation as it is, he looks even more ridiculous right now in the tight denims. The guy's pal is pulling on his shoulder – 'Come on, let's go' – but he's a fair solid build and he's no budging, and it's pretty obvious that the jacket cannot be his because it's way too small for him. In an instant the two men are barging out the room, pushing past the name badges, and it is over, just like that. Beans looks shook up. He is fairly shook up himself; but, through it, a small feeling of elation.

Nobody is moving, and it's Beans who is the first to speak, looking out the door through the bodies. 'Psychies,' he says, going over to the box and starting to root about, still after his socks.

On the way back to the park, carrying a new blanket and their cleaned clothes in carriers, Beans doesn't talk about what has just went on. He patters on as normal, like nothing's happened, telling him instead about the holidays he went on as a wean. Mick has the incident on his mind but. Wondering if Beans noticed his part in it even. 'Fair Fortnight, ye mind it? We'd go to Rothesay. Always there, nay discussions. One time my maw says let's go someplace different this year, maybe go see her cousins and that in Irvine, but the da he tells her we're going to Rothesay and that's that.'

Mick smiles. 'That's where we went, ye know, Rothesay.'

Beans stops in his tracks and a man on his mobile phone almost walks into him.

'Fuck off, serious?'

'We did, aye. Every Fair, mostly.'

Beans is still rooted to the pavement, amazed. Residents diverting past them. 'Mind that station the Friday morning? The platform mobbed with all these Fair Invaders packing in and the conductors playing hell with ye if ye got too close the edge – but what could ye do, eh? There was nowhere else to go!' He starts chuckling. 'Who ye go with, the parents, brothersisters?'

'No. Mean, my da died when I was wee, so it was me and my maw just. These other guys she was with sometimes, but mostly it was just us.'

They walk on in quiet for a while. If the two of them are in fact ages, then it's actually possible they would have been there at the same time. He is tempted asking him what years he used to go, but he stops himself. Something about Beans, this sense that he doesn't want pinning down and it's the better no to push him on things. Who's he to talk but? He who bloody cloys up at the barest mention of anything that might make him have to remember.

Beans is still on at it as they get back into the park. Ye mind the fiddle player on the Wemyss Bay ferry? Ye go the Punch and Judies? The pleasure boats? The tackle shop and dangle your line through the cracks in the pier? Mick is listening, but he's trying as well to figure out how they are going to make up the price of a bottle and get through the rest of the day.

'Once or twice we stayed in a caravan but most times my maw would be thumbing it through the small ads for one of they rooms that families rented out for the holidays. And see my da, he was a bevvy-merchant, right, and he was always away to the whisky booths or else he was there drinking in the room. But this landlady I mind we had, she knew what like the score was, and I don't know if it was cause it was her weans' room normally or what it was, but she starts into him this time – "Ye can't bring your drink in here, this is my house, a terrible man ye are" – and all this, and me and my maw and my wee sister are sitting there like three pounds of mince, thinking he's gonnae belt her, a pure certainty that he will. But he doesnae. He gets up just and he lets himself out the door, away to the whisky booth, and the three of us and the landlady staring at each other with nay clue what to do next.'

He is sitting on the bench, laughing, as if it's a happy memory he's just recalled.

'Amazing, eh, you going to Rothesay, no think?'

Without the money for a drink, it leaves a hole in the afternoon, so they decide what they'll do is go up the river and pay the swan a visit.

The gate has a new padlock on it. 'Bastards.' Beans strains over the palings, then is off scootling down the path. The swan is out. Or maybe she's been evicted too. The nest is still there, but the whole area has been cleaned up: the cans and the rest of the rubbish gone, and new wiring over the tunnel entrance. They sit down on the veranda and throw chuckies at the floaters, Beans starting up about the Fair again. It is all there in what he's saying – the Winter Gardens, the beach, Italian ice creams – but for some reason there is something queer about how he's telling it, as if it's no true somehow. Like he's heard all this off somebody else but he thinks it's his own memories. Or he's making it up. Maybe it's just himself but, trying to find holes in it. Maybe he doesn't want to believe it's true.

Later, they have a walk down the water. Beans tries it on, tapping passers-by for a few coins, but without much luck. They don't have any change on them; or they don't speak. Head down. Eyes to the tarmac. No a total disaster though. Eventually they come past a young pair kisscanoodling, who give him a two-pound coin.

The gloaming is come on when they return to the park. They drink the single can that they've each got, and take their positions, Mick on the ground with the blanket, Beans up on the bench. Without much superlager inside to numb him up, it is impossible to get to sleep. The cold nipping, and this unsettling feeling going through him in waves that is related he knows to the bringing up of old memories. He must doze off at some point though, because he is dreaming about a paddleboat and a boy fallen off the side when he is suddenly woken up – noise, heat, and a great blaze of fire above him that he realizes, through the flames, is Beans.

He is stumbling, flapping about, his chest and arms ablaze. Mick blunders to his knees, the fire crackling, a smell of petrol. 'Keith,' he shouts, uselessly, pushing him onto the ground and only then clocking the group of men stood on the play area. Watching; walking over. The guy from earlier, a can in his hand, laughing. Beans is thumping his hands on the grass and Mick tries to roll him, this kind of growling noise coming out of his throat, and his face damp, pieces of skin peeling off his neck. The hat – if it caught fire – and he scrabbles to pull it off him, Beans's eyes pleading, crapping it he's going to die. And Mick is thinking it too but he knows, in that instant, rocking the body on the grass, that his own fear is for himself. The men are stood over them. One of them puts an arm out and lager is pouring down, hissing on the dying flames. He is powerless, he just keeps rocking the great charred mass back and forth, burning his hands, until the fire is almost out, and he tries then to take the jacket off but it is too tight – more laughter – so he tears at it and it comes apart in pieces. One of the men suddenly puts the boot on, kicking Beans in his side. Then another of them catches Mick in the stomach and he is keeling over, bent double on the hot grass, no able to breathe.

They are away, running down the path, jumping the gate. 'Keith. Ye alright, pal?' Stupit question. He's alive but. The lips are quivering in his raw bleeding bawface; wet, red patches on his chin and cheeks. Mick pulls off the shreds of his jacket and his shirt, trying no to look at the body, then he takes off his own coat and rests it on top, lying down beside him, his hands stinging, too done in the now to move or think about getting somewhere safe.

30

Beans is sat up on the bench, quiet. He's got the coat draped over him like a blanket, but underneath it's possible to see what's left of his clothes, stuck to him in black tatterings on his chest and belly, patches of red wincing flesh, skin bubbles.

'Ye're well fired, then.'

No the right thing to say. He isn't amused. Just sat there, staring ahead. He's got his woolly hat back on, turned now a darker shade of red. Below it, one of his bug-ladders is burnt off, a few blackened stems of hair poking out from the blistered skin, and the bottom of his ear is yellow and gluey with pus, like an upturned clam.

'Want something to eat?'

Beans shrugs his shoulders just. Gives a kind of snort. Clear enough what he's meaning: who's going to get it, well? Mick stands up and goes to the bin. It hasn't been emptied yet from yesterday and it's overflowing: a magazine and an empty Lucozade bottle sticking out the top. The best he can find though is a bit of brown banana left in its skin and a few crisps in a bag. He takes them over to lay beside Beans on the bench, but he doesn't even turn his head. All the life is went out of him.

He sits again on the bench, the crisps and banana between them.

'I've seen a guy on fire before,' he says then, just to be saying something. 'A welder. Just pure unfortunate, really, cause he was doing this job that he had his mask on for and as well one of these flame-retardant suits, but see that was the problem. He starts jigging about and nobody knows what he's up to at first, they think he's dicking around, but actually a spark is got inside the suit and nobody can see that his clothes is on fire cause, like I say, the suit's flame-retardant.'

Beans isn't listening. His head is sunk down, looking at the grass. There is a scorched patch in front of where they are sitting.

'Anyway, so by the time his mate's clocked what's going on the poor guy is almost fried, and when he comes back from the hospital he's got third-degree burns and everyone's telling him he should go the courts but he says he's no gonnae because it was his own fault for no doing the neck studs up.'

'This supposed to be cheery?'

Mick turns round, relieved. 'Right, sorry.' He smiles. 'Sorry. See what I mean is it could've been worse.' Beans is looking now at the banana and crisps, not moving. His lips are swollen and bluish. 'Worse,' he says, in a quiet voice.

There is the problem of food and also, now, the problem of where to stay. They don't discuss it but it's clear enough they need to move from the park. As well, Beans is in blatant need of some medical attention. When Mick says they should go the hospital, however, he just gives a wee laugh. It's the only thing he responds to all after-noon. The rest of the time he just sits there in silence, pulling the coat around him and covering his wounds, but Mick can see well enough what like the state he is in: his face and neck hugely swollen by now, and the top of the coat soaked with whatever it is that's run-ning out of his sores.

Later, Mick gets up and tells him he's going off to find some food. He starts down the road, looking in the bins. A few people watching him as he gets grubbing inside them but he's too hungry to care, pulling and digging at all this stuff that the residents have decided isn't fit for them any longer: magazines, a bunch of flowers, news-papers with this picture of a politician type on the front. There is food too, plenty of it. Sandwich cartons, some with just the crust left, but a couple that there's actually an entire half-piece in there. Unfuck-ingbelievable, really. In another bin he finds a Japanese roll left in one box and two more with these pink pickled frillies on the side. He gets it all into a pair of sandwich cartons and leaves back to the park.

He lays it all out on the bench. Beans nods his head slightly – one eye is half closed, the lid above it pink and inflamed – then he stares off again without touching the food, back into whatever it is he's thinking.

They wait it out the afternoon until the light starts to change and Mick gets them on the move. Beans doesn't argue. He doesn't do anything, just keeps cloyed up, loundering slowly behind as they go down the road. They come again to the doctor's practice. He leads Beans down a path to the back of the building. All the lights are turned off and the car park is empty, so he lays the blanket down under an archway by the back door. He sits Beans up against the wall and sets off for more food.

Strange but it's gave him something of a punt up, what's happened. Fucking terrible, of course, he's a terrible bastard to think it but it's true. He feels more of a purpose about him. It's down to himself the now. Showing Beans that he's no just some leech that can't get by on his own. He can be useful. He is being useful. After a long walk he finds a full bin round by a kebab shop. A few looks but so what? Go fuck yourselves. On the way back, it starts to rain. He gets a hurry on, clutching the warm carton of collected chips and doner meat under his jacket.

Beans has moved. The blanket is laid out still, an empty carrier beside it. The rain tearing out from a gutter, hammering onto the concrete.

He eats half the food. Watches the yellow flowers over in the bed, nodding, drooping. Puddles growing in the car park. Which gives him an idea, and he gets up to go on another bin search, eventually finding an empty Coke bottle. Nobody on the street but. When he returns to the pitch he props the bottle with a stone out in the rain.

With the damp, and no overcoat, he sleeps fitfully the night, waking frequently with the same familiar sense of alarm. The blanket bare next to him. By morning, the rain has stopped, and the bottle is filled up quite a bit, stood there in the half-light of the glistening car park. Beans is gone still. He stays there, awake, the sun coming up and the sound of traffic increasing on the road, until eventually there's no choice but to move on before anyone arrives.

He sits on top of a wall across the road, watching the entrance to the car park. The cleaner arrives. He watches the dim shadow of him through a window, slowing passing the mop. Doctors. Patients. A woman with a screaming snapper in a pram, halting and shouting at it to get shut up.

There is curtain-twitching going on behind him. He can see the movement in the corner of his eye when he turns his head to look down the road. Next thing the meat wagon will be blaring up the way, nay doubt. Well, get to fuck, then, he isn't doing anything; he's just sat there. But then what happens, it's no the polis, it's the man of the house opening the door and coming out. 'Excuse me.' The wife in the doorway behind, in her dressing gown. He's got a T-shirt on – DUBLIN MARATHON *FINISHER* – and he means business: it's his wall, get the fuck off it. 'Excuse me, can I help you?' Mick starts to laugh. The residents don't know what to make of that though, they're exchanging glances, wondering what's their next move. Aw, sod off, and he hops down from the wall, gets walking away down the pavement. That's him, then. No use waiting there any longer, so he decides to go to the river and check the veranda.

No sign of him. A hundred places he could be.

He spends the night at the doctor's. Cold, shaking. Panic sticking the boot on at every turn and keeping him from sleep.

The familiar places: the river, the park – he even starts toward the day centre one morning, but then as he's on the approach he turns about. An ache is growing inside him, taking over the whole of his body. Hunger, for one thing. Something else but. Too big. It's too big. A sense that is inseparable as well from needing a drink – a pure desperate fucking need for one. So he starts going up the coach station again. It takes him a long while to walk there, using the wee bus stop maps and getting lost all the time but so what? Kills the time. Can ye spare any change, madam? Spare any change, sir? They can't. Or some of them can, but most of them give him turned shoulders and the silent treatment. He doesn't care. He needs a drink, simple as that, and everything else – it's all a great blank space above the clouds, himself lying there on top with the hands behind the head and the blanket underneath him, slipping and floating across like he's on a magic carpet. Any change, sir? Ye don't? Nay danger, don't worry, don't worry. An auld hen, her hands tucked together, that way auld ladies do, fingering in her bag. God bless ye, madam. A man gives him his apple and he goes over to Newcastle to eat it, hid inamongst the legs and dragged suitcases as the driver appears with his cup of coffee, climbing onto the coach and getting the doors open. A few moments of noise and bustle. Singsong voices. A wee man walking past, joking with his mate. Somebody he minds him of. Who? Sure there's somebody, and then he does mind – Ken – and he smiles at the memory. A great guy. About four foot two in his work boots, and a smile like a shopping trolley pulled out the river. One of the platers at Swan Hunter. This great singing voice he had on him, always belting out something or other – 'You ain't seen nothing like the Mighty Quinn' – that was one he was always giving it, because Newcastle had this striker at the time that was banging in thirty goals a season.

The bay is thinning out now, a line of people forming outside on the coach park.

The other thing about Ken, most people never guessed until it was too late, he was a serious hardman. He'd bring in his own pieces every day, which the wife had made for him in these neat paper bags. Ham and pease pudding. Every day. He was aye particular about it. What sandwiches you brought today, Ken? And it was funny because he never knew you were kidding, he was that proud of the wife's pieces. So one day this plater's helper called Tommy Lambton thinks it'll be a great joke to take the pieces from under his work bench and hide them while he isn't looking. Come lunch break and Ken's raging. Which of you's took em, then? And suddenly he's got the whole plating squad lined up, blank-faced, because in fact nobody does know where they are, until eventually young Tommy can't hold it in any more and he starts knotting himself – they're here, Ken, and he hands the sandwiches back, fair squashed and grubby by now. That's the end of it, as far as anybody thinks. But later the lunch break Tommy is in the canteen sat down eating, yapping about the great trick he's pulled, when in steps Ken, who comes toward the table and, calm as a waiter, picks up Tommy's plate and walks off with it. Then they're all following him through the yard like he's the Pied Piper, Tommy included, quiet as a mouse now and with this black-affronted look on him, as Ken goes up to the launching berth and tips the food into the water. Then he hands the empty plate back to Tommy and leaves, all the rest of them watching this pie case slowly floating down the Tyne. One guy joking that it just goes to show how much filling they put in those bloody pies.

He laughs at the memory of it. A woman reading her magazine

in the next bay, frowning at him. Chichester, she's going to. Course she fucking is. He gets up and leaves her to it; resumes with his collecting.

There is enough for a couple of cans and a sausage roll. He goes up the river, the old spot, looking out over the power station and the tollie tug. He doesn't stay long though. Even with the drink, he can't get relaxed. Not on his own. The panicky feeling is there, the heart going, some part of him always on the alert now it's only him to keep lookout, and as well nothing to distract him, nobody in his ear giving it the problem with bird-murdering farmers and all the rest.

The park is empty. No weans, or mothers, nothing. It's a pretty dreich day but. The patch of charred grass is still there, less black than it was, but just as dead. He moves on. Down the road he nicks into a pub to go for a pish, but it's dead inside and the landlord cops onto him before he can get in the toilets. Another pub opposite but, and he slips in unnoticed. He washes his face, and nabs a toilet roll from one of the cubicles.

Further on there is a subway station, and he sits down by the cash machines without too much of a thought but that he needs to sit down, so he may as well do it here and tap some money into the bargain. Pure murder on the arse after a while though, even with the blanket and his carrier of clothes underneath him. Thickets of legs, coming in waves, up the stair from the subway. He doesn't look at them. No up at their faces. He keeps his eyes on their ankles and their shoes instead. Without the body and the face on top, the feet take on a life of their own, like it's the feet themselves that are wanting to get a hurry on, them that are annoyed at having to swerve around him. That's fine but. Fine. Feet, he can deal with.

The first afternoon, he makes 87p. The next day, the weather is better and he gets there earlier. Somebody drops him a baseball cap, which he puts on to shield his face from the sun. Another gives him a cup of tea, and when he's finished it he leaves the empty cup on the ground next to him. His earnings almost double. Chink. In it goes. Like pressing a button. He spends his nights in the usual spot behind the doctor's, awake already and away early the morning. Sandwich, superlager; easy enough, the routine, and it gathers around him like a fog, guiding him and protecting him. Inside it but, thoughts and memories appear suddenly like figures out of the mist – he tries to lose them, give them the body swerve; always the same race between the reminders and the drink.

He's slept right through and they are come to move him, the light up and a crowd of blue jackets moving through the car park, one of them picking up an empty bottle of superlager, Beans not there, these rub-ye-ups grabbing at his legs – come on, come on – a man craning down toward him, his face tight with disgust.

The buses. A much better idea. Good and bad points but, obviously. Good and bad. There is a stretch of road with four or five bars knuckled together, and he learns after a couple of tries elsewhere that this is the best place to get on, wait while they're closing and the stops are birling with drunkens trying to cram and heave through the doors. Once on, up the stair and to the front is the best spot, a bit of extra space for the legs and the pilot's view out the window. The smell of chips and vinegar. Kebabs. Listening to the songmakers away at the back. It's only when the front's been took and he has to sit further down that people start putting the mix in. A lassie on her mobile phone sat next to him with her face turned to the window, speaking in a quiet voice and no realizing or caring that he can hear what she's saying. Another time, he falls asleep right in the thick of all these posh, clammering English boys, and wakes up to them laughing, the aisle full of legs and the one sat next to him wearing his baseball cap. The rest of them in knots about it. He sees Mick awake and turns toward him, grinning, takes the cap off slowly and puts it back on Mick's head. He closes his eyes. Too tired to do anything. 'Fuck off.' But that just sets them going again.

When the bus gets further out of the city and it starts to empty, is when he can sleep. Sometimes he'll have a carrier with some cans and he'll drink them up against the seat in front until he's knocked himself out and he sits slumped against the window, eventually the lights shuddering and turning off. Then shuddering on again. The bus starting to move, back toward the city; tired-looking African and East Europe types getting on, staring silently ahead, keeping to themselves.

No uncommon that a fight will break out. He tries to keep out the way, but one night there is one that kicks off across the aisle from him, a proper frontpager. Two pale lads laughing and shouting, going at the staring matches with anybody that looks over. One of them lights up a fag, the smell of it drifting through the bus. Right in front of them, this great belly man in a rock music T-shirt and a kind of perm haircut tumbling over the back of his seat, and the two lads start pishing about, kidding on they're going to set the perm alight. Then the smoker starts blowing smoke past his ear, leaning in so close it looks like he's about to kiss him on the neck. The big guy is getting irritated, tapping the foot and muttering away in a language that's no English. The whole thing kicks off the instant one of them touches the back of his head, and he jumps up and turns around, suddenly clambering onto the seat and standing on it. The two lads totally blindsided, sat staring up at him.

'You wanna see my poothy?'

Giggling from somewhere up the front of the bus.

'You wanna see my poothy, hey?'

The lads don't know what to do; they're sat watching, rigid and seething, and then suddenly the big guy starts into a lap dance, practically in the one boy's face. 'You wanna see my poothy?' And it's more than the boy can take, leaping up and getting the hands around his neck, pushing him back over the next seat and exposing the giant belly from under the T-shirt. Men jumping in now, a young guy in front of Mick standing up but his girlfriend pulling at his arm trying to stop him. There's four or five of them holding the lad back, his mate one of them, but the boy's beeling still, desperate to get at the lapdancer, who is walking away down the aisle by now. The veins standing out on his forehead and the whole face looking like it's going to explode from the skin – eyeballs, teeth, the lot. And then it does. A couple of girls in front screaming as his nose busts, wee red missiles flying everywhere.

31

'Tell you what, I'll give you a call after I speak to Kenny . . . He's coming on straight from college, I think . . . He won't have, but I'll ask him. Okay, got to go.'

The boy puts his phone into his jeans pocket and waits. The woman in front of him is literally taking forever. He glares at her back. When finally she does take her card out he steps forward, but she's not moving, she is staying by the machine, and now she is actually putting the card back in. Unbelievable.

When the woman at last shuffles off and it is his turn, he hesitates a second by the machine, unsure how much money to get – whether or not the plan is to get some food before they go in. He takes out thirty, turning away from the tramp on the pavement, and slips it into his wallet before he moves into the crowd of people streaming toward the tube station.

It is easier in the daytime. Mostly he can sit there for hours and hours without thinking about anything, watching the feet just and then sometimes, chink, and he'll look up at them walking away, a back of the legs and a backside, disappearing down into the subway. He never drinks in front of them. Common sense, that's all. He saves the bevvying for the end of the day when he leaves, and he always spends up whatever he's got, meaning the good days usually are followed by bad ones. Sat there the morning, turning green on the pavement. The sweats. The shudders. Shivering against the wall trying no to move his eyes, and the heart torn and flapping from the paranoia that is rising up inside him that any moment one of these pairs of feet coming out the subway are going to belong to somebody he knows. A total conviction building that Robbie is on the approach. He tries to fight against it but it's hopeless, hopeless, he hasn't the strength, he just wants to sleep, to sleep, to forget and let the brain go numb but he's too fucking sober and his breath is dying each time Robbie's haircut emerges up the stairs. He closes his eyes but it's impossible to stop the sense of him coming toward where he's sat; and then he has to look up – but he's gone, lost into the crowd.

The middle of nowhere. A bus depot. Quiet streets and closed shops. A car showroom; a cemetery; a golf driving range that it is easy enough getting round the back of and into one of the alcoves. It's actually quite comfy there on the spongy green felt with the wooden roof over his head, looking out over the field with its distance markers and a tractor perched at the side.

Screw the buses. There is an office block close to the subway, a big concrete one with dark, morning make-up streaks down the side of it. It is set back from the road, and there's a large, covered doorway at the top of some steps, in front of a revolving door. The lights kept on the night, so it's no the darkest, but see maybe that's in fact a good thing, because even if he is visible, so as well is any other cunt that wants to come along and get acquainted. He huddles in against the doors and gets drinking. Big, frequent gulps, anxious to be bevvied quickly, obliterate the memory. Through in the reception there is a grand flower display, an empty desk, and on the wall beside it a black-and-white TV screen flicking between images of the building: vacant corridors; an office floor; the bare insides of a lift. Nobody anywhere. It looks like the nuclear bomb has gone off. Fucking Trident, man, crank up the engines, float her up the Clyde. But then, the queerie shot of himself, bundled in the doorway. The only survivor. He gives a wave and sees his arm moving. Just him, then. The rest of the world is finally went away. Cheers. The head swimming now. Cheers to that, well.

The cleaners come when the clock in the reception is showing just the back of six, and he has to get up and move on. They are alright about it, being fair, but it's obvious that staying put isn't an option. It is cold, that time the morning, and he is stiff and sore from the ground and the drink, so he walks around for a couple of hours to get the blood going before making his way to the subway. A giant bruise is looming all down his side. He hitches up his shirt and jacket and he can see that the whole area is raw – no a great purple job, but kind of flamed and scarlet, like a rash. Maybe it is a rash, actually. Either way but. He isn't keen on investigating.

The streetlights are still on, and the pavements almost deserted. A few unchancy types. A damp, pink jogger labouring by. He comes after a while to a high street, and there is more action: shutters ratcheting up; a delivery van reversing; the soaked front patch outside a newsagent's. He is a ghost. Nobody seeing him. He walks on down the pavement. An Asian man in a butcher's coat is opening out a board by his shop window: *Star Buy – medium fresh chicken. £2.50 kg.* He starts chuckling. Medium fresh chicken. Good luck with that one, pal. And then he sees that the guy is an exact Asian John Virgo, serious, he is, and that just makes him laugh the more. The delivery van is parked outside. The back doors are open, and two more Asian men are handling what looks like a skinned sheep, hung over the one guy's shoulder as he goes into the butcher's, dark stains all down his coat. The limbs on the animal joggling lifelessly, like a tired wean over a da's shoulders. As Mick walks on past the van, he sees the second guy stood inside it, twisting another carcass out of a pile and lobbing it toward the back doors, where it falls on the wooden boards with a wet thump.

Up the way, a charity shop is open already. A business type stood outside, fingering through a row of books on a trolley. He steps up and stands in beside him, pulling a book off the trolley and starting to give a flick through the pages. A sideways glance from your man, but so what, serious? He slots the book back in and gets reading the spines, and halfway along the row his gaze is checked.

He reaches to take the book but his hand is shaking. A noise coming up his throat but he is only dimly aware of it, the man looking at him, walking away. *Remember*, by Barbara Taylor Bradford – 'An Unforgettable Tale of Passion and Suspense'. He looks up. Through the window, a woman is bent over, rummling inside a plastic bag, and he slips the book under his jacket and moves away.

Somebody brushes against his arm and his body stiffens, the whole of him suddenly turned cold. He doesn't know where he is but there are crowds pouring down the street and he is searching through them, stupit, stupit, but he can't stop himself, desperately trying to mind her face, but he can't.

32

There is somebody coming toward him. A man. He's on the approach from the road, coming up the steps, a carrier in his hand, and Mick is started to tighten, the bevvy no taken hold yet and this cunt in front of him all too fucking real.

'Would you like a sandwich?'

He is holding one out toward him, like a bone.

'It's fine, take it. There were some left we didn't sell.'

He looks at the sandwich in the guy's hand, tightly wrapped in cling film.

'What type is it?'

He brings it to his face, inspecting the filling.

'Not sure. Prawn, I think.' He holds it out again.

'Ye have any beef?'

The man gives a wee laugh and pauses, then gets rustling about in the bag.

'No. He brings out another. 'Tuna?'

Mick shakes his head. 'I'm alright.'

He is staring at him. 'You don't want any of these sandwiches?'

'No.'

A wee lift of the eyebrows.

'Okay, then. Fair enough.' And away he goes. The Master of Sandwiches. Fuck you, pal. Who's he getting annoyed a person doesn't want to take his leftovers? He doesn't like fish sandwiches. That simple. The smell of them. One of the only things he can mind about his da, he used to eat these tins of pilchards, and the stink when they were opened, it was honking.

Sandwiches. Always fucking sandwiches. They never come and offer you a bloody bottle, do they?

★

He is sat on the blanket staring at the book, the sun gone behind the clouds. He takes his cap off and looks out at the pavement. An empty can rattling along the fence with the wind.

'Fuck me. A man of riches.'

He looks up. It is Beans. Stood over him, grinning, peering into the cup. He bends down and sits against the wall next to him. His neck and the side of his face are red and leathery, his ear a great black scab.

'Check you – in the money, eh?' He points at the cup. There is the rumble of a train underneath the ground. He is stretching himself out, sticking his legs onto the pavement. Mick closes his eyes. Tries to make sense of things. It's too much an effort but, and he opens them again, looking across. Beans has got a blue jumper on, a tear down the side of it, his head turned away toward the cash machines; a big peel of skin coming off behind his ear. A moment later and he is lumbering to his feet.

'Come on. Ye hungry?'

Mick doesn't move. The eyes fixed on him from under the dirty red hat.

'No. I'm sticking it out here.'

'Aw, right.' He stays there, dawdling, pedestrians trying to get past. 'I'll see ye, well.'

The rest the afternoon is sunny and he gets quite a few drops. He doesn't feel relieved, or angry, or anything, about Beans. As if he wasn't really there, he imagined him just.

He is real enough though. He appears again as Mick is about to get leaving, a carrier of lagers with him. Mick gets up his things and they are away up the road together to find somewhere to drink it. Simple as that. Back into the routine without so much as a word about all this time that's passed. Easier just carrying along with it. And immediately he is feeling safer. Which is stupit, obviously, seeing as all the unchancy situations he's been in it's because Beans has put him in them. He's got the beers in but. The one thing he can always be relied on for. They sit on a bench in a drab concrete square and get drinking.

'See me, I wouldnae beg. Mean, begging's fine – I've done it myself.' He is scratching at his throat. 'But thing is ye're a sitting duck. I'd rather go on the broo. And see, if ye do well then they move ye on just. They don't want you making more money than they are making, know?' He chuckles, beer bubbling between his lips. 'Plus piles as well. Fucking piles, man, it's a killer on the arse.' Mick lifts the can to his mouth. The superlager is already kicking in. Drowning it all out.

Beans approves of the office block. Good and sheltery, is his verdict. And he likes being able to see himself in the television screen too. He spends most of the evening until he collapses watching himself in it, waving, dancing, mooning. Mick sits and watches him. The guy is a pure marvel, serious. And no for the first time, he finds himself wondering: who is he? How long has he been living like this? No that you could ever get a straight answer out of him. Impossible. The truth is but, it's difficult to imagine him any other way, to imagine him as a young man, a wean. No watching him the now, anyway, blootered on the superlager, pulling bits of skin off his face.

'Where is it ye went, then?'

Beans straightens up a moment, the eyes narrowing, like he is trying to remember.

'No, see I didnae go anywhere.' He starts laughing. 'I was on my holidays. Rothesay. That's where I was.' He is falling about laughing, and that's the last either of them say about it.

They settle into a pattern. The square, the office block, and then going their ways until Beans comes to pick him up at the end of the afternoon. One night, a couple of people come up to them at the office block. Hard to tell if they're Hallelujahs, or sandwich brigade, or what they are, but Beans soon enough scares them off, great drunken guard dog that he is.

Asleep. Dreaming. The image hits him like a scud in the ribs, repeatedly, no going away. Her hair draggling wet over the tops of her breasts and the bathwater seeping into the pages of her book. Turning the pages over with damp fingers. But the picture is wrong, it doesn't fit. She is too young. She is the girl in the ship-launch photograph; before they were married. He can't stop looking at her.

33

They stop at the lights alongside a heaving pub. There are men packed in the doorways; smoking on the pavements. A row of bum cracks along a window seat.

'Champions League,' Martin says, putting the van into gear and moving on through the lights. The roads are not busy, and they make quick progress, turning onto a high street and scanning shop signs for the Superdrug. Martin is keeping fairly quiet. There is nothing awkward about it though, and she sips her coffee, eyes peeled out of the window.

When they do find the Superdrug, it is deserted. They park up outside and she looks at the sheet to check it's the right location. It is. They get out and have a scout around. The doorway is wet, clean and freezing. 'Bastards,' Martin says, and they separate to search down the street in opposite directions.

'Anything?' she says when they reconvene at the van.

'Nope.'

They set off again. Past another busy bar with steamed-up windows.

'Big match?'

Martin smiles. 'Quarter-final.'

'You should have changed your shift.'

He turns to look at her for a moment, then they both go silent as the van cuts through an empty street market, past bare stalls and tumbled stacks of cardboard boxes by the rubbish bins.

They have better luck at the next site. In the arcing entrance of a shopping centre, a young man is sat up amongst blankets and a large red sleeping bag. He recognizes them as they approach. Danny. This is the fourth contact with him, and on their previous visit he had told them that he would be happy for the team to make a referral. He seems quite bright tonight, smiling as they hunker beside him and explain that they have arranged a visit to a hostel, for him to get a look at the place and do an initial interview. He is pleased at the news. They organize a time that they will come and collect him, and he laughs. 'I've not got many plans going anywhere,' he says.

Danny, they learned on the second contact, is from Hartlepool. His mother died when he was sixteen, after which he went to live with his sister. The sister, though, had her own family and Danny moved out, feeling he was in the way, and, because he thought there was nothing for him to do in Hartlepool, he came down to London. There were a couple of people he knew that had moved down there, but after a short time of sleeping on the sofa of one friend, and not being able to find the other, he ended up without a place to stay, and has been moving from pitch to pitch for the last six months.

Buoyed by this development, they are both feeling quite cheerful as they get back into the van. They stop again on the high street so she can nip out and get them another coffee. Martin watches her through the entrance of the shop. As she turns to leave, she sees him, and he looks away while she comes back with the drinks.

Their next stop is behind a budget hotel, in a small complex of office buildings. There are a pair of men staying in the main office doorway, who they first visited a couple of weeks ago after a phone call from one of the hotel workers. That first time, the pair had been too drunk to talk with properly, but the next contacts had gone slightly better. They have come down from Glasgow, possibly together, although it has been quite difficult to build a clear picture. One of the men, Mick, keeps very quiet while the other, Keith, is obviously the one that does the talking for them both. They have no plans, and nowhere to go, that much is clear. As they come up the steps to the doorway now, the two men appear fairly sober, although they don't seem to recognize who they are. When Martin reminds them, Keith stands up and exaggeratedly shakes both their hands. He has severe burn marks on his face and neck, although he won't be drawn on how he got them. A fight, is the most he will say clearly.

The following week, when they meet the two men again, they have begun drinking, but Mick especially is becoming more comfortable with their presence. They learn as well that both men had been staying in a night shelter before they came here, but left when their belongings were stolen and there was some kind of argument with the management.

One night, they are sat in the parked van, eating doughnuts. Martin has sugar on his shirt-sleeve and on an impulse she reaches forward to brush it off, but he withdraws. A few moments later he restarts the engine, and they carry on with their round.

The police have notified them of an elderly man sleeping outside the underground station. They find him, and he is awake, but disorientated, and he backs away, shouting, as they approach from the van. He carries on shouting as they stand at a distance attempting to talk to him, and after a minute or two of this he picks up a shoe and throws it at them. They decide to leave him in peace and try again on another visit. The next time they come to the underground station, though, he has gone, and it is the last they see of him.

Danny, too, has moved off. There was no sign of him at his pitch when they came to take him to the hostel, and he does not reappear on any of the next few visits. The office call around outreach teams in neighbouring boroughs, but nobody knows anything. There is, however, some movement on Keith and Mick. After a couple more successful contacts, a referral is put in to a nearby hostel. The two men are brought over for an initial visit, and they are placed on a waiting list. Although Mick is at first reluctant to move, he seems to draw confidence from Keith, who, although unpredictable, has declared that he is very keen to move into the hostel.

One week, Mick has a bruise on the side of his face where, Keith tells them, he was kicked sitting outside the underground station. It has clearly caused him some distress, and she and Martin are growing concerned, especially given the experience of their previous accommodation, that the connection might break before their places become available. For the next couple of weeks, however, they remain where they are, and when the time does come to move them on there is not in the end too much difficulty getting them into the van, and inside the hostel.

Once there, both men become somewhat agitated, and it is not possible to complete the induction that night. It is agreed that the forms can be completed the following day, to give a clear night for the men to settle, and orientate themselves in their new surroundings.

It is a good result, and they leave the hostel relieved, walking quietly together back to the van.

34

He sits now on the edge of the bed, torpid, brainless. He was awake most of the night, listening, and has slept through the morning. Everything in the room is white: the walls and floor, the curtains, the wardrobe, even the bedside table, which is pushed now up against the door. It's like a hospital. A mental institution. He is hungry, but he's no even thinking about food the now because he isn't moving, he is not leaving this room; his eyeballs staying alert on the locked door in front of him.

At the end of the room there is another door, and through it, a small bathroom. En suite, bloody believe that? There's even towels and toiletries inside. A few times he gets up for a pish, but otherwise he stays on the bed. The room is silent. No sounds through the thick door, or the double-glazed window which looks out onto a road. Cars queuing. Shops. A sign on the second floor of the building opposite – *Mumtaz Carpets*.

Earlier the morning, somebody came for him. Renuka, she said through the door. He had missed his appointment with her. It is very important they speak before the end of the day. He presses his head into the pillow; keeps quiet. The heart careering for a long while after she's gone.

Sudden moments of clarity keep interrupting him, in which he knows what he is going to do: he's going to wait it out until dark and give Beans a knock, tell him he's for the off and going back to the pitch. But he doesn't know what room Beans is in. He doesn't know where they are either, for that matter – *Mumtaz Carpets* the only clue. And then all his energy for the escape idea will disappear immediately, the brain dreiching over again. He has the thought a couple of times, until, as if accepting defeat, he takes off his jacket and goes to sleep.

He doesn't wake until late the afternoon. The small clock on the bedside table, its wire stretched taut along the wall to the door, is the only decoration apart from a mirror and a plywood TV stand at the end of the bed. He stares a long while at the clock, then at the imaginary television. What now, well? He needs a drink, but the possibility of taking out his bits of smash and going on the hunt for an offie – it's too much of an adventure. Even in the silence, the locked door with the furniture pushed against it, he feels exposed. Defenceless. As if at any moment that door is going to open and some terrible calamity awaits him. He gets up and goes to the door hook for his jacket, puts it back on and immediately feels more at ease, a snail with his shell returned.

A chapping on the door and he opens his eyes.

'Mick.'

He hunkers down pretending to be asleep, suddenly feart she is able to see through the peephole.

'Mick, it's really important we have our meeting. Mick. We need to get your claims put in, or we won't be able to hold your place for you.'

He can see the shadows of her feet under the door. They stay there a minute or two, then she goes away.

She is back again the next morning though. From the sound of the shoe squeaks she is not alone this time, and she knocks more fiercely, her voice sterner.

'I'm going to have to unlock it if you don't respond.'

He sits up, breathing heavily. A few seconds later he can hear the key in the lock, and the door starts shifting and butting against the bedside table.

'Mick, you're going to have to stop obstructing this door.'

He gets up slowly, and pulls the table aside. The door opening, and he stands there stupidly in front of her. She is alone. Small, Asian. Annoyed.

They go through the empty corridor, and into another room on the same floor. She is his key worker, she tells him. She motions him to sit down at the desk and then she starts laying it off about his licence agreement and how he has to begin cooperating. He sits there silently trying to listen, or at least act like he's listening. When she is finished, they go out of the room for a tour of the other floors, him keeping the head lowered as they come past other people and she gets showing him inside all these doors he needs to know about: the canteen, the day room, the computer room. Through the window to the art room, a line of wonky clay pots humped on a window ledge.

She leaves him back at his room, and arranges a time for their next meeting. When she's gone, he gets warily down the staircase and through the reception, out of the hostel. On the busy road outside, he finds a minimarket and uses up what he has on a loaf of bread, a packet of ham and a four-pack.

Beans finds him the next day. He bangs on the door, calling his name; Mick squinting through the peephole at the giant, scarred bawface. He opens the door, half expecting the familiar grin – 'Breakfast?' – but instead Beans just walks straight in and sits on the bed.

'How's it going?' He is looking out the window. 'Decent view, that.'

'Okay. Yourself?'

'Fine. Fine. Only this cunt in the door next me, plays his stereo the whole time. Quiet in here but.' He looks about the room, then up at Mick. 'Been the canteen?'

'No.'

'Come on, well, let's go.'

He hesitates a moment but Beans is already out the door, summoning him away.

He stays close as they go down a floor and into the canteen. A few people milling about. Hard to tell which of them are the homeless. One or two obvious candidates but. A pale, thin girl talking to an older woman; a ramshackle beardie man in a wild assortment of clothing. They go up the glass counter and tell the guy what they're wanting. Both of them take the full works: scrambled eggs, sausage, fried tatties and beans, then they get sat at one of the small round tables, away from where the other people are clustered together.

'Who pays for this, well?'

Beans grins. 'You do, pal, so get beasted in.'

They don't talk as they eat. A murmur of quiet patter in the room. The pale girl comes past their table and looks at them, but he puts the head down, ignores her. Strange, but he feels easier with Beans. He keeps the world away, somehow. Mick looks over at him, eating and scratching away at his face and neck, something he keeps doing the whole time they are sat there. He's still got the woolly hat on, pulled down over his ears. No the less, it's visible enough that one of them is a write-off, the lobe dark and shrivelled into a wee currant.

Beans finishes his plate quickly, clattering the knife and fork down.

'How ye finding it, then?'

He shrugs. 'Okay. I've no really left the room.'

Beans nods. 'I know, I know. Seems – well, it's pretty comfy, eh? Still got to keep the edge but. Don't trust anybody.' And as he is saying it, he gets glaring past Mick's shoulder at two young men who are going up the counter.

'That's him.'

'Who?'

'The neighbour.'

The two men are laughing at something with the guy behind the counter.

'Which one?'

'Him there, that skinny one with a face like underneath a fridge-freezer.' He starts to get up. 'Come on. Ye got any money?'

'No, I've –'

'It's fine, I do, come on.'

They go down another flight to Beans's room on the ground floor. It is pretty much identical to his own. Beans goes into the bottom of the wardrobe and pulls out a couple of cans, hands one to Mick, and they sit down on the bed.

The hostel is not far from where they were. There is a large map of the borough on a wall in the reception, and he has a study of it one morning when there isn't much traffic passing through, only the woman on the desk, occupied at her computer.

He walks there the first time, getting sat in the old spot by the cash machines. Coming back that afternoon, he figures out there is a bus he can get that goes right down the road the hostel is on, and it's one of these bendy ones you can skip the fare onto. A bonus. Plus as well, thanks to the en suite bathroom, he's no boufing like he was, so his takings are on the increase.

Rare there are many people about on the corridors or in the reception. He has little difficulty keeping out the way. There are four floors, sandwiching the men and the women. Probably about fifty people in total, he calculates, but the only place he sees them usually is the canteen. A few looks but that's all. It's different here to the other places they've been. The scaffers don't all look like scaffers, for a kick-off. A lot of them are clean and normal-looking. Decent clothes. Even one black guy that goes around in a suit and tie the whole time, the hair gelled into a side-shed and his shoes polished as steel. There are groups, obviously. Wee cabals. He steers clear of them, even though there's none he's seen yet that look like they might be trouble. Quite a few of the men and the women mix together, in fact, and the atmosphere is pretty calm, orderly.

He copies Beans's idea of storing his lagers in the wardrobe. It's allowed, it says in his agreement, but the better to be careful. And nay chance he's leaving them in the fridge in the corridor kitchen, which he comes past on the way to his room, keeking inside at men from his floor, cooking, talking.

He meets with Renuka each Thursday in the small, cramped office that she shares – if the scattered papers and flyers are anything to go by – with Daniel Katongo, Complex Needs Worker. There is a shelving unit built into the whole of one wall, packed with box files labelled things like: Risk Assessments, Overdose, HEP/TB, Serious Incidents. They talk about his benefit claims, and where is his family, do they know where he is? No exactly his favourite subjects, so he usually cloys up and stares at the files or at the photos on the walls. One of a woman in a skirt suit shaking the hand of a bemused-looking old guy inside the hostel entrance; another of Renuka stood amongst a line of people in yellow T-shirts, their arms around each other's shoulders, smiling.

On their second meeting she had asked him if he's using drugs. No. He isn't. Alcohol? Sometimes, maybe – who doesn't? No like he keeps a bucket of electric soup by the bed. Does he drink in his room? He tells her he doesn't. Time to time, maybe. She's alright but, is Renuka, she doesn't put the boot on. She is helping him get a bank account and sort out his claims, arranging his interviews for housing and broo money. The first time he goes up the jobcentre is a pretty fucking dreadful experience. A cheery enough black woman with dreadlocks that deals with him but he's just too bloody shamefaced hardly to speak to her. He is leeching again. Him that once was pure sickened by the very idea of it, who watched others going down the broo office while he was too proud even to get off his bar stool, and now this. Moved from Beans to the broo. An unchancy pair, that's for sure.

Beans isn't having things so easy with his own key worker. Or, more likely, the key worker isn't. He's no comfortable sitting in they type of rooms, he tells Mick; he needs to get up and move around. Which is the first thing this guy Robin is in his ear about. Plus he hasn't been too forthcoming himself about the drink. He's told Robin he's teetotal. Robin says he isn't helping himself with this attitude, that there's services in the hostel he could start making use of – but once he's said that, Beans digs the heels in just and starts into the usual chicanery.

As well, there's been some argle-bargle with the neighbour. The skinny guy has been putting the mix in, or Beans has been putting the mix with him, it's hard to tell from Beans's account of it. Either way, this guy, even though he's quite young, he's obvious in with the bricks and he's pretty testy about what's his plate and what's his fridge shelf and all this. Something to do with the fridge getting flooded that started it off and now the two of them are at each other's throats at the flick of a switch. He fancies he's some kind of hardman, according to Beans, even though he's no but a scrawny wee fuck, and a couple of times the neighbour's tried to hang one on him, the last of which ended with Beans sat on his head. Robin is very unpleased about it all. They've got the zero-tolerance rules to aggression here, and if he carries on like this then he's out on his arse.

A slow, heavy sadness is weighing on him. He feels lost – adrift. Now that he isn't distracted by the need to keep warm, keep safe, keep fed, it's as though a layer of something protective is went away and now he's floating in space with nothing to shield him from his thoughts. Fragments of conversations, images, keep coming at him and he is powerless to block them out. Robbie. Craig. He lies on the bed or sits on the pavement with his eyes tight shut and waits for them to pass, but then all he's left with is this great unmoving solidness inside him. The drink no helping either; making it worse. Nothing to do. There is nothing to do. Sleep, that's all there is, but even that is become totally random now: sometimes he won't get more than two minutes at a time, awake for long stretches through the night, then other days he'll hit the pillow and sleep for fifteen hours straight. He needs something to keep the mind occupied. To get him off the bed. There is the day room, which has a TV and a pool table in it, and sometimes he thinks about asking Beans if he fancies going a game, but then he'll convince himself it's a bad idea – nay doubt the skinny guy will be there and it'll turn into a bloodbath. He could go up there on his own and watch a match, a film, but the idea of it straight away makes him uneasy, the thought of the room hoaching with people, eyes, noise.

He is lying on the bed one afternoon when it occurs to him that he's got the book. The Barbara. He gets up and takes it out from the bottom of the wardrobe, then sits with it on his lap for a while, looking at it. Trying to work out if he recognizes the cover. Maybe. Hard to tell. They were all pretty similar, from what he can mind, always these good-looking women on the move in expensive dresses. He turns it over and reads the back:

Television war correspondent Nicky Wells is a media superstar. Courageous, beautiful and renowned for her hard-hitting reports from the world's most dangerous trouble spots, her life is shattered when she loses the only man she ever truly loved – dashing English aristocrat, Charles Devereaux.

He chuckles. No Dickens, is it, hen? He flicks it open though, and gets reading the first couple of pages. By the time he puts it down to go the canteen and meet Beans, he's already a fair chunk into it.

The battle with the skinny guy shows no signs of stopping, but his own neighbours are fine. One side doesn't come out of his room much, and when he does he doesn't say a great lot. Mick passes him sometimes on the corridor, or in the kitchen if he's getting a cup of tea – quite long grey hair tied in a ponytail, and always the same green tracksuit on. They nod the head at each other, and get back into their rooms. The other side but is a different story. It's almost a month before they cross each other's path, but when they do it's immediately obvious that the guy is a yap. They are both going into their rooms when he stops in his doorway and turns to ask Mick if he's got a shelf in the fridge, before delivering pretty much his entire life story right there in the corridor as if Mick has just asked for it, which he hasn't, he's hardly said a word.

'I've been here a year, myself. I'm supposed to've got my flat but I was behind with my service charge and now they won't move me on, even though they know I'm good for it. I am. I was in the army. Infantryman, but I got injured, see.' He lifts up his jeans to show a dark scar on his ankle running all the way up to the knee. He looks at Mick; no clear if he's expecting a challenge, or for him to be impressed.

'Where were ye stationed?'

'Cyprus. But then I got injured, right, so I went and lived with my brother in Stockport. He's long distance with the lorries, so it worked out sound because I usually had the place to myself. You know those lorry parks? In Calais and wherever. Pretty much just brothels, honest to God, all these girls that work between the lorries. And the beds fold down off the sides so him and his mate are practically sleeping on top of each other. So what happens is, my brother, he's always got a cob on when he comes back from a run, he doesn't want me around, and eventually we have this big fight and he chucks me out.'

Mick stays quiet. Hard to put an age on him. He could be anywhere from twenty to forty. Behind him there is the sound of a television and a faint bogging smell coming through the open door, the walls covered in posters and magazine pages. He didn't know you were allowed to do that. Maybe you aren't.

'That's why I came down to London, because I had a friend I knew I could stay with. I knew him before I went in the army and he's always been pretty sound. His mates are an alright lot too.

There was always these parties. You wouldn't believe it, just wild, man, like the wildest parties you've ever been to. There was this roof, and you weren't supposed to go on it but everyone did, and you'd go up and there'd be the whole building out there on the lash. I remember one time somebody had got a pig – and like I'm talking a whole pig – fuck knows where they'd got it, but it takes about a dozen of us to drag it up there because it's as heavy as a car, I swear. Then once we'd done it, somebody goes, hey, let's chuck it off, so we get it to the edge and then' – he does a pushing motion with his hands – 'it hits the road and it must've exploded or something because it just sounded like this massive wet fart. And then this car pulls up in front of it, and a bloke gets out and stands there scratching his head, not a fucking clue what's going on – he thinks he's just knocked over a pig – and he never looks up but we're there on the roof absolutely fucking pissing ourselves.' Mick is started edging into his room, no sure when is the end to this story. 'What I didn't know though is that this lad, my mate, he's stealing from me. Fucking stealing, right in front of my face, honest to God. I come in one day and he's there going through my bag. Says he's looking for fags but he's lying and that's it, man, I'm fucking gone.'

The neighbour's name is Paul, he tells him before Mick's managed getting back into his room. He's okay. He's a yap but he's okay. They have the same conversation a couple of times. No too clear if Paul can mind he's told him already, or if he's honing the details just. They aye change anyway, the details. The next time he sees him, Paul is washing up a load of mugs in the kitchen, and it isn't Cyprus where he was deployed, it was Afghanistan. So what though? Even if it's made up, what does it matter? No like he's writing the guy's biography, and if he wants to keep talking about himself then that's fine, it's better than him asking questions.

A half-hour walk from the hostel, there is a park. No a scratty job either, but a big green one with ponds and boulevards and sunbathers. He takes to going up early each afternoon, to be doing something just, no just sitting in his room festering. There is a bench at the top of a large sloping lawn, in front of a rose garden, a bit out of the way. A view of the tennis courts, off to one side; and, in the distance, a group of homeless that he has to walk past on his way to the bench, who sit drinking by a plantation of young trees. East Europes, they sound like. Strange, it occurs to him as he's sat there on the bench, how there's none in the hostel.

He keeps on with the book. It's quite gripping, actually. This woman, Nicky, she meets an old photographer friend while she's reporting on the Tiananmen Square protests, and the two of them start getting increasingly friendly on each other, but she's still haunted by the death of the dashing English aristocrat. No the less, the photographer's got a farmhouse in Provence and there's the inevitable steamy lovemaking when she goes to visit. The relationship going from strength to strength, until she gets watching the news one day and she sees the dashing English aristocrat in a crowd. Not drowned, as it turns out, and so she sets off across Europe in search of him.

He finds himself sat up in the bed with the cup of tea and the plate of biscuits reading it. Sometimes it's no a tea, but there ye go, such is life. The book is a genuine doorstop and it takes him a few weeks to finish it. A strange mood that comes on him afterwards. A sense, which dogs at him and he doesn't try blocking out, of emptiness now that the book is gone.

35

A lot of the time now, he is having thoughts about the boys. Unsettling ones, which make him want to shut himself away in his room and go to sleep. The smallest thing can set them off. He'll be sat quietly drinking on the bench with nothing rattling about in the brainbox, the dull distant thwock of tennis balls over on the courts, when a toddler comes tottering toward him, falling onto her hands and lying there with the head up, silently looking at him until her maw is along to scoop her up and away. And then the thoughts will kick off. They don't know where he is. He is sat here on a bench in the sunshine and nobody knows it but himself; and a great wave of self-pity will come over him, the sense again that he is abandoned. No. No, he isn't and don't fucking try acting it any different, because if there's any abandoning went on then it's him the one that's done it. That is the fact of the matter, fucking go deal with it.

Renuka brings it up sometimes during their meetings. Does he have any feelings of blame, or guilt, toward his family? No, he tells her. And then he'll go silent while she moves on to talking about activities and employment and housing solutions.

Beans has joined the art class. Mick laughs when he tells him this, in the canteen while they're eating a watery chicken curry.

'No, see it's alright, serious. And it's good for the points too. That guy Robin is always on at me to join this or that group and get exercising the auld grey matter, so I thought, fuck it, why no?'

'What do ye do, paint?'

'Aye, paint, draw, all that. I've only been twice. Ye should come.'

The next time it's on but he gives it a bye, deciding instead to stay in his room and batter his head against the walls.

It's no until the following week, after a fair while of Beans protesting, that he steels himself and goes.

It is a bright room with a few large school tables put together into

a square. He sits on one side, next to Beans. There are four others –
two men and two women, who have obvious all been coming for a
while, because they're giving it the patter with the teacher, Chris, an
Englishman, twenty stone, white curly hair and glasses. An okay
guy, it turns out. Friendly. He asks Mick his name and tells him to
help himself to the tea and biscuits. As he's getting the kettle on, he
looks over the room. They are all busy with paintings that they've
started a previous week. The suit and tie man is here. He is humming away to the radio, each now and then quietly muttering
something to himself.

Beans has got a lot of paint onto his paper. There's parts of it
where he's went over a dried bit from earlier and the paint has
formed into a kind of ledge. It isn't clear what he's painting exactly.
The sea, maybe. A sunset.

'It's me on fire,' he says when Mick asks him.

'Aw, right. It's good, aye.'

There is nothing himself he can think of to paint, so he sits there
a while, drinking his tea and observing the others. The two women
stick close together, talking, occasionally a wee joke with the suit
and tie man. One of them is quite a bit older than the other, and it's
clear enough the young one looks up to her, leans on her. A mother
and daughter? No, how could that work? Maybe but. How does any
of it work? Fucked if he knows. The teacher is coming over again.
He asks if he's struggling for ideas, and then he says why doesn't he
try and think of something that he knows really well. Then he
moves on to Beans, and Beans is looking at him intently as the guy
examines his painting. It's good, he tells him. Maybe be a bit lighter
with the brush though. And away he goes to the other side of the
table to speak to the women.

He starts painting the QE2. It's quite a good likeness, actually,
except for he's done the mooring line too thick and it looks a bit like
there's a tail behind it. It's relaxing but, painting. Quietly getting on
with it, the mumble of the radio and the suit and tie man in the
background.

The next session he keeps going on the ship. Paul is there, sat
with him and Beans, they two yapping away while Mick paints and
listens. Both of them are agreed when he's finished it that it's a

decent painting. So too are the others, at the end of the session when the big fella asks them all to show the group what they've done. Detailed, the two women say about it. The young one has done a sunflower, and the other woman has done a picture of her daughter, who from the looks of it is black, so that rules out the young one unless she's had a mix-up with the paint.

They are allowed to keep what they've done, so he takes his painting to his room and puts it up on the wall. He has spruced things up a little with his giro payments and the room now contains: a collection of mugs, a mini television that he saved up quite a time for, a mat, a kettle, and as well two more Barbaras and a potted plant on the windowsill.

Something he thinks about quite a lot these days: what would she think if she knew? He is staying in a homeless hostel and the family is disintegrated. Of all the guilts putting the boot on, it's this which is aye the worst. This feeling that goes with it, crawing at him, that it's too late. That things are too far gone the now ever to be put back.

Each while, Beans goes into one of his maunderly phases. He'll cloy up and keep to his room or stay outside all day, until the point comes when he'll disappear, for days, sometimes for weeks. His key worker tearing the hair out wanting to find out from Mick where he's went to, but he genuine has nay clue either. Usually a fair bet the skinny neighbour and his squad have something to do with it though. One night, Beans is asleep in his room and a mob of them are outside in the corridor, digging him up, banging on his door every few minutes. The next night it's the same story, and the next, until eventually Beans snaps and he charges out the room with a wine bottle. A mighty scrap in the corridor, one guy's face getting ripped, then the polis arriving and the whole pile of them away in the meat wagon to the station.

Soon afterwards, Beans does the disappearing act. No sight or sound of him for two whole weeks until one evening he's suddenly there in the canteen, cheerily queuing up for shepherd's pie. No word about where he's been. The usual performance. Everything back to normal. After they've eaten they go up the day room for a game of pool, and Beans is once again full of the usual patter.

At one point, he is bent down about to take his shot, when suddenly he straightens up and starts into a life history of Chris the art teacher.

'Know he used to be a serious artist? Ten, twenty years ago. He was selling paintings and he was a proper somebody, mean, he was known in the art world. See but he liked a wee refreshment. A bevvy-merchant. So what happens, he's been to this party, an artist party, and he's driving himself home totally out the game, and he knocks into another car, a young couple on their way back from holiday. Dead. Instantaneous. Your man gets put away for a good long stretch, and when he comes out the clink he's totally hit the scrape. Too drunk to paint, and even if he could, the art world has gave him the swerve because of what's happened. So he's going about staying on people's couches, bedsits and that. Ten years, a total wipeout. Now he doesn't paint any more, but he does this class because he used to stay here one time. And he does them in the prisons as well. A decent guy, serious. Just the bottle, man, know what I mean, it ruins ye.'

He leans down, finally, and takes his shot.

Mick stands looking at him.

'How ye find out these things?'

Beans shrugs the shoulders just. 'Don't know. I keep my ears about the place.'

Both of them keep going to the art class. Most weeks it's painting – oils, watercolours – but sometimes they do other things as well, like pottery, T-shirt printing. Renuka is pleased that he's stuck with it. It helps with his move-on. Activities, jobseeking, reduced bevvying, it all counts toward it. They last two maybe haven't been quite so successful as the activities, but such is the way of things. Renuka seems happy anyway. He's been a couple of times to this room in the hostel where they've got some kind of link with the jobcentre and they try fixing you up on these volunteer schemes, training programmes and the like. Although to be honest, fuck that. Trainee. Him employed twenty years in the shipyards and now to get working for nothing. Even these jobs that he keeps applying for, the main reason he's doing it is there's no choice: they want to see work-related activity, as they call it, if he's to get his giro.

Strange to feel that way about it, when normally work has always been the answer. And he knows as well that he does need to get doing something, to get out of the building, get out of his room; but he's just no got the will for it. Back in the day, at least he knew it was going somewhere, the money. He needed it. There was a family to support and he went into work and could aye see what he was working toward because it was bloody right there in front of him: eighty thousand tons of it, sat on the water. But why apply for all these crappity jobs that you can't get anyway because apparently you're no good enough? And then even if you did get them you've still nay chance earning your rent, so you're never going to see any of the income because all you're doing is trying to tread water with the benefit money.

It goes up and down, how busy the art class is. Some weeks it's just him, Beans and the two women, but other times there might be nine or ten turn up. Some who are pretty decent at the artmaking; others who come just to sneak a mug of sugar under the coat and leave. One or two who spend the whole time in your ear giving it the life story, or – like Beans – everybody's life story but their own; and as well the ones who sit and barely speak a word. Probably there's a lot more of the quiet types staying in the hostel, just they keep themselves hidden. The yaps are about all the time, in the canteen and the day room, or hanging about the reception biting the receptionist's ear off, but the silent ones stay in their rooms. Mostly they're only likely to come out if there's a fire alarm – which actually is about three times a day – everybody gathering outside in the car park in their bedclothes and their baries; keeping to themselves, or pattering with the firemen that stand in groups waiting for the all clear.

He is outside Renuka's office for the weekly meeting. She is running five minutes late, she tells him round the door, and he waits in the corridor until she's ready for him. When he comes in she asks if he'd like a cup of tea, as is the routine, and he gets sat silently while the kettle boils and she finishes off tidying some papers away.

'So,' she says, sitting down and looking at him across the desk. 'How are you feeling?'

'Fine. Okay.'

'Good. That's good.'

She is looking right at him, like she's testing if he's telling the truth.

'I've received a letter, Mick, that I need to show you.' She reaches for a piece of folded paper from her in-tray. 'It's been forwarded to me from the Missing People charity – and I should just say right now that whatever happens from here is entirely up to you.'

Confusion. The brainbox jumbling.

'I know this must seem quite out of the blue, but you were registered as missing in February. Obviously the charity will have been making efforts to locate you, but the letter simply asks if you would like to get in touch with them to decide on a course of action.'

His head is spinning. He steadies his mug on the desk and fastens the hands tightly around it.

'Robbie?'

'The letter doesn't say.'

'How they find me?'

'It doesn't say that either. Here, would you like to see it?'

She passes the paper across.

He takes a moment and tries to read it. They would like him to contact them. They never disclose information about people's whereabouts without the missing person's permission. Missing person. He is a missing person. Course he fucking is, what else is he: a holidaymaker?

'It's up to you, Mick. There's a number of options.' She is looking at his hands on the mug. 'You don't have to do anything, would be one. Or, I could write back to them and say that you would like to initiate contact. But if you don't want to do that, or you don't feel ready yet, we could ask them simply to let your family know that you are safe and well, without saying where you are.'

He feels sick. Renuka is smiling faintly at him. The side of her computer that he can see flicks now to a picture of a wean by a swimming pool, and it's actually funny, the absurd pointedness of it, he could in fact laugh out loud only he's feart he might boak up onto her desk. She is still smiling, and he realizes what a massive cunt she must think he is. He has abandoned his family. He has

227

abandoned his family and now he is sat there at her desk and if he doesn't feel ready he may pass on a message to inform them he is safe and well. But if they want to know where he is then get to fuck, they can't.

They leave it at that. He is to have a think about it. He takes the letter and stands up to return to his room.

He barely sleeps that night. Or the next. He sticks the television on and keeps it quietly going in the background. The letter on the windowsill, weighted under the plant. How is it his decision? That's what he can't understand. How is he in charge of the situation, and they've no say in it? They. Is it? Is it they, or is it Robbie, or maybe is the whole of Glasgow out the now looking for him? The not knowing about any of it is what's chibbing at him. He keeps to his room, gets his own food in. Misses the next art class. The wardrobe stocked again with superlager, no that it does any good: it's lost the ability now to numb the brain. In fact it's bloody turbocharging it. February. They declared him missing in February. Which means he must have been gone a few months before they notified anybody. So what? What difference does it make how long it took or who did it or if Alan's involved, or if Robbie's had to keep coming back from Australia, or any of it, because it doesn't; what matters is what he has done, what he is going to do. The idea of making contact. Hello, it's your da, how's it going? Unthinkable. Totally unthinkable.

36

A girl is sprinting down a path through the park, her bandy legs looking like they are about to knock each other over at any moment. She passes the rose garden and begins to slow down, out of breath. A group of her friends are sitting in a circle in the middle of a wide, open area of grass, and she goes to join them.

It is hot, and she rolls up the bottom of her T-shirt, then she lies down and rests her can of Coke on her belly, the way the others are doing. For the last few days, the man on the bench has been there the whole time they have, and they've had to move further away from the rose garden. He never does anything though. He just sits there being drunk or falling asleep. They think he is probably mental. Sometimes he starts talking to himself, not loudly, like the mad woman who is always in the bus stop, but anyway you can see his mouth moving even though there isn't anybody next to him or anywhere near him.

There are quite a lot of drunk and mental people in the park. Further down the path, there is a group of Polish homeless men who lie on the grass by the little trees and get drunk. Sometimes they stand up and chase each other about, and once they came over to where her and her friends were and started shouting something in Polish, so they ran away and that's when they started sitting up by the rose garden instead. And, as well, there is a pub near the entrance on the other side of the park, where the drinkers come over the road to lie on the grass and take their shirts off to drink with their big red bellies out.

Most of the time since they broke up they come and sit and listen to music or talk or usually just lie in the sun. She is going on holiday to Spain in a couple of weeks with her family. They went last year as well, but it's not too bad, it could be worse. At least she's not going to stay in a caravan like Carolyn with her mum and brother and Shitface Anthony.

The days when it's not sunny she stays at home or sometimes Carolyn comes round and they watch TV, but usually it's hot so they go to the park. One time the hobo has a friend in a woolly hat that comes and joins him, and he is properly mental. Whenever anybody walks near them he starts shouting or laughing, but you can't understand anything he says because he is drunk too. Nisha saw him weeing into the rose garden, just standing on the grass and doing it over the little fence onto the flowers. Most days though the man that talks to himself is on his own. His face is all red and sunburnt. Even on really hot days he never takes his jacket off. If he is asleep and you get quite close when you walk past, you can see that the knees of his trousers are all muddy and his fingernails have got loads of dirt under them.

The last day before she goes on holiday is the hottest day all summer. No point going to Spain, really. When she leaves, the others are just lying on the grass passed out, and pretty much that's where they'll be when she gets back so it's not like she's missing out on anything. On her way back to help her mum pack their things, she stops and watches the tennis players for a minute, and then, because she is on her own, she takes the path to the other side of the park from where she lives, so she doesn't have to walk past the Polish men.

37

He tells Renuka to write back to Missing People. He is safe and well. He will get in touch with them when he is able. Pathetic. It makes it sound like he's been fucking kidnapped.

Beans is back heavy on the drink, and they are returned now to the old routine. Away up the park and into the superlager. A few times Beans puts the mix in with the East Europes by the trees – for some reason he's decided that's where he wants to be sitting, and what right do they lot have taking the best spot? A couple of shouting matches but Mick is able to pull him away and get over the other side of the park before they both get skelped. One night, they have been drinking all afternoon, the both of them totally away for oil, and they don't make it back to the hostel. They find a line of bushes along a path and collapse into it. The night is warm and still, and he lies there awake with the familiar warm weight of Beans pressed up against him. Safe and well. Blootered in a bush next to a madman, his head blaring with drink and sunburn, but he is safe and well, thank Christ for that.

When he is not up the park, he stays in his room with the television on, staring at it, or out the window. Thoughts about the wife, the family, hovering around him the whole time now. He doesn't try to hold them back, there's nay point, and sometimes it builds and builds until he feels like getting up and putting his fist through the window – but instead he just lies there on the bed, staring or greeting. That is another thing he's doing a lot of the now, greeting. It comes on him out of nowhere: sat absently watching a cookery programme and suddenly he's bubbling up and it will go on uncontrollably for a long while, until his face is as hard and sticky as if he's just woke up under a tree. He lets himself do it; he encourages it even, searching for how many ways he's failed her, trying and no being able to get a sense of her, and then blaming himself for that as well.

A chapping at the door. He ignores it. A few minutes later and it's there again. He tries to blank it out, but the heart is going and he knows that much more of this and his nerves will be that ripped he'll have no choice but jumping to his bloody death on the pavement below. He gets up and looks through the peephole. It is Paul. 'You alright in there, mate? Mick? Everything okay, mate?' He stays as still as he can and tries to control his breathing. After a while, Paul goes away. The sound of his door closing.

Renuka has been informed he's stopped going to the art classes and has missed his benefits interviews. She is concerned about him. His eyes and his face and the general honk of him nay doubt pointing to the drink. Is the letter still troubling him? Does he want to think about a different course of action? Aye, I think we should get the whole family down here for a visit, have a tour round the place; then wipe the slate clean, let bygones be bygones.

Paul comes in the kitchen one evening while he is waiting for a plate of food in the microwave.

'How's it going?'

'Okay, thanks.'

'Not seen you at the art class for a while.' He pulls a packet of ready-grated cheese out of the fridge. 'Fancy a knock on the pool table later?'

'Think I'll give it a bye the night, thanks.'

'No worries, no worries. If you do – just give me a knock, right.'

More and more, he is going over the time when she was ill. He tries to mind it, what like it was, what happened, how much of it he was there for. He hadn't finished working until a few months from the end – he couldn't, even after he sold the car, they couldn't afford otherwise – but he can't stop the thought of her alone in the house, in the bed, knowing she was going to die. See if they knew she wasn't going to live, why was he working? Who was he working for? The rent, bills, food, keeping things going, how could any of that have been for her? The smell of the house when he came in off a shift. Going up the stair and seeing her, alone, asleep. Or with Craig. There at the bedside with her. All the wee details, he strains to mind them. Who had called round the house; what had he cooked for her; when did it first come up, the talk of putting in a compensation claim?

As well, an image he keeps recalling. She is picking up the front door mat, taking it outside and shaking it. He recalls it over and over, screwing the eyes trying to make her turn round, see her face, but it is always the same picture: him looking from the doorway, watching her beat the mat on the gate and a cloud of white dust puffing out with each clout. He dreams about this scene and when he is awake he finds himself searching for it, until he doesn't know any more if it is actually a memory, or if he's made it up.

38

His benefits have been cut, and they are threatening to withdraw them on account of the missed interviews. As a result he has no money and he is got behind with his service charge. He keeps to his room. Reads a lot. A new Barbara he's picked up, about this successful businesswoman that owns a string of international inns. She is preparing for her daughter's wedding when she finds out she's suffering from this strange illness that nobody can diagnose, and the only way she can find out what's wrong with her is to go round the world uncovering all these secrets from her past.

All day and all night, even if he's no directly thinking about it, he has an awareness of the family out there, somewhere. Searching for him. Fine well clear enough, the message he's sent out, that he doesn't want to be near them. Pure torture, thinking about it, but that's what he's engaged in – here's my brain, my body, let them fucking stiffen each other. He isn't interested in deadening himself with the drink any more; the torture is more relieving. No that he's gave the drink the go-by but. He still gets to the offie with what little he has on his tail. It's too instinctive not to.

An anxiousness is welling inside him that he cannot leave them hanging like this; himself, hanging. To keep them thinking that he doesn't want to see them. Because he does; he does want to see them. Not all of them, obviously. But the boys – the pull of seeing them, it's undeniable, and it wrests and knots at him because no matter how strong it gets, that pull, it's never as strong as the one that is wanting to keep them away, to keep them from seeing him here.

Up until the letter he had been doing well, at least they seemed to think so, going the classes and up the broo office. He tells Renuka that he's going to start again with the activities, that he's cut out the drink. He goes to the next art class. Everybody says it is good to see him. Maybe they've been talking. Possible they know the score.

Unlikely but, seeing as he hasn't told anybody about the letter, even Beans, who has been going through his own dark patch of late. They have been doing clay objects, bowls, ash trays and that. He makes a small pot, and digs up some soil and a wee flower in the park to put in it; sticks it on the windowsill next to the other one. It dies a couple of weeks later, and he washes out the pot to use as a mug for tea and superlager.

To have something to focus on, something to do, it is good for the nerves. Paul is going to the art classes too and he takes him up on the game of pool. Mick cuffs him. No that Paul seems to mind. He's happy just being up there in the day room, it seems, talking. Amazing, all these things he says he's got up to. One story he tells him. Each fortnight when he gets his giro, he draws a twenty out the cash machine and goes straight up the supermarket. The security guards are always on his tail whenever he's there, so what he does, he tries to look as unchancy as he can, jinking in and out of the aisles, giving these shifty wee glances at the guards – then he grabs a bottle of champagne and something else expensive, a steak, or a pack of smoked salmon, and he slips them under his coat and legs it to the tills. Just as the heavy team are sweating and shouting up the aisle, he sticks them on the belt and pulls out the twenty, all calm and swaggersome, and the meatheads are left standing there just, panting and stupit. He's okay, is Paul. He's been on a script the last six months, he tells him, and he's trying to sort himself out. There is a woman that comes round quite often to visit him: his girlfriend, Monica, who he knows from when he lived up north. She's friendly too. A couple of times she comes in the day room and chats with them while they're playing pool.

Renuka and him talk about whether he feels ready to start with the move-on process. Yes. A pure certainty he is. She explains to him that he needs to get his service charge on track, and then she lays out how it works: that they get given a quota each year to put on the housing register; that it's no a very big quota; that it might take some time. Fine. Whatever it takes. He is compliant.

Posters go up around the hostel for an outing to an open-air theatre production in the park. Beans and Paul are dead set on going, so he puts his name down. A sunny day, when it arrives, and the play is in fact quite enjoyable. It's about this young Asian girl who is supposed to marry a guy she's never met, but she's fell in love instead with a white lad that works on the market. Racial differences. Arglebargling families. Eventually the pair try to escape and there's a tragic ending in a cash-and-carry car park. Pretty interesting, parts of it, although you'd think it's actually the ten of them from the hostel who are the real show, the way the residents stare at them from their blankets. Beans, at least, enjoys the attention – laughing loudly at all the jokes and getting up each while to walk a circle around the back of the audience, his hands clasped behind him, smiling and pattering away.

He meets Renuka in the computer room and she shows him how to go the internet and get looking at properties. Incredible, really, all that just there at the fingertips. She has to demonstrate a few times, the same patient way she explains everything else, writing notes on a piece of paper so he can mind for next time. They put in his bidding number and look together through the vacant flats. A few decent ones; a few genuine shitholes. She does another session with him, and he puts a couple of bids in. If he prefers, she can do all this for him, she says, but he tells her no, he's fine doing it himself. He wants to do it himself.

There's never many in the computer room. Sometimes one or two with the giant headphones on, listening to music; and usually as well the young woman from the art class, sat quietly getting on with her own things. He doesn't mind coming in here, especially now the weather is on the turn and the park is cooler and blowier getting. At least he is out of his room doing something. As well, there's the anticipation through each week of seeing if your bid's come in, followed by the inevitable finding out that you've went down again. One day he is getting up to leave, the same time as the woman is for the off, and they go out the door together. She slows down in the corridor, turning to speak to him.

'You're bidding for a council house, aren't you?'

'Aye. Ye doing the same?'

'Yes – four months.'

'Serious? Nothing?'

'Nope. Well, I went to look at one a couple of weeks ago that was just a dump. Everyone ahead of me had obviously turned it down.'

He's no heard her say this much before. Surprising how well spoken she is.

'You on the Clearing House?'

'The – mean, I don't know.'

'Well, maybe better not to be anyway.' They are come to the reception. 'Good luck with it.' She smiles, and goes toward the main entrance.

The longer goes on, the more restless getting he is. Nearly eight months is by now since they notified the charity that he'd fucked off and left them. To get on his feet just, be in a flat. Then he could face them. Face the music. Could he? See that's what he's been telling himself – that's what's been driving him through – but, if it comes to it, is he actually going to be able to look at them and no just wither in a heap at their feet? And as well, who's to say that they do want to see him? Consider that one a moment. There is a hollow feeling he gets when he starts thinking like this. Hard to stave off the drink but he's trying. A loneliness that circles about itself, because then he'll start thinking about Cathy, searching for her, this sense that she is there but out of his grasp; and it leaves him empty, longing.

He speaks to Renuka about the housing situation. The lack of a housing situation. She makes him a tea and puts her doctor's face on. The problem with the letting scheme, she says, is there's crap-all housing stock left in the borough. He can keep on as he is, and points-wise at least he's no badly stacked, but there's no guarantees anything will happen soon. Or, he can try for a private-rented tenancy. More likely he'll get something that way, but more likely as well that it'll be expensive and temporary and the landlord will be a bastard. No quite her words, but he gets the picture.

He asks her to stick him forward for it. At the same time though, he carries on with his internet bidding. The art class girl, Terri, is in the same boat and the pair of them are in there each week, talking about have you seen this house or that house. As well, Beans has got himself involved. No that they're letting him think about getting his own flat – Robin is still doing his box in at how he carries on – but he can't resist getting in the mix, telling Mick which flats he should

237

and shouldn't go for. Amazing, but he's pretty good at working the computers. When he gets bored of looking at the properties, he turns to his own screen and starts pulling up TV shows, news, underwear models. Anybody's guess how he's learnt to do it. In other hostels maybe. Nay point asking him. Sometimes it's easier leaving off the questions and just marvelling at the guy.

His benefits have been mostly restored and he is working at paying his service charge arrears. Still applying for the jobs that he's even less of a sniff of now after the missing period, and starting on something of an economy drive: less bevvying, more of the Barbaras. He is reading one about another female reporter, in Kosovo, whose colleague gets shot and she leaves the war behind to do celebrity photo shoots. This playboy artist she meets and falls for, but everything that's happened in the past continuing to plague her at every turn.

He keeps up with the art classes, and goes a couple of times to a film club that gets run in the day room by a chuckling retired Welshman called Peter. Sometimes as well there'll be an event going on in the hostel. One day, a visit from a member of the English royalty, or the aristocracy, or Christ knows who he is, but Mick comes down to the thing for the same reason everybody else does: because there's a free lunch going. It is an old guy with gold jewellery draped off his blazer, so maybe he's the Lord Provost or something. He shakes the hands, keeps the stiff smile on his face, eats a polite amount of sandwich triangles and mini sausage rolls. The weeks continuing to go by. The outside colder and colder getting and the heating turned up to blasting so that everybody starts wandering about the place in vests and shorts. Occasionally new people being admitted, led numb and shivery through the reception.

His art collection grows to include a fruit bowl with no fruit in it, a painting of a tree and another of Ibrox, a papier-mâché swan and a T-shirt with *Bluenose* stencilled on it. He is passing time, waiting, but when one morning Renuka knocks him up with the news that a private-rented flat is become available, he feels, at the same instant as relief, a sense of foreboding; unsure suddenly if this is what he wants, if it wouldn't in fact be easier staying put where he is.

39

There's no great ceremony about it, thank Christ. No staff lined up to pat him on the back and give him advice. Nobody at the door to collect and drive him away. He packs up his things into a large hold-all he bought in a charity shop and goes down to the reception, where Renuka hands him his new set of keys. She is arranging their meeting for later the week when Beans comes loundering in with a frying pan.

'That you, well?'

'That's me.'

'Good. Great.' He shuffles about a bit, and holds up the fryer. 'Here.'

'Ye got me a frying pan?'

Beans nods.

'Cheers.' He takes it, smiling. The coating is worn off the inside rim and it's quite possible he's lifted it – the skinny neighbour, more than likely – but no the less, no the less, and he stands there looking at Beans as a lump of gratefulness and fear together lands in his stomach.

Beans is grinning. 'Off ye go, well. Flatman.'

The bus goes past another parade of shops and he tries to recognize where he is. To mind which is his stop. No yet. He keeps the eyes trained for the boarded-up pub which is where he has to get out. Nobody is noticing him. Strange, that he's thinking they might, that all of them know the score somehow, when actually they don't even see him. There's the occasional wee keek over from a teenage lad across the aisle, but he realized a while back that he's just looking at the frying pan and papier-mâché swan which are rested on his lap.

He gets off and walks round the corner past the boarded-up pub, acting it that everything is normal and okay as he approaches the building and punches the code in. There is nobody about. He gives the lift a swerve and gets walking up the stair, his feet echoing against the grey painted steps. A couple of floors up, he stops on the stairhead and looks out through a narrow cracked window at the surrounding roads and buildings. Nowhere he recognizes. All of it alien, and he carries on up to his own floor.

It is a room and kitchen type of affair. The main room with a bed against one wall and a small shiny brown settee against the other. A plastic table with two chairs in the middle. When he first came to see it, the landlord said he should feel free to change things around however he wants, and him and Renuka had a wee chuckle about it afterwards. Bed this side, mini settee the other? Or mini settee this side, bed the other – what do you reckon? There is a doorless opening into the kitchen that he goes through now: toaster, microwave and a kettle, which he fills and flicks on. He puts the swan on top of the microwave and the fryer into the empty sink cupboard, then goes to sit down in the other room, listening as the kettle starts to boil.

No tea. Obviously. Or milk. Crap. He goes for a lie down on the bed instead. Closes the eyes, a heavy tiredness now come over him. A no unfamiliar situation. Careful. Just fucking be careful, my man.

He goes out later and finds a chip shop along the main road. Brings back a fish supper. Pretty decent, it turns out.

After sitting the mini television onto the table and fiddling about with it for a bit, he manages to get it up and running, and settles in to watch it. He should have minded to get napkins from the chip shop, because he's put grease marks over the settee, and he makes a note to wipe them off later. Nothing on the tellybox. Crap just. He gets up and goes to the window, looks out again at the city. It is still light outside, and he notices there's no blind. Another thing that will need sorting. Tomorrow, he can make a list or something. In that moment, the great grey expanse of the city stretching out in front of him, it feels all of it too much, and he leans forward to rest his head against the glass. He imagines Robbie and Craig stood there in the bare room, scrutinizing it. All of it, too much.

Ye battle on but. Ye battle on.

He keeps in and about the flat over the next couple of days. Staying busy. Going the messages for bread, milk, ham, beans, washing powder, loo roll. Normal things; normal people things. Then as well the wee chores: washing the clothes, getting them hung on the radiator and the back of the settee, cooking, washing up, pinning the pillowcase over the window. The evenings, he watches the television, eats, drinks a few cans.

On the third day, Beans comes round, the loudness of the entry buzzer surprising him as he's brushing his teeth, causing him to jab himself in the gums. He's at the bottom, the voice comes through the speaker, he needs pressing in. A surprise as well, Mick considers as he waits for him to come up the building, that he has minded the number.

He comes in and looks the place over from the doorway.

'How much is it, this?'

'Hundred and fifty.'

'Fucksake. Terrible.'

He goes up to the window and fingers with the pillowcase a moment, nods his head, then turns about. 'I'd go a cuppa.'

That day, and the next, they go up and down the high street spending his resettlement grant on bits and pieces for the flat. A broom, radio, hammer, nails, wire wool, a blind, bleach. He isn't too sure about the five packs of wire wool, but Beans is adamant it's an essential – keeps the mice out – so he gives in and buys it. He's keeping interested in all this, Beans, longer than he does most things. Possible that he is wanting to prove himself, let Robin see that he's no just some useless troublemaker. Mick is in the main room, investigating for gaps in the skirting boards, when there is the sound of something heavy scraping through in the kitchen. A moment later and Beans steps out, hands on hips.

'Place needs a paint, no think?'

The painting project begins the next day. Probably it isn't allowed in his contract, but so what, screw the landlord, no like he's going to do it himself, is it? Straight away, the place starts looking brighter. The radio on and a cold draught coming through the window, he starts in the main room while Beans gets stuck into the kitchen, his eyes red and squinting with concentration, specks of paint all over his hat and onto the kitchen counter. Mick grins, finishing round the window frame, at the idea of Beans as a neighbour. Knocking him up because he's run out of loo roll, giving it his wild stories, ear-biting him down the pub. No the worst thought, being honest.

It is Beans anyway that gets him acquainted with one of his own neighbours. They are coming out the lift on their way back into the flat, and there is a woman on the stairhead with a baby in a pram and a dog tied to one of the handles. Beans goes straight up to the dog.

'How's it going, big man, eh? How's it going?' He is bent down, patting the dog on the neck. 'He a Staff?'

'Yeh.' She snatches a look into the waiting lift.

Beans is pulling the dog's cheeks back roughly, no that it seems to mind.

'I had a Staff myself, a long while, I had him. He was a great dog. Walter. Like a fucking radiator, man – oh, pardon me.' He looks into the pram. 'True but. See that's how I called him Walter. Walter water bottle.'

She gives a smile, and presses the button as the lift doors close. Beans is moved onto the baby now though, waving at him with the big cabbage hands. 'Gonnae give me a smile, pal? Gonnae, eh?' It isn't looking likely. The baby is transfixed staring at the big red beardie face, trying to work him out, wondering if something frightening has happened to Santa Claus. The doors open again and she gets moving the pram inside.

'Nice to meet you,' Mick says, and she smiles briefly before the doors slide closed.

Awake, asleep, the awareness of Robbie and Craig presses on him all the time. What he would say to them. How their faces would look if they knew where he's been, where he is the now, that he is on benefits. One moment he is saying to himself: fuck it, I'm fixing this out, but then the next moment the whole weight of everything will be holding him powerless on the bed. Even if he was being offered jobs – and each week he goes up the jobcentre it is look-ing the more likely that it's never going to happen – how would he earn enough to pay the rent even? He wouldn't. And that's for a craphole like this. It would take years saving up for somewhere bet-ter. Just thinking about it makes him feel tired as hell, but he makes a deal with himself only to think about it when he's outside, on the move, and no when he's alone in the flat. Plus as well there's only one radiator in the place and it's pure nipping. So, when Beans isn't about, he spends whole afternoons taking these long walks, getting familiar with the local streets and grassy areas, turning it all over in his head.

How can you attack things full pelt when it's enough already just getting through the day-by-days? The way things have been, even the most wee things feel like an achievement, like he's winning. Shaving. Going the messages. Putting a blind up. They're effort enough as it is that the idea of getting those done and then saying – right, well, that's they sorted, now let's crack on for that warehouse job I've been passed over for five times already – it saps all the energy from him.

It's one of the things Renuka talks to him about when he sees her next. He takes a bus to meet her in a cafe for a chat about how he's getting on. She tells him he is at a contemplative stage of his Cycle of Change. A good thing, apparently. Important that he acts on it. Crucial. The next stage looming all the time over him. Does he feel ready? Almost, he tells her, his stomach dropping through his arse onto the bits of lasagne on the floor by his feet. Almost.

It is afternoon and him and Beans are sat in the flat watching television. Beans hasn't spoke in a while, and he is staring now at the adverts, scratching the backs of his hands, his eyes bloodshot, unreadable.

'Ye crabbit, eh?'

Beans ignores him.

'Hey, you,' Mick grins, digging him in the leg. 'Ye crabbit or something?'

He stands up suddenly. 'This is keech, let's go the pub, eh?'

'Sure. Okay.'

The nearest pub is a walk. Beans seems to know well enough where he's headed, and they walk on past the high street, down a couple of quiet residentials.

'I'm on the bell,' Beans says when they arrive, going up to the bar while Mick gets sat at a corner table. The place is quiet. A couple of men playing pool in a small room on the far side, and four regulars on barstools who eye Beans silently as he counts the smash in his hands and asks the barman what the pool table takes.

Mick watches as he goes and puts his coin on the table, the pool players exchanging glances as he does it.

They drink quietly for a bit, Mick staring at the slumped backs of the regulars and the tattered silver Christmas decorations drooping off the gantry. After a bit, he turns toward Beans.

'Know that dog ye were talking about – Walter – when was it ye had him?'

'Jesus, cannae mind.'

Mick takes a drink.

'What was it recent, like?'

'Eh?'

'The dog, was it a long while ago or was it recent?'

'Christ, a long while.' He stretches his neck round to look behind him. 'Fucksake, they no done yet?'

One of the pool players is walking back to the room with a couple of pints.

'What happened to him?'

'Copped his whack, didn't he.'

'Sorry, I didnae mean –'

'Fine. Fine. He was old, he'd done his stretch. I was in this place anyway, I had to give him up, they wouldnae allow dogs.' He turns round again. 'See that? Fucking kidding me?' He pushes his chair back and gets marching toward the pool room, where the two men are racking up for a new game. Mick sits watching, as if through a haze, a dream, the two men standing close together with their pool cues propped on the floor, Beans shouting, he can't make out what over the Christmas pop music. This song, he minds the video, the English comedian and the blonde lassie, what was her name? A line of angled heads at the bar, and Beans bent over the pool table, scattering the balls. Kim Wilde. That's her. Whatever happened to Kim Wilde? Beans away now out the pub doors. The barstool men slowly turning to look at him instead . . . *the Christmas tree, have a happy holiday. Everyone dancing merrily* . . . no these fuckers, serious, look at them. Jesus. He stands up. Gets gone.

Beans is already off down the pavement.

'Hey, wait up. Wait up a moment.'

But he's away. On the march. A cloud of breath above his head. Mick hurries behind, calling out, all the way to the high street. A bus pulling up – Beans makes a run toward it and hops on.

For the next couple of weeks Beans is even more unpredictable with his visits. He comes round twice, briefly, without any announcement, but then over Christmas he is there almost every day. They buy a chicken. Sprouts, tatties, superlager. They fix up a proper feast for Christmas day and fall asleep blootered in front of the television.

He makes Renuka a tea while she sits at the table and looks about the room.

'It looks good in here,' she says when he comes through with the mugs.

'Better, eh? Keith has been helping me get the place fixed out.'

'Good. Actually, that's something I was hoping to ask you about. Keith's key worker wanted to know if he's been round at all. His depression has been quite bad of late, and he's been absent from the hostel a few times. How has he seemed to you?'

'Fine, fine. Normal. He's been a great help, being honest.' He decides no to tell her about the business in the pub.

'Okay, good, I'll let Robin know.' She clasps her hands around her mug. 'So, you said last time that you'd been thinking about us being in touch with Missing People. Have you given any more thought to it?'

He takes a drink of tea and rests the mug on the table.

'Ye might say that, aye.'

40

He is there early, even with the traffic. Time enough for a wee set-
tler before he arrives. It is a big place, pretty empty the now in the
quiet after lunchtime. One of these bright-lit chain affairs, low leather settees around low tables. He gets sat on one of the few normal
table and chairs, near the middle of the room, facing the entrance.
A couple of business types in suits are stood at the bar, drinking
lagers and talking loudly. Mick takes a sip of his half. His giro isn't
due until tomorrow, and he's spent almost the last of his money on
new shoes and trousers. He didn't consider it. The thought then of
Robbie having to buy the drinks. Alarm starting to race through
him again and it's a few minutes before he can get it under control.

He continues to drink slowly. A pure battle no to neck the thing
but he manages to keep nursing it, while the businessmen move
onto the spirits and the bar staff have a short argument what music
to put on, and so he isn't anywhere near as well on as he'd want to
be when, early himself, Robbie walks in.

He hasn't seen him. He's gone straight to the bar, standing in
next to the businessmen and saying something to the barmaid. Mick
stays sat. He looks the other way, toward a television screen with no
sound because all you can hear is the music that is playing over the
speakers. He cannot move; his whole body is turned to mince. On
the screen there is a wee video of footballers on a training field and
the rolling news underneath – the big story from the English League
One is that the Carlisle United manager is for the chop and another
guy is lined up already for the hot seat. He turns around. Robbie is
coming toward him. A pint in his hand, approaching the table.

'Robbie.' He tries to get standing up but he is rooted.

Robbie stands on the other side of the table, looking at him. His
face – he sits down and Mick cannot look at it so he fixes his gaze on
his hands instead, resting flat on the table. How steady they are, his
son's hands.

'How are ye, Rob?'

He knots his own hands together around his pint, and they look like an ale jug, one of they old-fashioned type of ale jugs. A stupit thought to have the now. Stupit. Will he no speak? Is he going to sit there without speaking for the whole duration, however long that will be, the duration, perhaps a fucking lifetime? Mick glances up at him. He is greeting. No bucketfuls, but his face is tightened and the eyes are welled up, and Mick has to look away – will Rafael Nadal overcome his knee injury in time for the Australian Open? At the moment, his chances aren't looking too rosy.

'I don't know what to say to you.'

'Ye don't have to say anything, son.'

The two businessmen are away, one of them laughing and putting the arm around the other's shoulders a moment, then withdrawing it, clapping the hands together. Off blottoed back to the office for an afternoon's work. He looks at Robbie, who is watching them leave.

'I'm sorry, Rob.'

There is silence as they take a moment to consider each from their own side of the table how pathetic it sounds.

Robbie turns back toward him.

'What, were you homeless, Da?'

'If that's the word.'

'What else is the word?'

'No, well, it's that one, aye.'

'Mean, you were on the street?'

'Some of the time.'

'Jesus.' He is staring now at the table. 'Didn't you think I would've helped you?'

'I know ye would, son. I know.'

Robbie is screwing his eyes, scowling. 'We didn't know if you were alive. Most of them thought you were dead.'

He hasn't drunk any of his pint.

'I sent a letter.'

'Oh, yeh, your letter. Suddenly I get this letter and me and Alan are come to stay in fucking Heathrow for a month but nobody there knows where you are either, only that you were calling yourself Mick Provan and you got the sack.'

247

The barmaid is coming toward them. She is carrying a large black drinks tray which she sets down on the edge of their table, and picks up Mick's empty glass to put on it. She hovers by them for an instant, looking like she's about to say something, until she seems to clock that the atmosphere's no the best and she walks away.

'Alan was with you, then?'

Robbie shakes his head slowly. 'Fuck off, Da. He's been bloody great. Do you know it's him that was paying the rent arrears after you abandoned the house?'

He closes his eyes, or the elastic has went. His insides are turned to liquid, the bones alone holding himself on the chair, somehow. How is that? How are they holding him on the chair still? He was fixing things out. He was out the hostel and into a flat and he was fixing things out. He opens his eyes; sits upright in the seat. The thought comes to him suddenly that he is glad he hasn't shat himself.

He tries to say something but no words come.

'Do you understand what I'm saying? Craig's there telling him to –'

'Robbie,' he interrupts him, 'look, I'm sorry but, mean I don't think I can hear all this the now. I'm sorry.'

'What? What is it not a good time or something?' Robbie stands up. 'You're right.' His voice is shaking. 'You're right.'

He steps out from the table and tucks his chair back under. Then he turns, and starts to walk away.

He stays there, sitting. The bar is empty. After a few minutes the music is turned up loud, no paying customers left for the bar staff to worry about, only one old guy on his own sat staring at the sports news.

The rest of the afternoon is a wipeout. The door locked; television on. Renuka and Beans no calling round, or if they do he doesn't notice.

He is in and out of sleep the night, the television on in the background, an educational programme he tries to get listening to, occupy the mind – how does the criminal justice system work? – it's boring enough but it doesn't knock him out, and he lies there gazing at the spasm of blue light on the ceiling.

The next morning he is stood in the kitchen waiting for the toaster to finish when the entry buzzer goes. It is Renuka.
She comes in and sits with him at the table.
'I spoke to Robbie yesterday evening. I gather things were difficult.'
'They were.'
'It isn't going to be easy, obviously, as we said before.'
He nods.
'He's quite keen though, your son, to keep trying.'
'Ye think?'
'Well, yes – he's sat in a cafe down the road waiting for me to call him. He wanted to come straight here, but I told him I needed to speak to you first.'
She is smiling but he turns his face away from her. Out the window, it is started snowing.
'What did he say?'
'He just said that you both need to keep trying.'
He looks round at the tiny room: the unmade bed and the child-like paintings on the wall above it.
'I don't know I'm ready, Renuka.'
She is nodding. 'I know. The thing is though, if you leave it like this, things will only be more difficult the next time.'

She is right. They will. Plus as well the boy lives on the other side the world, so nay doubt he'll need to be going back anytime soon; and he is reminded again with a crawing of the stomach that he has come away from his family for this, for ten minutes in a chain bar and the da to tell him he's no wanting to see him still.

'The stupit thing is, I was that bloody terrified going there, I just needed to see him the more.'

She is nodding again. Patient as ever. Plotting where all this puts him on his Cycle of Change; or thinking he's a bastard just, who knows?

He comes in the flat with Renuka and stands in the doorway looking at him.

'Robbie. Come in. Want a cup of tea? Renuka?'

Robbie and Renuka wipe the slush off their feet and go in the main room while he takes the kettle over to the sink to fill it up. He can hear him treading through in the other room, inspecting, judging. Renuka telling him that it's his father that's fixed the place up, with the blinds, the paint job, and Robbie keeping quiet; whatever he's doing in there he's no saying anything about it.

He moves the television onto the floor and they sit down all three of them around the table. Get drinking their teas.

'So,' says Renuka, 'I can be here, or not be here – just tell me which you'd prefer.'

'No,' Robbie says, 'stay. It's fine. Yes?'

He nods.

'Look, Da, yesterday – I didn't mean to be difficult. Just there's things I don't understand.'

'Aye, course.'

'I don't know where to start.'

'No, me neither.'

Robbie is looking at the art work on the wall above the bed.

'You an alcoholic, Da?'

'No.'

Renuka is keeping quiet. It would look better, he realizes, if there weren't the empty cans of superlager on the floor by the bin.

'Just I don't understand how it's happened. If I'd known how things were, I would've stayed. Course I fucking would. Why didn't you say anything? I've felt that fucking guilty.'

'Christ, it's no your fault, Robbie, I didnae know any of this would happen. I should've answered your calls, you're right. Things got on top of me just.'

'Know you've lost the tenancy now? Alan couldn't keep paying it forever.'

He is glaring at him. Challenging him. Mick keeks down at his tea. The mug is chipped already. Pound-shop tollie, what do ye expect?

'I'm no going back, son, if that's what ye mean.'

A long period of silence. Much tea drinking. Renuka glancing from one to the other of them, weighing up when is the right time to step in.

'That's another thing I don't understand,' Robbie says finally.

He waits for him to go on, but he is gone quiet, looking at the table.

'What's that? What ye no understand?'

'That's where she is.'

He looks up, but the face isn't angry, he just looks horrendously fucking sad, which of course sticks the boot on a hundred times worse; and, together with it, he is seized with a feeling of desperate closeness to the boy, of wanting to be close to him.

'That's how I couldnae be there, Robbie.'

There is another stretch of quiet, broken again by Robbie. 'See, even if I can get understanding it, I can tell you for sure, Craig won't.'

Renuka is giving him a pitying look and it seems at that moment like she's about to put her hand on his. He withdraws it, gets it under the table.

'He knows he didn't act right, Da. Neither of you did. When I was staying with him, he said that. But then when you didn't come back, it – he – it was too much for him, I think.'

'Yous two come to blows?'

Robbie gives a wee smile. 'You might say that.'

There is obviously more but Robbie has cloyed up, gazing out the damp window.

'Either of you go another cup of tea?'

Robbie shakes his head. 'No. Thanks. I think we should call it a day for now, okay?'

'Right.'

They all stand up.

'Where ye staying?'

'I'm in a hotel in King's Cross. My flight's booked for next week. I can't leave them any longer.'

Renuka stays in the main room as he steps with Robbie to the door.

'I am glad to see you, you know,' Robbie says, and moves to put his arms about him. Mick comes forward uneasily. It is awkward and odd, being touched, and he stiffens up immediately. He can feel Robbie's chin on his shoulder. After a few seconds, they pull back, and Mick is about to say that he is sorry but he stops himself. He worries how he smells.

'I'll call round again tomorrow, okay? You should get a phone.'

He comes early the next afternoon. They sit on the tiny settee drinking coffee with the television on in the background. There is too much that needs saying to be able to say a lot, so they keep fairly quiet. He does anyway. Robbie is more conversational, if that's the word for it – more an interrogation, which it seems at times he's trying to hold himself back from but he can't; all these questions that he needs answers for. Why didn't he tell anybody he was leaving? Why did he go to London? What happened at the hotel? Why did he write the letter and then not make contact again, even when he was homeless?

If there were straight answers that he could give, then it would be easier. Why *did* he go to London? Why did he do any of it? Christ knows. He needs to be fair but, to be open, so he attempts to tell him at least some of what he's asking, even if he is light on the details.

Later on they try again going for a pint. They give a bye to the bearpit up the way, and walk a while longer in the other direction until they come to a decent-looking place next to a private gardens that is white with a covering of untouched snow. His giro is come and he's able to get the round in. Robbie of course is quick enough asking him how he's living, so he tells him. Whatever he thinks about it, he keeps it to himself. A few others in. A couple of old English boys in ties and blazers. There are things that Robbie wants to tell him: how it's been, all this time without knowing where he was. He was staying with Craig at first, he says, but then it got too much and he rented a temporary place for himself. Eventually he had to go back to Australia. His job. The family. Mick is wanting to ask him about Jenna and Damien, but he can't bring himself to. Before he returned, Robbie tells him, he went down to Newcastle, wondering if maybe that's where he'd went. Trying to dig out anybody he might have worked with; persuading landlords and bookies to let him put up these posters that the charity had printed. The rare time he did find anybody that minded him – how he had to explain the whole story to them about what had happened.

He doesn't want to hear any of this but he knows he has to let him say it. He certainly doesn't ask who it was Robbie found that used to know him. The thought of his mugshot up in a string of pub lobbies, there for every bevvy-merchant to have a gawp at – it's no exactly something he wants to get thinking about.

That evening, when they come back from the pub, he overhears Robbie in the kitchen, talking on his mobile phone. The tap is on while he washes up the plates from their curry carry-out, and Mick is through in the main room with the television on, but he can hear well enough.

'. . . he's got this flat, he's . . . Yeh, I know, I know, but I want to . . . No, it's fine . . . No, he's on benefits.'

The tap is turned off then and Robbie is saying goodbye. He turns the television up louder. Afterward, when Robbie has left, he wonders if he had meant him to hear.

The following morning, Robbie comes round with a new telephone in a cardboard box. As they get opening it, Robbie says that he's spoke to Alan. He wants to come down and see him. Mick keeps quiet and concentrates on the box as he is told this.

'Don't worry. I told him it's too soon. He can wait, but you're going to have to see him sometime, with all he's done.'

'Aye, I know,' he says, even though there's absolutely nay fucking chance in hell he's ever going to let that meeting happen. 'And Craig?'

'I've spoken to him, yes.'

'Doesn't want to see me, eh?'

'He's relieved we've found you, Da.'

'Right.'

'He is.' He puts down a handful of phone entrails. 'He's going to find it difficult that you don't want to be in Glasgow, like I said.'

They get on with taking wires and parts out of the box, arranging them on the floor, and they let the subject go quiet. One thing's for sure: these telephone manufacturers don't like making life simple. Even the phone isn't a phone yet: it's in blocks of plastic that need fitting together. Robbie gets reading through the instructions leaflet, and Mick is started on screwing the handset together, when the buzzer goes. He gets up and answers it. Beans. For a split second he considers telling him it's no a good time, but then the great cargo of guilt that he's carrying everywhere is straight away weighing upon him, and he changes his mind.

This is the first he's seen him in a while. A nervousness builds as he waits for him to come up the lift that he won't be sober, that his clothes will be clatty. He has told Robbie that there is a guy he's known, who helped him when he was on the street, but the most he's said when Robbie's asked what like he is, is that he's from Paisley and he's something of a queer ticket.

Beans is puzzled at first that there is somebody else in the flat.

'This is my son, Robbie.'

'Yer son? Oh, right. How's it going?' He puts a hand out, and Robbie shakes it. 'Keith. Ye come to stay?'

Robbie glances over at Mick, understanding then that Beans obvious isn't up to speed with the situation.

'I'm here visiting for the next couple of days. I'm stopped in a hotel in King's Cross.'

Beans is giving him a quizzical look.

'Where ye from? You an islander?'

Robbie grins. 'Naw. Govan.'

Beans doesn't look convinced. 'That's a strange accent ye've got. I'm no being rude.'

Mick stands in the kitchen doorway, observing the pair of them.

'No, don't worry, my wife tells me the same. I've been living in Australia for ten years, that's how I sound like this.'

Beans laughs. 'I knew it. I knew there was something strange about you. What's all this?' He has spotted the dismembered phone next to its box and is going toward it. 'See me, I'm good with telephones.'

He gets immediately trying to put the thing together. With no little success either. Making Robbie see him over the different coloured wires and screwdriver heads, demonstrating how it's done. Robbie is clear intrigued by the guy. Right from the kick-off there is an easiness between them, which in fact shouldn't be too surprising: he's pretty straight down the line like that, Robbie, takes people as he finds them.

The phone is fixed out in no time. Robbie gives it a call off his mobile phone to check it works. It does. He is connected. He is attainable 24/7 and nay excuses. Robbie notices then that he has a message from Jenna and he goes in the kitchen to make them a cup of tea and get reading it.

'Who's Jenna?' Beans asks when he's gone out the room.

'His wife. They've a wean too, a toddler.'

Beans goes quiet a moment, thinking.

'He come over to see your flat, then?'

'No exactly.' He may as well tell him the score. 'Turns out I've been on this missing persons list for quite a while. They were looking for me.'

Beans is nodding slowly. 'That's good. They've found ye. That's very good.'

The last two days of Robbie's stay pass quickly. The temperature is dipped to freezing but he's bought a new two-bar heater and they keep most of the time to the flat, or the pub, Beans joining them for a pint but keeping on pretty good behaviour. The last afternoon, when Beans goes off, they get wrapped up and go on a long walk, at one point passing the subway station, Mick keeping quiet as they move by. It is good, being around him; he enjoys his company, always has. Strange how you forget. No that it's perfect but.

Obviously. There's moments when he can feel Robbie is gone quiet and he knows that he's thinking about things, withdrawing from him. Fair enough but. Fair enough. Robbie doesn't bring it up but he knows that he is missing the family, and from what he can tell when he's talking to Jenna in the kitchen, she's feeling the same way.

The morning of his flight, they sit in a cafe along the high street eating ham, egg and chips. Robbie says he wants him to come over to Australia for Easter.

'I've talked to Jenna about it. It was her idea, actually.'

Mick looks up at him without speaking. Robbie's got that face on him that says he's ready for a fight if one is needed.

'That's kind of you, son. See but –'

'I'm paying for your flight.'

He shakes his head. 'It'll cost a fortune.'

'I know. Tell me about it. But you can't afford it and I'd be paying the fare to come over here anyway. And this way you'll see Jenna and Damien.'

Hard to argue with that, but he tries.

'See, I'm no long in the flat yet, is the thing. I don't know if I'm allowed.'

'I've spoken to your key worker and she says it's fine.'

He winces at Robbie using the word.

'Fucking hell. Da, I'm only talking about a couple of weeks, it's not like I'm asking you to come out and live with us.'

'No, course, I know that. Just it's a big thing, is all. I'll need to think about it.'

It is decided but, and he knows it.

The next few days he is thinking about it constantly, sitting in the flat or on one of the afternoon walks, worrying. Guilt, money, the whole caboodle. An agity excitement that breaks through but when he imagines being there. Seeing the grandwean – although of course he understands well enough that part of that is because Damien is too young to understand any of what's happened. Unlike his maw. He is nervous about the thought of seeing her, what she must think, all this time that Robbie has been gone from them because of him. If he could be employed by then, it would be easier. Obviously he couldn't afford the flight still, but maybe he wouldn't feel like such a bloody leech – he'd be able to pay for things when he's out there. It isn't looking too rosy though, the job search. It's enough of a struggle convincing them that he is a reliable, time-keeping, non-bevvied type of individual, let alone that he's qualified for anything. He goes into the office and sits waiting for his turn, never with the least expectation any more that anything will come of it.

One afternoon when he is returned from a hailstorm, there is a flashing red light on the telephone. It takes him a while retrieving the message, but when he has, it is Robbie, saying that he's wanting to speak to him so he'll call back later the evening.

When he rings again, Mick is in the middle of cooking tea. He turns the grill down and wipes the grease off his hands before going through to answer.

'Craig is coming,' Robbie says.

'Eh?'

'Craig. He's coming over here for Easter.'

There is silence on the line.

Jenna probably in behind, listening.

'Da? You hear what I said?'

'He know I'm coming?'

'He does. He needed a bit of arm-bending, but he's coming.'

. . .

'Da, it'll be fine.'

'The Highlanders as well?'

He can hear Robbie chuckling. 'No. It'll just be us.'

He goes on to explain the arrangements: where he'll be staying, the food they're going to eat, the trip down the coast they've got planned with Jenna's sister and her own baby. He doesn't take much of it in. Robbie says that he'll call again next week when he's booked the flights. He puts the phone down and goes back through the kitchen to get the grill turned off. The tops of his hash browns are burnt, but he plates them up as they are, with sausages, beans, and goes to sit down at the table and eat, as the hail starts up again outside, tapping and scratching against the window.

42

He is on the bus, the top deck, looking out for any signs of a toy shop. He'd tried down the high street but with no luck, so he decided instead to get a bus into the centre. Even now though, it's no looking likely. He gets down the stair and steps off. Wanders up a busy shopping street for a long time – clothes stores, fried-chicken shops, pharmacies, junk stalls – nothing. In the end, without any particular thought, he goes into a sports superstore.

It is a massive warehouse-type shop floor, mobbed out with swivel rails of trackie bottoms and luminous shirts. There isn't much of an order about it, and he has quite a difficulty getting through, squeezing between the huge bulging roundabouts of all this noticeably unsporty-looking clothing.

In one corner, where football and rugby boots are displayed on a wall, he finds a giant basket full of mini footballs. He rummles about through them on the off chance there's a Rangers one, but course it's all Chelsea and Tottenham and Man United, although he does eventually find a plain one, no team markings on it. Probably it isn't the best present for a toddler, but it's no bad. No bad at all. He decides he'll get it, and looks up the way, trying to plot a route through to wherever it is he has to pay. Radio station music playing loudly through giant corner speakers. A shop-assistant boy bent over, bundling up fallen heaps of shirts from the floor. Snooker cues, mounted on the wall like rifles. He snakes his way through, moving past the shop assistant. The clink of metal hangers going onto the rail – and an image comes into his head, distinct, vivid, the wife shopping. Out of nowhere. He puts a hand out to hold the rail, disorientated, needing to sit down. A buffit-step type thing by the wall, next to three cardboard cut-out snooker players with their arms folded, serious looks on their faces. He parks down on it and closes his eyes. Tries to hold on to the image. He can see it clearly. She is fingering through a line of tops, swivelling the rail around.

Her face. It is a study of concentration, looking down with a frown, a wee double chin pressing against her throat. Pulling out and discarding the tops back into the wrong place on the rail. He has started greeting. The suddenness of it. An overwhelming feeling of emptiness that he lets come over him, and he stays sat there a long time, minutes, hours maybe, fuck knows.

He opens his eyes. The cardboard snooker players stood around him and the shop assistant looking over, a grimace of confusion on his face. Probably he doesn't even know he's doing it. He gets up and wipes the eyes, gives the boy a wee smile. 'Don't worry, pal, I'm away the now.' And he gets walking off, squeezing hard on the mini football, to see if there's any tills through this bloody jungle.

It is going to be another hot day. Already there are people putting up parasols and windbreakers on the beach, arranging cool boxes and pulling down trousers. There is not much wind yet, but the light breeze that comes off the sea is welcome as he jogs along the uncrowded promenade, past hot-dog vans and ice-cream stalls whose shutters are now being opened and awnings stretched out.

Where the promenade angles toward the town, he turns away onto the beach. He wipes his forehead, looking out over the sea: small still boats moored in the harbour, gently flapping banners mounted on buoys to advertise sea trips, hotels, the amusement arcade. The pleasing crunch of pebbles under his trainers. He continues down the beach, enjoying the stillness of the early morning. Seagulls. Waves sucking back through the shingle. A circle of pensioners doing knee lifts. Further on, along the base of the high wall – above which a line of bars and clubs looks out onto the sea – there is plenty of evidence of the previous night: broken pint glasses, cigarettes, fish-and-chip wrappings, a belt. He smiles, stepping up his pace as the beach arcs round and a long stretch of coastline comes into view – the pier jutting into the ocean, and, in the distance where the beach has ended, miles and miles of rocks and landslips and high, windswept farmland.

He has a sweat on now, continuing along the base of the town wall. He approaches a part of the beach where the pebbles thin out to reveal small patches of sand. On one of these, a short way ahead of him, there is a body reclined against the wall. He begins to swerve around it, keeping the same speed, until he is almost alongside, at which point he slows, turning to look at the man. Something unnatural about the way his body is positioned. Bent double; unmoving. It is fairly common on his Sunday-morning runs to see late-night revellers passed out on the beach, but this man is clearly homeless; that much is obvious from the state of his clothes. He is wearing no shoes or socks and his feet are hugely swollen and purple, a dirty red woollen hat pulled down over his face, which is bruised and bloodshot, a pink scar running down his cheek and neck and under his coat. He stops, just for a moment, and then begins again into a jog, following the brief wet curve of sand over a stream before it turns again to pebbles, and he continues on towards the pier, where the dim drone and convulsing lights of the amusement arcade have already started up.

Acknowledgements

I would like to thank Mary Mount and Peter Straus, my editor and my agent, for making it easy, even the difficult bits. Also to Joe Pickering, Jenny Hewson, and everybody else at Penguin and RCW, all of whom I feel very fortunate to work with.

For his early advice on the book that I thought this would be, thank you to Paul Chambers, and for what it did become, to Corin Pilling at the Cardinal Hume Centre, and Simon Hughes, together with all the staff and residents at St Mungo's Mare Street.

I am grateful to Bruce Biddulph for all that you shared with me, and to John Dolan and Jim Moohan of GMB for your willingness to help with my research. Furthermore, and especially, to Jimmy Cloughley and all at Clydebank Asbestos Group, whose aid and advice continue to support so many of the victims of asbestos and their families.

To my family, and the Tiptons; to David Vann (who had the idea for the title); and, more than anybody else, to Tips. Some of this book comes, however indirectly, from you. And thank you for helping me to make it better, even down to the bloody acknowledgements.

To Dream Again

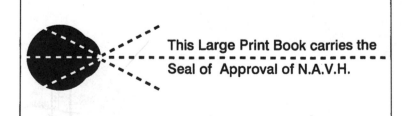

This Large Print Book carries the
Seal of Approval of N.A.V.H.

To Dream Again

Sally John

Thorndike Press • Waterville, Maine

Published in 2002 by arrangement with Crossway Books, a division of Good News Publishers

Thorndike Press Large Print Christian Romance Series.

The tree indicium is a trademark of Thorndike Press.

The text of this Large Print edition is unabridged.
Other aspects of the book may vary from the original edition.

Set in 16 pt. Plantin by Myrna S. Raven.

Printed in the United States on permanent paper.

Library of Congress Cataloging-in-Publication Data

John, Sally D., 1951–
    To dream again / Sally John.
        p. cm.
    ISBN 0-7862-4088-1 (lg. print : hc : alk. paper)
    1. Drug traffic — Fiction.   2. San Diego (Calif.) —
Fiction.   3. Large type books.   I. Title.
PS3560.O323 T6 2002
    813′.54—dc21   2001057797

To my children,
Elizabeth and Christopher

This one is for you, kiddos,
with gratitude for the memories of girls'
basketball and a green truck,
and for filling my world with more delight
than I ever could have imagined

He heals the brokenhearted
and binds up their wounds.

Psalm 147:3, NEW INTERNATIONAL
VERSION

Prologue

Terror flooded her dream, then spilled out into the night.

Cat St. Clair bolted awake and jerked upright, flinging aside the tangled covers.

She quickly flipped on the bedside lamp, picked up the cordless phone, grasped the pillow, and clutched it to her side. It was a familiar routine, finished almost before her eyelids opened.

Her heart pounded. She gulped for air and pulled at the neck of the clingy nightshirt damp with perspiration. With a sweeping glance she inspected the now brightly lit corners of her bedroom. Through the open door a dim light assured her that the shadowy, hulking form had fled the apartment.

Again.

She punched all but the last digit of a phone number, then stopped.

He would only say, with just a hint of a sigh, "Catherine, this is becoming tiresome."

If he answered.

The last time, he hadn't answered. At

7

3:16 A.M. he hadn't answered his phone.

The time before that, someone else answered. At 2:30 in the morning a feminine voice had answered his telephone.

Cat shuddered and took a deep breath. The time before that, he said it was becoming tiresome.

She pushed the OFF button and laid the phone on the nightstand next to the clock radio. It was 3:53. Hugging the pillow with both arms, she scooted down and curled up under the covers, her face toward the open doorway. Slow, gentle tears meandered sideways down her cheeks.

Tiresome, yes, but less often also. That was a fact to hold onto, a fact that promised she would get through this.

Thankfully, she never remembered the nightmare's details, only a sense of having been pursued by a large, vague, dark form. She shuddered again.

Think about work! Think about work . . .

Yes, that would do it. She would plan her day at the motel.

The new employee was coming, a temp to fill in as second-shift maintenance supervisor. First on the agenda would be to introduce him to the staff, show him around, give him keys . . . No, first she should go in early and work on the budget. Then there was that ongoing tiff between some of the Housekeeping ladies. She'd better get them together and take care of it soon. What about the paint order?

She yawned and continued the mental checklist. Her eyelids soon grew heavy in the bright light.

One

Dominick stopped dead in his tracks just inside the small office. His heartbeat ricocheted violently. It felt as if ice pulsated through him, then burst out into droplets of cold sweat.

The young woman sitting behind the desk was her.

No two ways about it.

The nameless stranger now rising to greet him was the one he had been searching for, the one he wanted so desperately to meet.

But not now. Not here.

She smiled at him. "Hi." The corners of her eyes crinkled.

He hesitated. Those eyes were what he remembered most vividly, and even at this distance he saw that his memory had not conjured the image. They were like sunlight dancing through honey.

She stretched her hand toward him across the desk. "You must be Dominick D'Angelo." She grinned. "Did I pronounce that correctly? Dee-ANN-je-lo?"

She didn't recognize him. The thumping panic in his chest ebbed, and he stepped forward. With a slight cough, he loosened his vocal cords. "Uhh, yes, that's it." Her handshake was firm. "Nice to meet you, Miss, uh . . ." He tilted his head to read the brass name plaque beneath his arm. ". . . Catherine St. Clair."

"Thank you. Please, have a seat — and call me Cat." She sat back down.

In spite of his still-tense nerves, Dominick automatically slipped into his professional mode as he settled into one of the two armchairs facing her desk. *Name association.* "Cat. As in the curious one?"

She chuckled and shook her head. "I hope not. Actually, the nickname stuck because apparently I napped and purred away my preschool years. Easiest kid in Poway history."

"That's a community just up the freeway, right?"

"Right, about twenty minutes. I take it you're not from the area?"

"No."

"Well, welcome to San Diego, and welcome to your new job at Castillo de Cala."

He noted her perfect Spanish accent. *Castee-yo day cah-lah.*

"Castle by the Cove." She spread her hands in an arc as if encompassing the whole property that lay beyond her office

11

walls. "The most fun family vacation motel you'll find on Mission Bay. Will you excuse me for just a sec?" She swiveled in her chair to face a computer that sat atop a credenza behind her desk. "If I don't finish up a few figures here, I'll lose track."

"No problem." He took a silent deep breath, gave his shoulders an internal shake, and started cataloging.

There was a faint citrus-like scent in the air. Her perfume. Her hair was a dark brown with hints of a deep reddish hue. Chestnut. It fell to just below her collar in a casual, layered cut. She wore a short-sleeved, white silk blouse that set off her lightly tanned arms. An expensive-looking pale green jacket hung on the back of the leather chair. Gold watch, oversized face. One ring, right hand, dark red stone. Garnet? Focusing beyond her shoulder, he saw that what looked like a spreadsheet filled the computer screen as her fingers tapped across the keyboard.

He surveyed the office. Small — just long enough to accommodate two chairs inside the open door, just wide enough to walk around one side of the broad, oak desk. Walls papered in muted shades of beige stripes. Infusing that light citrus fragrance were whiffs of warm, sea-scented air that drifted through two open windows behind the computer. They framed a patch of blue sky and flat-leafed subtropical plants.

In the ceiling above the desk was a covered attic opening. He thought of the architectural design of the place. True to its name, the Castillo resembled a castle with its stone walls. It even had two imitation turrets. This office was in a corner of the lobby building, so one of the turrets must be right above them.

The desktop was neatly organized. The only personal items besides the name plaque were a fat, glazed pot that held pens, a pink camellia floating in a crystal bowl, and a green bottle of S. Pellegrino sparkling water.

Cat swiveled back around, her quick eyes catching his. "Well, did I give you enough time to get over the shock?"

His breath caught, and he forced a word past the heartbeat that had jumped into his throat. "Shock?"

Her chuckle was low, like the clear, confident alto voice. "I won't hold it against you. I see that look on a lot of faces. I go through this with everyone new to the staff. No one expects me to be the assistant manager because I'm not at least fifty years old and I'm not a man. All right, here goes."

Again his momentary panic subsided. She

was still unaware of who he was. What must have been his startled expression only implied to her that he hadn't expected his new boss to be a young woman.

She folded her hands on the desktop, her direct eye contact holding his attention. "As assistant manager, I answer to Ron Hunter, the manager who hired you. He answers to the real bosses, the owners. If there's something you're not comfortable discussing with me, I don't mind if you talk to Ron. But I prefer that we communicate directly as much as possible, especially when we work together." She smiled. A dimple in her left cheek deepened. "Which we're scheduled to do Tuesdays through Saturdays, 3 to 11 P.M." She raised her eyebrows, waiting for a response.

He lifted a shoulder and felt a grin tug at his mouth. A genuine grin that he didn't hold back. "Well, what can I say to such a disarming invitation? I look forward to answering directly and only to you, Miss St. Clair."

There was a knock on the open door behind him. He turned to see a petite, longhaired blonde walk in, clapping her hands.

"Bravo! Can we keep him, Cat?"

Cat smiled. "I think so. He did answer

well, didn't he? Dominick, this is Cissy Owens, front desk manager. Cissy, meet our new temporary maintenance jack-of-all-trades, second shift. And it's pronounced dee-ANN-je-lo."

"D'Angelo." The young woman kissed her fingertips in the gesture of a chef. "Umm, sounds like a pasta dish I'd order in a restaurant. A particularly delicious pasta dish. No offense."

"None taken." He stood and shook her hand. "Nice to meet you."

"Likewise." She squeezed his hand a moment longer than necessary and batted long black lashes over her green eyes. "Welcome aboard, Dominick D'Angelo. So, are you married, engaged, or otherwise involved with a significant other?"

"Cissy," Cat intervened, "you really beat around the bush too much. Try to get right to the point. Did you come in here for a reason?"

"Oh yeah, Trent called. He said he'll be here at 5:30."

Cat's eyes closed briefly. "Thanks."

Cissy nudged her elbow into his ribs. "Well?"

He winked down at her. "No, no, and no." *Fact. On all three counts. No wife, no fiancée, no one special. Uninvolved.*

"Really? Not even a semi-significant other?"

He shook his head. "Not even."

"So nice meeting you, Dominick." Cissy took a backward step toward the door. "So very, very nice."

Cat wadded up a piece of paper and whizzed it past his ear. "Go!"

"I'm gone!" Her spiked heels clicked as they hit the hallway's rustic stone tile.

Cat grinned. "As you can see, we're extremely professional here. Please, sit back down." Her eyes shifted again toward the door. "Tara!" She jumped up and hurried around her desk to embrace a little girl who had walked in. "How was Sea World?"

"It was awesome!"

A breathless woman arrived at the door. "I'm sorry, Miss St. Clair. She couldn't wait —"

"No, no, it's all right. If my door is open, you're always welcome to come inside."

The small girl tugged at her arm and held out a paper bag. "I got something for you."

Dominick settled back into his chair and watched Cat's interchange with what appeared to be motel guests. Her features were striking. Her mouth, now a circle of surprise, was wide, expressive beneath broad cheekbones. The teeth were shiny white,

16

straight. Probably full of braces at one time.

She was as tall as he remembered, maybe five-nine or ten, the top of her head about level with his shoulder. The hair was different, though, of that he was sure. No bouncing ponytail. She looked feminine in the silk blouse and pale green, straight knee-length skirt and low pumps, but it wasn't a delicate femininity. There was a solidity about her. Healthy, athletic . . . like someone you'd find on a Wheaties box.

"Bye!" Cat waved a black and white stuffed animal as the visitors left, then shut the door and leaned against it, smiling. "I'm sorry. Where were we?"

Her eyes rested on his face, and for a split second his mind stalled again. He had once held a honey jar up to the sunlight, trying to recapture that color. *Dear God, I can't do this.* "Uhh, I was saying I'll be glad to answer to you even though you're female and under age fifty."

"That's all the further we got?" Sighing in an exaggerated manner, she walked back around the desk and sat down. "At least you're getting paid for this time. Why don't you tell me what you learned from the manager so I won't repeat things you already know."

He thought back to yesterday's interview

17

with Ron Hunter, the so-called official interview at the motel, not the earlier one at the agency. "I learned your regular second shift guy had surgery and might retire after he recovers. For now you need someone to fill in for him as a temp. My job is to follow the maintenance supervisor's schedule, take care of emergency repairs, close down the pool at 10:45, generally be available for whatever needs to be done."

"Exactly. Which is why we asked the temp service for a Jack-of-all-trades."

"Ron said I had to keep up with the 'Jill-of-all-trades.'"

"Jill?" Cat's eyes widened. "What in the world is that? Ron's never called me that."

He smiled and lifted a shoulder. "My interpretation." *Turn on the charm, D'Angelo. She'll never recognize a charming man.* "Jill, also known as assistant manager, hostess," he counted off on his fingers, "activities director, baby-sitter, lifeguard, waitress, maid, shuttle van driver. Did I forget anything?" He glanced at the camellia on her desk and grinned. "Oh, yeah, gardener." He was on automatic pilot now. He could do this. He had to do this. It was his job.

A blush deepened her complexion, and she waved a hand in dismissal. "That's all just part of assistant managing. What I

18

meant was, are you familiar with plumbing, wiring, hammers, paint brushes, pool chemicals? Shuttle van driving and the route to the zoo?"

"You got it." *Fact.*

"Good. And you kind of look like a security guard."

"I do?"

"Well, what I think one should look like." She squeezed her fists together and stuck out her elbows.

Oh . . . my build, Dominick thought. He chuckled, relaxing his face, trying to look pleasant and not like a security guard.

"So we can call you that too, if the need arises. The security people don't come in until we go home, but once in a while we have problems early in the evening. Anything else?"

He noticed that her hand stroked the stuffed whale now sitting on the desktop. "Shamu fan?"

She burst into laughter. "Not about me! Come on. I'll show you around so you can get started."

If she didn't implicitly trust Ron's thoroughness and judgment, Cat would have protested rather loudly the hiring of one Dominick D'Angelo.

19

The guy was scary-looking. Naive Cissy flippantly compared his name to a menu item, while Cat was hoping the Mob wasn't moving into her castle.

He strode beside her now as they followed the sidewalk through the courtyard between the two double-story, guest room buildings. On the positive side, he was the epitome of what you'd want walking with you down a dark alley late at night. Over six feet, probably by at least four inches. Trim waist. Arms and chest that filled out his short-sleeved, blue denim work shirt in such a way that there was no question of his strength. Deep, low voice.

Not that there were any dark alleys on the grounds or for that matter an abundance of troublemakers. For the most part the guests were pleasant young families on vacation.

She and Dominick reached the pool area at the end of the courtyard. "I'll show you where the chemicals are stored. The key is on your ring there, marked *pool*."

He pushed open the wrought-iron gate and stepped aside for her to walk through. "Sounds appropriate."

Cat led him along the end of the crowded pool, past the concrete bathhouse to a small shed. She thought of Cissy's immediate attraction to him. No doubt the young woman

20

would say it was his rugged good looks. Cat, on the other hand, would call his looks a little rough around the edges and wondered if his 5 o'clock shadow was there most hours of the day like it was now at 3 o'clock. She also wondered if a brush would calm the thick black hair that grazed his collar. And what about his nose? The bridge of it was a little crooked. Now how had that happened?

His eyes were a clear gray. She had sensed only a sporadic connection through them. It was as if they alternately froze over and then melted, like the ice at the indoor skating rink. His infrequent smile didn't seem to be related to the melting. All that combined with his size gave him the security guard look.

Oh, well. He seemed cooperative enough. He'd either get over the macho-guy-must-answer-to-female-boss syndrome or move on as temps often did. She wondered how he got along with Hispanics. "Dominick, do you speak Spanish?"

"*Por favor, gracias,* and *buenos días.*" He shrugged.

"That'll work. Miguel understands English fairly well. He's on second-shift maintenance with you, part-time. And many of us are bilingual, so it's easy to find help if

21

there's something you can't communicate."

They continued past the playground and miniature golf course toward a sports equipment shed. "When you close up the pool, it's a good idea to check to make sure the bicycles are locked up — this door here. Unless Kevin's working. He's very dependable."

"Is that the end of the property?" Dominick pointed behind the shed.

"Just beyond the basketball court, where that marina begins. The place is basically a rectangle. This is the southwest corner." They turned and headed back north along a sidewalk that paralleled a small beach area on the quiet cove. "This," she gestured toward the guest room building on their right, "is what I call the Castillo's west wing."

"I take it the other building across the courtyard is the east wing?"

"Of course." She smiled. "They're looking a little worn. That off-white color used to be white, and the turquoise trim is really hunter green."

"How many rooms are there?"

"Ninety. It's a small place and not a true resort. We don't have room service or gift shops or any luxurious amenities. And the restaurant's menu caters to kids, not gourmet types. It's a popular place though.

Quite a number of local families visit regularly, just for a short getaway or for holidays. We always do special things on the big holidays. We're reasonably priced and near all the touristy things, so we do get a steady flow of out-of-towners."

"Another turret." He looked toward the restaurant in the distance. "And you've got life-size armored knights and a stone fireplace in the lobby. Where'd the castle motif come from?"

"Oh, the original developer had a daughter who loved the Cinderella story and always asked what was it like after she married Prince Charming and moved into the castle. So he built her one."

"Hmm. Creative."

She chuckled. "I made that up. We don't know where the idea came from, probably a frustrated Hollywood producer-turned-developer. But it works. We've been catering to families for sixteen years now."

"You've been here that long?"

"Well, no, just six years. Three at the front desk and doing those other Jill-of-all-trades things, part-time, while I took more classes in business. My dad wasn't comfortable with just the hotel management degree. He thinks the job market is too unstable. So now I'm qualified to do all sorts of things

I'm not very interested in."

They reached the restaurant, two sides of which were table-filled patios. "Cissy will show you inside later. We all get a discount here. Let's go behind to the maintenance garage. Most of what you'll need is in there. This is the north end of the property."

"What's over there?" Dominick nodded to where the sidewalk continued beyond the garage, still paralleling the bay.

"Well, that pile of boulders is an unofficial boundary and a busy place. See the kids climbing there now?" She smiled. "If the playground equipment ever wears out, I don't think we'll need to replace it. The property on the other side is a community center. They hold special cultural activities there. Much of the time it's empty, which makes the Castillo seem bigger and more private."

She showed him around inside the storage garage, then locked it back up. "Now on the other side of that fence," she pointed through the small grove of eucalyptus trees toward a tall privacy fence, "is the kitchen door and the service drive. But I want to show you one more thing this way."

They headed back the way they had come, then circled around the patio side of the res-taurant.

"Have you done maintenance work before?" she asked.

"Yes."

He sure didn't offer much extra information. She veered off the sidewalk onto a stone path. "This whole area is what we call the garden. It makes for a good shortcut."

In spite of the quiet stranger beside her, Cat took a moment to inhale the fragrant garden. Full of short and tall palm trees, flowering bushes and juniper, it was always a soothing place. They reached a narrow pond, spanned by a footbridge and full of enormous goldfish whose scales reflected glimmering sunlight as they slid through the water.

She stopped in the middle of the flat bridge. It was about four feet wide and twelve feet long, a couple of feet above the water. "Dominick, here's your first project. Can you fix this?" She wiggled the railing. "I think it's loose in these two places."

"No problem. I take it this is your castle's moat?"

Cat was surprised to see him smiling at her. "Well, yes. The closest we get to one anyway."

He nodded. "It works."

"I think so." She led him along a path that angled left and pointed to the right. "That way takes you onto the courtyard. This comes out near the lobby. Do you have any questions?"

"No."

They emerged from the garden and followed the sidewalk to the open lobby doors. "I think that's it. I have to get over to the dining room. Cissy will give you a walkie-talkie, and then you can get to work. If you need anything, she always knows where I am. And she knows as much as I do; you can ask her anything. So welcome aboard, Dominick."

"Thank you, Miss St. Clair."

She stuck her hands on her hips and frowned.

"Uhh, I mean Cat."

"Are you from Chicago?"

"Yeah. Does it show?"

"Mm-hmm. Formality and flat a's."

"I'll work on it."

"You can keep the accent, but it's okay to lighten up a bit. After all, this is California." With a wave she headed down the sidewalk.

A moment later she peered over her shoulder to watch Dominick enter the lobby. She smiled to herself. Cissy latched onto him, just as she suspected she would. Her coworker could be bold and brassy, but she was also kindhearted and fun. Guests

26

adored her. She was perfect as front desk clerk, the first person they saw as they entered the Castillo de Cala. No doubt under her direction, the new guy would soon be smiling more often.

Two

After leaving Dominick in Cissy's capable hands, Cat strode toward the restaurant. She stepped through an opening in the low bushes that separated the patio dining area from the sidewalks and greeted a waitress who was arranging place settings at the empty square glass-topped tables. Inside the dining room she found Mandi setting tables. She was an efficient college girl working for a second summer as hostess.

"Mandi, did Kara show up?" Passing a supply cart, Cat grabbed a handful of napkin-wrapped silver and began setting a nearby table.

"She just called in sick, but we should be okay. There aren't many reservations."

Cat grinned at her as they worked side by side. "But the rooms are full."

"If I were a guest on this beautiful Wednesday in July, I'd be at Sea World, eating their food and waiting for the special summer night shows."

"Me too. I trust your judgment, but Andy said he'd like some extra hours, and he'll be home for a while this evening. You can call

28

him if you need to."

"Okay. Hey, that new guy's a hunk."

"Mm." Cat set out salt and pepper shakers.

"Mm," Mandi mimicked. "What does that mean?"

She shrugged. "I think he'll do a good job."

"Oh, Cat," the young woman laughed, "how can you be so businesslike and so likable at the same time? Admit it, he's a hunk."

"Hunk definitions vary. And he's too old for you."

"Now you sound like my mother."

"Good." Cat patted her shoulder. "Like I've said before, extra mothers keep you healthy. I have to go." She wove her way through the tables.

"Cat?" Mandi called.

She turned.

"Thanks."

"You're welcome. I always liked setting the tables."

"Well, that too, but I mean for being an extra mother."

She smiled and gave her a thumbs-up sign. "See you later."

Cat relished all the details of running a motel. Everything from counseling an employee like Mandi to setting a table to soothing an irate guest pumped adrenaline through her. Vying for reviews in national magazines and a spot on the Top Twenty list, keeping the average occupancy rate at 75 percent, creating ad campaigns, coordinating schedules — all the business details suited her competitive streak. And the other side — creating a suitable environment for guests and staff — seemed a natural continuation of the life she'd always known. As an athlete and one of five children in a close-knit family, she understood team relationships and hard work.

She made a quick swing through the kitchen, checking on dinner preparations, then stepped out the back door and through the employees' eating patio. Even nitty-gritty details like making sure the large garbage bins were shut and in place outside the patio's tall fence were enjoyable because she perceived it all as a part of the process of managing a motel.

Alongside the dumpsters was the service drive, the area she had pointed out to Dominick from the other side of the fence as they stood outside the maintenance garage. She made a mental note to double-check his memory tonight, make sure he remembered to lock that door.

A late afternoon breeze scurried the ever-present brittle eucalyptus leaves across the concrete. Instead of retracing her steps through the restaurant, she turned right and followed the service drive to where it opened onto the main driveway and front lot. She hummed in her off-key way, jangling her bracelet-size ring of keys. She reached the corner of tall oleander bushes and headed right again, through the parking lot. Immediately she paused mid-stride. A silver, two-seater Mercedes was parked in a guest registration space near the lobby entrance.

Her humming halted abruptly, replaced by a low, strangled noise that was not quite a groan, not quite a sigh, not quite a curse, but somehow managed to express the emotions of all three.

It wasn't 5:30 yet.

Cat combed her fingers through her hair and moistened her lips. Should she go around to the employee entrance, duck into her office, freshen her lipstick, slip on her jacket, spray on a bit of cologne? No. The added touches would be unnoticed because of her tardiness. And it would be tardiness despite the fact that he was early.

Better to just go on in. If she'd worn the jacket, she'd have lipstick in her pocket. But

31

it was too warm for the jacket. She tucked her blouse more neatly into the skirt, smoothed the waistband, took a deep breath, and strode across the lot.

It doesn't matter, Cat. It really doesn't matter.

Trenton William Carver, Jr. He was her definition of — well, not hunk exactly, but rather Prince Charming, even now. Six feet tall, just right for her five-ten. A slender frame made, it seemed, for the elegant draping of professional, understated suits, ties, and white shirts with French cuffs. Light brown hair brushed back from a handsome face with smooth angles. Baby-blue eyes. Intelligent, focused, corporate attorney eyes that warmed when he looked at her. An income that promised a North County home, small-castle size. Maybe a Palm Desert condo or a sailboat. Certainly time off for babies.

Not the dark alley type.

The lobby doors were propped open. Without pausing, Cat entered and walked to the far end of the long registration counter. Sitting on the other side, Cissy looked up from the computer. She opened her mouth to speak, but Cat's face must have told her she didn't need to. So she subtly tilted her head toward the small accountant's office located behind her.

Cat swung around the counter, stepped into the office, shut the door, and dumped her keys on the desk. "Hi, Trent."

Seated at the desk, he glanced up from a paper in his hand. "Hello, Cat. Making rounds?"

"Mm-hmm."

"How are you?" He made eye contact now.

"Fine." She slipped into a chair across from him. Their conversations always started like this. Short, clipped sentences. Inwardly she fumed that her voice was breathy. Still, after all this time, after all that had happened, how could her heart skip a beat?

"Sleeping?"

"Mm, better." No need to mention last night.

"Good. Well, the inspection is just a little over two weeks away."

"I know."

"I thought we could do a trial run next Thursday."

"They're coming on a Monday. I thought we should do it a week from Monday."

"Cat, I don't want you working extra days."

Sundays and Mondays were her days off.

"I don't mind. You know I don't mind."

"It's not necessary. Please don't bite your nails. Here's a revised list. The Group agrees that the front building painting can wait, but the bay side has to be done."

"It'll be done. Frank painted the south end before his surgery. The new guy started today, so —"

"New guy?"

"Dominick D'Angelo. He's a temp."

"I thought you were going to do without?"

Cat shook her head. "We tried for ten days. It's too disorganized. Miguel couldn't handle it. He's a honey, but he's sixty-eight years old. Anything else on the list?"

"Just some minor details."

"I'm sure I can read them." She cleared her throat, venting the sarcasm that coated her words, and tried again. "Trent, you could have mailed this. Or called. I'm fine. Really."

He stared back at her, as if unsure.

"My report was all right, wasn't it?" *This time. This time it was all right, I know it was.*

"It was well done, Cat. I'm proud of you." He stood, snapped shut his black leather attaché case, and handed her the paper.

Classic linen. Twenty-five percent cotton fiber. Jacobs, Pemberly, Carver and

Carver's everyday memo stuff. "Thanks. We'll see you a week from Monday, then?"

Trent smiled and tugged at the white French cuffs beneath sleeves of subtle, charcoal gray stripes on black. It was never too warm for him to wear a suitcoat. "Thursday, Catherine. And don't worry about the painting." He squeezed her shoulder as he walked past. "Have a good evening."

"You too." Cat blinked rapidly, trying to read the paper in her hand, trying not to inhale the Obsession-laden scented air. The ache in her jaw suggested she loosen its clench, but it wouldn't budge. Not just yet.

Dominick stood at the check-in counter and shook Trenton Carver's hand. Only one word was needed to describe him — yuppie.

"Mr. Carver," Cissy explained, "represents The Bennington Group."

Carver smiled. "Nice to meet you. Cissy, I'll be back next Thursday for a mock inspection. You can spread the word. Goodbye." He strode out the door.

"Bye." Cissy leaned across the counter, watching him go.

"So who's The Bennington Group?" Dominick asked.

"Oh, they own the place." She glanced

over her shoulder toward the accountant's office.

Cat was sitting in there, only one crossed leg in view, swinging. It occurred to him that it was a nicely shaped leg.

Cissy looked back at him. "They're in Phoenix. They own a lot of different things. When they bought the Castillo two years ago, Trent's law firm represented them."

"He's an attorney then?"

"Yeah. He did the sale, then there was a lot of legal stuff when The Group got out of the chain's franchise. Then there's all the INS paperwork."

"Immigration?"

She flipped her long blonde hair off a shoulder and leaned over to open a drawer. "We have immigrant employees. There's like a zillion documents to keep track of for employment eligibility. Cat knew more about it than Trent." She rummaged through the drawer. "Anyway, now he's kind of their liaison, I guess you'd say. Checks up on us now and then. Helps Cat with some things."

Dominick picked up the handwritten note he had been asking Cissy about earlier when Carver emerged. Now he noticed that Cat's leg had stopped swinging. "Well, thanks for deciphering this for me."

Cissy smiled at him as she pried the lid off a brown plastic prescription bottle. "Anytime. Barry's handwriting is a pain. Usually he'll be here when you come in. He had some appointment. Cat!"

She stood in the office doorway. Her eyes seemed unfocused as they swept across the empty lobby and passed over Dominick before finding Cissy at her side.

"Here." The younger woman lifted Cat's hand and poured something from the bottle into her palm. "Two?"

Cat dropped her chin in a sort of half nod. With hesitant steps she walked from behind the counter into the hall area and turned left toward her office.

"What was that all about?" Dominick asked. The assistant manager's changed demeanor was too obvious for him not to mention it.

Cissy shook her head. "Oh." She ducked into the office and came out with Cat's large key ring just as the telephone rang. "Dominick, take these to her, please? Meet me at 6:30, behind the kitchen. Good evening," she said into the phone, her voice lilting. "Castillo de Cala."

Dominick could see Cat at the end of the hall outside her office door, wriggling the locked knob. She leaned her forehead against the door. Puzzled, he hurried toward her. "Cat . . ."

She peered at the keys through half-closed lids. "Thanks." She fumbled with them, her left hand still clutched around whatever Cissy had placed there. Her fingers trembled, and the key missed its slot.

He placed his hand over hers and unlocked the door.

"Thanks." Her voice was lower than usual.

He followed her inside. "Are you all right?"

"Headache. Ibuprofen." She held open her palm, then swallowed the white pills with a drink from a mineral water bottle. "Prescription strength. Cissy's my drug dealer." Massaging her temples, she sat and closed her eyes. "Hazards of the job. I'll be all right in a few minutes. Umm, we have to paint the bay side of the back building."

"That would be the west wing." He remembered Carver saying he'd be back on Thursday. "By next Thursday?"

She managed a small smile. "You're quick."

"I paint quick too."

"And I thought you'd have a hard time with a female manager."

"None whatsoever."

Cat's eyes opened then. "I'm sorry I misread you."

"No problem." That honey color, all shimmery liquid now, was doing something to his insides. He took a backwards step. "Do you want the door shut?"

"Yes, please. Dominick?"

He paused.

"No matter what Cissy tells you, Trent is a good man." She closed her eyes again. The fingers at her temples wiped at the tears that slipped through.

Quietly, he shut the door.

Cissy told him about many things. As he suspected, she was a wealth of information and, having a bubbly, flirtatious personality, was eager to share all she knew.

They sat on the kitchen patio at an aluminum picnic table. There were two such tables, both empty at the moment except for the two of them. A tall wooden fence separated the area from the service drive and the storage garage. He had eaten the night's special, hamburger and fries, taking his dinner break the same time as Cissy, as she had suggested. The sun was low; the fence threw long shadows. It was a typically mild July evening.

"Does Cat get uptight like that every time

Carver shows up?"

Her green eyes widened. "This is nothing! You should have seen her four months ago. Migraines. We'd have to take her home. She even used an empty room a few times, but don't spread that around."

"Doesn't she do a good job?" He thought back to his conversation with Ron, the manager. He hadn't mentioned any problems in this area. He'd indicated the assistant manager was efficient. And what Dominick had seen so far confirmed that. She gave the impression that the motel was her home and other employees were more like family or team members. Guests were pampered in every sense of the word. It wasn't a snobbish performance, just an easy flow of friendly words, smiles, genuine attention to everyone. And despite her earlier tossing of a paper wad, there was a distinct air of professionalism about her. She was treated with respect, he felt, not simply because she was the boss but because of the way she conducted herself.

"Oh, Cat's naive but generally does a great job, which is really surprising considering her background."

"What's her background?"

Cissy leaned across the table and lowered her voice. "Silver spoon stuff."

Dominick pondered that for a moment. "You mean rich?"

"Filthy. Big house up in North Poway. Big family. Her dad owns a huge construction company. The house is on like seventy-five acres. Can you imagine what seventy-five acres is worth in southern California? Anyway, you get the picture. No concerns as a kid. Fairy-tale world. Which is why she's so naive. School was easy. Basketball was easy." She sipped her coffee.

"Basketball?"

"She played year-round — expensive camps and traveling leagues — then played at USD. Small, private college." She rubbed her fingertips together. "Why was I telling you this? Oh, yeah. Easy life. So when Carver dumps her, she falls to pieces."

"They dated?"

"They were *engaged*."

"What happened?"

"I don't know. They're both extremely closed-mouth about their private lives. What I know about her I mostly pick up here and there, just bits and pieces from her. We're not exactly what you'd call tight. No silver spoon in my background. Anyway, I discovered by accident they were dating — happened to see them at a restaurant about a year ago. Then last Christmas he gives her

41

this humongous diamond. *That* she talked about. She was ecstatic, floating on air for about three days.

"Then her sister calls in, says Cat's sick. She's gone for ten days. When she comes back, her long hair's cut off. She looks sick; she's lost weight. Calls Carver five, six times a day. Gets these migraines, at least two a week for a while. Moves from her old apartment, which I know she was crazy about, into a different one in another neighborhood. Things start to fall apart around here, but Carver and Ron cover for her." Cissy shrugged. "I'm not one for coddling spoiled brats, but I admit, I did too. I figure she's better than somebody we don't know. Then one day, I think it was in February, she shows up without the ring. I remember thinking Happy Valentine's Day to you too. Men." She snorted.

It would have sounded like a soap opera, just street noise to be ignored except . . . *Christmastime. Long hair.* Something tugged at his thoughts. He filed it for later. "What happened?"

"I don't know for sure. She just said they weren't right for each other. Rumor has it he was seeing someone else and forgot to break it off before he gave Cat the diamond."

"Hmm."

"Men can be such —" She smiled and touched his forearm. "Sorry. Present company excluded. Where are you from?"

"Chicago." *Fact.*

"How'd you get here?"

"My truck." *Fact.*

"Ha, ha."

"Got tired of snow, so I headed west. Ended up here about a year and a half ago." *Fiction.* "It's a great place."

"Where do you live?"

"Mission Beach, just a little hole in the wall." *Fiction.* "How about you?"

"Pacific Beach. We're neighbors!"

He smiled. "So are you engaged, married, or otherwise involved with a significant other?"

"Thought you'd never ask. No, no, and no. Well, sorta no."

"Ahh. What do you do in your spare time?"

"Party. How about you?"

"Party." *Fiction.* He winked and stood up. "I'd better get back to work. Don't want to get fired my first day."

"Cat won't notice what you do tonight. Here, I'll take your tray for you." Cissy stuck her empty salad bowl on it. "Stop by later and I'll introduce you to the night manager. She does the accounting. And the security

43

guy will be in just before 11. He'll want to meet you."

"Okay. Thanks."

Dominick went out through the opening in the fence and walked to the storage garage. He paused beside it and looked out over the calm inlet. It was a warm night. A few families lingered on the small beach.

His mind replayed Cissy's chatter, sifted through it for pertinent details. Given the girl's personality, he reminded himself that much of what she said was more than likely a mixture of fact and fantasy. Her interpretation of Cat's life would be biased. Perhaps the "silver spoon" hadn't been there at all.

What haunted him, though, was the story that directly involved Cissy, the one that didn't leave room for interpretation.

Christmastime ... six months ago ... Cat St. Clair's life falling apart ... long hair cut short ... emotional upheaval, migraines. There has to be a connection, but does it have anything to do with —

Oh, dear God, what have I done?

Three

It was never too warm for Trenton Carver to wear a suitcoat. He only perspired when he played tennis.

Thinking about that, Cat grinned to herself, dipped her right hand into a pail of water, and splashed a palmful onto the lump of wet clay that spun before her on the potter's wheel.

What really made him sweat was when she beat him at tennis.

She laughed out loud at her thoughts and then again just because it felt so good. It was like a vigorous mental broom sweeping at those sticky cobwebs that kept rebuilding themselves when she wasn't paying attention. They filled her mind with confusion, dread, and bitterness. A few good belly laughs would vacuum them up once and for all. *Oh, well. Maybe someday.*

She sat alone in the "pot shop," a long room at the back of an old rambling warehouse downtown. The row of potters' wheels sat mute along one wall. Only hers hummed as she bent over it, elbows braced against her knees. Shelves and worktables were everywhere else, flat surfaces that held an array of pottery in all shapes, all stages. Wet, dry, in-between. Some hidden under plastic. Gray, terra-cotta, bisque, greenware, glazed, unglazed. Bowls, platters, animals, casseroles, vases. In one corner were a dozen or so barrels, each containing a different shade of liquid glaze. A small room off to the side housed the kilns.

There were other rooms used for various art classes — painting, drawing, sculpting. At the front of the warehouse, art galleries with large plateglass windows faced the street.

Cat's fingers nimbly shaped a bowl. With one hand against the exterior, the other inside, she pressed evenly as it flew around and around on the wheel. Gray droplets splattered everywhere. Two hands, equal, working as one, creating something new from a formless lump. Something beautiful, durable. Practical and real, and yet a work of art.

That was it. She and Trent were two separate people, working in love on a relationship, one that was to have been durable and real and practical. A beautiful creation. When one felt pressure, the other provided the support necessary to keep the thing from caving in. When heat hotter than a kiln

46

engulfed it, it would only grow stronger. Because it had been properly prepared, it wouldn't explode.

Yeah, right.

She had followed the rules, played fair, worked hard, prepared properly — and what happened? *Kaboom!* Trent couldn't handle one lousy nightmare.

Her foot let up on the pedal, slowing the wheel while she surveyed her work. Oh, it would do. They were all getting lopsided pots these days. Annie and Elli said no one else had her critical eye — the bowls, vases, and casseroles were wonderful. She tapped the pedal again, setting the wheel in slow motion, and her fingers gently fine-tuned the lip.

She really was all right, as she had told Trent last night. Two months ago she would have squished the clay back into its original lump. Four months ago she didn't have the wherewithal to enter the studio, let alone sit at the wheel. Time did heal wounds. Thank God.

Thank God? A lot of good it had done to follow His rules. If He had cared, the nightmare wouldn't have happened in the first place and she'd be studying honeymoon brochures and choosing delicate china patterns for when the in-laws visited. Her family, of course, would use pottery, St. Clair pattern. She would not be sitting alone in the middle of the pot shop spinning out yet another bowl her sisters didn't need but said they did. It was to have been a September wedding . . .

Thank You, Jesus, for Your death and resurrection. I really do understand and accept it, but I'll take charge from here.

Mother said Cat was more in love with the idea of love than with Trent. Cat disagreed but did admit to herself that she was less angry with him for letting her down than she was with the fact that life just didn't work out the way it was supposed to when you followed the rules. Her heart probably skipped a beat when he came by because of profound disappointment, not in anguish that Trenton Carver had found someone else.

She really was fine with that development. It was only natural. She had glimpsed her once, sitting prettily in the Mercedes. In Cat's imagination the girl was wealthy and knew which fork to use without asking. She doubted the girl played tennis, but if she did, she'd never allow herself to beat Trent. The only Bulls she would know of were in Spain, and she'd break a nail just picking up a basketball. She certainly wouldn't be the type to enjoy a belly laugh.

48

Cat stopped the wheel and stretched her back, glancing at the clock on the wall. Her hands and forearms were crusty gray, covered with dried clay. She had time to glaze four other bowls that were ready before going home to change for work.

Work. How she loved it! She loved making the guests feel at home. She loved leading the other employees, encouraging them to do their best. She would love to complete the entire painting project, just to show Trent she really was fine. At any rate they would pass inspection this time, unlike the last one.

That one was just three months after the incident, when the nightmare still burned. Now, almost seven months after her traumatic experience, she could handle an inspection. It seemed the only thing she couldn't quite handle was Trent's friendship visits disguised as business. The migraines and sleepless nights were fading, but tension always filled her when she saw him, his handsome face always reminding her of what she had lost.

Dominick studied the report. It didn't exactly read like Cissy's silver spoon version.

Catherine Michele St. Clair was thirty, born and raised in Poway. Parents were Betty, an elementary school teacher, and

49

Stan, an ex-Navy man, a construction worker who had started his own company twenty years ago. A small company that paid its bills. Nothing to warrant a filthy-rich reputation. Two brothers, two sisters, Cat in the middle. Basketball guard in high school, all-state team; athletic/academic scholarship to SDSU — San Diego State University, a state school, not the private one Cissy had mentioned. Her income as assistant manager was average. Her credit rating was excellent; no unusual purchases or outstanding debts except for a school loan. Small savings; checking account was appropriate. Rent for an apartment in the Clairemont area was high, but probably average. No car payment. No arrests. Not even a speeding ticket.

Funny how these things said nothing about wholesome, healthy good looks suitable for a Wheaties box; outgoing; hums tunelessly; honey-colored eyes that unfocus when the ex shows up.

He flipped the paper over. He could have guessed — Cissy Owens was prone to exaggeration, her perspective tainted with envy.

He skimmed the other pages. Everyone looked clean. All the Hispanics were documented, legally employed. The food and laundry services were well-established.

Nothing suspicious. Which meant everything and everyone was suspicious. The activity would more than likely involve the delivery trucks. He'd begin there.

Last night he had worked with Miguel. He liked the old man who spoke little English. This afternoon they were starting early in order to begin the painting project. In Spanish the man had told him he would cut off his right arm for *la gatita*. The kitten.

Cat.

He picked up the phone at his elbow and punched out Dr. Adam Parker's private number. After seven rings his friend answered with a grunt.

"Sorry to wake you, bud."

Another grunt.

Dominick knew it was all right. Adam had told him more than once that he was always available, even after a twelve-hour shift of emergency room surgeries. No doubt last night had been one of those. "Missed you this morning. Waves were great."

"Hold on."

He heard creaking bedsprings, shuffling noises, then kitchen noises. Adam's wife Megan would have prepared the coffeemaker. He imagined his friend now moving the carafe aside, holding his mug directly under the basket of grounds as the

51

steaming, mud-colored water dripped into it. A few minutes ticked by, then he heard a clunk and a chair scraping.

Slurp. "Okay. What's up?"

"I found her."

Adam didn't reply.

He waited. He couldn't say the words, even now. His friend would know what he was referring to.

Adam sucked in a breath. "Oh, dear Lord."

"Exactly. I think it's something to pray about?"

"Of course. What happened?"

"She didn't recognize me." Dominick paused.

"But you told her?"

"I can't yet."

"I see." Adam sipped his coffee. "You're sure it's her?"

He thought of her eyes. "I'm sure."

"You have to tell her. You can't live with this."

Dominick rubbed his forehead. "I know, but there's a catch. This makes her a suspect."

"Again."

"Yeah. So maybe the first time . . ."

His friend sighed. "I don't know how you do this."

"I don't think *how,* just *why.* Tell Meg?" He always sensed that Adam's wife's prayers counted the most.

"Sure. How about Sunday brunch?"

"See you then. Thanks."

Cat hung her dress on the hook attached to the back of the door, locked it again, and stepped into the manager's office, right next to hers.

"Hey, Ron."

"Hey, Cat." He swiveled around in his desk chair to face her with a smile. "Early again, I see."

Although she was in fact early today, Ron's usual greeting didn't necessarily refer to the time. The teasing phrase had served to carry them through that brief period a few months ago when he often stayed late because she seldom arrived on time. It was his way of allowing her to make mistakes and not worry about jeopardizing her job. Cat would always be grateful to him.

She had admired him for years, trying to mimic his laid-back attitude that somehow kept the staff on their toes. He had survived eight years at the same motel, including the bumpy ride of ownership change. He was forty-something with thinning blond hair, an easy smile, a wife and two young children. "How was the soccer game, coach?" she asked him.

"We won, three zip." Ron eyed her T-shirt and shorts. "You must be going to shoot hoops. Those don't look like painting clothes."

"Painting?"

"Miguel and Dominick got here before 1. That makes four guys out there painting this afternoon."

"Wow. As Cissy would say, can we keep him? So, what do you think of Trent's revised list?"

"We could pass inspection today. Well, maybe tomorrow. We've taken care of everything except that painting job."

"I'm going to get the whole thing done, Ron. Front and back, east and west."

He raised his eyebrows. "Go for it, girl."

She grinned. "You don't think I can do it."

"On the contrary, I bet you can with Dominick. He seems like a worker. And Miguel . . ." He made a slashing motion with his left hand. "He'd cut off his right arm for you."

She laughed. "He's my honey."

"But no sixteen-hour days for you, Cat."

"Well, only one or two if —"

"No! N-o — no."

"Okay, okay. You didn't tell me much about Dominick. What other kinds of work has he done?"

He shrugged. "The temp service said his references are good. I get the impression he's lived all over, done all kinds of things."

"Ah, an unsettled drifter. Or maybe he's running from something. You don't think he's a convict, do you? He has that rough look about him. Have you noticed his nose? And his voice is sort of raspy. You know, like he's strained it." She headed toward the door. "Maybe from singing. That's it. He's a wild, hard-rock singer, tired of life in the fast lane."

"See you, Cat."

"Bye, Ron. Have a nice evening."

She strolled along the sidewalk between the buildings, greeting a groundskeeper who was mowing the grassy area near the patios beside the guest rooms. The area was empty for the most part. Being the middle of the afternoon, the majority of guests had either checked out, hadn't checked in yet, or were off sightseeing. She rounded the corner near the pool and waved to a few mothers with their children. At the equipment shed she entered the side door, then rummaged through the assortment of balls until she found the women's-size basketball.

She figured the teenager in charge of the booth must be outside working on the bicycles, but then through the large open window she spotted him halfway along the west wing, beyond Dominick and Miguel, with a paintbrush in hand. As she walked that direction, she heard singing and chuckled. *He is a rock singer.* Then the words reached her ears, one voice in Spanish and one in English: "Jesus loves me this I know, for the Bible tells me so." *Well, probably not rock.*

When the verse ended, she called out, "*Qué tal,* Miguel, Dominick!"

"*Qué tal, señorita!*" Miguel, standing near a patio door, waved his brush at her.

Dominick called down from the top of a ladder, "*Qué tal, gatita!*"

She laughed. "You're being tutored!"

"Yep. I mean, *sí.* What do you think?"

What she thought as she watched him climb down was that his muscles were for real. He wore a white T-shirt with the sleeves cut off. And she noticed she could see the back of his neck. His unruly hair was tucked up underneath a navy blue cap perched backwards. As she suspected, yesterday's 3 o'clock jaw shadow was a 2 o'clock one today. "I can't believe how much you've finished already."

56

He stood beside her and looked up at the second-floor balcony above the first-floor patio. He and Miguel were painting hunter green around the doors. The stucco walls had already been painted white. "First shift had some extra time, so they sprayed the white. I think they got about three-fourths done."

"Maybe we really can do it."

"Finish this side by next week? No problem."

She glanced at him out of the corner of her eye. "I was thinking the entire building by two weeks from next Monday."

"Hmm."

"What do you think?"

"Oh, a week from Saturday."

Cat took a deep breath and spun the basketball between her hands, avoiding his eyes. "What about the east wing too? Double overtime."

"Hmm. Actually, money's overrated in my opinion."

She tossed the ball and caught it. "Okay. How about, umm, a season pass to the Chargers?"

"I'm not a big football fan."

"Padres?"

"Nah."

She looked up at him and, raising her

voice in mock exasperation, asked, "Well, what would it take?"

He narrowed his eyes at her. "A new longboard."

She hugged the ball to herself, calculating. New surfboards cost hundreds and hundreds of dollars. Maybe she could pay half, finagle Ron into budgeting extra —

"Cat, I'm just kidding."

"But I think I can —"

"He's not worth it."

"What?"

"Nothing. How about dinner? If we finish in time, you take us. For Italian. We'll stuff Miguel with pasta, put some meat on his bones." He wiped his hand on his jeans. "Deal?"

She shook his hand. "Deal. What if you don't finish in time?"

Quickly he made a slashing motion with the side of his left hand against his right arm.

Cat burst into laughter.

"It's the least I can do." He climbed back up the ladder. "I suppose you want Charger tickets?"

"Lakers."

"The right arm would be easier."

"Okay, dinner. Some gourmet fish stuff, though."

He gave her a thumbs-up sign. "You got it, *mi gatita.*"

Cat headed toward the basketball court located behind the equipment booth. Dominick wasn't only quick at painting. He had picked up on the fact that preparing for the inspection was a personal challenge for her, an opportunity to prove herself to Trent, so important that she would even consider buying a surfboard to meet it. She wondered what Cissy had told him about Trent. Probably her usual number, an exaggeration. "He's not worth it" was somewhat of a strong reaction.

Dominick D'Angelo certainly was turning out to be an interesting addition to the staff.

Four

Cat shoved the black plastic trash bag with her foot over the kitchen doorstep, clicked off the lights, then pulled the door shut, turning the handle to make sure the lock was secure. With both hands she grasped the bag's handle and hoisted it over her shoulder. She made her way quickly across the darkened patio and through the fence opening into the service drive. A few moments ago the Friday night bread delivery man had driven off.

It wasn't part of her job description to greet the bread man. He had his own key and was capable of doing his job alone. Neither was her nightly stroll through the empty restaurant and kitchen at 10:15 part of her duties, tidying up what only someone with a subtle eye for detail would notice. Her family called her a perfectionist for a reason. But then again this garbage wasn't exactly subtle. The staff had to have tripped over it in order to walk out the door.

"Umpf." She pushed the bag through the opening in the huge, metal bin. A waste disposal service would pick up the motel's trash tomorrow morning. If they came as early as they sometimes did, the breakfast crew wouldn't have been able to get this bag out in time.

She walked through the other fence opening at the end of the drive, then meandered through fragrant juniper bushes and eucalyptus trees, heading toward the sidewalk that paralleled the small beach and inlet. Moonlight glittered off the water's surface. It was a nice, clear night, a change from the usual mistiness.

Cat never minded doing the extras, though she should probably talk to the staff about this. It was against regulations to leave the trash in the kitchen, and this wasn't the first time it had happened. Had it always been on a Friday? It seemed to her that the bin was near to overflowing those other times, just like now.

There was a rustling noise to her right. Something moved quickly toward her —

Sheer terror shot through her, bolting her feet to the ground, choking the scream in her throat.

"Cat." A large shadow stepped beside her.

"Oh!" she cried out loudly, her hands flying to her mouth. She recognized Dominick, but the jolt of fear was impossible to contain. She gulped for air and screamed, "Don't — don't ever do that!

Oh! . . . I mean . . ."

He touched her arm. "I'm sorry."

She couldn't catch her breath. Her chest felt as if it would burst. Tree trunks swirled before her.

"Cat, sit down." He steered her a short distance along the sidewalk to a wooden bench, then sat beside her, speaking gently in his low, almost whispery voice. "I'm sorry. I didn't mean to scare you. Try taking deep breaths. I thought you had seen me. I was inside the garage — I'd just turned off the light and locked the door."

"Don't —"

"Deep breaths. That's it."

"Don't ever," she rasped, "*ever* do anything like that again."

"I won't. I promise. How about if I wear bells on my shoes?"

Her giggle sounded like a choking noise.

"That's better. Hey, I've got a new Jill-of-all-trades name for you. Jill the midnight trash collector."

Through the shadows thrown by the dim pole lamps, she could make out his grin. "It's — it's not midnight."

"Close enough. Seriously, is it safe for you to be wandering around on the edge of the property so late? This beach is public, right? And the sidewalk is open — anyone can use it."

"There's never been a problem." Maybe she should start carrying her Mace with her, even here at the castle. She became aware of her right hand clutching his shirt at the shoulder. "Sorry." She let go, smoothing the wrinkled fabric. "Sorry I yelled at you too."

"No problem. Are you all right now?"

Well, no, she wasn't, but that was a long story. It would explain her overreaction to this, but . . . she seldom talked of it and besides, she didn't really know this guy. She cleared her throat. "Uhh, yeah, I'm all right. I always feel so at home here, so safe. You know that feeling, like when you were a kid and you'd sit in the backyard counting stars?"

"My backyard was an alley in the big city. Not many stars."

"Ah ha!" Cat recalled her early impression of him. "Was it a dark alley?"

"What?"

"I knew there was a dark alley in your life. You just have this look about you, that security guard look. When we first met I thought you were the type I'd want walking *with* me down a dark alley." She chuckled. "I didn't think about what'd it'd be like to have you walking *toward* me."

"I'm sorry." As he looked at her, half his

face was in darkness, the other half bathed in moonlight.

"I know. Don't worry about it. I'm all right now. My heartbeat's almost back to normal."

"Will you forgive me?"

She bit back an urge to make light of the question. His serious tone combined with that particular choice of words struck her as incongruent with her image of him — the independent, uninvolved, drifter sort. He sounded like a Christian! "Dominick, there isn't much to forgive, but of course I do. Have you been to the pool yet?"

"I'm headed there now. I can walk you back to the lobby first."

"Normally I cruise around the property —"

"Because it's like your backyard."

"Yes. So I'm going your direction." They stood and followed the walk between the beach and the restaurant's patio. "I don't want to run into you again from the other direction."

"Now you can't keep bringing that up if you forgive me."

"I couldn't resist."

"Mm-hmm. Do you normally take out the trash too?"

She shrugged. "Well, when I find some left in the kitchen, I do. I often roam around, just tidying up here and there."

"There's another one. Jill the tidier-upper."

"Ha, ha. Okay, here's one for you. Jack the dark alley walker."

"Hmm. Is that good or bad? For scaring or protecting?"

She glanced at the profile of his strong angular nose and chin. His arm above hers appeared massive in the lamplight. It could go either way. He could easily intimidate. "Whatever's necessary. You grew up in the city then? Not a suburb?"

"Right."

She wondered how to get him to elaborate. "With no backyards. So where did you feel safe?"

He was silent for a moment. "That's a good question. I'll have to think about it. What was your backyard like?"

Cat smiled. "Oh, it's wonderful."

"Present tense?"

"Yeah, it's still there. You can't see the neighbors, and it's deserty, with sage and manzanita and rocks and lizards and hills. Scrubby trees." She felt an odd sensation, like a longing to show it to Dominick, the big-city dweller. "There's a dry creek bed — it's been dry forever, I think — and my dad built this little flat footbridge across it."

"Do you live there?"

"No, my parents do. My dad grew up on the place. His parents had avocado groves, but most of the trees are gone now, and most of the property has been sold. It's the original house though. Mother and Dad added on to it when our family kept growing."

"You have a lot of brothers and sisters?"

"Two of each."

"Where are you in the lineup?"

"Right smack in the middle. There are about two years between each of us. Anne is the oldest, then Ben, me, Doug, and Elizabeth. A, b, c, d, e. Dad wanted Frank and Gloria, but Mother said no way. Now they've got nine grandkids."

"Frank and Gloria?"

"Felicia and Grant are in the bunch, but that's where it ends." She chuckled and glanced over at the newly painted west wing as they passed. "This looks very nice, by the way, already. Oh, good evening!" she called out to a couple sitting on the balcony outside their second-story room.

"Hello!" They waved back to her.

"See, Dominick," she turned to him, "there's always someone around. It's just like a big family here. Nothing to be afraid of." *Nothing to be afraid of.* She repeated the words to herself, clinging to their promise.

"Except Jack the dark alley walker," he murmured.

"Well, yes, I will have to watch out for him," she teased. They rounded the corner by the sports equipment shed. Kevin, the teenager working tonight, stood outside leaning against the doorway, watching two groups still on the miniature golf course. "Hey, Kevin."

"Hey, Cat. Hey, Dominick."

They chatted for a moment, then continued on, past the low wooden fence that surrounded the small course and the colorful, gimmicky figures at each hole. There were tiny dragons, knights, moats, castles, an ivory tower with a princess in the window. Just beyond that they reached the chain-link fence that surrounded the pool area. Dominick pushed the gate open and let her go ahead of him.

While he went into the bathhouse to turn off the lights and lock the doors, Cat settled into a lounge chair. It felt good to sit still. Dampness hung thick in the night's cool air. She pulled her cardigan more tightly around her neck and wrapped her dress more snugly around her knees.

She watched two children climb from the other end of the heated pool. Their parents swathed them in large towels. She often took a vicarious pleasure from eavesdropping on families like this one. There was such a comfort in the thought of their being on vacation, swimming late at night, laughing about the cool breeze and goose bumps, making plans for tomorrow, leaving behind the ordinary. Oh, there were times, of course, when she recognized that the threshold of too much togetherness had been crossed, when the kids whined and parents snapped.

Dominick walked around the pool, lining up the deck chairs against the fence. She thought she really hadn't learned much about him. Except for that moment of genuine concern in his voice when he asked for her forgiveness, he was rather stoic. He could easily pass for their security guard, in both the demeanor and the muscle departments. His face was usually closed — no emotions showing there, like what the Secret Service guys always looked like in photographs with the President.

Not like her. Everything showed on her face; she couldn't help it. Happy, sad, mad, whatever. Her eyebrows always moved, her voice fluctuated, her mouth was too wide to not be expressing something at any given moment.

The family walked by her and said good night.

Cat leaned back in the chair and looked up at the stars, dimmed by the moonlight and the city's illuminations. Then again, Dominick did have friendly moments. He flirted easily with Cissy. He seemed to enjoy painting with Miguel. And there was that teasing bet. Or was it teasing? Would he really expect dinner? Oh, probably not. Even if he didn't finish the job, she would see that he got extra on his paycheck, just for the effort. Enough maybe for a new longboard.

"Dominick . . ." She looked at him as he approached. "Do you surf?"

"No. I just thought a board would look good in my place, propped up in a corner."

He could be a smart aleck too. "Ha, ha. Where do you go?"

"Usually near the Crystal Pier. Pacific Beach. Bright and early."

The hotel phone, on the outer wall of the bathhouse, rang, and he went to answer it. A moment later he returned. "Cissy needs to see you before she goes."

"On my way." Cat stood. "Amazing. She always knows where I am."

"I can walk with you."

"No." For a second, gazing down the empty, dimly lit courtyard between the two buildings, foliage blocking her view of the lobby in the distance, she hesitated. "No, but thanks anyway. See you tomorrow."

"Good night, Cat."

Just like my backyard. Just like my backyard. Crossing her arms to hold the cardigan shut, she hurried along the sidewalk, humming, pushing at the fear lingering on the edges of her mind. It hadn't been there much lately, had it? And never while she was at her castle. If Dominick hadn't surprised her, it never would have slipped into her consciousness here, would it?

She bent to pick up an empty soda can.

Jill the tidier-upper. Jill the trash collector.

Trash. It suddenly occurred to her that the trash containers weren't visible from the maintenance garage — the fence was in the way. If Dominick were in the garage, he couldn't have seen her shoving the trash bag into the bin.

Oh, she'd probably missed something in the conversation. She sighed. That had been happening a lot in recent months.

Cat heard the commotion from her office late Saturday afternoon. She hurried out to the lobby to see what was going on.

Cissy met her as she rounded the corner. Behind her were a man and woman, obviously distraught. "Cat, we're missing a little boy."

"Did you alert everyone?" Most of the staff had walkie-talkies.

Cissy turned back toward the check-in counter. "Maintenance, Housekeeping, and Kevin know. I'm calling the kitchen now. This is Mr. and Mrs. Lansky, the parents."

"Let's sit over here." She led the couple to a group of chairs in the corner. She saw the fear on their young faces and tried not to reflect it, although she felt as if she'd been punched in the stomach. "By now everyone is surrounding the property and is out looking for your son. What's his name, and when did you last see him?"

The father answered, "Brendan. He's six, and about an hour ago he was gone."

"From?" Cat prompted. She noticed now that Mrs. Lansky was pregnant and was wringing her hands.

"The room," he said. "I was out on the balcony, my wife was napping. Brendan was watching television. I went inside and he was gone."

She glanced at her watch. "So he probably just wandered out the door?"

"I guess. We've checked all his favorite places."

"It's a big place, lots of nooks and crannies. You couldn't be everywhere at once. I'm sure the staff will find him. They *can* be

71

everywhere at once. He is your child, right? Both of yours?"

They looked at her in surprise.

"I just want to make sure there's no parent who wants custody."

"Oh, no," Mr. Lansky replied. "He's ours. He's got my big ears and his mom's red hair."

Cat smiled to herself. He should be easy to spot. "Good. Does he do this often? Go exploring by himself?"

"Not really. But he is an independent little guy."

Cissy joined them and handed her a walkie-talkie. "Well, dinner's been put on hold. All the cooks and waiters are out looking too. I sent the busboys both directions along the beach walk."

"Does Dominick know?"

Cissy smiled briefly. "He was my first thought too. Must be the muscles."

"Secret Service look."

"Yeah. I'm going out to the side parking lot. Jan's covering the phone for me." She left.

Mrs. Lansky sniffled, and her husband stood. "I can't sit."

"Of course not." Cat handed him the walkie-talkie. "Take this with you." He strode out the door. "Mrs. Lansky, is there something Brendan wanted to do that he hasn't done yet? Or something he wanted to do again?"

"Oh, everything. He loves this place. I get so tired these days in the afternoon, and Dan had work to do. We're on vacation, but he has to do his computer stuff! I told him to take Brendan on the bikes, but he said it would have to be later. He couldn't get a bike by himself, could he?"

"No, I don't think Kevin would give one to a little boy by himself. And they're locked up."

"He hates television, but his dad told him to watch for a while."

"So do you think Brendan was maybe a little upset?"

"Definitely." His mother shook her head. "He's a good-natured boy, but his feelings would be hurt that his dad told him to leave him alone while he worked."

"It makes sense then that he would just take off by himself." Cat felt a sense of relief. "I'm sure we'll find him soon. I think I'll go look around. Do you want to wait here? Cissy will be right back, and when someone finds him, they'll call her."

Mrs. Lansky nodded.

Cat found another walkie-talkie behind the counter and walked out a side door onto the patio behind the Housekeeping entrance.

Dear Lord — okay, I'm calling a truce. Will You do this one? Not for me, but for this family? Don't let Brendan be hurt. Please take care of him, and help us find him.

Foxhole prayer.

Jesus said I could ask You this stuff.

Was there something else she wanted to ask? No . . .

So I'm asking in His name for Your help. Amen.

Cat wandered across the patio. Straight ahead was the east wing of rooms. So many bushes to hide behind. Would he be hiding?

At the sidewalk she turned right. A few more steps brought her to a stone garden path.

Of course he'd be hiding. He was mad at his dad for putting him off, for hurting his feelings. He would hide from that stern face. Any face that declared, "Not now — I'm working even though this is vacation" would appear stern to a child. And he would want to hide from that uncomfortable feeling of anger toward the one who takes care of him. How do you hide from an uncomfortable feeling like that?

Cat stopped in her tracks.

Well if, like Brendan, you don't watch

television, you do it on the inside. You detach within. You use your imagination.

Oh, Father . . .

She hurried along the winding path between bushes and flowers and small palm trees. Although the garden wasn't huge, the vegetation was dense enough to block views from one end to the other. When the stone path forked, she veered to the right. Ahead was the pond. At its most narrow point, the twelve-foot bridge spanned it.

"Brendan?" she called. "Brendan?"

Carefully, she picked her way through stiff junipers and ducked under a drooping palm frond. Reaching the side of the bridge, she knelt. In the small space under the bridge between the path and the pond's edge, a little red-haired boy lay curled like a kitten, fast asleep.

"Hey, Brendan." Glad she was wearing slacks, Cat crawled toward him. The bridge was too low for her height, so she found a fairly flat spot nearby, sat cross-legged, and pressed the button on the walkie-talkie. "Cissy, I found him! We're under the bridge."

She could hear muffled cries before Cissy replied, "Mom and dad are on their way!"

The little boy stirred.

"Hi, Brendan. My name's Cat."

75

"Cat?" He sat up.

"Yeah. Your mom and dad are coming. Did you get lost?"

He stuck out his lower lip and shook his head. "I know my way back."

"Ahh. Just needed some time alone, huh?"

"Yep."

"Do you like chocolate-chip ice cream?"

He nodded.

"Did you know they've got some in the restaurant? And they've got those humongous," she held out her hands to demonstrate, "waffle cones. And I work here, so I'm going to tell them that you can have one right now for free and they should put extra globs of whipping cream on top. Would you like that?"

"Mom won't let me before dinner."

Cat smiled. "I think she might today. Did you go to the zoo yet?"

They chatted until his parents arrived, accompanied by various staff members. Relief was evident in everyone's smiles as they watched the reunion. Mrs. Lansky cried, and Mr. Lansky swore he'd put the computer away and they'd take a bike ride. Brendan wanted his ice cream first. Naturally they agreed.

Cat waved good-bye, then sat back down

on the ground, leaning against the wooden bridge's support beam, holding her head in her hands. *Say thank You. Say thank You,* she told herself. *No. I'll cry if I do. I don't want to cry anymore. I don't want Your love anymore, God.* She wiped at the corners of her eyes and blinked rapidly. *You are so rude, St. Clair,* she thought.

"All right," she spoke aloud, softly. "Thank You."

Above her sniffle she heard whistling, and then Dominick came into view, walking from the other side of the bridge. "Cat, are you still down there?"

She had to clear her throat before answering, "Yes."

He spotted her, then sat on the slats just above her, his legs dangling over the side, under the railing. He wore his paint clothes, splattered jeans, sleeveless T-shirt, backwards cap, sloppy tennis shoes. "We're all having ice cream. It's a celebration. Shouldn't you be there since you found him?" He folded his arms on the railing and leaned over.

"I'm coming. Just had to sit still a moment."

"Does this happen often? Lost kids?"

"Not often. This one was scary. An hour and a half or whatever is a long time."

"How did you find him?"

"God." It slipped out without a thought.

Dominick grinned. "Really?"

She shrugged and pulled at a weed under her leg. "Yeah, I guess. Actually, we're not on speaking terms, but I did ask Him for help."

"I didn't know you could do that. But I'm new at this."

She glanced up at him. "New at what?"

"Faith. Jesus. Praying."

He was a Christian then. She found a rock to fiddle with. A stone. A stumbling stone. She'd be one if she opened her mouth.

"Anyway," he continued, "I didn't realize you could talk like that. That you can say you're not on speaking terms with the God who created the universe."

Cat tried to detect a reproof in his low voice. She concluded there wasn't one. What she heard was the wonder of first love. "Well, I don't know if you can, but I am. It's between Him and me. It's —" She laughed nervously and ran her fingers through her hair. "I don't want to talk about it."

"But can you tell me what happened after you asked Him to help?"

She blew out a breath as if she'd been holding it for a long time. "I guess I thought about when I was little and I'd get my feelings hurt. Happens a lot when you're in the middle, you know. The older ones go off and do things. The younger ones need Mom and Dad more than you do." She was quiet a moment, remembering. "I always felt loved and wanted, but I was spoiled. So when my feelings got hurt, I'd go out to the backyard . . ." She met his grin with one of her own. ". . . and sit under the bridge."

He laughed. "No way."

"Yes, way!"

"And do what?"

"Well . . ." Her face felt warm. "I'd just get lost in my imagination, making up wonderful places for families to live in. I'd make up stories about them, and I'd build castles out of rocks and dirt and . . . whatever. Then I'd feel better."

His laughter grew louder.

She grabbed his foot and yanked it. "You can't tell anyone!"

He hooted.

She yanked again. "Promise!"

He caught his breath. "Only if you tell me, were you the little girl who always wondered what happened after Cinderella married Prince Charming and moved into the castle?"

"So what if I am?"

Dominick grinned and stood up, leaned

over the railing, and stretched his hand out to her. "It's just perfect — you being manager here at Castillo de Cala."

She put her hand in his, and he pulled her to a standing position. "Assistant manager," she corrected, looking into his gray eyes. When his face dropped its Secret Service expression, like now, it really was a very nice face.

He kept his hand wrapped around hers. "They'll want to thank you. You will go eat ice cream?"

She nodded. Only then did he let go of her hand.

"I have to get back to painting. Don't want to get fired." He walked a few steps, then turned back. "Hey, Cat."

She climbed up to the bridge. "Hmm?"

"He's still listening, isn't He? Even though you're not on speaking terms?" His eyes seemed to bore into her from clear across the bridge.

"Good question. I'll have to think about it."

He waved and strode down the path.

What she'd have to think about was why she so easily opened up to this stranger, Dominick D'Angelo.

Five

"I was a regular Mr. Motormouth." Dominick concluded his description of his encounter with Cat at the footbridge.

Across the patio table, his friends Adam and Megan Parker stared silently at him.

"I mean, when she said God helped her find the kid, it was like something inside of me clicked on. I wanted to hear all about how she relates to God. I just couldn't shut up. I *have* to shut up."

Meg burst into laughter and thrust an arm above her head with a resounding, "Yes!"

"What?" He turned to her husband, who only contorted his face in reply. "What?" he repeated.

Adam snorted, and Dominick knew he'd have to wait for an answer. As his friend's loud guffaws filled the whole outdoors, he shook his head. The Parkers had moments like these. He didn't know if it was their tendency toward wackiness or an expression of sheer joy. Like now, joy seemed inconsistent with the subject at hand, but they were wacky enough to find it at the oddest times.

He couldn't help but smile at Megan's elfin features all scrunched up in laughter. Except for big brown eyes, she was tiny with delicate features and short brown hair that usually stuck out in all directions. She only sat still on Sunday mornings. Other hours of the week were filled with volunteer work at a homeless shelter and being her husband's best friend. Her wardrobe was down-to-earth, their home modest and miles from the ocean. It always amazed Dominick that, given her talents and inability to have children, she had never pursued a business career or at least spent the good doctor's salary more flamboyantly.

Dr. Adam Parker towered over his wife. He looked like the California native surfer he was — an athletic, blue-eyed, and sun-bleached blond. His nights were spent doing emergency surgery at a nearby hospital.

Which was where Dominick had met him two years ago. He remembered seeing those piercing blue eyes as if from a great distance, just before he lost consciousness. When he awoke three days later, they greeted him. During the weeks he spent recovering in the hospital, Adam befriended him. A relationship developed during follow-up office visits, and as the healing progressed, they began meeting for breakfast, surfing, and racquetball. Dominick owed his life twice to the doctor, once for removing the bullets and once for telling him about Jesus Christ.

Meg dabbed at her eyes now with a paper napkin, and Adam's roar subsided into chuckles.

Dominick tried again. "I'm serious. I can't talk to a suspect like that."

Meg jumped up, ran around the table, and gave him a quick hug. "Oh, Dominick, we know you're serious. Deadly serious." She patted his cheek and looked straight into his eyes. "There's just this new tenderness about you. It's such a joy to see. Don't you think you can have a heart for the bad guys and still do your job?"

"I can't be tender when I'm on a case."

"Why not?" she challenged as she sat back down, her eyes never leaving his face.

"I'm a character who fits a role that's necessary for the moment. If I'm tender, I spill my guts, I'm me, and then I can't be a drifter working a temp maintenance job."

"I think," Adam intervened, "that the something you felt click when Cat — Is that her name?"

He nodded.

"I think what clicked when she mentioned God was His Spirit in you recognizing His

83

Spirit in her. Sometimes Christians sense an ability to communicate about things of faith even when they don't know each other. Does that make sense?"

"Yeah. Go on."

"That's the tenderness Meg is talking about." Adam leaned forward, an eager expression on his face. "It's authentic, and I don't think it's going to go away. But it doesn't have to be specific. A drifter working maintenance as a temp can have a heart for God and a concern for others just as well as he can surf and live in your apartment and drive your pickup and eat pasta until it comes out of his ears. Right?"

"Okay. So far."

"But, understandably, you can't tell her yet exactly just how God got your attention, right?"

"Right, and if I keep running off the mouth like yesterday, I'm bound to."

"Dominick, your discipline is still in place!" His words tumbled out. He was clearly excited, grasping the meaning of this new development. "You've only lost the ability to mask your concern and compassion."

Meg added with a wink, "And besides, I've never known you to talk too much."

"And," Adam continued, "let's back up.

In the first place, this is an answer to prayer, remember? You wanted to find this woman. We've been praying specifically for that for months. God's brought you this far. We can trust that you'll have the opportunity to tell Cat everything at the right time."

Dominick looked down at the table cluttered with the remains of Sunday brunch. What they said made sense, but he still felt unsettled. Why would answered prayer so complicate his life? "I just . . . I just didn't anticipate these circumstances."

"Hey, bud, that's when God does His best work. When things are unpredictable, we can't manipulate them as easily."

He thought about what his friends had been teaching him the past few months, that there were many facets to faith and that sometimes there was nothing to go on but the knowledge that God was in it. He gave his friends a small smile. "This is just part of the adventure you keep telling me about, huh?"

Meg grinned and nodded exuberantly. "That's what we think. So what's she like?"

Describe Cat St. Clair? Now here's an easy one. "Friendly. Straightforward. Confident. Professional. Kind. The front desk manager is a little jealous of her, but for the most part the staff seems to like her." He thought a moment. "You know what it is? I just figured it out. She accepts everyone. She makes everyone feel significant, from the little rugrat who tromps on the flowers to the college waiters to the Hispanic maid who never went to school to me, the aimless drifter."

"Oh, I want to meet her!" Meg exclaimed. "And what does she look like?"

"She has eyes . . ." Dominick stopped. If he told them about those eyes that sometimes mushed his insides, or that dimple in her left cheek, they'd go into another laughing fit.

"Good," Meg prompted, "she has eyes."

"Uhh, nice ones. She looks like a Wheaties box photo. Athletic."

"Healthy, all-American?"

He nodded.

Her eyes widened. "This is a suspect?"

"Meg," he said, "looks and personality are not measuring sticks. Believe me, I know."

She frowned. "That is so sad. How do you know whom to trust?"

"I don't. I assume they're all guilty until proven innocent."

"Adam," she turned to her husband, "he can't keep doing this. Talk to him."

Adam squeezed his wife's hand while

looking at Dominick. "He's good at what he does, love. And he's needed in that capacity."

"I appreciate your concern, Meg, but I'm all right. I've been at this sort of thing for ten years. After a time, it becomes second nature. You and Adam are teaching me to trust. I'm learning to separate work from the rest of the world. I'm learning to accept the evil in the world and do what I can to fight it without losing sight of a good and trustworthy God. I just can't build an authentic relationship with Cat St. Clair at the moment. This operation might take a few weeks. After that I can open up with her." He paused. "Unless she's behind bars."

Meg's curls bounced as she shook her head in an exasperated way. "Okay, okay. So I suppose you want me to pray that you'll shut up?"

"You got it."

Adam yawned loudly. "Isn't it time for you two to get going on your outing?"

"Sorry, bud." Dominick stood. Saturday nights in the ER were usually his friend's most difficult. Sunday mornings, like today, he often went to church anyway, then needed the afternoon for sleep. "Wanna ride with me, Meg?"

"No, I'll drive too. That way you won't

have to backtrack. Adam, leave the dishes."

"You talked me into it, love."

Dominick watched as the two hugged and kissed. An expression of their obvious love after twenty years of marriage was always a sight to behold.

He and Meg were meeting a group of kids from the homeless shelter at the zoo this afternoon. It wasn't the first time she had convinced him paperwork could wait. "See you, doc. Tomorrow?"

"Sounds good. Kiss the orangutans for me."

"Dominick," Meg said as they walked through the kitchen, "one thing — you cannot refer to the children as rugrats."

"Megan Parker, you are so persnickety. Can't I keep some of my vocabulary?" She had taken on the challenge of cleaning up his language with a vengeance these past few months. "It's authentic, at least."

"It's atrocious. Try lamby-pies."

"I can't say lamby-pies."

"Ha! You just did, big guy!"

"Then meet me on Friday, Mother, at the pot shop." Cat cradled the phone between chin and shoulder as she hooked the strap of her denim overall shorts. "We can eat Chinese at Horton Plaza."

"Will 11 work, honey?" her mother asked. "That'll give me time to do a few errands and —"

"And miss rush-hour traffic and have time to fix dinner before your meeting." She laughed. Her schoolteacher mother's summer schedule made hers seem dull. "I know, I know. Eleven is perfect. I gotta go. Put Daddy on."

"All right. I love you, Catherine. Stanley!"

Still holding the cordless phone to her ear, Cat knelt and rummaged through a pile of clothes and shoes on the closet floor. She found one comfy old Birkenstock and slipped it on her bare foot.

"Hey, Kit-Cat!" her father's voice boomed.

She winced and tilted the phone a few inches from her ear. "Hey, Daddy. How you doing?" Her right hand found the other sandal, and she sat on the floor to buckle the straps.

"Great. We got the Timber Oasis project."

"No kidding? That's fantastic!"

"I think so. How are you? Don't say fine."

Cat smiled. She couldn't dodge a subject for long with her dad, so she seldom tried. "I'm not bad. Trent came by unexpectedly the other day, and I only got a minor, minor headache."

Her dad grunted in reply.

"Anyway, I have a favor to ask. I was roaming around the pond yesterday, and I thought it sure would be nice to sit down and relax and not be sitting on the hard ground —"

"You always liked sitting in the dirt."

"Well, I still do, but I'm thinking of the guests. Can you make us a park bench? Or two? Not elaborate ones like you did for Mother. Just basic, rustic jobs."

"Sure. When do you want them?"

Construction was her father's business, and he'd gladly build her anything. But he was a busy man. "The inspection is two weeks from tomorrow. I thought it'd be a really special touch to have those in the garden for it. I'll come up and stain them."

"Nah. We can do it. Probably have them there early next week."

"Thank you! I'd better go. I'm meeting Elli and Jason at the zoo."

"That's what I heard. Give my grandson a bear squeeze for me. Elli too."

"Okay, Daddy. Bye. Love you."

"Love you, too, Kit-Cat. Good-bye."

She continued sitting on the floor. For a gruff, straightforward kind of man, her dad could be subtle with her, and for that she was grateful. The mention of hugging her sister and nephew, which he knew she always did anyway, was his way of voicing concern about her hug quota. If she didn't get it filled — and that meant at least one good solid wrap every couple of days — a distinct irritableness crept into her personality.

She had always been that way. She didn't know if it came from growing up in a demonstrative, loving family or what, but even through her teen years any grumpy, out-of-sorts feeling had a quick fix in her father's bear hug or her mother's slender arms that gently rocked her. By adulthood she had learned to recognize that feeling and mask it when necessary. But Daddy would always detect it. Thanks to Trent's departure from the relationship and not seeing her folks for the last two weeks — not to mention the upcoming inspection that sat like a barbell on her shoulders — it was probably there today in her voice.

She bit her lower lip, cutting off the sob before it formed, and stood, tossing the phone onto the rumpled bed. It looked as messy as the closet floor.

Oh, well! Her internal voice rose on the *well.*

Cat stepped into the bathroom, shoved aside a wet towel with her foot, briskly ran a brush through her hair, then hurried through the small apartment. It was a suffocatingly small unit with only three windows. The combined kitchen and living room was as messy as the bedroom closet floor. Shoes, clothes, magazines, and newspapers lay here and there. Two sealed cardboard boxes of books still unpacked after three months were stacked near the couch. On the floor next to the round dining table sat a group of brown-leafed plants. The counter, a minimal dividing line between kitchen and living room, was covered with various forms of pottery awaiting the final step of sanding on their rough bottom edges. Today's breakfast dishes were in the sink inside last night's popcorn bowl that sat atop yesterday's breakfast and lunch dishes.

Oh, well! Late Sunday nights were good for catching up on dish washing. She certainly didn't have anything else going on. What had she heard once? Something about if your desktop was a mess, it indicated a disordered inner life. Actually, her desk at the motel was in order. What did that mean about her inner self — a clear desktop at work but her living space a disaster area? She didn't think she wanted to know.

Kitchen cabinets above and below a countertop ran along the same wall where the door was. The one organized spot in the whole place was at the end of that counter where she always kept a large celadon-colored platter she had made years ago. In it lay her purse, keys, sunglasses, pens and pad, a to-do list, and a migraine prescription bottle. She grabbed what she needed now, unlocked the chain, two deadbolts, and knob, and headed out the door, carefully locking up half of what she had just undone. She strode down the single flight of carpeted steps.

Small but secure. Just what she had wanted and needed. Security here was expensive and mediocre though. Gone was her reasonable rent, along with a private front door on a plant-abundant courtyard. No more patio or assortment of friendly neighbors, many of whom kept the same strange hours she did. No more intriguing characters at the twenty-four-hour laundromat across the street or the café down the block.

What she had instead was a double set of security doors front and back of the eight-plex that required a key or someone from the inside to open them. Only dense, ankle-height ground cover filled the small green area through which the sidewalk cut. The side drive and carport area was nearby and well-lit. Fellow apartment dwellers were seldom seen. And it was all tucked into a residential neighborhood, the nearest business a gas station three blocks away.

She had needed this, though, needed to get away from the nightmare memories that haunted her other place. The fears. The breakup with Trent.

Maybe she'd outgrow the need in time. If God answered her parents' prayers, she would. They still had hope. At times it was only clinging to their hope that kept her going in between the hugs.

Cat slid into her tangerine-colored, small sport utility vehicle. The Tracker had been a gift from dear Trent, one he insisted she keep. And being utility-minded herself, she did. The higher rent didn't leave much for car payments.

She drove toward the freeway while steering her mind back to her parents. A rush of gratitude flowed through her. In the aftermath of the nightmare, they supported her with loving tact and subtlety, never overbearing in their concern or their opinion on what she should or shouldn't do. Space and hugs. It was a winning combination.

The odor in the children's petting zoo always overpowered Cat's sister Elli, even when she wasn't pregnant. She sat on a bale of hay outside the chicken-wire fence, holding a handkerchief over her nose, while inside Cat and little Jason meandered among the goats.

Her three-year-old nephew resembled his mother. They both had chubby cheeks, brown-black eyes, long black hair, and short legs. Younger than Cat by four years, Elizabeth was the baby of the family but was ahead of her in the marriage and children department. Her husband Jim was out of town on business, which gave the women just a little more time than usual together. Besides being sisters, they were the best of friends.

Jason squealed in delight as a goat nuzzled him. Cat heard a nasal laugh come from Elli's direction and scooped up her nephew before he was knocked down. It seemed a good moment to whisk him out of there. The place was getting too hot and crowded even for her. Although her sister was only about six months along, she was probably suffering.

Tickling him so he wouldn't notice the departure, she carried the boy through the double set of thick screened entrance doors. She pulled open the second and walked right into Dominick.

"Well, hi!" She smiled. Jason wrapped his

arms and legs around her and stared quietly.

"Cat! Hi." Sunglasses were perched on top of his hair. Two small children were at his sides, each holding a hand. Someone jostled him from behind, and he moved aside.

A small woman with curly, brown hair walked around him, two youngsters in tow, and laughed. "D'Angelo, you're holding up traffic."

"Blame my boss. She's coming out the wrong way."

"You're his boss?" The woman's voice was incredulous, and her eyes widened. "No, no, no. You're much too pretty and too young to be this ruffian's boss." The two little ones tugged on her arms, and she followed them through the door with another laugh.

Dominick winced. "That's Megan. She's in charge of this outing." He held up his right hand, "This is Mikey," then his left, "and Andy."

"Hi, Mikey and Andy." She noticed they wore yarn necklaces with name tags attached. They were about five or six years old but had a sober grown-up expression behind the grins on their undernourished faces. Similar-appearing children holding adults' hands were making their way around them. "This is my nephew, Jason. Oh, and my little sister Elizabeth behind you. This is Dominick

96

D'Angelo, the new guy at the Castillo. He's the one doing the big painting project."

"Nice to meet you, Dominick."

He glanced down at Elli. "Nice to meet you. Well, we're off to feed the goats. See you Tuesday, *Jill*." A small smile lifted the right corner of his mouth.

"Bye, *Jack*."

Jason reached for his mother. "Mommy . . ."

"Oh, Jase, let Aunt Kit-Cat hold you. Mommy's too hot in here. Who's Jack and Jill?"

Cat bounced her nephew on her hip and headed down the sidewalk. "Uhh, inside joke. As in jack-of-all-trades. Let's go get some ice cream!"

Jason giggled and squeezed her neck. "I want chocolate!"

"Chocolate!" she echoed. "Elli, are you okay?"

She replied with a wan smile and nodded, wiping her forehead with a hankie. "You spoil this child too much."

"That's what aunties are for, right, Jase?"

"Right!"

"If Mommy says no, then you can always . . . ?"

"Call Aunt Kit-Cat!" Jason yelled.

"Give me five!" They laughed and slapped hands.

A short time later, in the main part of the San Diego Zoo, they sat under an umbrella at a round table. A light breeze gently fanned them as they ate ice cream cones.

"Cat, you never mentioned Dominick to me."

"Yes, I did. I told you we have a new temp who's being a big help with the painting job."

"Like I said, you never mentioned Dominick to me."

"What does that mean?"

Elli wiped Jason's mouth with a napkin. "Well, he's attractive. Really, really well-built. Intense eyes."

Cat shrugged. "Did you see his nose?" She touched her own. "Little askew."

Her sister sighed and made a wry face. She wouldn't press that it was time for Cat to get on with her life, but she'd come close. "And a few tiny scars. Is he married?"

"No. He's a drifter type, just a temp, just in town a short time. I suspect the man is not the marrying type."

Jason leaned over and licked his aunt's cone. "It's dripping."

"Cat, he's taking homeless kids to the zoo."

She met Elli's eyes. "Is that what they were?"

She nodded. "I saw the name of a shelter on the back of one of their name tags."

"Okay, I admit it. It impressed me to see him holding those two little boys' hands. But I'm not —" She took a breath. "I'm just not interested, Elli."

"I know." Her sister reached over and squeezed her arm.

Jason's sticky fingers grasped her wrist and pulled her melting ice cream to himself. "Aunt Kit-Cat, you should eat ice cream, not fingernails."

Six

Tuesday afternoon Cat absentmindedly brushed a layer of dirt from her desk with a paper towel. Someone must have used her office and left the window open to blow so much of it around. It seemed to her this had happened a couple of other times also. She'd have to ask the Sunday-Monday staff about it. She didn't mind sharing this room, but she had too many other housekeeping and maintenance details to be bothered with tidying up after others.

From a drawer she pulled out a clipboard. Attached to it was the checklist she had created, a combination of her own ideas and the official inspection report. Today she would go through it all again. She would make sure every millimeter of tile grout throughout the lobby was dirt free, every guest room's shower stall sparkled, every formerly leaky faucet was dry, every light switchplate factory-fresh without one fingerprint smudge, every inch of carpet shampooed, every blade of grass neatly trimmed —

She burst out laughing. No wonder her

apartment was always a disaster area! She had this place to take care of.

She started with Cissy at the registration desk.

"Uh-oh," the younger woman greeted her. "Denim jumper, bobby socks and tennies, and the infamous, fluorescent lime clipboard. It looks like serious work time. I'd better warn the others."

Cat waved the clipboard above her head. "Right! It is getting-down-to-business day. Hold my calls. And move out of my way!" She scooted behind Cissy and began systematically reviewing the work station. Computer, printer, paper, pens, forms, calendar, telephones, room keys, pamphlets. "Cissy, have I ever mentioned you're welcome to come organize my apartment anytime?"

"Oh, once or twice."

"Thanks for doing such a great job out here."

"You know I love it."

"Maybe we could have fresh flowers on the counter when the big guys come for inspection? And replace that hinge there." Pointing with the pen, she indicated a cabinet door beneath the counter and then the large brass-plated letters on the wall that spelled out Castillo de Cala. "And make

101

sure those are straight. It's a little dusty in that space beneath the counter." She smiled and wrote notes on the clipboard. "Other than that, it's perfect. As usual."

"What about my new reservation program?"

Cat sighed loudly and scrunched her eyebrows together. "I know that's more important. Supposedly it's on its way. I'll try to get an update." She found a notepad on the counter, jotted herself a reminder on the top sheet, then tucked it into her pocket. "Will you call Mandi and ask her to get the restaurant staff together at 3:45 please? And can you find Dominick? He should probably go through this with me."

"Sure."

While Cat strolled through the lobby checking for fingerprints on the knights' armor and dust on the rough-hewn end tables, she heard Cissy speaking into the walkie-talkie.

"Yo, handsome! Are you there?"

The other voice was drowned in static, but Cissy's instructions were loud and clear.

Muttering to herself, Cat finished the lobby inspection and circled back to the counter. "Cissy, that was inappropriate."

"What was?"

"I know the general consensus is he's a

hunk, but flirting in public over the walkie-talkie isn't professional."

"Oh, Cat, no one's in here." She flipped back her long blonde hair.

"That's not the point."

"Do I have your permission to go out with him?"

"You don't need my permission, Cissy, you know that. Just keep it on a professional level here."

"Yeah, yeah. No huggy-kissy stuff in the lobby."

"Not even behind a tree. Consider the entire property as being in public and therefore off limits to any display whatsoever of a relationship beyond a business one. Okay?"

"Got it, *Miss* St. Clair." Her tone was borderline huffy, but she recovered quickly and smiled. "Do you want a Band-Aid for that finger?"

Cat glanced at her hands. "What — Oh, that's professional-looking." She laughed at her left ring finger. The jagged end of the nail was covered with blood.

Cissy pulled a box of bandages from a drawer and found one for her.

"Thanks." Cat set down the clipboard. "So, are you going out with him?" She winked.

"Well," she looked beyond Cat's shoulder

and grinned, "I'm working on it. Hi, hand-some! I mean, Mr. D'Angelo."

Cat raised her brows and leaned sideways in order to intercept Cissy's eye contact.

"Just giving you a hard time." The younger woman held up her right hand. "I'm done. Scout's honor!"

Dominick joined them. "So which is it? Handsome or mister?"

Cissy wiggled the hand she still held in the air. "Just Dominick. Hello, Dominick. Good-bye, Dominick." She meandered down to the other end of the long counter and busied herself.

Cat smiled at him as she picked up the clipboard. "Hi. How are you?" He wore his paint-spattered jeans, but she noticed he had turned his cap right side around and had put on a short-sleeved blue denim work shirt over the T-shirt.

"Fine."

"I'm doing my version of an inspection, and I thought it'd be a good idea for you to come with me. That way you can make your own list and tell me how unrealistic I'm being when I assume it can all be finished by the day after tomorrow."

"No problem." He wore his Secret Service look, his gray eyes never wavering from hers.

She thought he didn't resemble that man who two days ago escorted children around the zoo. "Did you get the goats fed?"

He nodded slightly. "Every last one of them."

"Good. Will it seriously set you back if you leave the painting for an hour or two?"

Cissy giggled as she walked back toward them. "He'll just come in again at 9 A.M." She reached across the counter and tapped his arm with a clipboard. "Here, you'll need this."

"Dominick!" Cat was flabbergasted. "You came in at 9 this morning?"

"Wanted to get an early start."

"But 9 A.M.?" She did some quick mental calculations.

He shrugged. "No reason not to."

"That's six hours' overtime!"

"Miguel and I don't want overtime, just dinner."

"Miguel came at 9?"

"No, he came about noon."

"I can get you some overtime."

"Don't worry about it. Shall we get started?"

"What were you, a Marine?"

"Hardly."

"Don't you have a life?"

"Hey, Cat," Cissy interrupted, "are you going to tell him?"

She turned to the other woman. "Tell him what?"

"About you and your inspection mode. It's starting to show."

For a moment, Cat didn't comprehend. "Oh, right. Dominick . . ." She tilted her head, closed her eyes, and in a singsong tone delivered a prepared speech the other supervisors had already heard. "Don't take anything I say for the next two weeks personally. If I see one blade of grass out of place, I may totally lose it. I'm a little uptight because I failed the last inspection, and I am absolutely determined to pass this one."

"Excuse me, but I thought you were the *assistant* manager?" he asked.

She opened her eyes. "Number two has to try harder."

He burst into laughter. "Weren't you the one who told me to lighten up? Remember, this is southern California."

She was glad to see his face soften. It helped smooth her own edginess. "Let's go. Thanks, Cissy." They walked outside and headed down the sidewalk. "I have to talk to the restaurant staff first. Will you check in the kitchen? They were trying to unclog a sink this morning, and some lightbulbs need to be replaced."

From the corner of her eye, she watched him write on the clipboard. "Dominick, I apologize. Obviously, you have a life. I just saw you with homeless kids at the zoo. Do you spend much time with them?"

"No. Just when Meg comes up with something like that outing and needs an extra pair of hands. I'm not all that altruistic. Left to my own devices, I'd be surfing or moving on down the coast."

She thought Meg must be one special lady to him. If that was his type, Cissy didn't stand a chance. "But you came in six hours early to paint."

"That doesn't involve people."

"Ultimately it does. The guests here are affected, the owners, and me." She chuckled. "Definitely me. Oh, this will be so fantastic if you finish! Promise me you won't move down the coast until after the inspection?"

"Well, I don't know. I don't often plan that far in advance. This may call for another bribe."

"You name it."

"I'll think on it."

"So why *down* the coast?"

He shrugged. "Never been to Mexico. How about you?"

"It's beautiful. Desolate and deserty, but

with such friendly people. We used to drive down to Rosarito for rock lobster. I've camped right on the beach further south. And Acapulco is gorgeous. I go into Tecate all the time; it's inland and not far from here. There's so much poverty and sadness. You'd like it, a perfect home for your altruistic heart, Jack."

"Mm-hmm." He opened the door for her. "What about the drug trafficking?"

She walked inside ahead of him. "What about it? If you believe everything you hear, you'd think it was going on right out your back door. It hasn't interfered with my travels at all."

They spent the next hour and a half combing the grounds, then stopped to compare notes outside the back lobby entrance. Sufficient progress had been made on every possible detail. Cat felt confident that things were under control and even caught herself breathing a prayer of thanks.

"That's better," Dominick said.

"What's better?"

"Your dimple's back, and you haven't bitten a nail since we were at the pool."

She laughed. "I'm kind of easy to read, huh?"

He grinned. "Yeah, now that you mention it, you are. If we're done here, I'm going to get back to painting."

"Sure." She watched him walk down the sidewalk, his large frame moving with athletic grace. "Hey, Dominick, thanks," she called. "You're making this bearable."

He gave her a thumbs-up sign as he rounded the corner. "Just doing my job."

He certainly was an interesting character, Cat thought as she turned to go inside. At that moment a man burst through the door. She took a step backwards to get out of his way.

"I'm looking for the manager!" he barked. He was tall and middle-aged, with graying hair and a matching mustache that outlined a frowning mouth.

"I'm the assistant manager, sir. What's the problem?"

"Where's the manager?" His voice rose.

"He's gone for the day, but I'm here." She smiled her sweetest. "If you'll just tell me —"

He made a noise of disgust. "This is not what I signed up for. No room service, no bar, not one !%@#! thing for my teenagers to do, the !%@#! ocean is not at our doorstep, no !%@#! MTV . . ."

Inwardly she winced at his adjectives. "I apologize for the misunderstanding. We try to make it clear that our facilities are on a quiet cove that families with young children enjoy. We will find you a more suitable place and refund your money. Did you just check in?"

"You won't find a place —"

"Apologize to the lady," Dominick's voice cut in.

Cat glanced over her shoulder and saw him striding toward them. His eyes were slits and his jaw set. He was decidedly more intimidating than this irate guest. Quickly she soothed, "It's okay, Dominick. We can just —"

"It's not okay." His voice was a rumble, like a volcano about to erupt. "Mister, I repeat, apologize to the lady."

Cat thought it best to stay out of it. She bit her lip.

The man's mustache moved, but no words came from him. At last he noisily cleared his throat. "Excuse my rudeness. My wife and kids are disappointed."

"Of course they are," she said. "That's understandable. I promise, we can take care of it. If you go to the registration desk, Cissy will help you, and I'll be right there."

As the door swished shut behind the guest, she turned toward Dominick, still glowering behind her. She touched his forearm, an intuitive gesture to defuse the

110

tension. Beneath her fingers the contracted muscle felt like a band of steel. "Hmm," she teased, "I was going to suggest you can borrow the armor from the knight in the lobby." She patted his arm. "But I don't think you need it."

The corner of his mouth lifted, and she felt him relax. "Didn't mean to spoil your fun."

"Oh, this was much more fun. I don't think he can sue us for that little exchange." She recalled Dominick's friend Meg at the zoo referring to him as a ruffian. "If he hadn't apologized, you wouldn't have done anything, would you?"

"Probably just ushered him into the lobby."

"Probably?"

He raised his eyebrows as if not sure.

She caught her breath, wondering how to tell him that combativeness was inappropriate. "Dominick, I can handle these situations. I appreciate your knightly effort, but I really was okay."

"I know you didn't need any help. It was just his screaming at you that . . ." He paused and looked away. "The last time my dad did that to my mom, I punched him. Haven't seen him since."

"I'm sorry. How old were you?"

"Ten." He shrugged. "That's life. You'd better get inside."

"Oh, yeah, right. Thanks."

Hurrying along the corridor toward the lobby, she wondered how in the world God had gotten this guy's attention. It must have been something along the lines of earth-shattering.

He needed a drink.

No, he didn't *need* one, he *wanted* one. A stiff one.

Elbows propped on bent knees, Dominick placed his hands over his face in an effort to blot out reality for just a few moments. It was dark now. He sat on the ground, behind large bushy oleanders against a wooden fence that allowed a cracked view between its slats of the service drive just outside the kitchen's patio. It was where he had hidden the night he surprised Cat after she placed trash in the dumpster.

Father God, help me. Remind me that You are all the reality I need. Help me figure out who's involved. Give me a chance to tell Cat the truth. Soon. In Jesus' name, Amen.

Cat.

She was getting to him. Working in close proximity on Tuesday, scouring the property in her meticulous way . . . He swore he could still feel the imprint of her long, cool fingers on his arm, calming the fire in him with that simple touch, with her gentle teasing about armor.

Why did he tell her about his dad? He had told only two people in twenty-five years about that incident. One was his little brother who had been at the neighbor's at the time. The other was his friend Adam.

Today he had watched her from a distance walking with Carver and Hunter, the manager. Clipboard in hand, she resembled an ad geared toward top female executives. Hair just so, the usually straight layers wavy. Black suit with white silk blouse, small gold earrings, just enough heel to accentuate her shapely legs. She looked focused, in control, not on the verge of a headache. When he questioned Cissy about the different reaction to Carver's last visit, she explained that when Cat had at least a week's notice and the visit was strictly necessary business, she could handle it.

The trial inspection had been conducted early afternoon. He knew when it was over. She came running to where he and Miguel painted, grinning and yelling, "Game time!" She had changed into shorts, T-shirt, and high-tops. A group of girls followed. He recognized them as the twelve-year-olds' softball team staying at the Castillo. From the top of the ladder, he noticed some of the younger staff members — housekeepers, waiters, cooks — noisily making their way down the sidewalk.

She clambered up a couple of the ladder rungs and yanked on the cuff of his jeans. "Come on! The other team wants you cuz you're tall."

"What's going on?" he had asked.

The grin on her face kept the dimple firmly in place. "Trenton William Carver, Jr. has declared we are in good shape, so we're celebrating. We always celebrate around here with basketball. Come on. It's mandatory!"

He spent the next hour enjoying the strangest game of basketball he'd ever played. There were people of all ages and lots of laughter. He soon learned it wasn't a foul to hug someone to prevent them from shooting. Cat hugged everyone. Even him.

He had never met anyone so wholesome who wasn't afraid of him.

Now he mouthed another prayer. *Dear Lord, I pray that she's innocent.*

At the sound of a truck braking on the other side of the fence, he turned silently and looked through the sliver of space between the boards. It should be the Thursday night produce delivery.

He had a good view of the truck because the driver had backed in. Spotlights mounted on the fence lit the driveway. The man unloaded several cartons marked *Oranges*. Around 2 A.M. when the night security guard slept in a corner of the housekeeping room, Dominick would investigate the kitchen to see if indeed oranges were in them.

After a week here, the suspicions were still vague. The Castillo was part of a route, of that much the agency was almost certain. Was it drugs going north, money going south, a collection point? Monday night's bread delivery appeared more than a practical amount in his opinion, but he hadn't been able to search the kitchen. The Friday-to-Monday night security guard didn't nap like tonight's guard. He stayed alert — all night.

Tuesday morning the vending machines were serviced, and laundry was picked up and delivered. He had missed both.

Who helped from the inside? Night security? Daytime maintenance? Registration clerks? Cissy? Not sharp enough. Part-time college kids? They were either users or were too serious about school to risk anything illegal. Kitchen staff?

The driver returned, and Dominick saw that Cat was on his heels. Her clear voice carried. "Bring me some Saturday. Please?"

The man's reply was muffled as he climbed into the back of the truck.

"Well, try hard, okay? I'm going to Tecate early Monday morning. They really need it this time." She accepted a small box marked *Avocados* from him.

"Yeah, I know, Cat," the driver replied. "I'll see what I can find."

Something twisted in Dominick's stomach. *"I go into Tecate all the time."* He remembered her talking about Mexico. Why Tecate? Nothing there but a brewery. And cocaine.

He gritted his teeth and fought down the image of Cat's fresh face grinning up at him, the dimpled cheek.

It was time to sever his emotions from the job at hand. Special Agent D'Angelo had better plunk himself back into the driver's seat and lock all feelings in the trunk. Then he'd better find a place to bury the key, far from any honey-colored eyes and disarming personality that threatened to take up permanent residence in his heart.

He had work to do. *Father, help me do it.*

116

Seven

Cat focused on the heavy freeway traffic zipping eastbound on the 8. The car's top was down, and her hair flew in the wind. She wore sunglasses and visor to protect her face from the hot sun, a white cotton shirt, and khaki shorts.

A box of goodies nestled in the seat next to her. Today it was carrots and potatoes, extras the produce delivery man had managed to scrounge up for her. In the back were gifts from her mother's church circle — cereal and disposable diapers. It wasn't much, but it would be appreciated as much as a rainstorm after months of drought, and it would not go to waste. The orphanage workers were smart managers, and the children ate whatever was available.

She seldom missed one of her semi-monthly trips. Two Mondays out of every four she headed down to Tecate, Mexico. Her interest in the place began the Christmas she was fifteen years old. Mother had found an organization that played Santa at one of the orphanages, asking the children what they would like and making their lists available to Californians who then shopped, wrapped, and donated those items. Mother, of course, wanted to deliver them too, and she did, taking along her five children.

The smiles, hugs, game of basketball, and primitive conditions burrowed their way into Cat's heart and stayed there. Mother, disgruntled that Santa received more attention than the King whose birth they celebrated, formed her own loosely knit organization — friends who gave what they could, when they could. Through the years many subsequent trips were made.

Not all the children were orphans. Many just had to live there while parents worked elsewhere. Unable to provide homes for them, they would often visit on weekends.

That above all was what bound Cat to them, but Trent never seemed able to grasp that and often questioned her motives for regularly visiting the orphanage. Many times she had explained, "Trent, *I* am an orphan. Except for the grace of God and Stan and Betty St. Clair, I could have grown up in that environment."

He would pooh-pooh the explanation, reminding her she was born in the States and it was highly unlikely that environment could have been replicated here. That really wasn't the point she was trying to make. But no matter how she worded it, he just didn't get it.

An image of Dominick D'Angelo came to mind — little boy hands tucked into his large ones. Would *he* get it?

Trent visited the orphanage with her once, cringing the whole time, even while he smiled politely. Another time, just to be ornery, she begged him to let her drive his Mercedes down there. Horrified, he recounted stories of car accidents and the *federales* confiscating American automobiles. Eventually he joined in her laughter and kissed her . . .

Sometimes she would stare at her reflection in a mirror, noting the complexion a shade deeper than her siblings, the dark hair, eyes "the color of maple syrup," in Daddy's words. And she would wonder what mixture of blood ran through her veins.

Besides the true royal blood, that is. She smiled to herself now. When her parents had explained the concept of adoption into God's family by accepting who Christ was, it was a simple one for her to grasp. It was what they had done for her. They took her into their home and asked only that she accept the gift of love they wanted to give her.

The past, where she had come from, didn't make a difference — with her parents or with Jesus.

The green freeway signs now directed the way to Jamul, but Cat navigated by rote, circling along a couple of exit ramps and onto Highway 94, which soon narrowed to a divided four-lane with stoplights. The roads and scenery had changed drastically through the years, with developments springing up like sagebrush through the dry earth. She turned at an intersection, following the highway southeast where it soon left the heavily populated areas, shrank to two lanes, wound up and down rock-strewn hills, and shot through valleys flung with breathtaking vistas. Some S-curves were sharp, and she had to downshift, taking them at thirty miles an hour. Still, it wasn't a long trip. She usually could make it from her apartment and across the border within forty-five minutes.

She moved through Jamul in the blink of an eye, then Dulzura, population all of 700, and Barrett, which was only a sign on the highway.

She took advantage of the sparse traffic and enjoyed the scenery. It reminded her of her childhood home with abundant fragrant wildflowers and scrubby bushes greener than average if the winter rains had been heavy like this year. Distant, higher hills appeared a hazy turquoise dotted with white boulders and an occasional house. The vast expanse of sky was cloudless, the blue unbroken except for an occasional soaring hawk crying in its mournful way.

Seemingly in the middle of nowhere, a border patrol building came into view on her left. It was an immigration inspection checkpoint. A variety of at least ten official vehicles lined the parking lot — cruisers for highway speed, Explorers for off-road excursions, vans for hauling — all painted white with the telltale green stripe and lettering, *Border Patrol.* Two officers stood alongside the road, stopping everyone headed north. That point sometimes slowed her homeward drive.

About twenty minutes later she turned right onto Tecate Road and soon entered Tecate, California, basically just a spot at the top of a hill — a small strip mall, a border crossing, and an intriguing view of Tecate, Mexico. The border consisted of a small building off to the right and a prominent red hexagon sign with the word *Alto* rather than *Stop* on it. She sat for just a few moments as the Mexican guards greeted the occupants of three cars ahead of her before waving them into Mexico.

This wasn't the shoppers' mecca that Tijuana was. Crossing the border here was much less complicated and time-consuming and therefore much easier for her purposes. Even when there was a line of cars when she headed back and each had to be stopped and sometimes searched, it was nothing like that place.

"*Señorita* St. Clair!" The guard's teeth glistened brilliant white against his black mustache. He leaned across the passenger's side. "*Bienvenido!*"

"*Gracias,* Alberto!" Cat chatted with the young man who more often than not was at this post on the Mondays she visited. When another car approached behind her, he sent her into his homeland with a smile. She knew not everyone received that.

It always hit her when she first drove along the narrow street — an immediate sense of being inside someone's private, colorful, cluttered house. Not one inch was unused space. Her eyes couldn't put order to what she saw, bombarded as the scene was with signs, buildings, cars, plants, and people. Even above it all, the sky was crisscrossed with thick telephone and electrical cables.

The median strip was packed with

flowers, squatty palm trees, and signs. Along the right curb, cars were parked bumper to bumper, block after block. People — sitting, walking, and standing — filled the narrow sidewalks outside the storefronts. These ran nonstop down both sides of the hill, all different sizes, colors, and shapes with names and descriptions painted in large letters on their stucco walls, rampant bougainvillea twisting between them.

The scene crowded out all thoughts of Trent and the upcoming inspection. Driving toward the orphanage, she knew this was the best way to spend her day off. She'd get her "*abuelita* fix," and all would be right again with the world.

Dominick's soft shoes silently hit the pavement. He spotted the Jeep parked across the street from Cat's apartment building, in view of the carport where that orange car of hers stuck out even in the dark, kind of the way a whale in the Chicago River would. When he opened the passenger's door, the dome light didn't go on. He slid inside.

"She went to an orphanage."

"An orphanage?" Dominick stared at the young man sitting behind the steering wheel. The dim glow from a distant street-light didn't reveal much of his expression.

"An orphanage. Real tough cookie you got here, D'Angelo."

He heard the sarcasm in the other agent's voice. "What else?"

"*Nada.* Little kids, basketball, loud singing in English, a bunch of women. She delivered some boxes. They dug into them outside on a picnic table. Carrots, potatoes, cereal, and — are you ready for this? — disposable diapers."

Dominick leaned back against the seat and rubbed his forehead. Brent Engstrom, agent-in-training under him, had spent the day tailing Cat. "Orphanage," he muttered again. "What does a good-looking, single woman do on her day off? Drives through miles of desert to an obscure little town in Mexico and visits orphans. Makes perfect sense to me."

"They seemed to know her. You could tell this wasn't her first time. Shoot, the Border Patrol knew her."

"Border Patrol?"

"Yeah. Going down, the guy leaned into her car, laughing and smiling. I sure didn't get that from him. Coming out, the U.S. guys just waved her through, a hi-how-ya'-doin' wave. Then she parked, ran over to the

Mexican guard, and gave him something wrapped in a napkin. He pulled out a pastry-looking thing and started eating it."

"So she did take something from the orphanage?"

Engstrom shrugged. "Some woman who looked about a hundred years old handed her a Burger King bag when she was leaving, then they hugged each other. That's what she pulled the pastry from."

"Did you watch her car?"

"Nobody went near it. I left for ten minutes, fifteen max. Had to find a bathroom. The only stop she made was at a grocery store down the street here, then home by 5. She's been inside ever since. I tell you, it's just all too innocent-looking to be a cover. I felt guilty watching her. Don't you think she's got a wholesome face?"

Dominick ignored the question. Had he ever been that wet behind the ears? Of course he had. He could hear his own voice saying almost the exact same words. *Too innocent-looking to be a cover.*

Fifteen minutes unaccounted for. Regular trips to Mexico. Familiar with border guards. A bag with unknown contents. Attractive, smart, friendly, single woman alone on her day off.

"What's she like?" Engstrom interrupted

his thoughts. "Is her personality as whole-some as her looks?"

"You'll find out soon enough. Are you checking into the motel Sunday?"

"Yeah. I'm supposed to be a family man on business from L.A. The wife and kids will be down later in the week."

"Okay. I'll get her car tomorrow, have the crew go over it with a fine-tooth comb. Hadacek relieving you?"

"At midnight."

"Why don't you go get something to eat?"

"Food? I don't need food. This is the fun part. Thirteen hours straight, my eyes glued to one car —"

"Get out of here. Take my truck." He dug into his jeans pocket for the keys. "It's two blocks back."

The younger man opened his door.

"Hey, Brent — about covers."

"Yeah?"

"You never, never know."

Dominick settled back into the seat and glued his eyes to Cat's car. They would watch it until she arrived at the Castillo to-morrow. If she carried anything, it'd be un-loaded there. If somehow they missed something between now and then, there'd at least be a clue. False flooring, a hidden com-partment, residue. He'd find it. And he'd find her wholesomeness a cover . . . or not.

Guilty until proven innocent. You never, never knew. The one time he thought he knew, he almost got himself and two others killed. She was an attractive bundle of fun, loving and totally innocent-looking. He fell for her hard. That was one scene he wasn't about to repeat.

Not even with this Catherine St. Clair who visited orphans on her day off.

"Dominick, you don't have to do that."

He forced himself to meet those honey-colored eyes across the desk and give her a small smile. "But let me, as a token of my appreciation. Like I said, the car wash has this great deal going today. They did such a good job on the shuttle van, it'll last until inspection next week. And besides, your car's dirty. It doesn't look orange anymore."

"Tangerine." Cat opened the large Burger King bag he had noticed on her desk. "Here, have a *buñuelo*. My *abuelita* makes them for me, and they're the best in the world."

The illogical mental leaps of women never ceased to amaze him, but he tried to just go with Cat's flow. "Thanks. *Abuelita?*" He bit into the crispy, cinnamon- and sugar-coated tortilla-like strip. It melted in his mouth.

"Grandma. Well, she's not really my

grandma. Everyone calls her that. I went to see her yesterday in Tecate, which explains one reason my car is so dusty. Had to get my *abuelita* fix." Her half-smile looked absent-minded, as if her thoughts were miles away.

"What's an *abuelita* fix?"

"Oh, hugs and food. She prays for me, reminds me to read my Bible." Another half-smile. "Coming from a gentle grandma in Spanish, it gets my attention for some reason."

"Grandmas are like that." A fleeting image from his childhood came to mind. She had been a generous woman, like this one before him. "Cat, I picked up my check . . ."

She stacked papers on her desk, all business now. "Sorry it doesn't cover all the time you've put in. I don't have that much clout."

"Well, I appreciate what you did do. Now can I get your car washed for you? I'll use my dinner break time."

"Goodness, don't worry about that. We owe you time." She opened a drawer and pulled out a key ring. "Thank you. I know I won't get around to cleaning it this week."

He accepted the keys from her. "It'll make the employee parking lot look better for inspection."

She chuckled and finally looked at him.

"And I thought *I* went overboard. I'll pay for —"

"It's a gift. I won't be gone long."

Dominick headed out the back door. Cat had been preoccupied either with her visit to Mexico or the upcoming inspection but was not concerned about letting her car go. That was a good sign.

The top was down, as usual. He climbed in and adjusted the seat.

"Buttering up the boss?" Cissy sauntered toward him across the lot.

"Can't hurt, huh?" He grinned and winked, buttering her up, front desk clerk style. How did she know everything? Flighty as she was, this girl certainly kept her eyes and ears open.

She stopped beside the car. "Did you know Trenton Carver gave it to her?"

"The ex-fiancé?" That explained why there were no car payments. It sounded better than a hidden stack of cash.

"Yeah. Imagine getting a brand-new SUV for nothing. Makes me wonder if he let her keep the diamond too. Maybe it'll show up on a necklace someday." She trailed her fingers along his forearm. "Got any plans for tonight?"

"Just waiting for you to ask." He slipped on his sunglasses and started the engine.

"There's a big party in PB. It'll go till dawn."

"What's the occasion?"

"Tuesday night. Care to go with me?"

"Sure. How about I meet you there? Gotta feed my goldfish."

"Okay. I'll give you directions later."

He drove off and shoved aside the thought of a party in Pacific Beach. It would mean booze, smoke, deafening music, the whole gamut of drugs, sugarcoating his rebuff of Cissy's advances while his internal antenna tried to pick up leads on dealers.

Forty minutes later Cat's car was torn apart. Seats and doors lying on the garage floor, hood up, tires off. Glove compartment contents were spread nearby. Except for proof of insurance papers and owner's manual, it all looked like the paraphernalia from a woman's purse.

The head of the inspection team ordered the crew to put it back together. "It's clean, D'Angelo."

"No trace of —"

"Nothin'." He chewed his gum harder. "Zilch."

"Okay." He sensed the hope rising inside him and tried to ignore it. "I need it washed, waxed, and vacuumed."

"Nooo problem. Vacuum's over there;

hose is outside, around the corner. Junior here will help you." He nodded toward Engstrom and turned on his heel.

Brent Engstrom elbowed him in the ribs. "There's a full-service car wash half a mile from here. How'd you get her car?"

"Long story." He glanced at the younger man. He had a stocky build, deep brown eyes, and a buzz haircut. "Boils down to charm. Thoughtfulness. Human kindness."

"That's not in the manual. Guess that's why I get to hang out with you. Gives me a chance to learn the unprintable stuff. So what do you think?"

What did he think? "The facts are — You know what they are. Unless she made you tailing her —"

"Impossible."

Dominick allowed himself a grin. "You're that good, huh? Okay. You said the office phone tap has come up with nothing. So unless she's simply looking the other way while drugs or money exchange hands at the motel, she's clean. And one extremely naive manager."

"How will you go about figuring that one out?"

Something that felt like the surf pounding in his chest yanked his train of thought off the track. He'd have to get close to her, spend time with her. Catch the nuances in those eyes. Memorize the cadence of the low voice. Brush the hair from her forehead. Hear her heartbeat like his own. God help him. He turned to Brent. "I just have to lay on the charm so thick it'll make a guy choke."

Eight

"Let me get that!" Dominick yelled as he hurried across the parking lot.

"I can do it," Cat replied. She gripped one end of a wooden park bench, her ever-present lime green clipboard perched on its seat. The other end was held by a teenage boy, an employee of her father's. "There's another one in that truck."

"Got it."

Cat smiled to herself as she and the boy edged along the sidewalk, the heavy bench sagging on her end. No doubt Mr. Big Muscles could flip the other bench across his shoulders and easily catch up before they reached the garden path.

The benches were great, smooth and clear-stained pine, five feet long, with wide armrests. As promised, her dad had them made. Her dad still spoiled her, but he thought it didn't hurt since she knew it and appreciated it. She should go visit the folks, but this Sunday was out, being the day before inspection. It would have to wait until the week after.

When the sidewalk turned to a stone path

surrounded by huge, semitropical plants, she told the young man that was far enough and thanked him. Dominick could move it for her once she decided exactly where to place it. As she suspected, he was right behind them. Catching her breath, she noticed not even an "umpf" came from him as he gently lowered the bench from his shoulder.

He smiled. "Got a new one for you — Jill, heavyweight champ of the Castillo."

"You can have that title, Jack." She flopped onto a bench and picked up her clipboard.

"Why didn't you let me carry it?"

She shrugged and felt a tightness pull across her back. She must have strained it. "I had to do something physical to prepare for the inspection. I helped clean two rooms earlier. I'm thinking of running home to get some paint clothes."

He pointed a finger at her. "That's my department, and it's under control. I noticed the St. Clair Construction sign on the truck. Anybody you know?"

"My dad. He had these made." She patted the wood. "Nice, huh? I'll let you move them."

"Lead the way."

They meandered around the garden,

imagining scenarios of guests walking along, spotting a bench, welcoming the opportunity to pause and enjoy the birds and flowers.

Dominick stood under a palm tree. "How about here?"

"No way. Your back's to the pond. Over here."

"Nobody'd even see it there. How about this?"

"Too close to the bridge." She shook her head. "It's gotta be an alone place, for reflection."

"From what I've seen, a hiding place for when the kids get crabby is more like it."

They went back and forth until she finally noticed the corner of his mouth, lost in the 5 o'clock shadow, lifting ever so slightly. He was teasing her. "Dominick! Stop it!"

He laughed. "I'd say you're a little uptight, Jill, boss lady."

"So? I already told you I would be, but you're making it worse! Just put one," she stomped to the edge of the pond and pointed, "here."

"Yes, ma'am."

While he retrieved a bench she walked along the path, then called back, "And here!" She studied the list on the clipboard, waiting for him.

He walked by, balancing the second bench on his shoulder, then reached over and gently pulled her hand away from her mouth. "Cat, I've got a better idea for you than carrying benches and chewing finger-nails."

She frowned, bunched her fingers into a fist, and held it at her side.

He set down the bench. "Basketball."

"What?"

"Let me see your list."

"No —" she started to protest, but he whisked it from her hand.

"Let's say you get the benches in place," he winked at her glare, then held the clip-board high, beyond her reach, and read, "and let's see here, call the florist, do this Mandi chat . . . mmm, organize your files — ah, and get the maintenance guy — yours truly — to promise to wax the lobby floor late tonight." He looked at her. "Let's say you do all that, and then you give yourself a break."

"I'll take a break next Tuesday, when this is all over. Now may I have my clipboard back please?" She held her hand out for it, palm up.

Dominick took her hand, turned it over, and examined it. "Your nails won't last until next Tuesday. And the staff won't either without your dimple. That's what keeps us going." He tilted his head, raised his brows, and pressed his lips together, waiting.

The sense of turmoil in her mind stopped. Okay, he had her attention now. She stared back at him.

"One on one, 9 o'clock." He squeezed her hand ever so slightly before dropping it, then gave back the clipboard. "I'll meet you on the court. I'll spot you ten points." He headed down the path.

She found her voice. "You'll spot me ten?" she called. "Ha! You'll need twenty."

At 9, changed into shorts and T-shirt, Cat met him on the lighted court. She knew it was the dimple remark that got her there. Ten sweating minutes later, she knew she should have figured this out for herself. It had been too long since she had pushed herself to physical limits, cleared her head, awakened the endorphins, clarified her perspective.

"Foul!" Dominick held the ball.

"You wimp. I barely touched your arm." She knocked the ball from his hand, but he recovered it quickly and made a layup.

Spectators gathered around the perimeter of the blacktop. Cat grinned when she heard distinct female voices cheering for her.

They played seriously and evenly. Too

evenly? He was head and shoulders taller, agile, and obviously stronger than she was. "Time out!" she called. They faced each other, panting. "D'Angelo, is this the best you can do?"

He wiped his forehead with his sleeve and nodded.

"Pretend like I'm not your boss." She dribbled and, seeing his split-second hesitation, stepped around him and tossed off a jump shot. She figured it would be her last one.

The score soon grew lopsided.

He cornered her while she dribbled. "Hey, boss lady," he teased, "shouldn't you get back to work? There's that inspection."

"What inspection?" Cat bounced the ball between his feet and beat him to it but was laughing so hard she couldn't do anything with it. "I quit!"

He braced his hands against his knees, breathing hard. "Mission accomplished?"

She nodded and smiled. "Thanks."

"Thank you. Your dimple's back."

Later that night the thought struck her that maybe God truly was still listening. What an odd way to bring a new friend into her life.

They played again Friday night. After that

first game, Dominick noticed Cat had warmed toward him whenever they met, seemingly by coincidence. She was predictable, which made her easy to find on the property. She responded to his friendly overtures. His charm.

He rammed his fist into the sand and gazed out at the ocean. Hints of the morning sun's heat touched his back. In his peripheral view he saw a surfboard lowering next to his.

"Morning, Dominick."

"Hey, Adam."

His friend plunked down next to him. "Your words say hello, but the expression on your face says get lost. Care to talk about it?"

He shook his head. He really didn't. Adam's concern only reminded him of how filthy he was. He was grateful the guy waited awhile before breaking the silence.

"Meg will want to know. Things are pretty bad, huh?"

"I'm getting out. Soon as this is over."

"That's cool."

"Adam, I think she's innocent, but I don't know that for a fact, and now I'm pretending like I want to be her friend, and she's falling for it hook, line, and sinker."

"How are you doing that?"

Dominick lifted a shoulder. "Anticipating her needs. Being there when she needs help. Listening when she wants to talk. Suggesting ways she can be less stressed out about her job. Playing basketball with her."

"Just paying attention, huh?"

"Yeah, basically."

"Do you want to be her friend?" Adam asked. "I mean, is she someone you'd choose to be friends with if you met her in a different setting?"

He didn't respond.

"You don't know, do you?" Adam's voice sounded exasperated. "Take a minute and think about it. Just be a man, not Dominick D'Angelo, special agent for the Drug Enforcement Administration. Here you've got a woman who, from your description, makes others feel special, and she's attractive in a Wheaties-box way. Athletic. She knows Christ."

Cat doesn't matter, he thought. *She isn't the point.* The point was, how could he separate himself from what he did? Impossible! He had no other identity.

"And her eyes do a number on you."

"I didn't tell you about her eyes."

"You didn't have to."

Dominick laid back on the sand, arm propped under his head, and stared at the

140

blue sky but saw only dark lashes and honey-colored eyes that crinkled when she laughed. He had it bad, and Adam could tell.

"Look, Dominick, I know you got taken one time, and it hurt. But you now have a relationship with God, and you can believe that He brought you to this situation. If you like her, then like her and stop feeling guilty about it. If she's responding, maybe she needs a friend just like you."

"She doesn't even know who I am."

"I don't think that matters at this point. She knows you better than you know yourself. She's seeing you from the inside. That's where your real identity is. And you want my opinion?"

"No."

"You're seeing her from the inside. You're seeing the real Cat St. Clair. That's what's drawing you to her." Abruptly, Adam stood. "The bottom line is, it's just too weird that you found her under these circumstances. God has put you there for a reason. Now answer the question."

"What was the question?"

"Would you want to be her friend if you didn't have to be?"

Dominick sat up and brushed sand from his hair. "I think if I think too long about it, I'll think I'm falling in love with her. Does that answer your question?" He squinted up at his friend.

A smile spread slowly across Adam's face. "I wonder why I had to ask it."

By Saturday night Cat admitted to herself that Dominick's shaggy good looks and friendly demeanor were growing on her.

She lived and breathed inspection preparations that week, neglecting her apartment more than usual, the pot shop, Elli, and eating. At least the basketball games had provided a stress outlet. That helped along with manager Ron's kudos. Visiting Tecate had helped. She had even read a few Psalms. But she was still knotted up inside. The Castillo was her life, and if it didn't pass inspection this time, she and Ron would be standing in the unemployment line come Tuesday morning. Maybe she could go to Dominick's temp agency.

She drummed her fingers on her desk. This line of thinking was going nowhere.

It was late, almost time to go home. The painting was done, except for some trim work in the southeast corner. Dominick had promised to come in tomorrow and finish it. The man really went overboard helping out. Where had he come from? It was such a pleasure to meet someone with his work ethic. The funny part was that from his looks, you'd expect the exact opposite. On the other hand, impeccably dressed, polite, and wealthy Trent should be a role model for gracious, overboard giving.

He probably billed the hours he spent on dates with her.

She caught herself smirking. *Oh, let's not go down that road.*

Cat headed outside. She might as well try to walk this off with one more round of the property.

She followed her usual route but didn't go inside the restaurant. Instead, she breezed past its patio side, then down along the west wing and beach area. As she neared the equipment booth, she heard glass breaking and loud voices from the direction of the pool. She ran toward it. In the distance, shadowy figures crashed through the gate. Since it was after-hours, the lights were dimmed. *No one should be in that area!*

"Hold it!" she yelled. Nobody stopped.

Another figure stood near the pool. Cat ran that direction and realized it was a girl. When she reached her, she heard her crying and saw she was holding her upper arm. "What happened?" she asked. A quick glance about the area told her what had happened. Turned-over chairs, a table, and broken glass glimmering in the low lamplight. Simple. Kids had been breaking rules. "Are you hurt?"

The girl whimpered, and Cat helped her sit in a lounge chair. Her hand felt something warm and sticky. "Let me see." She moved the girl's hand and bit back a gasp. Even in the semidarkness it was obvious she was bleeding profusely. "Lie down. I'll get a towel."

She ran the length of the pool to the bathhouse, a doorless concrete block. There was no time to use the phone. She flipped on the interior lights and the exterior spots, grabbed a towel, and ran back. She held up the girl's arm, wrapped the towel around it, and pressed firmly. Why hadn't she carried a walkie-talkie?

"Cat?" It was Dominick.

"Oh, thank God! I think we need an ambulance."

"I'll call."

She soothed the girl, who continued to cry. She appeared about thirteen. Cat finally got her name, but she didn't give a room number. The towel was soaked through. "Dominick! Bring more towels."

He returned, knelt beside her, and helped replace the towel. "Guess a tourniquet won't help." The cut was too high underneath her arm. "What's her name? I'll go call the front desk, see if we can find her parents."

She continued soothing the girl, never letting up on the pressure. At last she heard the sirens.

"Cat, are you okay there?" Dominick rushed past. "I'm going to meet them, direct them to this end of the parking lot."

"Go."

It seemed an eternity. The girl stopped crying, and her eyes closed. Cat prayed. At last the paramedics arrived. They nudged her aside and took over. Another eternity passed.

"Is she okay?"

"She'll be fine, ma'am."

Cat and Dominick followed them to the ambulance. As the EMTs were lifting the stretcher into it, the parents showed up. It seemed like they hurried from the parking lot; they must not have been in the motel.

Cat's job was over. Silently she and Dominick returned to the pool. "I'll hose it down," he said.

Cat tried to nod, but there was a rushing sound in her head, and she couldn't make it stop. She went into the women's changing room and stood at the sink before the mirror. Blood streaked her face, soaked the front of her chartreuse silk blouse and beige slacks. Her hands were red. She turned the hot water on full blast, vigorously pumped the liquid soap onto her hands, and held them under the stream. The water turned pink and then blurred before her eyes.

"Why can't people just follow the rules? No glass in the pool area. Do not enter after-hours. Do not run. Simple, simple rules! Why can't they just follow them?"

As he hosed down the pool deck, Dominick heard the sobs above the spray whooshing across the concrete. He knew she was coming unglued.

He lowered the hose, directing the cleansing stream toward the grass beyond the fence, and hurried into the open bathhouse.

"Cat . . ."

She was talking to herself, tears falling down her face harder than the water from the faucet that she held her hands under. In between sobs he heard "rules" and "stupid" and "AIDS."

He found a towel and went to her. "Cat, let's dry your hands." He turned off the water and clasped her hands within the towel. The front of her blouse was almost completely covered with blood.

"Dominick, why can't people just follow the rules? They're so simple! No one would get hurt —"

"It's over, Cat." He unbuttoned the denim work shirt he wore over a sleeveless T-shirt. "Here, get rid of your blouse and put this on."

He went back outside to put away the hose. He could hear her still crying.

She emerged, buttoning the shirt that looked like a big robe on her. In her hand was a rolled-up white towel with a corner of her bright green blouse poking through. She shoved them into a nearby trash can. "What was I supposed to do?" Her voice rose, her words rushed together. "Tell her to stop bleeding for a minute while I go hunt up some latex gloves? 'Maybe there's some down in Housekeeping, I'll be right back'? Why can't people just follow a few stupid rules? I should have had a walkie-talkie! Oh, why don't I carry it all the time? I always think I can handle everything! Idiotic —"

He went to turn off the lights. She was scared. He thought of her broken nails and cut skin and hepatitis and HIV. As he walked back outside, he prayed, *Dear Father, protect her.*

She stood hugging herself, whining managerial-type orders to him in an unnaturally high voice. "You know, we have to scrub the deck with special —"

He wrapped his arms around her, cutting off the flow of hysteria-edged words. "I know. It's all taken care of. You probably saved her life, Cat. Everything's all right. Shh."

It felt right to hold her, to press her forehead against his chest, to tighten his arms around her trembling shoulders. When her crying slowed in only a few moments, a twinge of disappointment surprised him.

"You okay?"

She nodded against him.

"Come on then. It's time for you to go home." He released her.

She was quiet as they walked through the courtyard, abnormally quiet after such an outburst. In the brightly lit lobby she mumbled a thank you. He watched her walk rigidly down the hallway, arms crossed over her stomach and head held at a stiff angle. It was the way she had walked that time after Carver's visit. Cissy had given her something for headache pain, but Cissy wasn't here tonight. Was this the same thing?

He stopped to tell the desk clerk that the girl's parents had arrived, then hurried to Cat's office. She was digging through a large handbag on the desk. "Want me to get you something?" he asked.

Her breathing was labored, and the tears were spilling over again. "No." She rummaged in the bag, her obvious frustration growing, then groaned and sank into the chair, leaning her forehead against the bag. "It's not here."

"What isn't here?"

"Migraine stuff. I don't need it because I don't get them anymore."

"Have you got one?"

"Mm-hmm."

"I'll take you home." He helped her to her feet.

Without protest she leaned on his arm all the way to his truck. He half lifted her up into it, where she immediately laid down on the bench seat.

Ten minutes down the freeway he remembered that he knew where he was going, but he hadn't been given that information by her. He had been to her place that night with Engstrom, but she didn't know that. "Cat, what's your address?"

She mumbled something.

There, that was covered. *Man, what a night!*

Not wanting to have his truck towed away, he parked in the carport slot where her car had been, then flicked on the dome light.

"Cat, where's your key?"

She pushed herself up, unsnapped the handbag, and slid it toward him. Her hair was mussed and her eyes puffy slits.

He hesitated. He was accustomed to searching personal items that did not belong to him, but for the first time it seemed like an invasion of privacy.

Gingerly he picked up the large purse and peered inside. The scents of leather, minty gum, and her subtle, citrus-like perfume wafted out. It was so like her, basic and wholesome. And, so like her, a ring of keys was attached to a clip just below the opening. Miss Jill Assistant Manager was organized. He almost smiled in relief.

He helped her out of the truck and to the back of the square building, where he unlocked the door. Inside, as they climbed a flight of stairs, she leaned heavily against him, clutching his arm. They stopped outside a door on which was a peephole with a silver number 3 attached above it. He unlocked it with another key. The doorknob turned, but the door didn't budge.

Cat, leaning now against the wall, pointed to another lock, a deadbolt. He fiddled with the keys again and at last got the thing unlocked and ushered her inside.

She flipped a light switch, opened a

kitchen cupboard, pulled out a prescription bottle, and handed it to him. He twisted the cap off and poured two capsules into his palm. She took one and disappeared around a corner.

He swept his gaze over the combined kitchen and living room, trying not to feel as if he were snooping, which he knew was exactly what he was doing in this case. Ever since that moment he held her at the pool, it seemed professional habit kept bumping into a mishmash of feelings. He wasn't sure how to act. Friend or DEA agent on duty?

Familiar with the appearance of her office and now her purse, her home was surprisingly a cluttered place. Dishes were in the sink. On the other side of a counter covered with an assortment of pottery, he saw clothes and reading material strewn around the living room. He looked in cabinets, stepped to the half-empty bookshelf and read titles of hotel-related books, peeked through the blinds and saw the top of the carport.

Cat came from a short hallway that must lead to the bedroom. She still wore his shirt and now white sweatpants. She trudged on bare feet to the refrigerator, a cloth bag in her hand. He realized it was an ice bag and offered to fill it for her. While he did so, she picked up a cordless telephone and started punching in numbers.

He took it from her, handed her the ice bag, and pressed the off button. "It's after midnight, Cat. Who are you calling?"

She closed her eyes. Her voice was barely a whisper. "Trent."

"Why?"

She turned away and shuffled to the couch.

He knew this was none of his business, but he followed her and repeated, "Why?"

She rested her elbows on her knees, pressing the bag against her forehead. Tears slid beneath her lashes. "To come hold me."

The two steps it took to reach her side crossed something more significant than the short distance between them. Dominick knew it the instant he sat next to her and she leaned into the circle of his arms.

Nine

Red light danced behind her closed lids.

Cat groaned and rolled over to her other side, burying her face against the back of the couch.

Couch? She groaned again.

Awareness came slowly, as it always did after a migraine. First was the obvious give-away — that drugged feeling. Thoughts formed like cobwebs in a dark closet, threads hanging with no form, so little to grasp and comprehend. The metallic taste on her tongue begged for a toothbrush scrubbing, the first thing she would do as soon as her legs and brain connected.

She rolled over again and let the sunlight tease open her eyelids. Why was she on the couch facing west, not in her bed facing north? Sunlight . . . west . . . Good grief! It was afternoon. Whoa, back up. What *day* was it? Sunday. At least she wasn't late for work. Normally this would be a day off, but with the inspection coming . . .

She felt warm, peered down at a blanket, and kicked it off. Why was she wearing sweatpants and — and — Her eyes were wide open now, and she clutched the large piece of denim she wore. Dominick's shirt?

Last evening came back to her now. The accident at the pool, herself in the bathhouse, nearly hysterical, throwing away her blouse and the towel. Soaking the beige slacks in her tub. They would never be the same.

She studied her hands, the cracked skin around the short nails. *What kind of germs had seeped in there?* A sense of dread washed through her, then settled like cold fingers clutching some inner part of herself, a fitting companion to that other constant fear, the one that was now over seven months old.

Oh, God, where are You?

She had been feeling better, coping better these past couple of months. How could she still so totally lose it?

She groaned again and willed herself to ignore the frustration and instead consider the facts. The past two weeks had been the most draining she'd put herself through in a long time. She had felt up to the task and so pushed herself to the limit. When Ron wasn't paying attention, she had put in a few twelve- and ten-hour days. But by last night she was running on empty.

Tears of frustration smarted her eyes. When would she ever just get over it? When would she not succumb to a migraine over some accident that truly was beyond her ability to prevent? When could she throw away the prescriptions, those drugs she couldn't function with or without?

She wiped the corner of her eye with the shirt sleeve. A faint scent of soap cut through her thoughts. Irish Spring maybe?

The cordless phone rang on the coffee table at her side, but it was ringing for a third time before she managed to pick it up and push the on button.

"Cat, it's Ron. You're not coming in, are you?"

Well, she had planned on it. "I thought —"

"Stay put. Dominick told me about last night. The girl's fine. And I mean she's fine, Cat. She's an extremely healthy young girl, okay? And everything is under control here. The painting is even done. How are you?"

"All right," she lied.

"Well, I know you got one of your headaches, so I want you to promise me you'll stay home and not push it. You know you'll be better for it in the morning, and *that's* when I need you."

She closed her eyes and imagined the Castillo. It had looked perfect yesterday, but would it stay that way without her there today? Had Dominick completely cleaned up the pool area? Her head throbbed. "I promise."

Deep laughter filled the receiver. It wasn't just the manager's. "She promises not to go anywhere!" More laughter.

"What's so funny?"

"You *can't* go anywhere. Your car's here in the lot!" he roared. "Oh, sorry. We couldn't help it. Dominick's here — he wants to talk to you. Don't worry about anything. I'll see you tomorrow."

"Hmm."

"Hi, Cat. You feeling better?"

"Uh, yes. Thanks for bringing me home."

"You're welcome. I'll come pick you up tomorrow, unless you want your car today? Never mind, Ron says you're not going anywhere today, so your car stays put. So, what time tomorrow?"

"Uhh." What was his schedule? What was hers? Why —

"Eight o'clock early enough? The bigwigs are coming at 10."

"Okay."

"Need anything else?"

"Uhh, no. Thank you."

"See you in the morning then." The line went dead.

She clicked the phone off. Maybe she'd just sleep until tomorrow. Maybe it'd all go away between now and then.

She turned back on her side and smelled the soap again.

Dominick D'Angelo. Jack-of-all-trades to the rescue. At the pool. In the office, understanding that she was in no shape to drive. At home, unlocking the door, opening the bottle, filling the ice bag, not letting her make a fool of herself by calling Trent. At her side. Holding her until the fear and the pain floated away on the drugged sea.

She hadn't been aware when he left. Now she glanced around the apartment. The lights were off; the ice bag was on the counter, cap off. The quilt from her bedroom covered her; a pillow was under her head. He was like that, attentive to details. Attentive to her needs.

Trent wouldn't have come anyway. He had stopped coming a long time ago. His voice would still have been a comfort, but nothing like —

Cat tried to stop the thought from forming, but it kept coming, riding the coattails of a warm, snug, carbonated fizzy feeling.

Nothing like those massive arms of Dominick holding her gently against his chest. Nothing like his deep voice laughing just now through the telephone, scattering any discomfort or embarrassment she might feel over last night, anticipating and promising to take care of her need for a ride tomorrow.

She combed her fingers through her hair. He was a drifter sort, had a good friend named Megan, and drove a pickup truck. And Cat was, as the phrase went, on the rebound.

She wrapped his shirt tightly around herself. This could be dangerous territory, and she had absolutely no business entering it.

At 7:55 the next morning Cat found Dominick outside her apartment building, arms crossed, leaning against his truck. What she had thought was a nondescript exterior now looked bright emerald green. He seemed to be into clean vehicles this week. It wasn't bad looking for a pickup — full-sized cab, short bed, a model of fairly recent history, not many dings.

As she approached, he slipped off his sunglasses and slid them into his shirt pocket, another denim like the one she carried. He wore neatly pressed khakis, and his thick black hair was damp and almost looked as if it had been brushed.

He smiled. "What would you do if I whistled right now?"

"Fire you."

"That's what I figured." His ice gray eyes were twinkling in the sunlight. "What if I said you're looking especially lovely and professional this morning?"

"I'll buy that." Her ears felt warm. "I mean — Oh!"

"A little nervous, are we?" He chuckled and opened the passenger's door for her.

"Thank you. Here's your shirt." *Duh,* she thought to herself, *like he can't see.* She laid it and her bag on the seat and realized she was stretching upward. She eyed the height of the floorboard. Her ivory suit skirt and heels were not going to make it, but she lifted a foot anyway, then set it back down on the concrete.

"Need a boost?"

Cat turned toward him. "I could just stay home."

"And miss all the fun?" He placed his hands around her waist, bunching up the suit jacket. "Duck your head."

She balanced her hands on his shoulders as he lifted her onto the seat. "Thank you."

He shut the door and leaned through the open window, his face sober. "You forgot something."

Her breath caught in her throat; a mental checklist raced through her mind. Everything was done. "What?"

"Your dimple."

"That's not funny. Just get in the truck."

He laughed and walked around to climb in the driver's side. "You'll be fine." He started the engine. "You look terrific, the epitome of an assistant manger. The Castillo is in tip-top shape. Ron says everything is under control. I do have one question though." He glanced at her as he stopped at a red light.

"What?" She heard the exasperation in her voice.

"Your files." He turned to her, his brow furrowed. "I hope they're not as messy as your apartment?"

Her jaw dropped.

Dominick smiled and drove through the intersection. "I mean, that could be a problem, you know?"

"You're fired."

"For what?"

"You can't talk to me that way."

"What way? Just stating a fact?"

"My housekeeping habits are off-limits, bud."

"Well, if they're related to this inspection, for which I have put in almost as many hours as management —"

"For three weeks!"

"Three *crucial* weeks." The corner of his

mouth lifted ever so slightly.

"Dominick, stop it! If I laugh, I'll start crying."

He glanced at her. "Take a deep breath."

She did as he suggested while keeping her eyes on the freeway traffic. "Okay. I'll be fine." It sounded like a whimper. She cleared her throat. "I'm fine." She took another shaky breath. "Anyway, why are you here? This is your day off. Ron could have picked me up."

"He's busy." He paused. "With your files."

She burst into laughter. The carbonated fizz bubbled again. If she had made this trip by herself, she would have been a mess by the time she reached the Castillo. "Thanks. I think you're making this less difficult."

"Good."

From the corner of her eye, Cat peered at him. "And thanks for, umm, for taking care of things Saturday night. And me."

"No problem. A guy's gotta look after his boss. Especially since she promised to take him to dinner."

The painting challenge! "Oh, yeah, dinner." He was serious about that?

"Miguel and I thought tonight would be good, since the three of us have it off."

"Tonight?"

"Unless you have some other plans to celebrate passing inspection?"

"No. I was just hoping not to be having a pity party."

"You're sure? Carver won't want to take you to dinner?"

"N-no." She looked out the side window. "It was stupid of me to want to call him. We won't be going for dinner. Or anything."

Dominick reached over and nudged her hand from her mouth. "I bet you'll want to celebrate. So, how about you, me, and Miguel? What's your favorite Italian place?"

She thought for a moment. "I have a few, in the Gaslamp District downtown. Have you been there?"

He had. For the remainder of the drive they discussed the variety of menus and the ambience of the district's sidewalk dining. They decided on a particular restaurant. As he parked at the motel, he said, "Shall I pick you up about 7:30? I'll get Miguel first."

Miguel or no Miguel, this resembled a date, which was more than she wanted to try to handle just now. "I'll meet you there. At 8?"

"All right. Wait, don't move." He ran around the truck to open her door. "If you jump out on those heels, you'll be in the emergency room instead of on the inspection tour." He grasped her waist again.

"Thanks." She retrieved her bag from the seat and glanced up at him. "And, umm, well, thanks." Her heels clicked across the parking lot.

She had considered wearing flat shoes and slacks, but the thought of what Trent liked nagged at the back of her mind. Trent and the other testosterone-type owners. There was a very real possibility they would admire her in a skirt more than they would the completed painting job. At the very least this suit would make a favorable impression. Was she being unfair, manipulative, untrue to herself . . . or just plain practical?

"Hey, Cat!" Dominick's voice broke through her thoughts.

She turned around.

He placed a finger on his left cheek and smiled.

She returned his smile and gave him a thumbs-up sign. *Dimple. Okay — dimple, skirt, and high heels. And my best efforts. Let's do it.*

Ten

Cat ran across the downtown street, then hurried along the sidewalk, dodging passersby. No heels tonight. She moved freely in an ankle-length black knit dress, her bare feet wrapped in comfortable espadrilles, the long purse strap across a shoulder. It was 8:10, and she had parked three blocks away.

Even if she had been early, she would have raced. It was as if fireworks were exploding inside her, ricocheting great bursts of energy that sent her legs flying, her heart laughing, and her arms aching to be flung around someone. She had hugged Ron and the housekeeping ladies, but that was hours ago. Elli hadn't been available all afternoon, and Cat hadn't had the time to drive to her parents' home.

At the restaurant she stopped near the maitre d's outdoor stand. A group of people blocked the entrance to the sidewalk dining area, which was surrounded by a three-foot-high wrought-iron fence. The typically beautiful, cool summer evening meant that even a Monday was crowded.

"Oh!" she cried aloud in frustration.

Stretching, she peered over heads and spotted Dominick standing and waving at her from the far corner. "Oh!"

She couldn't get through. And she couldn't wait another moment. She stepped back out of line and ran along the sidewalk. "Dominick!" she squealed when she reached him. Balancing with a toe on the fence crossbar between them, she reached over and threw her arms around his neck. "We did it!"

He hugged her back and laughed. "Told you so."

"Help me over this thing." She bent her knees, lifting up her heels.

His arms tightened, and he hoisted her smoothly over the low fence. "Do you always make such a grand entrance?"

She smiled at nearby diners who chuckled in their direction and slid onto the chair he pulled out for her. "I'm sorry I'm late. Where's Miguel? I need to hug Miguel too."

Dominick sat across from her and folded his hands on the small, linen-covered table. A votive candle glowed from a glass bowl between them. "He couldn't make it. At the last minute one of the grandkids got sick, and they needed him at home. I was at his house when it happened, too late to reach you. I hope you don't mind?"

She was struck then with his dark good looks. He wore a black suit, white shirt, and red tie. In the dim light cast from the restaurant's interior through a large window, his black hair shone. It was combed off his forehead. She knew it wouldn't stay there. "Uhh, no, of course not. That's, umm, too bad. You look really different. Nice. Really nice."

The right corner of his mouth tucked itself into the recesses of his shadowed jaw. "Thanks. Bet you thought I didn't own a suit."

"Never thought about it. Oh, I feel like I'm going to pop," she giggled.

"Here comes the maitre d'. You could hug him. Then maybe he won't throw you out for climbing over his fence."

A man wearing a tuxedo and a small, formal smile appeared at her side. "Good evening, ma'am, and welcome." He handed her an oversized menu, then turned to Dominick, eyebrows raised, and said something in Italian.

Dominick replied, and the man left.

"You speak Italian?" she asked.

He shrugged. "My grandmother spoke nothing else, so I know phrases. And I can read a menu."

"What did he say?" Why had she never

noticed his thick eyelashes before?

"He said you were worth waiting for."

"He did not."

"All right. Truth. He said you were prettier than I described you, and he hoped I was proposing tonight because any woman who climbed over fences would not be available for long."

"Dominick!"

He chuckled. "I asked him to bring you an S. Pellegrino."

That he knew which sparkling water she preferred was more unnerving than his compliments. She held the large menu in front of her face. He placed a finger on it and pulled it down.

"I haven't said congratulations yet. Congratulations." He smiled.

"Thanks. I tried to find you when it was all over."

"I saw the entourage leave and heard you scream, so I knew the verdict. I left. After all, it was my day off. What'd you do?"

She touched his arm. "I appreciate your coming in when you didn't have to. Well, after I finished screaming, I shopped for staff gifts. And —" She pointed a finger at him. ". . . and, no wisecracks now, I cleaned my apartment and got ready for my — for dinner." Again she held up the menu. She had almost said "my date." It must be the adrenaline still pumping from the excitement of passing inspection that caused this fluster. It had nothing to do with the S. Pellegrino set before her now or the attentive friend sitting across the table. Wearing a suit.

"Cat, do you know yet what you'd like?"

She shook her head. "I can't think straight. What do you recommend?"

They discussed a few items, and then he ordered for them, the Italian flowing from him without hesitation.

He listened to her babble on about the inspection, through the soup and salad courses, until at last she ran out of breath. As steaming dishes of pasta were served, she held up her hands. "Okay, I'm done. This was a major ordeal for me. Sorry."

"Don't apologize. I've enjoyed watching it all come about, and I'm glad you succeeded."

"Well, we do have to make some changes in order to meet the budget. Umm, this is great."

"It is. My *nonna* would be impressed. Are you firing me for real then?"

"No. Actually, we want to hire you full-time, permanent. Are you interested?"

He raised his eyebrows.

She rushed to add, "I don't have to know tonight." The thought occurred to her that the word *permanent* wouldn't be in this man's vocabulary. No doubt he'd be moving on soon. But she didn't want to hear those words just yet.

He gave her a small smile. "I'll think about it. So how's the conversation with God going?"

She shrugged. "I was wondering, how did He get your attention?"

Dominick looked down at his plate. "I was in an accident about two years ago."

"A serious one?"

"Yeah. Anyway, the doc and I became friends. He surfs with me sometimes." He looked at her now. "Remember meeting Megan at the zoo? He's her husband."

"Oh." *Ohh! Megan has a husband.*

"They sort of adopted me, and I just sort of kept watching the way they lived. I admired them, and they told me about Jesus. How about you?"

"Nothing so dramatic as a serious accident. My parents included Jesus in every decision, every meal, most conversations. He was part of our life, and I understood at an early age what He had done for me and that I could accept Him or not. I saw no reason not to or to put it off for later. Even now . . ."

She toyed with her fork. "Mother and Daddy think it's a faith-stretching time for me. I haven't turned my back on God — I just don't want to look Him in the face. I feel as if He let me down."

"So it's hard for you to trust Him?"

She nodded.

"What happened?"

She met his eyes. The gray was melted ice tonight, concerned, curious. She hadn't noticed the Secret Service look about him for a long time. "I call it my nightmare. You really want to hear it?"

"I really want to know all about you, Cat St. Clair."

That fizziness bubbled inside her again. "Well, since I already offered you dinner and a job, I guess you're not just being polite, huh?" she teased.

He grinned and pushed aside his empty plate. "No, I'm not just being polite."

"Okay." She took a deep breath. "About seven months ago, right after Christmas, Elli — you met my sister at the zoo — Elli and her little boy and I were at Bay Village, that outdoor mall just off the freeway on Friars Road. Jason's favorite place is the fast-food restaurant there, so we stopped in. They got in line, and I headed toward a table in the back. This — this big guy with a gun . . ." She stopped and bit a fingernail.

Dominick gently pulled her finger away from her mouth, placed her hand on the table, and covered it with his own. His thumb stroked her wrist.

She cringed. "All of a sudden I felt a yank on my ponytail. Then there was this gun in my face. People were screaming, and he was shouting at me. A policeman yelled something about the wrong one. They ran off. It was all over within a split second." She let out her breath. "I guess I fainted. My head hit the floor. I've been a basket case ever since." She shook her head. She'd spare him the details, about how fear had totally affected everything she did. "It's no big deal. I should be over it by now."

He squeezed her hand. "Of course it's a big deal. You weren't seriously hurt, but I imagine you were scared to death. That doesn't go away overnight. What did he look like?"

"I don't know. It happened too fast. He wore sunglasses and an army green jacket. He had a full beard. He was just . . . just big. When he turned, I saw hair pulled back in a ponytail. It's pretty much just a blur."

"Where does Trenton Carver come into the picture?"

She stared at him. *How did he — ? Oh,*

probably Cissy. Although Cissy didn't know this story, she would have told Dominick something about her odd behavior and the broken engagement. "Trent didn't want to be engaged to a basket case. It didn't fit the job description." She bit her lip. "No, that's unfair. I became extremely fearful. I had nightmares. I got my long hair cut off. I moved out of my apartment to another one. I had migraines all the time. I still haven't set foot in that mall again. I wasn't the woman he had proposed to. He couldn't or wouldn't go through it with me. Probably a little of both. We decided not to get married."

"I'm sorry."

"The hard part is, I've always followed God's rules, and this is what He let happen. I wanted to marry Trent and have a big family. What was so wrong with that?"

He squeezed her hand. "What happened to the guy with the gun?"

She shrugged.

"Didn't you tell the police?"

"No. In the first place I wanted to totally forget it ever happened. And I know he just made a mistake. Elli and I figured he was an undercover cop and I happened to fit the description of somebody he was after. He was just trying to do his job. Phoning the po-

172

lice wouldn't change what had happened. God could have taken him another direction."

He removed his hand from hers. "Do you want some coffee?"

It seemed an abrupt change of subject. "Uhh, sure." Her hand felt empty.

He signaled the waiter and ordered it. "The bottom line then is that God let you down." He looked at her. "What do you think it would take for you to get back on speaking terms with Him?"

She fiddled with a spoon. "I used to think if Trent changed . . . you know, and we got back together . . . But it's more than that. I'm just so afraid. Of *everything*. If I weren't afraid — if God could rewind that split moment when my life fell apart, like — oh, I don't know — walk me back through it and swing His divine sword at all the fears and banish them and tell me why it had to happen . . ." She looked back at him. "That might do it. In the meantime — ice cream!"

The waiter set silver bowls of spumoni before them along with the coffee.

"Thanks, Dominick."

He grinned. "You're paying for it."

She grinned back at him, then sobered. She had just told him everything, including her innermost feelings. "Not many people know my story. Only Trent and Ron and my family."

He reached over and brushed hair from her brow. "It's safe with me, *mi gatita*."

Later, after dinner, they both drove to the Castillo. Cat was pleased that Dominick wanted to accompany her. It seemed only appropriate after his weeks of hard work that he would be nearby while she personally thanked staff members. And she wanted to give his gift to him there.

She smiled to herself, watching him saunter toward her across the parking lot. Appropriate had little to do with it. She was enjoying his company, probably beyond what was appropriate, given his drifter status and her rebound status. But that exact combination made him less of a threat. He'd be leaving, and she was just taking advantage of an available male shoulder to lean on, no strings attached. Maybe that was what had granted her heart permission to notice his manliness tonight and to trust him with the nightmare.

A shiver went through her. She didn't know why she had done that, told him about that day.

God knows. Her mother's voice popped into her mind. The phrase was from a children's book she had often read to them, something about mysteries in nature. Every page asked the question, "Who knows how this and that can be?" The only answer of course was, "God knows, that's who!" Mother used it to answer the countless unanswerable questions that arose in the lives of her five children. It wasn't a flippant retort; the four words were packed full of assurance.

It reminded Cat of something from the Proverbs. "There are three things which are too wonderful for me. Yes, four which I do not understand: the way of an eagle in the air, the way of a serpent on a rock, the way of a ship in the midst of the sea, and the way of a man with a virgin."

That last one she certainly didn't understand. Dominick strolled toward her now, and that carbonated fizziness effervesced through her. Absolutely, totally illogical.

His demeanor was nonchalant with suit coat open and flapping in the breeze, hands stuffed in the pockets of his slacks.

"For a temp," she teased, "you sure act like a permanent employee, coming in at all hours, any time of day or night."

"Maybe it's the company." He winked.

"Mm-hmm." She turned to go inside. "You sure know how to make points too."

He opened the door for her. "Did I mention names?"

"No, you didn't. Excuse me for assuming it was present company."

"Did I say it wasn't?"

Cat laughed and stopped beside the door to Housekeeping. "I'm going this way."

He waved and headed down the hallway. "I'll be in the lobby."

Her first hug and gift certificate went to a second shift housekeeper. Afterwards she meandered through the courtyard toward the pool and sports equipment shed where Kevin should be. She and Ron had decided they wanted to give tokens of their appreciation to the staff. It would strain the budget, but this moment called for it. Cat had spent the afternoon shopping for the people she knew well enough to make their certificate a little more personal by purchasing it at a favorite store of theirs. Tomorrow she would see Miguel and Mandi and others, but tonight she wanted to catch a few who wouldn't be around then. And of course she wanted to hug Cissy as soon as possible because she played such a major role in keeping things running smoothly.

The Castillo felt like Cat's to care for again. It had passed the test. With the inspection cloud no longer hanging over her, she could relax in maintaining the status quo and could pursue the creative side of making the motel a memorable place for guests. The owners had approved a new ad campaign of hers, something that had slipped through the cracks after she and Trent parted ways.

She gazed up at the stars. Saturday's migraine indicated it wasn't over yet. But it was *almost* over, of that she was certain. *Thank You, Lord.*

Where had that come from?

She continued down the sidewalk and, out of habit, made her rounds, greeting a few guests along the way. Since she hadn't brought her keys, she skipped the restaurant. Dominick met her as she came around the front of the building.

"Cat, who else delivers on Monday nights besides the bread guy?"

"Nobody. Why?"

"I just saw an unmarked white van fly out of the service drive."

"Maybe the bread truck was out of commission and he used a private van." She glanced at her watch. "And came early."

"I think we should check it out. I got the keys from Cissy."

They walked to the back and entered through the kitchen door. Cat flipped on the lights. "No bread yet."

After a quick search inside and out, they concluded that nothing appeared out of place. "Probably just kids out cruising," he offered.

Back in the lobby Cat hurried around the front desk to hug Cissy. "Oh, thank you, thank you, thank you, Cissy."

"Hey, just doing my job."

Cat gave her an extra squeeze. "No, you're not. Here — a token of my appreciation and Ron's." She pulled an envelope from her tote bag.

When Cissy opened it, her usually aloof appearance melted away. "Cat! This is — this is unbelievable. Thank you!"

"You're welcome." She handed an envelope to Dominick across the counter. His certificate, too, was a larger amount than one would commonly refer to as a token. She and Ron had added their own personal funds to these two.

He didn't open it. "Cat, dinner was more than enough."

"Ron and I don't agree. So there. You're welcome." She replaced the kitchen key in a drawer and pulled out one to her office. "Now I'm going home. I'll see you two tomorrow." She smiled at them and left.

As she walked away she heard Cissy say

something about a party to Dominick. As she unlocked her office, he strode up.

"Cat, thank you." He held up the envelope's contents. "This is . . . I don't know what to say."

She smiled at his loss of words and opened the door. "It's not enough for a new longboard, but — Why is my light on?" She dropped the shopping bag on the desk and noticed a trace of grime. She wiped her finger through it. "Whew! Now I know I'm tired. Tonight this place can stay dusty."

He followed her back through the door and pulled it shut behind them. "I can take you home."

After locking her door, she patted his arm. "I'm fine, Dominick. Just walk me to my car. And could you put this back at the front desk for me?" She handed him her office key.

"I'll follow you home."

"No."

"For my peace of mind."

"You must watch too much television."

They walked silently until they reached her car. "You said you were afraid —"

"I said I'm getting better."

"You should be afraid, after what happened at that mall, and this time of night. Let me —"

"Dominick! I drive home every night at this time."

He let out an exasperated breath. "But are you afraid?"

She opened her door and climbed in. "That's not the point."

"Then what is the point?" He leaned inside, preventing her from shutting the door.

"That I do it by myself." She stared at him with clenched jaw, suddenly feeling very tired.

He didn't blink or budge.

"I'm just getting used to doing it by myself. Don't make it easier for me."

"I'm following you."

She placed the key in the ignition and turned it. "You're fired if you do."

"Compromise. I'll call you."

"All right." She pushed his shoulder. "Now close the door."

"At least you've got the top up. Lock the doors. Thanks for dinner. And the gift certificate."

"Dominick!"

"Bye." He smiled and shut the door.

Cat drove quickly from the lot and toward the freeway. Her mind begged for sleep, but a dizzying anticipation won the debate. She'd rather talk on the telephone with

Dominick D'Angelo into the wee hours of the morning.

"Want me to follow her?" Brent Engstrom's soft voice came from near the employee entrance. His black sweater and slacks blended into the shadows.

Dominick stopped just outside the door. "She'll be fine. We have to check something. Wait, let me make sure Cissy's not headed this way." He cracked open the door. If the desk clerk saw him again, he'd have a difficult time dodging another party invitation. He'd rather run into the security guard than that little spitfire.

He motioned to the other agent to follow him inside. They quickly slipped into Cat's office and shut the door.

"You're lookin' pretty spiffy, boss." Engstrom spoke in a stage whisper.

"Hmm," he grunted. In the dim light coming through the closed blinds, Dominick maneuvered his way around the chairs and switched on the desk lamp, then climbed on top of the broad desk, pushed up the attic covering, and slid it aside.

"The charm must be working," Engstrom continued. "All dressed up, cozy dinner. Sounded like you even had a little disagreement. Must be serious if you're having a spat already."

Dominick poked the top of his head through the attic opening and stretched his arm into the dark. "Rule number one, Engstrom — shut up." His hand fell on something soft, covered in plastic. "Got a flashlight?"

He handed a tiny one to him. "When do I get to be the charming guy instead of a married dork with an imaginary wife — What'd you say?"

Dominick didn't bother to repeat the expletive. "It's here." He eased himself down from the desk. "Take a look."

He listened at the door while the younger man peered inside the turret.

Why did Cat come in here? Just to drop off that tote bag? She was surprised. Of course she was surprised. I was right next to her. What's she gonna say, "Oh, they've left attic dirt on my desk again while digging into the stash"?

Engstrom let out a low whistle. "Five kilos?"

"Let's go."

They quickly replaced the cover, turned off the lamp, and made their way out to the edge of the lot and stopped in the shadows near Dominick's truck.

"Brent, were you around when that white van was on the service drive?"

"Yeah. It just pulled in and made a U-turn. Odd thing, though, its lights were off. Couldn't get the plate number."

"You okay checking out the bread delivery? This guard's thorough."

"But predictable. I got his routine figured. If he changes it, my cover is the wife and me had a spat, and I needed some milk to calm my nerves."

"And knew how to pick a lock. Okay, whatever. I'm leaving then."

"Better make that phone call, clear up your little spat."

Dominick walked around his truck.

"Hey, D'Angelo, the stuff in the turret?"

He paused and looked over his shoulder.

"It still doesn't prove anything, right? Miss Wholesome Athlete maybe is just incredibly dumb?"

Dominick wanted Cat to be innocent. Truth was, the other agent was right. Over 200,000 dollars' worth of cocaine hidden a few feet above her desk didn't prove a thing. Something inside of him relaxed. "Could be, Engstrom. Could be."

Eleven

Twenty-four hours later, Cat and Dominick had again lingered in the parking lot. Instead of discussing whether or not he would follow her home, they discussed meeting at an all-night coffee shop. Sleep was the furthest thing from her mind and, apparently, his.

Twenty-four hours after that, they skipped the discussion and just met in the same booth they had sat in the previous night.

Sitting across the table from him, she figured maybe he felt sorry for her the night of the pool incident. Then, just to be nice, he called her on that dinner bet. After that enjoyable evening, it was a natural — albeit quick — progression to longer conversations when they met on the job . . . his wondering if she ate after getting off work at 11 . . . a mutual craving for stuffed French toast . . . inside jokes . . . Jack and Jill completing each other's sentences. Something had clicked between them. She couldn't deny it.

Cat's internal monologue tape was stuck on replay when she wasn't near him. *Go slow.*

Just be friends. Temp guy, temp relationship. Go slow. Just be friends. When she saw him looking at her, though, with that slight lift of the corner of his mouth, it was as if the reverse button clicked on, and static filled her head.

Of course she was at a disadvantage. He caught her attention at an incredibly vulnerable moment, when the migraine had struck that night. Before that he was just another person. No, not quite. His hard work, gentle teasing, and basketball challenge pruned the weeds choking the path that led straight to her heart. When she looked up, he was standing on the path, staring at her.

A shiver went through her now.

"Cold?" he asked and rubbed her arm. "You've got goose bumps. I've got a flannel shirt in the truck. I'll get it."

She shook her head no. Truth was, she'd rather have him across the table from her. His wild black hair fell across his forehead and in the back touched the top of his short-sleeved gray sweatshirt. His shoulders filled the booth, blocking from view the occupants at the table behind him.

Already his face had etched itself into her mind's eye, and she could see it even as she read the menu. There wasn't the symmetry of Trent's handsomeness here. It was rather

. . . craggy. She suspected his nose had been broken at one time. There were scars — a slit just below his left eyebrow, and on his forehead a ridged line with stitching marks. The shadow of a thick beard never lessened. His lips were a bit off center because the right corner always tucked itself up when he smiled. There was not a spare ounce of flab. His face was a solid extension of the rocklike muscular shoulders and neck. Discipline and character, yes, but this was not a small-castle-in-the-suburbs future now staring at her.

"Where's your dimple?" His gray eyes crinkled.

"Same place as your Secret Service look."

His hand went still on her arm. "My what?"

"Your Secret Service look. You probably don't even know you do it. Cissy and I noticed it right away. Of course your build has something to do with it, but your eyes get kind of serious now and then, like they're watching out for the President."

"I see. And where does that put your dimple?"

She smiled. "I don't know."

He moved his hand aside as the waitress served their food.

In between bites, Cat added, "We have a

couple of other theories about you. Are you interested?"

"I didn't know I warranted theories."

"You're so different, it makes you mysterious. We assume you came to California all on your own without friends or family or job. And you're old enough to know better. It's not as if you're a young kid trying to find himself. We've never met anyone like you."

"Hmm."

"You're either a rock singer incognito or a convict."

His eyebrows shot up. "I don't think I want to know any more."

She laughed. "Okay, tell me something about yourself. Then you'll be more real to me. Tell me about, umm, when you were a little boy."

"Like . . . ?"

"Like remember I asked you where you felt safe? I said I did in the backyard, and you said your backyard was a dark alley. Think of a place."

Dominick sipped his coffee.

She saw his eyes go cold but decided against telling him she had found his Secret Service look.

"Okay," he said, "but this is just between you and me."

"Agreed."

"The safe place was in the kitchen with Ma hugging me while she cooked. And with Vince, my little brother, at the table doing homework. He'd be doing *my* homework while I was busy explaining why I'd had another fight."

"You'd been in a fight and your mother would *hug* you?"

He chuckled, and his eyes softened a little. "After she yelled at me for fighting."

"And your dad wasn't around?"

"Not after . . . not after I was ten."

"I'm sorry."

He gazed over her shoulder, his jaw locked. "It's okay. It was safer after he left."

She remembered what he had told her when that guest had shouted at her, when she thought Dominick would punch him. He had told her the story of punching his dad. "Are your mom and brother still in Chicago?" she asked.

He smiled, and the ice melted again. "Vince is a hotshot stockbroker with a beautiful wife and two great kids. Ma lives in a condo in a nice neighborhood. I try to get back at least once a year."

"When did you leave home?"

"Ahh, too many long stories, Cat. Another time. I was wondering, are you and Cissy friends?"

She shrugged. "We have fun together at work. She's perfect as the front desk manager, and we have a good rapport. But outside of the Castillo our interests are so different, we don't socialize. She's kind of on the wild and crazy side, in case you haven't noticed. And I go to Padres games."

"And Lakers?"

She smiled. "Maybe once a season my dad and I make it there."

"Your voice just got real soft. Sounds like you and your dad are close?"

"Yeah, we are. Besides the fact that my brothers aren't as crazy about basketball as I am, Daddy and I just get along in general. He's a special man."

"Obviously. He makes park benches for you just in time for inspection. I imagine you're spoiled rotten."

She heard his teasing tone. "So what if I am?" she countered.

"No problem." He grinned. Then his face sobered. "At first I had a hard time calling God 'Father.' You know, with my background. But I have glimpses now of being spoiled rotten by Him."

"You do?" Surprise raised her voice.

"Did you see the sunrise this morning?"

She laughed. "No! You did?"

"I was surfing. How about the sunset tonight?"

The chuckle died in her throat. At the display of such tenderness on his strong face, her breath caught.

"And those are just the little things He gives me."

Somewhere from deep inside a warmth began to grow. It was as if a flood of liquid sunshine washed through her. Dominick heard God's whispers. He shouldn't. He was too independent, too unsettled, too scarred by the childhood he hinted at, too physical. But he did hear! Why couldn't she?

"Your French toast is getting cold."

"What? Oh." She turned her attention back to her plate.

"So tell me what else you do. What would you be doing right now if we weren't here?"

She glanced at her watch. "I'd be sleeping."

"It is getting kind of late."

It was after 1 A.M. Last night she had gotten home at 1. She peered at him through her eyelashes. He didn't motion for the check. She didn't hurry her eating.

"What will you do tomorrow before work?"

Again she glanced at her watch.

"Sleep," he answered for her.

She laughed. "Yes. And I'll go to the pot shop."

His eyes narrowed.

She grinned. "You know, pot shop — where potters make pottery. Need a bowl or a vase?" She told him about her friends there and her love of shaping clay.

"And what do you do on your Mondays off?"

She imagined him in a kitchen in the middle of a rough neighborhood, his mother hugging him after he'd been in a fight. He was a good candidate to join her. "This week I'm going to Tecate. Will you come with me?"

"To visit your, what was it, *abuelita?*"

"Oh, there's much more than my *abuelita* in Tecate." She would surprise him.

Before Monday came, Cat and Dominick met two more times at the coffee shop after work.

They also met at the potters' studio. On Thursday morning he came, and she helped him throw a pot. Her hands on his, she guided them round the wet lump of clay on the wheel, shaping what she called a man-size cereal bowl. She was surprised at the agility of his large hands, surprised that her heart beat in sync with the spinning wheel.

191

And they met on Saturday morning at the pier. They ate breakfast at a nearby outdoor café, his hair still wet from surfing. He made her laugh with his stories of how he had learned to surf. She asked if he had been athletic in high school, if he had played football. She realized her inability to comprehend his childhood when he smiled softly and mentioned something about fighting and hanging around street corners. She wondered then about gangs but did not ask.

All these hours together were in addition to the eight they spent in close proximity at the motel. It seemed a natural progression of a new friendship. Neither hesitated when the other suggested a meeting.

On Sunday they went their separate ways, she to see her parents, he to see his friends Megan and Adam. Cat didn't know what he thought, but she knew she needed a breather by then. It was getting more difficult to tell herself to go slow. She admitted to herself she felt an attraction that went beyond friendship. Dominick crowded out her fear and loneliness, Trent, and sometimes even sleep. He made her laugh, held her hand when she started unconsciously to bite her nails, and made her think about God.

It wasn't that he directly questioned her struggle with faith. It was that she caught glimpses in him of such pure awe at comprehending the fact that the Creator of the universe knew him, Dominick D'Angelo, by name and cared about him. She was intrigued by that, perhaps almost envious of that in him.

On Monday morning he parked his pickup at her apartment building. She insisted on driving. He sat beside her in her open Tracker, wearing shorts, T-shirt, baseball cap, and a wary look in his squinting eyes.

"Where are your sunglasses?" she asked.

"Forgot them at home. Now what exactly are we doing in Tecate?"

She smiled. "Hmm. I thought you had an adventuresome spirit, one that doesn't need to know the outcome."

"Sure, I'm adventuresome. That's why I let you drive this go-cart with me in it on the freeway."

"Ha, ha. Just wait until we get on the winding two-lane. That's the best part."

Less than an hour later she parked and escorted him through an unmarked gate. When the shouting children ran across the dirt courtyard toward them, he grinned at her. "A school?"

"Sort of. An orphanage."

He fit in easily. They delivered canned

goods, sang songs, joined in their lunchtime. The children as well as workers adored his antics and his halting attempts at their language.

Sometime later Cat sat under a shade tree with Rosa, the elderly woman she called *abuelita*. They watched Dominick kneel on the ground while the children wrestled with him. When they knocked him over, something deep within Cat broke apart, and the laughter she hadn't known for so many months was at last released. It was a cleansing, unadulterated delight that flowed from her in tears and loud unladylike bellows. He lifted his head between the small arms that hugged him and smiled.

She had hoped for a favorable response to the children. Her hope was a mere fraction of what he gave. This was compassion, boundless and glorious.

Rosa put a hand on her arm. "He makes you laugh, Catalina."

She looked at the white-haired woman whose aged face crinkled in a smile. "*Sí, Abuelita.*" As always, they conversed in Spanish.

"The other one didn't."

She patted the woman's hand. She had often sensed that Rosa did not care wholeheartedly for Trent.

"This Dominick has known pain. It's in his eyes. That is why he can give such joy."

He approached now. She wasn't embarrassed when Rosa said to him in Spanish, "You are the man for Catalina. Take good care of my little one, and do not forsake your Father's word."

To Cat's surprise, Dominick leaned over and tenderly kissed Rosa's cheek.

When they left, a tiredness filled Cat, the comfortable kind that comes after a hard physical workout, like hiking up a mountain. She handed him the keys, which he accepted without a word.

"Dominick, did you notice a restaurant all by itself, on the highway just this side of Jamul? It's called El Coyote. Shall we stop?"

"Only if we have enough time to get to the pier before sunset."

"What?"

In reply he simply touched her face. "Catalina. It's pretty in Spanish."

He drove, and she napped until the sound of gravel under the tires woke her. They were at the restaurant.

As they ate in the quiet courtyard surrounded by colorful potted plants, she told him about her first trip to the orphanage and how she fell in love with it. It seemed a small thing to bring gifts and spend a little time with the people there. She was sure she received more than she gave. Dominick understood. She didn't have to tell him more.

He asked for the check instead of coffee and stood. "Let's go."

"Where to?"

"The sunset. I think Rosa told us to watch the sunset from the pier."

She laughed, glad he didn't ask what Rosa had really said because she couldn't tell him and she couldn't lie to him.

They made it in time. She closed her eyes as he maneuvered her car into a tight squeeze of a space she never would have attempted. They hurried along the sidewalk to the pier, glad to see the white wrought-iron gate still unlocked at the entrance. Although open to the public during daylight hours, the Crystal Pier was private property. Dominick grabbed Cat's hand, and they ran between the rows of white motel cottages that lined both sides of the first half of the pier.

He slowed down when she couldn't keep up. At last they reached the far end where a small crowd had gathered to await the sunset. They spotted an opening at the wooden rail. He nudged her forward into a tight fit between others standing there.

"Kind of like parking the car," she mused.

He stood behind her, his hands resting on

her shoulders. Nothing but the railing and the vast expanse of ocean separated them from the sinking sun. They observed it silently. She thought of how he had described this as a gift from God. It was obvious. Low on the horizon, all shades of purples and pinks streaked through the clouds. Below them, the red-orange sun dissolved into the ocean. Day turned into night. On the other side of the earth, night turned into day.

The crowd began to disperse, but she stood still, not wanting to break the spell of the sunset's beauty — or of this physical and emotional closeness to Dominick.

He dropped his hands and moved to her side. "It was a good day, Cat. Thank you."

"I'm glad you went with me." *More than glad.* The mental cobwebs were at last swept away. She was all right. There was abundant life after the nightmare. She smiled at him. "Thank you for being a friend."

In the deepening twilight they stared at one another for a few moments. He leaned toward her and hesitated.

Cat held her breath. "This wasn't supposed to happen."

"You're telling me," he murmured. And then he kissed her.

Maybe Rosa had told them to watch the sunset after all.

Twelve

"You're cleaning!" Elli exclaimed as she stepped into her sister's apartment. *"Cleaning?"*

Cat shut the door and hugged her. "Well, hello to you too. Where's my nephew?"

"With his dad. Jim's working at home this morning, so I'm doing errands without my little appendage."

Cat cleared books from a dining table chair. "Sit down. How's the littlest appendage doing?"

Elli patted her abdomen and propped her feet up on another chair. "Just fine. He or she was kicking half the night."

"Want some iced tea?" Cat busied herself in the kitchen.

"Thanks. Hey, nice tabletop. I haven't seen it since you moved in."

Cat served the tea and asked small-talk questions while scrubbing the sink. That lasted less than five minutes.

"Okay, Cat, what gives?"

"Nothing."

Elli giggled. "That was a quick response. Sit down and look me in the eye and say that."

Cat wiped her hands on her gym shorts, then fiddled in the silverware drawer.

"C'mon, sis, you haven't really cleaned or organized this place in the four months you've been here, so I take this little spurt as a significant development. What happened?"

She opened a cupboard and began rearranging spice bottles. Fourteen years of sharing a room with this sister and a lifetime of being there for each other through all the highs and lows meant she couldn't hide from Elli. She had been up since 5 A.M. hiding from herself.

Not that she had slept much, trying to make sense of her totally emotional, illogical response to a man who was in no way, shape, or form her type. After last night's sunset there were whispered words of going slow, a silent ride home. At the apartment door they had simply stared at one another, still speechless. It was as if the kiss ended everything. Or just began —

"Catherine Michele!"

She sat down. "Dominick went with me yesterday, to Tecate."

"The big guy from the zoo? The one you had dinner with after the inspection?" Her dark brown eyes danced with anticipation.

Cat nodded.

"And?"

"Well, I don't know exactly, except I like him." She sucked in a breath. "A lot."

Elli clasped her hands to her chest. "Oh, Cat, that's wonderful! It's time. Go ahead, be excited and care about yourself again and clean your apartment."

"I'm *cleaning* so I don't think about him."

"Why not think about him?"

"Elli, I'm on the rebound. It's like he's just there instead of Trent. I'm barely standing on my own two feet again. If I care about him, then when he leaves I'll fall flat on my face. I can't handle that again. I can't even *think* about trying to handle that again. I'd be lost. Probably forever. I'd never be —"

"Whoa! What do you mean 'when he leaves'?"

"He's just a temp and not just as in employee. We're going to offer him a permanent position, but he's a drifter. It sounds as if he's lived all over, and he talks about heading south, I'm sure before winter. Just him and his surfboard. He probably lives in a room with his board and a sleeping bag and a hot plate!"

"Cat, slow down. What do you know for a fact? Other than he's lived beyond San Diego and he now works as a temp?"

"I know his hair is as long as mine and he drives a pickup!"

Elli burst out laughing and reached across the table to put an arm around her. "Well, I'd say we know for a fact that he's no Trenton Carver."

Cat rested her forehead against her sister's. "Maybe you better pray about this, El. I get that fizzy feeling whenever I see him. Or think about him."

Her sister sat up. "You haven't prayed about this? Oh, Cat, Cat, Cat! When are you going to talk to God again?"

"I don't know."

"He knows what He's doing!"

"I still don't like what He did. I played by His rules, and . . ."

Elli sighed in a frustrated way. "Life is not a game of basketball. You know better than that."

"You have everything you want or need."

"I know. And I understand that I cannot fully appreciate what you feel. I didn't lose what you lost that day." She squeezed her hand. "I am just so thankful no one was killed."

Cat looked at her. She could still read terror in her eyes whenever Elli remembered that day at the fast-food restaurant in the mall. Her sister had heard the screams and from a distance turned to see a man pointing a gun at Cat. She had described it as a split second with the feel of an eternity, torn between rushing toward her or racing away with her son.

"You know I'll talk to God for you. For now."

She nodded, slightly calmed after unloading on her sister.

"Fizzy feeling, huh?"

Cat rolled her eyes.

"Remember the house rules?"

"Of course." House rules were their parents' boundaries set when they were children. They had been fair as well as permanently engraved in their minds.

"Number 12?" Elli asked, examining her fingernails.

Cat's jaw dropped open in surprise.

"Aha! He kissed you!"

"El, I'm thirty years old!"

She laughed. "Number 12 is forever. First kiss, you gotta bring him home for a Sunday dinner to meet the fam."

Though non-interfering, they were a close-knit family. And despite her independence Cat knew she needed their support. She met Elli's challenging glare with one of her one. "If you breathe a word of house rule number 12, I'll tell Mother about you-know-what."

"You wouldn't dare."

"Would too."

Their semi-serious argument eventually disintegrated into giggles. It felt so good to laugh again.

"D'Angelo, you with us?"

Smitty's sharp voice cut through the cottony sensation in Dominick's head. "Yeah." He pressed the heels of his hands against his eyes. Nothing would focus this morning just twelve hours after one sunset and one kiss had plunged him into an ache he wouldn't have imagined was possible. But almost simultaneously with that plunge, he had skyrocketed into an overpowering sense of total release from that ache. After a sleepless night, he knew the two were inseparable. And he knew that Catherine St. Clair was responsible for opening his heart to both the ache and its release.

"D'Angelo!"

"Huh?" Dominick sat in the Drug Enforcement Administration's field division office. Across the table sat Brent Engstrom, the newest recruit, and Robert Smith, the Special Agent in Charge or SAC. Smitty was a lean and mean type and at the moment short on temper.

"I want it tied with the AFO," he insisted again. The Arellano-Felix Organization, also known as the Tijuana Cartel, was responsible for importing multi-ton quantities of cocaine through the Baja area, from Colombia to Mexico to San Diego.

Dominick shook his head. "Who doesn't want it tied to them? We told you, we're done. The Castillo is small potatoes, Smitty, the end of a route before a few kilos hit the street. It's gotta be umpteen steps removed from the Cartel. Combined with this," he riffled a stack of papers, information collected from the DEA, FBI, Border Patrol, and Customs, "we can shut down a very short string of very small potatoes, but that's it."

"Let's say," Engstrom interjected, "I stick like glue to the bread man."

He gazed at the young agent and recognized the attitude. When had his own adrenaline stopped pumping when he looked evil in the eye? When had he given up on saving the world? Rather than one turning point, it had been a slow chipping away by life's realities — evidence turning to jelly in the hands of an inept prosecutor. A woman he thought he loved setting him up. Relocating at the drop of a hat. Eating and sleeping according to some sleazeball drug dealer's schedule. Submitting to random drug-testing because handling coke and meth and weed meant you had easy access and maybe you forgot how to say no. Learning never-ending new twists on money laundering. Posing, fusing fact with fiction, lying . . .

Grabbing an innocent bystander by her bouncing ponytail and sticking a gun in her face.

He had to get out. His debt was paid.

"Engstrom," he explained in a quiet voice, "think it through. Say you follow the bread man. He goes to his brother-in-law's for Sunday dinner, backs his car into the garage, picks up five kilos. You know where it's going, you found it in the turrets at the Castillo. So you follow the brother-in-law. His source is some friend's garage. Let's say you keep going and eventually are led to a warehouse and someone delivering. You hang out with that guy a few weeks until he drives into TJ.

"You decide to break the rules big-time — this isn't watching a woman on her day off visit an orphanage two miles across the border — and you go into Mexico. If you've talked with the wrong authorities — and nine out of ten times they're on AFO's payroll — you're dead. If you haven't talked and no one's looking, you find this guy's taking orders from someone who doesn't have a clue who the bread man is or AFO's phone number, let alone a face from the inner circle.

205

"If after all these months you should by some quirk happen to get close enough to prove a link, some Mexican official will have egg on his face and they'll want to extradite you in order to prosecute you. In the meantime, your proof gets lost in enough red tape to wrap up the Rose Bowl."

Smitty and Engstrom stared at him in silence, and then the younger man raised his hand. "What about the one out of ten times?"

Smitty burst into laughter and clapped Dominick on the back. "You need a vacation. It's all true, but," he turned to Engstrom, "tell us, Boy Wonder, what's our mission?"

"To combat drug trafficking, sir!"

"Right. First I need you to help wrap things up in Logan Heights, probably by next Monday. Then go shut down the Castillo operation and the two others related. Coordinate it with Rehder and Frenell. How many arrests?"

Engstrom counted on his fingers, "Bread man, two bus boys, one security guard, one kitchen staff. The assistant manager is an unknown."

"Cat's not in on it." Dominick's stomach knotted.

"We can't rule her out yet," the younger

agent disagreed. "I don't want her to be part of it either — she's the straightest-looking chick I've ever seen, so wholesome I don't even want her to *know* what's going on. But the stuff's in the turret above her desk."

"She's not in on it." His adamant tone left no room for doubt.

Smitty frowned. "This isn't personal? You're sure beyond anything you've ever been sure of in the past?"

He knew what situations his boss referenced. One was years ago, but the lesson from being set up by a woman he cared for had been well ingrained. The second one Smitty had been involved with, the incident from just seven months ago, the one that had forced him to order Dominick off the street for a time.

"Yes, sir, I'm sure. It's not personal, not related to anything in the past."

Oblivious to the undercurrent, Engstrom continued, "Then the front desk manager must be. One of them has got to be coordinating efforts."

"Cissy?" Dominick turned in surprise. "She's too flaky."

Engstrom grinned. "Someone once told me you never, never know about covers. I take it that includes flakiness."

Thirteen

Dominick thought Cat was avoiding him. The fact was, he was avoiding her. The boundary line had blurred, the line that kept authenticity out of reach in order for him to role-play the charmer. Blurred? After that kiss he couldn't even find it anymore. It was probably far behind him. He had unconsciously, easily stepped over it somewhere between a pickup basketball game and stuffed French toast in the middle of the night. Until he got his bearings, it was best that he avoid her.

Therefore, they hadn't talked much at work this week, hadn't spent any off-hours together, had agreed after the sunset that . . . that what?

That it wasn't supposed to happen.

He glanced now at his truck's sideview mirror, signaled, switched freeway lanes, and rehashed Monday night.

"Dominick," she had whispered. They stood at the end of the pier as the sky darkened.

He leaned toward her again, to catch her words before the wind flung them out to sea.

"I — I can't get involved."

"I know." He knew she was fragile, and he of all people knew exactly why. He knew she wasn't ready and would never be ready for the likes of him.

But then she had brushed her lips against his cheek. Her soft hair touched his face, filling him with the sweet, citrus-like scent of her perfume. In his mind he cried out to God, begging for her healing, begging that he would be a new man in Christ, one she could trust.

If he didn't step away, he would kiss her again.

He took a step back. "Cat, I care for you. I can't ignore that any longer. But I won't pressure you. Tell me what you're comfortable with."

"Just being friends. Going slow?"

"Seeing what happens?" Tentative solutions.

"Yes."

The early evening stars were twinkling by then, and he couldn't see those honey-colored eyes, but they were branded into his brain. They would always be a part of him. Not to confess his sin and his love at that moment had demanded a discipline from him that he had never before known. Even now he could still feel a splinter in his hand from clutching the pier's old wooden railing.

The day in Tecate had been magical. No, Meg would say it had been supernaturally orchestrated. Any lingering doubts of Cat's wholesomeness, any professionally sound restraints were swept away that afternoon at the orphanage when he heard her laughter.

Given that discussion of five days ago, that agreement to go slow, why was it that at this moment she sat in his truck as he drove them to her parents' home for Sunday dinner?

It was first, of course, because of those eyes. And second, it was because when he was with her he was that new man, more alive than at any other time. He was like the grimy city, and her smile was a cleansing rain shower and the pristine sunlight all rolled into one.

"Why do you drive a pickup?"

He diverted his eyes now from the freeway traffic for a fraction of a second. Her knowing smile told him she understood that he loved his truck. He grinned. "Why wouldn't I drive her? She's an F-150 four-by-four with regular cab, short bed, rad set of chrome wheels, and thirty-inch tires."

Her laughter filled that regular cab as well as his heart, and he wondered how he was supposed to go slow.

"Daddy will like it."

Twenty minutes later he met "Daddy," and he prayed the man would like something about him.

"Nice to meet you, Dominick!" Stan St. Clair was his height, barrel chested, steely-gray-haired. The man's forearms were as thick as his biceps. As he held Dominick's hand in a viselike grip, he announced in a foghorn voice, "If you hurt my Kit-Cat, I'll kill you." His blue eyes twinkled, his mouth smiled, but there was an air about the man that said he was serious.

Dominick had never felt so intimidated in his life.

"Stanley!" Betty St. Clair pushed aside her husband and took Dominick's hand in hers. There was a softness about the petite blonde that gave him an immediate sense of being in first grade. "Aren't you glad you're not a sixteen-year-old boy? He always greeted the girls' boyfriends like that too — scared the living daylights out of them. Welcome to our home. I want to hear all about how you and Catherine met."

Cat rescued him before he had to answer. She showed him around the house and introduced him to siblings and in-laws and children. His mental camcorder, normally second nature to him, took a while before clicking on. Stan St. Clair had shot normalcy right out of the water.

Eldest sister Anne had medium brown hair, height, and weight. Husband John was occupied in the garage assembling bicycles. Felicia and Grant were the cutest twins he had ever seen. Today was their fifth birthday.

Brother Ben was tall, skinny, red-haired, married to someone in the kitchen. He worked with his father at the construction company and, like Anne, had three children.

That made six kids.

He remembered Elizabeth from the zoo, the short, raven-haired, pregnant young woman. Friendly husband, salesman-type, Jim. Shy little Jason.

Seven and one on the way.

Doug was in the Navy, in Japan. His wife Penny was here, a studious-looking mother of two.

Nine kids, all under the age of eleven. And one on the way.

Cat steered him through the house. It was a rambling, hacienda affair with a red-tiled roof, U-shaped with a covered porch that ran the length of the inside of the U. In the center of that was a flagstone patio, with a fountain and potted flowers everywhere. Distant hills were visible.

Inside the house was dark wood, Spanish style with high, beamed ceilings, a cool oasis in the desert's hot afternoon. Walls were covered with family portraits. He lingered over an area devoted to Cat. Definite Wheaties box material from the age of five when she wore a shiny pink athletic shirt and white shorts, a soccer ball tucked neatly in the crook of her elbow, the other hand propped on bent knee.

"Dominick . . ." She pulled on his arm. "I want to show you the bridge before the game."

"What game?"

"Basketball. It's a family tradition whenever most of us are together."

He followed her across the patio and noticed a basketball court off to one side.

"Daddy built that for Ben, but of course I was always under my brother's feet. All of my free time was spent either on that court or down at the footbridge."

They trudged down an incline full of scrub brush and large boulders. The rock-hard soil was blonde, as if the sun had bleached out the earth itself. Desert heat dried his throat and warmed him all the way through to the bone marrow. It took only a few minutes to reach the bridge, but it wasn't visible until they were almost upon it.

"Isn't it great?" she asked.

He smiled. It was about six feet long, simple wooden planks placed crossways over two beams, all covered in flaking red paint, without a railing. It spanned a dry creek bed that looked about five feet deep at this point. "Uhh, sure. It's fantastic."

"Come on!" She punched his shoulder. "It really is. Here, you have to sit beneath it to get the full effect."

He scrambled down the bank behind her. They sat cross-legged, facing each other in the dirt. It wasn't as hot here in the shade of the planks and a nearby tree.

"If you follow the creek bed," she pointed to her left, "it winds up into the hills where the avocado groves used to be. It's a housing development now."

"So, this is your safe spot?"

"Mm-hmm. Except for the occasional rattler."

He looked over his shoulder.

"Don't worry. We always keep a snakebite kit in the house."

He peered over his other shoulder. "I was hoping you'd have a Daddy-bite kit."

She laughed. "Oh, and this," she pointed

to an arrangement of stones near her feet, "is a castle." Her tone was final, as if she had shown him everything.

He knew that in contrast to him, she *had* shown him everything. She had opened to him the corners of her heart.

"Dominick?"

He saw concern on her face.

"I know they can be overwhelming at first. I just . . . I just wanted them to meet you."

Oh, dear God. "Cat . . ." He exhaled. "I've never . . ." He swallowed. "This is like a foreign country to me. All those people under one roof, related and laughing. All this space. With my background, I don't exactly fit in."

"Yes, you do." She shifted her weight to her knees, braced an arm against him, and quickly kissed his cheek. "Thank you for reminding me how special this place is. I sometimes forget. God has given us so much, not just in material things. Did you figure out we're all adopted?"

"What?"

"All five of us are adopted."

There was no resemblance between the siblings! Where had his mind gone? It had turned to mush somewhere between Stan St. Clair's handshake and these honey-colored eyes now just inches from his face.

"That's why you don't look alike."

She smiled. "Duh."

"All five of you?"

She nodded. "Pretty amazing when you think of all the biological families represented here. Mother and Daddy weren't able to have children, but they desperately wanted them, and so they found us. We're all two years apart, all came here as babies, all California natives."

He brushed hair back from her cheek. "Where did they find you?"

"In a crack house in Los Angeles."

For a split second his mind hit empty space, quickly displaced by a rushing wind of incoherent thoughts. *Born in a hell. Fresh. Wholesome. Suspect? How could I ever — ? Honor student. All-star athlete.*

"Well, the police found me. Daddy knew somebody who knew somebody on the force. Actually, I might not be two years behind Ben. The doctors guessed at my age. There was an unidentified dead woman, but there were no records of her giving birth, no relatives found. They really couldn't figure out where I came from. I was just this scrawny little thing — can you imagine me a scrawny little thing? Daddy held me for twelve months straight. It was the only place I was content. I think that's why he still gets

216

a little overprotective."

Dominick listened to her matter-of-fact description, and then coherency fled again. He cupped the back of her head with his hand and could think only of that dimple and the generous mouth that made it appear. Tenderly he kissed both.

A distant bell clanged, slowly bringing him back to the present.

Her lips brushing his, she murmured, "Game time."

He lifted his head. "Cat, I can't go slow. Do you know what you're doing?"

She frowned.

"When you sit close and kiss me and thank me and tell me everything about yourself?"

"Just being friends?"

He pulled her to himself. She could be so frustratingly . . . wholesome.

"Dominick," she said, her voice muffled against his neck, "this is my safe spot, and you're sitting in it. That makes you part of it."

Straightening, he placed his hands on her shoulders and looked at her. "You feel safe with me?"

"Completely. Maybe God doesn't want us to go slow."

He blinked. "You're talking to God?"

"Well, I'm thinking about it. I don't understand how I can feel so close to you when if I'd had my way, I'd be addressing *wedding* invitations today. Maybe that guy with the gun was an angel in disguise, saving me from a huge mistake with Trent."

His heart skipped a beat, and he closed his eyes. *Angel in disguise?*

"I mean, I don't think anymore that you're just filling up the hole that Trent left."

He forced himself to meet that shimmery honey. "Why do you think that?"

"I brought him here once. He never sat down in the dirt. And he never ever asked where they found me."

The obvious way God was answering his prayers was almost frightening. No doubt about it now. It was time. She had to know the truth.

Dominick traced her jawline with his finger. Did she truly feel safe with him as she'd said? He would push her to the edge and see. She wanted a divine sword to banish the nightmare. He knew God would hand it to him, but he could not wield it until she totally placed herself in his hands. If she did that, the plan he had devised could work. If it did, the fears would be gone, and their relationship would find its one chance of moving forward.

And he really wanted it to move forward.

With a quick prayer and great effort, he slipped his voice and his facial expression into professional mode. "Catherine Michele St. Clair, do you trust me?" He saw in her eyes then what he knew he could put there, a flicker of fear.

"Y-yes."

"You're absolutely sure?" He touched the worry crease between her brows.

"Dominick . . ." She swallowed. "I trust you. Even when you get that icy, Secret Service look on your face that reminds me I really don't know a whole lot about you."

"Good girl. I want to walk you through the nightmare."

She stared back at him.

"We'll go to the mall, into the restaurant, stand on the spot."

"I can't," she whispered.

He held her with his eyes. "I'll stay with you."

"I can't."

"I know you can't. But if you trust me, I can do it for you. Do you trust me?"

She laid her head on his shoulder.

"Please. Let me do this for you."

"Why?"

He kissed the top of her head. *Because I'm*

the only one who can. "Cat, you know I'm new at this faith business. But I do understand that God loves you, and He doesn't want you to be afraid of this anymore."

"I'll . . . I'll pray about it."

He wrapped his arms around her. "All right."

Fourteen

It was Friday morning. Cat meandered through the quiet pot shop, rolling up the sleeves of her oversized denim shirt, idly inspecting other potters' work. The place resembled a library. But instead of books, the floor-to-ceiling shelves were stacked with mugs, bowls, platters, vases, and knick-knacks.

In the five days since Dominick's offer, she had successfully avoided praying about it. To a large degree she had avoided even him. Whenever she'd catch a glimpse of him in the distance, she'd turn and go the other way, then tell herself how silly her behavior was. And then her heart would race while her practical mind shouted, *He's not your type!*

Yesterday she had joined Elli at her Lamaze class and afterwards for lunch. Her sister, of course, launched a full-court press before she even had time to open the menu.

"Cat, he's perfect."

She rolled her eyes. "Who?"

It was Elli's turn to roll her eyes. "Dominick!"

"Hmm," Cat grunted as she studied the menu. "He's . . . He's . . ."

"He's what?" she prompted.

"Perfect. Except for the fact that he doesn't in any way, shape, or form fit any dream I've ever had for my life!"

"You're not still on that kick about a North County castle-type house and a big family of athletic, straight-A kids and never a financial concern?"

"Wellll . . ."

"Did you see him talking to Dad? Going over each other's pickups like a couple of mothers talking about their babies? And then Dad skipped his usual twenty-questions routine during dinner. Mother thinks he's wonderful. All the kids liked him —"

"Jason was standoffish with him."

"Jase is going through a quiet period. He can't figure out the deal with my big tummy and the baby talk. Anyway —"

The waitress interrupted them at that point, but Elli got right back to it after they gave their orders.

"Mother and Annie and I think you two make a striking couple. You look better with a guy bigger than Trent. He's just too slick to go with your earthiness, you know, your bone structure."

Cat stared out the window.

"So when are you seeing him again, I mean besides at work? Like as in a date?"

"El, slow down! If I think this way I'll just get all fizzy-feeling inside again."

"What's wrong with that?"

"I can't see where I'm going. It's like I used to feel life was a garden path. All I had to do was keep the rules and skip on down it. Then out of the blue it gives way to this abyss and I'm clinging to the sides. So I've decided *that's* real life, not the garden path garbage. Only I'm not plunging headfirst without looking anymore. I'm holding on and taking it one step at a time so I can see where I'm going."

"God knows where you're going."

"God says we can make choices, right? Well, I choose to trust only as far as I can see. If I start praying about it all, I know what He's going to do. He's going to make me let go of the grip I've got and then I'll feel like carbonated soda and not in control, and when Dominick changes his mind, I'll lose mine for sure." She covered her face with her hands.

"Whoa, Cat. Maybe *you'd* better slow down. You're that crazy about him?"

She nodded.

"Ladies," the waitress boomed, "need

223

some Kleenex here?"

"No, thanks," Elli answered.

Cat sniffled and lowered her hands. "We're fine. Just a couple of goofy females talking about men."

The waitress chuckled and refilled their iced tea glasses. "Coulda guessed that. Have a nice day."

Her sister studied Cat's face, waiting.

"El, he . . ." She pressed her lips together. The words refused to form.

"He what? Good or bad?"

She lifted a shoulder.

"Cat, it's obvious he's attracted to you. If he cares about you, it's probably more on the good side."

"The mall. He wants to take me there."

Elli's eyes widened. "You told him about that?"

She nodded. "He thinks I should get over the fear."

Elli blinked and thought a moment. "And get on with your life." She slapped the tabletop. "He's right! You can't really get into a new relationship until you let go of all that past horror. You're so much stronger than you were a few months ago, Cat. Maybe you're ready for it now."

"I guess that's what I thought, the part about a new relationship. If I do it, then

Dominick will mean even more to me and — Oh, can we just change the subject? I have to think more about it."

"And pray about it. You know they're usually one and the same when you know God." Elli caught the frown on Cat's face.

Now, in the pot shop, Cat pushed her sister's words to the back of her mind. She'd mull them over later.

She picked up the bowl she and Dominick had formed together. She smiled, remembering how they laughed at his attempts. Despite its dubious beginnings on the wheel, it had survived the first firing and was in the bisque stage, ready to be dipped in the glaze. With deft strokes, she wiped a sponge around the bottom, spreading a liquid form of wax to prevent the glaze from adhering to it. That breathing space would keep it intact during the next firing.

As often happened here in this artistic, creative environment, Cat's logical thought processes tangled with a fanciful slant. She liked clear-cut rules to follow, and when something like this lopsided bowl caught her attention, she had to admit that not keeping the rules sometimes worked.

The ill-formed piece should have exploded in the kiln.

Dominick D'Angelo didn't fit the form

she had decided upon long ago. He was too tall, too muscular, from *Chicago* of all places, not interested in a salaried professional career, evidently had not grown up in a church. And he drove a pickup. His influence over her should have fizzled by now. He shouldn't be this close to her thoughts. *All right, heart.*

She would apply the glaze to the bowl — there was nothing else she could do — and see if it endured the second firing.

If she allowed their friendship to be glazed, to be coated with the attractive things — laughter . . . candlelight . . . hand holding . . . anticipation — would it survive the unknown, inevitable changes?

Only time would tell.

She studied the string of colored tiles, trying to choose one for his bowl. The grayish green of celadon? His gray eyes came to mind . . . his green truck. A red? She thought of the tie he wore to dinner . . . the rose he had laid on her desk last night.

Obviously the glazing of the relationship had already begun. And she was decidedly enjoying the process of it.

She grasped the bowl with long-handled tongs and stepped to the barrel of deep blue liquid. Blues brought absolutely nothing to mind about Mr. D'Angelo. She quickly dipped the bowl in and out, then set it on a shelf and headed down an aisle toward the huge plastic bag that held the clay.

She disagreed with Dominick and Elli. The nightmare didn't fit in anywhere. It had nothing to do with what was going on here. It was in the past; she was getting over it. Five years from now that mall would be no big deal to her. She was fine with her life as is. No reason to complicate matters with prayer and working through some ugly fear. If she prayed about it, she knew she would agree to walk with Dominick through the nightmare because . . . because she trusted him.

Cat halted in the aisle, her eyes focused internally. That was it. Why did she trust him? Because she sensed that somehow he really could absorb her fear. The only way he could do that was supernaturally. He believed in God as she did, in the supernatural power of God walking in human form as Jesus, bringing the kingdom with Him for the here and now and forever, to replace all their fears with His love.

Dominick reminded her of what Jesus must have been like to the people who lived with Him. As a man who built things and walked great distances, His physical strength was a given. People would be at-

227

tracted to His friendly demeanor, His attention to detail, His concern for others, His storytelling that made them think as well as laugh.

Dominick was all of that. He showed concern for things Trent had never noticed about her. He even mentioned her middle name, which she hadn't told him — he'd probably seen it in her mother's cross-stitched piece amidst the mass of photographs he studied. Photographs that Trent had merely glanced at once.

Her family had enjoyed him. He made them laugh with his stories. Mother learned that his family called him Nicky, his brother was two years younger, his mother knitted for the needy, he attended a church downtown. Other than that, they knew only that there was integrity in the way he spoke of others and observed the world, humility in the way he listened to the little ones and helped in the kitchen.

And Cat sensed there was a divine sword available to him, and he would fight with it for her.

Which was why she was not going to pray about it. If her fears were banished, what would she cling to? She'd lose *all* control and race headlong into the emotional upheaval of falling in love and planning the future with hope, this time knowing full well that God could nix it at any point. If she had a choice in the matter, she didn't want to ever be in that position again.

She wiped her eyes with her sleeve and strode over to the bag of clay. She dug inside and pulled off a fistful, slapped it onto a tabletop and viciously pressed the heels of her hands into it, kneading it, crushing air bubbles.

Trent seemed still full of air bubbles, as if he hadn't been crushed enough by life. When the intense heat came, he didn't look so good. His character was splotchy; there was not enough depth in him to care for her above himself. He had never made her feel *cherished* or *safe*. When Dominick kissed her under the bridge, she was the most special woman who ever walked the earth. When he wrapped his muscular arms around her, it was his inner strength that protected her from the world.

Cat lifted a shoulder to rub the sleeve against her eyes again. *Uh-oh.* Tears were a bad sign.

Oh, Lord!

The following afternoon Cat pushed open the door marked *Housekeeping*. As usual, bleach-scented humidity and a dull thumping of the industrial-sized clothes dryer greeted her.

With hesitant steps she walked between floor-to-ceiling shelving units packed full of linens, cleaning supplies, and miscellaneous hotel room items. She heard a radio, soft strains of jazz mingled with the laundry noise. Where the room opened into a wider area, she stopped. Dominick sat writing at a desk, his back to her. His broad shoulders dwarfed the desk and chair. She noted that his black, rather shaggy hair was probably longer than hers, long enough even for a ponytail.

He set down his pen and folded his hands on the desktop. He seemed to be waiting, and she wondered if he sensed her standing six feet behind him. He was like that, attuned to details most people missed. A whiff of her perfume, a shadow, a slight shift in the air, even the pounding of her heart. Like Jesus, he knew her, probably knew she stood there, but he was the consummate gentleman. He would wait for an invitation before speaking.

"Dominick?"

His shoulders drooped, as if he exhaled a breath held for a long time. He swiveled in the chair to face her. "Hmm?"

"I've thought about it." On its own accord, her forefinger slipped into her mouth. "I — I don't want to do it."

"Did you pray about it?"

"Sort of."

"Doesn't count."

She bit harder on her fingernail and turned to leave. "Well, it has to."

"He's waiting to talk to you, Cat." Dominick was immediately beside her. He braced his right hand on a shelf near her head, cutting off her escape. "Just like I've been waiting all week. What's holding you back?"

She leaned against the shelf and stared at the top button of his plaid shirt. If she just didn't look at his face . . . "I like it where I am."

He placed his other hand on the shelf above her and leaned toward her, tilting his head until she had to meet his eyes. "I don't think we can move forward until you deal with this situation."

She blinked rapidly and whispered, "I know. That's just it."

"Are you saying there's nothing between us?"

No! Yes! No! "I don't *want* anything to be."

He smiled. "I think that's a moot issue at this point, *mi gatita*. We'll take it one step at a time, and this is the first step. A necessary one. Uncomfortable, I know. We'll get it over with tomorrow."

She bit another nail. His deep, whispery tones were doing something to her spine.

He pried her hand away from her mouth and gently kissed each fingertip one by one. "Would you like to go to church with me first? We'll let God adjust our perspective, ask for His blessing, eat lunch, and then just do it. Hmm?"

She winced.

He held her hand against his cheek and took a deep breath. "Cat, this is for me as much as it is for you. Will you do it for me?"

In his gray eyes she saw something new. Somewhere between the ice and the meltdown was pain. How could he care that much for her welfare? She nodded.

His eyes closed. "Thank you."

"Elli was with me."

"Is she afraid of that mall or shadows in the dark?"

She shook her head. Neither was her sister afraid of prayer.

"I'll pick you up at 10 —"

"Well!"

They turned to see Cissy just inside the door.

"This is certainly professional!" The sarcasm in the young woman's voice was unmistakable. "Or does it mean inappropriate behavior is appropriate as long as it's done in Housekeeping?"

Dominick chuckled as he lowered his arms and straightened up. "It probably means you'll uninvite me to your party."

"You got that right, mister!"

Flustered, Cat finally found her voice. "Cissy, did you want something?"

"There's a phone call for you, *Miss* St. Clair." She turned on her heel and walked out.

Cat moved toward the door. Her head was beginning to pound.

"As I was saying," Dominick's voice held traces of laughter, "I'll pick you up at 10:15."

"All right. I think I'm going home now, after I take this call."

"Are you okay?"

She turned, her hand on the doorknob. "Yeah. It's just been a long week."

"Call me if you need anything."

"I'm supposed to say that. I'm the manager who's leaving five hours early."

"Don't worry. We'll take care of things."

"Maybe *you* will, but you'd better keep an eye on Cissy. A scorned woman is not nice." She opened the door.

"I didn't mean to scorn her. I'll tell her.

233

Hey, Cat, will you wear your red jumpsuit?"

"I don't have a red jumpsuit."

"I thought you were wearing a red jump-suit?"

"Oh, I threw that thing out. I knew I'd never wear it again. Bye."

"See you."

As she strode across the hall to her office, she dismissed the idea that she had never mentioned to Dominick what she had worn the day of the nightmare. She must have told him and just forgotten. Instead, she replayed his comforting "Call me if you need anything." That would get her through the night.

Fifteen

Sitting in the pew next to Dominick the next morning, Cat felt as if life were rushing along a roller coaster track with some unseen person at the controls. Forget slipping along a steep slope — this was turning into a totally unpredictable wild ride.

Here she was sitting in a church of all places with some guy she barely knew, thinking about doing something she desperately did not want to do. Why was that?

Because Dominick D'Angelo had lovely eyes and treated her respectfully and obviously cared for her welfare and made her laugh when she didn't want to and gave her space and hugs in just the right amounts? Probably.

Dominick now slid the hymnal into its place on the back of the pew in front of them. His shoulder brushed hers. The sheer solid presence of him flooded her with security.

She looked around and felt another reassurance in the grandeur of the stately old church. Located downtown, it exuded a different ambience from what she had known growing up, but Jesus was here too, and people worshiped Him. Was it His sheer solid presence that reassured? Was it okay if she just basked in that for a while?

This roller coaster ride must be what it was like to be carried on the updraft of someone else's prayers. She knew, of course, whose prayers those were, and she knew Whose hands were at the controls.

Cat felt Dominick's finger brush at the corner of her eye. She blinked back the tears.

"You all right?" he whispered.

She nodded. "I'm ready."

He tilted his ear toward her.

"I'm ready," she repeated.

He smiled and reached for her hand.

Goodness, she hadn't held hands in church since she was a teenager and her dad wasn't looking.

A short time later they stood on the sidewalk outside at the edge of the crowd, waiting for Dominick's friends to make their way over to them. She remembered Megan from the zoo. Her husband towered above her, decidedly more surfer than doctor in appearance.

"Meg, Adam, this is," Dominick paused and stared at her as if unsure of exactly who she was. ". . . Catherine St. Clair," he finished softly with a smile.

They greeted her warmly, both shaking her hand.

"I'm so glad to see you again," Megan exclaimed, her brown curls bobbing. "We've been hearing about you for such a long time. He calls you Cat. May we?"

"Yes."

"Will you two come for dinner tomorrow night? Please, please? You're both off from work, right?"

"Well . . ." Cat glanced at Dominick who raised his eyebrows, leaving the decision to her. "Yes," she said, "I'd like that. Thank you."

"About 6 then? Here . . ." Meg scribbled on a business card. "Call me if something comes up. Our number is unlisted." She handed it to Cat with a smile and leaned toward her. "I didn't think there was a woman alive who could get Dominick's attention. You must be very special, and I really want to get to know you. I'm glad you're coming."

They parted ways with promises to talk at length tomorrow.

As Dominick and Cat strolled to the parking lot, they discussed where to eat lunch. Their halfhearted conversation finally convinced them they weren't hungry.

They shrugged at each other and climbed into his truck.

The mall was tucked between two freeways, its entrance off of Friars Road. Cat hadn't driven on that road for almost eight months now, often taking circuitous routes to avoid it. When Dominick signaled for its exit from the freeway, her heart raced.

"My dad," she gasped, "tried this once."

He shifted as they came to a stop at a light.

"We got as far as that next light." She remembered screaming.

"Was that a while ago?"

"In January." Begging. *Daddy, take me home!*

"Long, long time ago. Another lifetime."

Crying. *I can't do it!*

They approached the next intersection. Dominick reached over and squeezed her hand. "I'm with you now."

Screaming until Daddy had no choice but to turn around, take her home.

"And I'm bigger than your dad."

Cat's breath caught in a strangled giggle.

"Well, sort of. Take a deep breath. Younger anyway."

She closed her eyes as he turned into the parking lot, a tightness in her chest allowing only shallow breaths.

"Back in January," his low voice soothed, "I don't think the divine sword was ready yet. It was still in the blacksmith's shop, getting shaped for today."

She unhooked her seat belt, scooted across the bench seat toward him, and buried her face between his shoulder and the back of the seat, crossing her arms against her midsection. The truck came to a stop, then the engine cut.

"This is a big day for you, Cat. And it is going to be as bad as you imagine, but you will get through it. Trust me?"

She nodded.

"Let's go to that fountain in the center, then you go on ahead, into the restaurant. I'll follow you. I think you need to do it by yourself."

By myself? She didn't answer. From the fountain to the restaurant? There were too many storefronts in between. It was too far.

He kissed the top of her head. "I'll be nearby."

"It's too far." Her voice was muffled against his shoulder.

"It's where you walk with God. There's no other way."

She looked up at him. "You said you'd do it with me."

His eyes held hers. "When you get inside the restaurant, I'll be there to hold you, and you won't have to be afraid anymore. Ready?"

She shrugged.

"You can do this, Cat. I'm with you, and God is right here with us."

They sat quietly for a few moments. She sat up and nodded. He took her hand as she slid from the truck.

On that day almost eight months ago now, the wide walkways along the mall had been filled with festive Christmas trees and fake snow villages. Silver garlands and red bows entwined the lamp poles. The winter weather had been its midday warm in the sunshine, sweater cool in the shade. The store windows displayed after-Christmas sale signs.

Cat had worn a favorite red jumpsuit, her hair pulled casually back in a ponytail. A new diamond sparkled on her left hand as she and Elli swung little Jason between them, entertaining him through the inevitably tedious ritual of returning wrong-sized gifts alongside hordes of post-holiday shoppers.

Today the crowd was sparse. Cat wore a simple white dress. In spite of the summer heat, goose bumps covered her arms.

Dominick walked beside her, his dark hair set off by a white polo shirt tucked into black dress slacks, a somber warrior look on his face. She edged closer to him, trying to breathe deeply and calm the dread that filled her, trying not to remember that day. She wasn't successful.

At the fountain located halfway down the sprawling mall, they stopped. Dominick took both of her hands in his. "Doing okay?"

She shook her head no.

He wrapped his arms around her and gave her a quick bear squeeze. "You go on ahead now." He glanced around.

"Walk with me."

"Then it wouldn't count. Let God walk with you, Cat. Talk to Him." He rubbed her arms, smoothing the chill bumps, and smiled. "I'll be close by, but I can't do what He can."

"But you'll come into the restaurant?"

"I'll come into the restaurant. That will be the toughest part." Quickly he kissed her cheek. "Go."

She took a backward step, then a few sideways steps. He gave her a thumbs-up sign, and she turned. *Oh, God.*

The fear was tangible. It was as if window shades in her mind were being pulled down one at a time. Darkness closed in.

Father! I can't do this alone!

The black lightened to gray.

Cat looked over her shoulder. Dominick wasn't there. She stopped and turned around in a full circle. Nowhere. He was nowhere!

"I'll be nearby. I'll be nearby."

He had to be there — he promised!

She crossed her arms over her waist. Thick blackness crept in again, now blocking even her eyesight.

"I will never leave you nor forsake you."

Promises. God was here just like Dominick. Unseen but here. And available. If she cried out, Dominick would come. She knew it. And so would her Father.

Oh, God, I need You. I don't want to be afraid anymore. Help me!

The mental shades lifted. A flower bed at her feet came into focus.

Cat continued down the sidewalk. God was as real as Dominick, and even nearer. He had always been there, waiting to answer her because He loved her . . . more than her parents, more than Trent . . . more than Dominick.

A hymn from the morning service sprang to her mind, and she began humming. *"Prone to wander, Lord, I feel it, prone to leave the God I love; here's my heart, O take and seal it."*

The scent of greasy french fries slowed her steps, churned her stomach. It was her little nephew's favorite place. How many outings would she miss with that child if she kept avoiding it?

With a shaky breath she walked to the glass front of the fast-food restaurant. It was an innocuous place, as usual full of friendly faces, all ages, talking and laughing at tables, in aisles, in line at the counter located at the rear, not far from a straight line of colorful booths shaped to look like train cars.

Eight months ago as they had entered, Elli and Jason went to stand in the food line while she headed to save a place on the "twain." He liked the locomotive the best, but it was most often taken. When its occupants that day began gathering their things, Cat bounded between tables toward it and then . . .

Not yet. Go inside first, she told herself.

She noticed a family approaching the restaurant. When someone opened the door, she stepped behind the group and followed them through it.

She was inside.

The crowd noise and the greasy smells were overpowering. Her heart thumped erratically. The sides of the room slipped from view as if she had tunnel vision. She saw only the path that led to the spot where terror had first entered her life.

Terror is not from Me.

It wasn't a voice but a distinct impression. *Dear Lord, dear Lord, dear Lord. Help me!*

A child bumped into her. Unintentionally, she moved.

Her breaths were shaky and her steps unsteady, both taken beyond her own willpower.

She reached it, that spot halfway between the counter area and the train, at the end of an aisle alongside a post, amidst people coming and going and eating and talking. She stopped.

An urge to turn around assaulted her. If she had turned that day, perhaps things would have ended differently. But she hadn't turned, she hadn't known there was a reason to turn . . . She resisted the urge.

The memory flashed vividly now. She sensed that she shouldn't fight it. It had to be replayed step by step.

She remembered the vicious tug on her ponytail. Her hands going to her head. Her cry of shock. Her body bending, turning slightly into the pull. The gun barrel inches from her face. The massive army green jacket filling her vision. The harsh voice barking unintelligible words.

Her screams.

Another voice. "Wrong one!"

Wrong one, wrong one, wrong one.

The pressure released. The gun was removed. The army green retreated.

His face. Nothing. A glimpse. Full, dark beard. Sunglasses . . . wire-rimmed, aviator shape. Red and white bandanna across the forehead, covering the hair.

The back of his head, bandanna tied above a ponytail. Blond? Dark? Red?

In less time than it took to tell the story, the intruder had crashed into her world and then vanished. With him fled all comprehension of God. A great nothingness engulfed her.

And then the blackness.

The blackness didn't come now. There was no escape.

Oh, God! she prayed. *Oh, dear Father! I lost You here. Let me find You again. Please let me find You again.*

Tears streamed down her face, and she felt a softness inside that hadn't been there for a long, long time. She wiped at her eyes. Things were going to be all right. They really were. Now that she was actually standing here, she knew the nightmare could become just a frightful memory. Over time even that would diminish.

Knowing she would cry, she had tucked a hankie into a pocket. Now she took it out and dabbed at her eyes. There was one more step. She had to turn around and see that nothing was there, prove to herself that the ghosts were gone. She heaved a sigh and peered over her shoulder.

Dominick stood directly behind her.

She smiled at him. "I'm okay," she whispered.

"Good. We'll finish it then."

She saw then the army green jacket he carried.

Her smiled faded, her skin prickled. What was he doing? Did he think they had to re-enact the whole scenario complete with props?

As he shrugged into the coat, his head tilted, revealing the black hair tied into a short ponytail at his neck.

It was black hair! Black hair. Black hair . . .

He reached into a pocket, pulled out sunglasses. Wire-rimmed, aviator shape, reflective lenses. He slipped them on.

Blood pounded in her ears.

"Cat, you forgot to tell me about the bandanna." He wrapped a red and white kerchief across his forehead, over the top of his head, tied its corners at the back. "But I was wearing it, wasn't I?"

He caught her before she fell, his arms around her waist, bracing her against himself. Her knees refused to lock.

"I'm sorry," he whispered in her ear. "I am so sorry."

The nightmare terror bombarded her. A battle raged in her head; lightning flashes pierced thick blackness. Her heart thumped in her throat, choking her until all breath was gone. Still she saw his face, the glasses and grim mouth just inches from hers.

"Breathe, Cat. It's okay. It's okay. Come on, sweetheart. Breathe."

At last she emitted a strangled, "No!"

"Hold on, it's okay." He pressed her head to his chest.

She clutched his jacket. Against that rough olive green cloth that had haunted so many of her hours awake or asleep, she sobbed. "Not you! Not you!"

"Hey, mister!" a gruff voice exclaimed behind her. "What's going on?"

"My wife's not feeling well." The lie came swiftly. "Can we use the back door? I need to take her home."

"Yeah, sure. This way."

Across the floor and into the parking lot she moved awkwardly beside him, his arm around her waist, her face buried against his shoulder, her hands clinging to the jacket.

247

Her sobs deepened. Each breath became a strangled gulp for air.

He lifted her into the truck. She huddled against the door, helpless to stop the flow of tears, unable to think coherently.

"Cat, please."

The next thing she knew, she looked up, and the truck had stopped.

"Talk to me?"

Talk! She didn't even know who he was! Her eyes were almost swollen shut. He was a watery blur across the seat. "Who are you?" She choked on the words. They sounded garbled to her ears.

"Let's go inside your place. I'll explain everything. Please."

"Who are you?!" she shrieked now.

He pulled off the bandanna and sunglasses. "I'm Dominick D'Angelo. I'm an agent with the Drug Enforcement Administration. I work undercover. Last December I was after a dealer who was spotted in that mall. I heard the description. Female, tall, red jumpsuit, ponytail. And then I saw you. Cat, I am deeply sorry and . . . I love you."

She opened the door, jumped out, and ran to her apartment building without a backward glance or thought, intent only on getting away.

Sixteen

Was everything a lie?

Of all the questions disturbing her head since yesterday, this was the one they all came down to, the one Cat needed answered. Now, at 7 o'clock Monday morning, she asked it again as she stood on the pier watching distant surfers bob in the ocean's gentle roll.

Dominick was out there somewhere. She had to ask him.

After leaving him outside her apartment, she had cried uncontrollably for a long while. In time she sensed a cleansing effect. Everything poured from her — eight months' worth of bottled-up disappointment and fear and anger, the hardness of her heart built on her willfully turning her back to God day after day.

She faced Him finally because there was no one else to face. Nothing made sense, and so she read the Bible, the book of Job, reminding herself that whatever happened, God deserved her trust and devotion. It was the only thing that mattered in life. It was life. At long last she prayed again.

There was no question of forgiving Dominick for his initial mistake, the incident at the mall. Despite the fact that her life had been turned upside-down and she had been angry at God, she knew the nightmare occurred for some beneficial purpose. She truly believed the gunman was an angel in disguise.

But that Dominick had betrayed her was beyond comprehension. When had he first recognized her? Why hadn't he told her? How could he behave like a concerned friend — actually promote their relationship! — while concealing his true identity? How could he kiss her? And how could she fall for it?

And what in the world was he doing at her Castillo working maintenance?

Again, though, there was no question of forgiving him even for this. The Bible's teaching was clear. But it would take a long, long time.

She had called Elli, but there was no answer. She could not talk to anyone else. Angry as she was that she didn't understand, only Elli knew her well enough to let her vent her confusion and not hold her responsible. Daddy was out of the question. He really would go after the man.

Megan Parker.

Cat had found her phone number tucked in her purse. Did she know who he was?

The woman answered midway through the first ring.

"Megan? This is Ca—"

"Cat! I'm so glad you called! How are you?" The compassion in her voice said she did indeed know who he was and then some.

Fresh tears sprang to Cat's eyes as she clutched the phone. "Who is he?"

"Didn't he tell you?"

"Yes, but . . ." She bit her lip. "Why?"

"First, can you tell me what happened this afternoon? He promised to call but hasn't. That means he's very upset. He told us he was going to walk you through that horrible situation at the mall."

"You knew about that?"

"Oh, honey, it was a major event in his life. He didn't have anything to do with Jesus until that happened."

Cat sat down on the couch, pulled her knees up to her chest. "Was everything a lie?"

"No, no, no. He loves God. He is everything he appears to be except a temporary maintenance employee. He cares deeply for you. He has been in agony these past six weeks or so, not being free to tell you what he does for a living."

"Why couldn't he tell me?"

"I don't know. He doesn't tell us the details of what he's working on."

Her breath caught. "He's at the Castillo *working* on something? Some *drug* thing?"

"I assume so."

Dear Lord! "I'm so confused, Megan."

They had talked awhile. Cat was thankful for her new friend's comfort, for encouraging her to just talk to Dominick. Megan gave her his unlisted phone number, but Cat couldn't even make the effort to get up for pen and paper. Last night had been too soon to speak anyway. She needed time to absorb the shock of yesterday. She needed distance between learning the truth and deciphering what to do with it.

Megan also reminded her of his surfing habit. Now, this morning, she had become almost frantic to ask him that one question: Was *everything* a lie? She scanned the ocean for Megan's description — a black wet suit with faded red short sleeves, on the north side. Elbows propped on the wooden rail, she leaned over and focused far below the pier on the long, staggered row of surfers who waited patiently under a gray sky. The possibilities of finding him or not finding him both filled her with a dreadful anticipation.

Images of him flashed like a mental slide show. Dominick teasing her about picnic benches, playing with the children at the orphanage, painting on the ladder, dribbling the basketball, holding her while the migraine pounded, celebrating the inspection over dinner, sitting under her bridge. Dominick kissing her on this pier, agreeing it wasn't supposed to happen.

But all along he must have known who she was while she didn't have a clue who he was!

She saw the beginning of a wave, like the humpback of a whale underwater rolling toward the surfers. Many paddled with their hands, moving into position to catch its curl at just the right moment. Some missed it and turned back out to sea. Some stood for milliseconds, then plunged below the water's surface, their boards flying skyward. Some stayed with it, racing just ahead of the crashing foam, a sheet of fiberglass keeping their bare feet atop the water.

It was impossible to tell where he was. Cat hurried along the pier, now dreading the thought of missing him. She should wait on the beach until he came out. Megan said Adam assured her that he would be here this morning.

She finally spotted him in the shallow water carrying the board under his arm, tugging at the back zipper's string. He stopped in the sand near a pile of clothing, set down the board, and peeled the wet suit from his arms, shaking water from his hair.

She approached as he bent and picked up a towel.

"Cat!"

"You sound surprised. That's probably a first."

In spite of her bitter tone, his slow smile lifted. "The first time was when I walked into your office."

She blinked, turned her head sideways toward the pier. "You knew me then?"

"Oh, I knew you. I had been looking for you for six months. It was your eyes I could never forget. I used to hold up a jar of honey in the sunlight, trying to catch their color."

She bit her lip. "Daddy always called them maple syrup."

"Well, I was looking at them with different eyes."

"I don't understand." She looked at him now. He was standing very still, watching her, the towel in his hand, water dripping from him. "I don't even know where to begin to ask how to understand."

"I know. I'm sorry. You have every right to hate me —"

"No, I don't have that right. I know you

made a mistake, and I forgive you, but I don't know you, and you know all about me. I am just so confused and angry. Was *everything* a lie?"

"No, ninety-nine percent of it wasn't. Let me start with the incident."

"Just tell me the one percent! What's not true?"

"Please. Give me five minutes? Please?"

"Don't manipulate me." She didn't hate him, but she knew she didn't trust him either.

"I won't. Just hear me out."

She waited, jaw clenched.

"Adam had been telling me about God for a long time. I listened to some of what he said, but I didn't really hear. When I held a gun to you and looked in your eyes, then I heard."

Her anger melted.

He took a deep breath. "Your beautiful, expressive eyes, Cat. I saw you asking, 'Why are you doing this to me?' And that's what I heard Jesus asking. You know, kind of like Saul on the road to Damascus? Why was I persecuting Him? Every day I chose to go my own way without Him, I was persecuting Him. I always hoped you would call the police, so I could thank you. I've been loving you for a long time, Catherine St. Clair, for that reason alone. You gave me a priceless gift, and I know what it cost you." His voice cracked.

She closed her eyes. This was too much.

"The only way I could make it up to you was to help you get over your fear at that place. I thought you were ready yesterday. I needed you to be ready because I was falling in love with you in a different way, not as the stranger who had changed my life forever. I mean, after I got to know you . . . well, what was there not to love?"

"Please don't say that. My life was ruined that day."

Dominick briskly dried his arms with the towel. "I think God only 'ruins' what He wants to rebuild into something even more beautiful." He bent and picked up a white T-shirt. "You know that."

She did, of course. "But it doesn't change my feelings, what I went through."

"No, it doesn't. Why don't you want to hear that I love you?" He placed his arms through the shirt sleeves, then gathered it in his hands.

Before he could slip it over his head, she reached out and touched a scar on his chest, toward his right shoulder. There were two short, pink, jagged slashes, close together. "What is this?"

"I was shot. That's when I met Adam. He saved my life."

"I thought you said you were in an accident." She met his eyes for a moment, and then he pulled on the shirt, breaking the contact. "Dominick, I don't want to hear it because I don't know you. It means *nothing* from a stranger. And you are still a stranger to me."

He swallowed. "Can we fix that?"

"I don't know. What are you doing at the Castillo?"

"It's almost finished. You don't have to worry about it."

"Tell me!"

"It's part of a drug run. Cocaine is dropped there, picked up by a few dealers."

"No!" she cried and covered her mouth with her hands.

"Cat, everything will be fine when it's over. We'll do what we can to keep a lid on the publicity."

She peered at him over her fingertips. "Who . . . ?"

"I can't say."

"Dominick, not my castle!"

"I will take care of it. You understand, it's imperative that you not tell anyone who I am. Absolutely no one. Not Ron or Trent or Cissy. Not your dad."

She nodded. "Do you have a gun?"

"It's part of the job."

"You can't take a gun to my castle!"

"We can pray I won't need to. Okay?"

She closed her eyes.

"Cat, will you meet me at Adam and Meg's tonight? They know me better than anyone. They can fill in the gaps. Please come?"

"I don't know." She lifted a shoulder.

"Think about it?" His head tilted in that gentle way that had become so familiar. "Pray about it?"

She winced, knowing at least one thing for certain. "Yes, I will do that," she agreed, then hurried away as quickly as she could drag her feet through the sand.

It was after 7 P.M. that night. She sat outside in a cushioned patio chair at Megan and Adam Parker's home, her legs curled up, wrapped in a sweatshirt to ward off the early evening cool that settled in with the chill that had lingered inside her all day.

"Is he always this late?" she asked.

Adam and Megan exchanged glances. Adam answered, "Dominick's schedule is unpredictable. We usually try to grab him after church."

"But he's always at work on time, sometimes early —" Cat realized it was his other job that got him there. "Does that mean he's working now?"

Adam nodded. "If it would help for you to ask us more about him, go ahead."

There was no pretense with these two, she had noticed soon after her arrival. They welcomed her like an old friend, offered her appetizers and drink, skipped weather talk, volunteered information about themselves. They asked her about the Castillo de Cala, about her family, her school. "Well," she raised her brows, "I guess that's why I came tonight. He said you could fill in the gaps. And there are gaps. I'm having a hard time figuring out how to process all this."

Megan stepped over to her and squeezed her hand. "I can't imagine how difficult this is for you. Do you remember when we met at the zoo? Dominick said you were his boss. I just assumed you were his DEA boss. He wouldn't let me near you after that. But I've been praying for you, that you can forgive him and trust him again. I don't like what he does, but they tell me it's necessary, that he accomplishes good." She returned to her seat.

"Mind if I start, love?" Adam winked at his wife. "I'm sure Cat has enough emotionalism to deal with."

Megan waved a hand at him and pulled a tissue from her pocket.

Adam chuckled. "Well, about two years ago I was on ER duty, middle of the night. A few guys were brought in, a couple of them in pretty bad shape. There had been a drug bust, a shooting. I worked on the one I figured was the bad guy. You know firsthand how grungy Dominick can look — long hair, unshaven, dirty, torn jeans. He was in tip-top physical shape, but still it was touch and go for a long time. When he woke up, we hit it off and began spending time together.

"He was, to put it mildly, an emotional wreck, and the recovery period was good for him that way. It gave him time to begin unwinding. He grew up in Chicago and has a younger brother. Did he tell you that?"

She nodded. "Did he live in a poor neighborhood with an alley for a backyard? And did he punch his dad, who left them afterwards?"

"He told you that?" Adam's tone was surprised.

"I didn't know that," Megan interjected.

"Cat, I can guarantee that whatever Dominick told you was the truth — he just didn't always tell you everything." He locked his eyes with hers. "Can you accept that?"

"I — I'll try."

"I don't know another man with as much integrity as he has. That's why he chose to do what he does. His childhood was harsh. He got into drugs early on. When his best friend died of an overdose when they were sixteen, he quit cold turkey. I don't think he's taken an aspirin since then. He almost killed the guy who sold them the stuff. Fortunately he got connected with some big-brother types, went to college, became a Chicago cop, then joined the DEA, trained at Quantico, lived various places doing undercover type work.

"I know he feels he's paying off a debt to his friend. He has a love-hate relationship with what he does. I don't know how long he can keep it up. What he did to you at the mall almost put him under. They forced him to take two weeks off, then stuck him behind a desk for a while. The whole time he kept searching for you. He hung out at the mall, kept checking with the police, hoping you'd report the incident."

"I went to an emergency room."

"Emergency room?"

"I guess I blacked out. My head hit the floor. I went to one up in North County. I didn't explain the incident."

Megan blew her nose.

Cat shrugged a shoulder. "It's okay. I

mean, it — it wasn't. I had migraines for six months, but now I know God was working in me."

Megan's curls bobbed. "He was doing His work in Dominick too. He wouldn't have been ready for you back then. When God finally brought the two of you together, you were a suspect again, so —"

"Suspect? *I* was a suspect? At the Castillo?"

Megan threw Adam a look of panic. He intervened. "Cat, he has to distrust everyone until he figures out who's involved."

She felt blindsided again, hit with another incomprehensible facet of Dominick D'Angelo. "But how . . . how could he think I was . . . ?"

"A long time ago he loved a woman who double-crossed him. He learned the hard way that no matter what someone appears to be, it may be just that, an appearance, not the truth."

She closed her eyes. "When did he stop thinking I was a suspect?"

"I don't know."

Her lids flew open, and she pleaded, "*Did* he stop thinking that way?"

"Oh, yes," Megan assured her, "yes, he did. Otherwise he never would have told you who he was. The last time I talked to him, he told me about your trip to Tecate. He even told me what the grandmother said to him, to take care of you. He wouldn't have told me that if he wasn't thinking the same thing."

"He told you what Rosa said? How did he know what Rosa said?"

"Didn't she talk to him?"

"In Spanish! She doesn't speak English, and he doesn't speak Spanish!"

The Parkers exchanged glances.

"He does speak Spanish?"

They both nodded.

"Oh, I can't think this way. It's just too complicated and confusing."

"Adam," Megan cried, "say something!"

He sighed. "It *is* complicated and confusing, Cat. None of us would deny that. The bottom line is, kids are dying from drugs. Dominick fights that day in and day out. He works with incomplete information. Sometimes he knows only that the bad guy is wearing a red jumpsuit or works at a motel. He betrayed you because he didn't know how else to protect those kids on the street. Every time he told you something like he lived in Chicago but didn't tell you he was a cop there, or like he knew some Spanish words but didn't tell you he was fluent, he died a little inside. And I know

263

that's true because he told me you're the most significant person in the world to him."

He stood. "Now, Meg, are we going to eat dinner or not? I'm famished." He walked over to Cat, pulled her to her feet, and hugged her. "That's from Dominick, God bless his rude soul."

She gave him a small smile. "Thanks. I was beginning to think your bedside manner is really lousy."

Megan hugged her then. "And this is from us."

Seventeen

"So where's your *'friend'*?"

Cat swiveled around in her desk chair to see Cissy just inside her office door. "Cissy! You startled me. I wish you'd knock when the door's shut."

"It was open." She sat in a chair, crossed her legs, and propped an elbow on the desk. "Pardon the expression, but you look like something the cat dragged in. Do you have a headache?"

"No, I just didn't sleep well last night. I'm a little tired. By the way, I need the to-date August figures for a meeting with Ron on Thursday. Can you get your stuff to me tomorrow?"

"Sure. Did you and your 'friend' have a spat?"

"What 'friend'?"

"Dominick." She flipped her long blonde hair off a shoulder.

Cat massaged her forehead. Maybe she did have a headache. So much had happened since Cissy had seen Dominick holding her hand in the Housekeeping room. She had gone from trusting him to total confusion regarding everything about him except the fact that his subtle Secret Service air was for real, just clothed in a different name — DEA Special Agent. And she wasn't supposed to tell. "He's just a friendly, hard-working temp. We're not *'friends'* as you say."

Cissy laughed. "Things didn't look just friendly and temporary with the two of you all snuggled up in Housekeeping." She threw up her hands at Cat's frown. "Hey, it's okay. He really isn't my type. I'm just a little surprised he's your type."

"It wasn't what it looked like." *Well, not exactly what it looked like . . . certainly not anymore.* "He was telling me something about God."

Cissy guffawed loudly. "God? Man, is he yanking your chain. Two weeks ago he was at a big party, smoking dope and drinking tequila at 2 in the morning."

Inwardly she cringed. Was this another side of Dominick D'Angelo . . . ? *No! Not drugs!* Nothing was as it seemed. What was it Adam had said? Dominick dealt with incomplete information. This was incomplete information. Could he *appear* as if he were smoking, drinking —

"Don't worry." Cissy leaned across the desk and patted her hand. "This rebound season will pass and you'll be fine. No more Trents or Dominicks. Anyway, he's not here. And he hasn't called us or the temp service. Maybe he's not so hard-working."

"He's still not here?" Cat glanced at her watch. It was 6 o'clock. She hadn't seen him since yesterday morning at the beach. He had never shown up last night at the Parkers'.

"Aha, you checked! You were looking for him."

"Cissy . . ." She stopped herself from accusing the younger woman of crossing the line of respect toward her boss. What made her think she was above reproach just because she happened to be in an assistant manager's position? "Cissy," she repeated in a different tone, "I apologize for not behaving professionally. We weren't snuggling in Housekeeping, but it was close enough to be just exactly what I told you not to do. I'm sorry."

The younger woman stared at her.

Cat saw behind the mask of bravado then. Cissy's face resembled a little girl's, a hurting little girl's. "Do you know God loves you?"

"Save it, Cat." She stood. "I've been on my own for a long time. We've got a couple of maintenance-type problems in rooms.

What do you suggest?"

"Where's Miguel?"

"At home. Family emergency."

She sighed. "I'll pull Chris from the restaurant after they slow down. He's handy with tools. Can it wait an hour?"

"Yes." Cissy shut the door behind her.

Cat distinctly remembered closing the office door before sitting down at her computer. Cissy often popped in, as if the door were open. Their good rapport had allowed her an easy access that had become Cat's biggest help during the unbearable days after the nightmare. There were times that if she hadn't covered for her, found her medication, led her to an empty guest room, or arranged a ride home for her, she would have been in trouble. Had she ever thanked Cissy for that? Really thanked her?

Probably not. The past eight months had been an intense focus on herself. Who else had she ignored or hurt along the way? What all had she missed?

Besides cocaine dumped at her castle?

She covered her face with her hands and held back a sob.

Who was involved? Everybody was so nice!

Oh, Father, please just fix it. And take care of Dominick, wherever he is.

★ ★ ★

By the next evening at 6 o'clock the strain was wearing on Cat. She pulled a compact from the desk drawer and applied more makeup, trying to cover the dark circles under her eyes and to press away the crease between her brows.

Dominick still hadn't been heard from. She had called the Parkers four times. Megan assured her this morning that it wasn't uncommon for him to be gone a week or two without communicating, but she promised to let her know the moment they heard anything. She made Cat promise the same, as if he would call her first. As if she were his friend.

Friends wasn't the word. Neither friends nor *"friends"* the way Cissy said it. Not even *acquaintances* described the weird set of circumstances that allowed them to meet. Twice. Only God could design such a criss-crossing of paths.

She snapped shut the compact.

Whatever.

Cat buried herself as best she could in work. There was enough to keep her occupied as long as she could force herself to concentrate on it. At 11, unable to keep Dominick from the center of her mind any longer and not yet ready to go home, she walked around the grounds one more time.

Where was he? Was he all right? How did she feel about him? How could she know what she felt when the only Dominick she knew was the temporary maintenance employee? And what was going on at her castle? She tried to turn all the questions into prayers. Her attempts felt like dismal failures. The old fear kept getting in the way, pointing the questions back into herself.

Back in the lobby, Cissy was waiting for her. "Well," she smiled, "it seems you have a new admirer already!"

"Admirer?"

"Someone named Adam just called. Ni-ice voice."

"What did he say?"

"He said, 'Please tell her that her angel in disguise is waiting.' " She waggled her eyebrows. "So, why is he your angel in disguise?"

Adam wasn't. Dominick was. She had called him that once, before she knew who he was. He must be there then, at the Parkers'. Cat took a deep breath. "Umm, I didn't recognize him as — as someone I'd care for." She shrugged. "But now I do."

"Wow, you work fast."

"Prayer works, Cissy. Not always fast or the way I want it to, but it works."

Angel in disguise. In a sense that was what she did know of Dominick. He was God's way of preventing her from marrying Trent . . . of smashing the imaginary castles she had built with her own hands without His blessing . . . of wounding her in the hope that she would turn to Him for healing. If that were true, it made Dominick D'Angelo a rather significant person in her life. That seemed a good place to begin knowing someone.

Before she could ring the Parkers' bell, Megan opened the front door and greeted her with a hug. "He's all right."

Cat heard tension in her new friend's voice. "But?"

"Well, he was hurt." She shut the door and tried to smile. "Adam thinks a couple of cracked ribs, says no big deal. He taped him to ease the pain. You know, I always imagine the good guys yell 'Halt, you're under arrest', and the bad guys freeze and hold up their hands."

"What happened?" A vision of Dominick being rammed hard enough to crack ribs flashed through her mind. "No, on second thought, I don't need details."

"Me neither. He's down there, in the den." She pointed at the hall that led from

271

the entryway. "He showed up here about 10:30. Adam's gone to the hospital now and wanted him to go, but you know Dominick. As long as he's awake and breathing, he doesn't need a hospital."

"Megan, I don't know Dominick. I don't really know the first thing about him."

She squeezed Cat's hand. "You can start now, if you want."

She hesitated a moment, eyeing the closed door at the end of the hall. Dim light outlined it; muted television voices came from beyond it. Walking toward it was more intimidating than going through the mall the other day. There at least she knew the fear that lay ahead. Now there was only an injured stranger, but she sensed that her attraction to him could very well turn her entire world upside-down. And that was the greatest fear of all.

Cat brushed her knuckles against the door.

"Meg, you don't have to knock." His voice was strained.

She pushed open the door and caught a glimpse of white bandaging where the top of his flannel shirt was unbuttoned. It was the sight of the rest of him, though, that halted her just inside the door and flung her flippant reply back against her throat. In a recliner, footrest raised, her big, dark-alley type sat motionless. With each breath he took, pain etched a new furrow across his face.

He closed his eyes and pressed a remote clutched under his hand on the armrest. The low volume on the television was muted. "What are *you* doing here?"

"Hey," she swallowed, "you were supposed to meet me at Adam and Meg's two nights ago."

He didn't reply.

"Not to mention, Jack, that faucets are dripping all over the motel and I've had to drive the shuttle van twice."

"Sorry. My schedule changed. My real schedule." He struggled with every word. "That feels good." He looked at her now through half-closed eyes. "To say that to you. 'Real' schedule."

She went to him and, taking his hand, sat on the floor beside the chair.

"Don't cry, Cat." With a small grunt as if the effort hurt, he reached over with his other hand and gently stroked her cheek.

Oh, how could she care for this guy she didn't even know?

"No more lies or half-truths. I promise. What are you doing here?"

"Adam called. I've been pestering him

and Megan since Monday, asking about you. He knew I was . . . concerned."

"What'd he say?"

"He left a message —"

"You didn't talk to him?" Barely audible as his voice was, it had an anxious tone.

"No. Cissy did. She thinks I have a new beau named Adam."

"What'd he say?"

"My angel in disguise was waiting."

A small smile lifted the corner of his mouth. "Good old tight-lipped Adam."

"Why did he say that?"

"So that only you would know it was me." He brushed hair from her forehead. "I told him about it the day you said it. It was my first ray of hope . . ." He stopped.

"Hope? For what?"

"That you'd want to get to know me. Who wouldn't want to get to know their angel in disguise?"

Yes, who wouldn't? She smiled softly. "I guess that's why I came tonight."

"Well, this is it." He leaned his head back against the chair, breaking eye contact. "This is my life. Gone for three days without a word. No regular sleep or meals. Still fighting, like when I was a kid. Sticking a gun in the face of an innocent woman."

"Dominick . . ." She laid her cheek on his

hand. "I forgive you for that."

"For that." He looked down at her. "I've been lying to you since the moment we met." His honesty was brutal.

A tear slid from the corner of her eye onto his hand. "Give me time."

He turned away. "Next week I could be told to move to New York, and I'd go. It's my work, what I signed up for. Impressed yet? I can tell you your dad would not be impressed." He rubbed his eyes. "I need to sleep."

"What about the Castillo? What's going to happen?"

"I don't know the timing — no, I do know, but I won't tell you. You'll be fine. It's nothing like what this just was. Please don't worry."

"What do I do?"

"Nothing, Cat, nothing. Just promise you won't worry."

Not answering, she stood, tired and more confused than ever. How could he hope that she wanted to get to know him and practically in the same breath consider moving across the country?

"Promise me."

She nodded.

His eyes closed. "Be careful going home."

"Bye."

She found Megan in the kitchen.

"Oh, Cat . . ." The woman took one look at her face and hugged her again. "He hasn't slept for forty-eight hours. Whatever he said, don't take it to heart."

"When exactly can I take to heart what this guy says?"

"I don't know. Leave it in God's hands. He's a potter, like you. And I suspect He's creating something exquisite."

Eighteen

Cat slept better than she expected, probably in relief that Dominick was safe. When she awoke, she lay in bed and tentatively directed her thoughts to God, thanking Him for those two things, sleep and safety. To her surprise, she immediately realized that something was missing from her usual morning awareness.

Fear.

The nightmare had lost its power. Trent and her castle dreams had been obliterated. Dominick D'Angelo was one big question mark on the horizon. She was a lump of clay and not the potter . . . And yet there was cause for hope. Her trustworthy Father had better plans than she could ever design.

She'd have to tell her parents their prayers were answered. They would be thrilled. But that would mean getting into who Dominick was. Who he was at the mall . . . who he was at the Castillo . . . what he did for a living. It would have to wait.

That decision made her uncomfortable. She didn't withhold from her parents. Maybe she could tell them only that Dominick had helped her go to the mall and that she wasn't afraid anymore. That could cover it for now.

A thought struck her. Was this just a hint of what Dominick dealt with day in and day out?

Dear Lord, please give him strength for this day. And how about a new job while You're at it?

She bounded from the bed, eager to start living without being afraid.

Cat wished she could talk with Elli, but that was out of the question for the moment. She was glad her sister would assume that as usual this week was keeping her necessarily occupied. Other friends came to mind, ones she had let drop by the wayside through the months. Some had offered help during the really tough time, but she had only wanted Trent and only allowed Elli. Now she felt like throwing a party in her ugly new apartment. Perhaps sometime soon.

Knowing the best outlet for her excess energy was a few extra hours spent in preparation for the Castillo's upcoming party, she left early. A few years ago she had created an end-of-summer festival, to attract families before they returned to school routines. Sign-ups were scheduled for a week from Friday. That Saturday would be filled with games and tournaments, ending in a hog roast and ice cream party and a swashbuckling fencing demonstration. Sunday offered an informal church service on the beach and late checkout time.

Later that afternoon she strolled around the property, writing notes to herself about what was needed for decorations. At the pool she stood and watched giggling children splash in the water. It was a beautiful, warm summer day. She hadn't noticed for a long time how refreshing it was to work outside under the bright blue sky. That was another plus for her job, being able to come outside at will, or for that matter stay inside when the winter drizzles came. Another was to wear whatever suited the role her agenda called for. Today, as assistant-manager-party-coordinator, she wore casual, multi-colored overalls and a fuchsia T-shirt without a second thought as to whether or not it was appropriate for the managerial half of the title.

Until she saw Trent walking toward her.

She scribbled furiously on the clipboard. The overalls were ditzy, faddish, definitely not classic, not *haute couture*, not — *Oh, dear Lord, do we really have to do this today?*

"Hello, Cat." All the blue from the sky and the swimming pool gathered in Trent's eyes. "You look great, like an end-of-summer festival, all wrapped up." He smiled.

She swallowed the *Huh?* and said, "Thank you."

"Do you have time now to talk with Ron and me? We're going over some budget items and need your insight. I realize you were scheduled to do it later —"

"No, now's fine."

Trent opened the gate for her, and they walked side-by-side through the courtyard. She noted with surprise that he was minus the usual suit coat. He and Ron must really be into the figures. But as usual he looked good in his long-sleeved white shirt, dark tie, and trousers. His light brown hair, neatly trimmed above the ears and across the neck, was cut so straight it could be used for a ruler.

"How are you?" His tone was sincere.

She stuck a hand in front of his face and wiggled her fingers. "Nails are growing."

"That's a good sign."

"Mm-hmm. And I went to the mall this weekend."

"Ah, shopping?"

She stared up at him. "*The* mall."

"*The* mall?" He thought for a moment, then his eyes widened. "You haven't been there?"

She turned away and bit her lip.

Trent pulled her arm through his and crooked his elbow. "I'm sorry, Cat. I'm sorry I didn't know, and I'm sorry I've let you down in so many ways."

She didn't reply. They had been through the apologies months ago.

He squeezed her hand. "It's the end of August."

She knew the date, of course. Because it was almost time for the festival, she knew the date, but she had buried the connection to the fact that it was almost September. Five weeks from tomorrow was to have been their wedding rehearsal and dinner. She had planned it to take place after this busy time at the Castillo — after the late summer's heat, when her parents' backyard captured that subtle shift of seasons and would provide the perfect early evening reception atmosphere.

He loved her, had loved her anyway, in his own way. It was his wedding too, his future.

She leaned her head against his arm. "I'm sorry too, Trent."

He stopped and drew her close.

With her arms wrapped around his neck, Cat felt she was in essence releasing him. She knew the headache wouldn't come this time, knew she could let the emotional pain go. She could forgive him.

He held her tightly for another moment. "Wanna have dinner?"

She leaned back to look up at him. "No."

He winced. "Maybe another time?"

"Maybe." She smiled. "Sometime."

"You have the most beautiful smile, Catherine. I will never ever find another smile like yours." With a dramatic sigh, he kissed her cheek and let go.

When they reached the lobby Cissy beckoned to her. She told Trent she'd meet him in Ron's office in a few minutes and walked over to the registration counter.

Cissy grinned. "Did you see Dominick?"

"Dominick's here?" Cat glanced at her watch, hiding her expression while she did some quick mental gyrations. What was she supposed to do? What exactly did she know, supposedly or otherwise? What didn't she know? What was he doing here anyway? Was it time *now?*

"Yeah, he looks like he's been partying a little too hearty."

"So," she searched for a nonchalant tone, "where's he been?"

"When I asked him, he just winked, you know like he does, shrugged, and asked what needed to be done first." Cissy giggled.

Cat interpreted the giggle to mean that the young woman's on-again, off-again Dominick infatuation was on again. "And you said?"

"He was fired." She giggled some more. "Seriously, I told him about the handrailing in the west wing."

"Okay, that's good." He was *working?* "I'll be in Ron's office." She hurried off, called "two minutes" as she darted past Ron's open door, then ducked into her office and shut the door. She had to compose herself.

What was he doing? She didn't think the charade needed to continue now that she knew. Wouldn't he just come unexpectedly, wearing some sort of official-looking suit and tie, flash a badge and announce who was to get into the paddy wagon?

Cat crossed her arms over her head and slid along the door until she sat on the carpet. No, he wore a ponytail and grungy army jacket and flashed a gun. And he got his ribs broken while fighting. The old terror engulfed her again.

Lord, I don't understand. I can't do this.

There was a soft knocking.

She stopped breathing.

Another knock. "Cat . . ."

It was Dominick. She stood, opened the door wide enough for him to step through, then shut it again.

"Cat," his voice was a low whisper, "sit down." He steered her toward a chair, then knelt before her, rubbing her hand between his. "It's all right. Relax."

She couldn't catch her breath, couldn't stop shaking.

"Relax." He smiled. "It's just me."

Me? Who is me? "Your smile," her breath came in a hiccup, "isn't right. The real one tucks in." She touched the right corner of his mouth. "Here."

His eyes closed briefly. When they opened, the ice had frozen over. "Undercover smile."

"Dominick, don't!" She threw her arms around him.

"Ouch!"

She sat back. "I'm sorry! I'm sorry! Oh, I can't do this."

Through clenched teeth he growled, "You don't have to do *anything!* Go about your business. I'll get a hammer and screwdriver and go about mine, and I will avoid you for the remainder of the day. That's all there is to it. Got it?"

She shuddered.

"Dear Father . . ." Dominick stared back at her, but he was praying. ". . . we need help here. She can't lie. Everything shows on her face. Please calm her so others won't be concerned and ask her what's wrong. In Jesus' name —"

"Amen," she whispered.

Gingerly he rose. "You could just go home. The place will stand without you here watching over it for one day. The budget can wait."

How did he know so much? She took a deep breath. "If I lose it again, I will. I promise."

"I was concerned about your initial reaction. You'll be fine, Miss Jill-of-all-trades." He winked and quickly slipped through the door.

Cat wondered if God answered Dominick's prayer with a gift of anger instead of peace.

The fact alone that he prayed confidently with her had a calming effect . . . until she thought of his pretend smile or his wink or not telling her what to expect. With those thoughts, the anger flooded her.

At least no one seemed to notice her condition, and that itself *was* the answer to prayer. She had made it through the meeting with Trent and Ron more or less intact. There were no surprises in their budget discussion, so she was well-rehearsed for that interchange. Twice, though, Ron did ask her if she felt all right, mentioned she looked pale. And Trent remarked that her hair looked fine, she needn't keep toying with it. She mumbled something about crepe paper for the festival.

Afterward he followed her into the hallway. "Cat, you will tell me if you change your mind? About dinner?"

She felt a vague notion that he interpreted her distraction as a hopeful sign for himself. If she weren't so unnerved, she probably would have laughed.

For the remainder of the workday she wasn't put on the spot. Thankfully she didn't see Dominick. No one saw panic on her face and asked what was wrong. She didn't have to decide how to circumvent the truth, which was that she was worried out of her mind because this man who was an undercover agent who carried a gun was the complete antithesis of Trenton Carver and yet had captured her attention in a way that Trenton Carver never even approached.

Not to mention that someone at her castle was dealing drugs.

No wonder she was angry. And where was God? According to Dominick, He was right there in the midst of it all, listening to a prayer about how she needed a peaceful countenance so Dominick's work would not be hampered.

It was after 11 now, and she should be going home. Instead she strolled down the dimly lit courtyard toward the pool. *This was her home too!* She had always felt a personal responsibility to the families who stayed here. Like a mother, she would make her rounds, locking doors, shutting off lights, symbolic to her of tucking everyone in.

This drug business added a whole new dimension to her usual concern. She had to make at least one more round, linger awhile, reassure herself that everyone was safe. If a room had been available tonight, she would have used it. If she had a couch in her office, she'd even consider sleeping on that. She simply could not leave.

It was anxiety that kept her here. And truthfully it wasn't anxiety *just* about the threat of what Dominick, probably along with other agents and the police, might do at any moment. It was about standing last night in the Parkers' hall and realizing that she was falling in love with a man she knew innately but not practically. It was about wondering what he was going to do about their relationship, what she wanted him to do. It was about not knowing if there was even enough between them to *do* anything about.

Yes, she was anxious, and she knew what to do about that, but still she hesitated to pray. This was the type of thing to leave totally up to God, trusting Him to work out the details.

The clincher was that a relationship with Dominick was out of the question. It was totally unimaginable, and totally unimaginable relationships did not fit her agenda. There were certain things she expected to occur in her life. A house, which her dad would build, inland. Three babies, hopefully a boy and two girls. All the sports for all of them. Car pool . . . make that minivan pool. Season zoo passes. Part-time work at the Castillo. She had a timetable, albeit about eight months behind schedule at the moment.

Well, she had come a long way in those eight months. What had she learned exactly? Following preconceived rules of the Christian life did not guarantee fulfillment of the agenda. Obviously God wanted more of a say in her agenda choices, wanted more of a hand in shaping her.

How would Jesus respond if He were in her shoes — those of an adopted daughter in a loving family, who enjoyed a job that utilized her talents and gave pleasure to others, who was afraid of the love she felt for a man because it might hurt, who didn't want to let go because God might have something else in mind?

Jesus would pray. He'd pray a lot about everything. He'd give love to others and accept love in return. He wouldn't worry about possible future wounds, because each day every need would be met. He wouldn't make up rules about if He did this, His Father would have to do that. He would trust in His *Father's* agenda.

She remembered the first time Dominick had talked about God, when they were by the garden footbridge. She had seen the look of awe on his face, the wonder at knowing that the Creator of the universe loved him. Had she lost that somewhere along the way? In the comfort of being able to talk to God as her Father, she had become casual, her worship routine. She had even had the audacity to snub Him for a time.

Now she strolled along the sidewalk that paralleled the small beach. Bay water lapped gently against the sand. Except for the reflection here and there of the few lamps that lined the walk, the water was black. The misty air obliterated the stars from view.

Obliterating the stars . . . but only from her point of view. They were still shining.

She knew that. She had always known that. She had just ignored the fact.

As she followed the walk, Cat began humming. Soon the words took shape, words asking for forgiveness, words uncurling her fist that clutched her perfect agenda, her castle dreams. It was so hard, but for the first time in her life she wanted to do it.

She reached the far northwest corner of the grounds, the pile of boulders that served as an informal boundary. Beyond, the sidewalk continued through a group of low buildings owned by some community group. This time of night it was always deserted, lending the Castillo an air of a large private estate.

Cat paused near the boulders, remembering her dream as a young girl of being a princess who lived in a castle and spent her days dispensing outrageous gifts. In a sense it was fulfilled, even if Prince Charming had fled the scene and business was precarious. For the time being she could still create a respite for others from the harsh world. Perhaps that should be enough. And as for Dominick — Well . . . ?

Well, he was still one big question mark.

Dominick crouched in the night shadows next to Brent Engstrom. They were behind the tall wooden fence at the end of the service drive, in the oleander bushes where last week he had trimmed away some of the thick leafy branches.

He shifted his weight and stifled a groan. It was at times like these that he considered thirty-five an old age, too old for this line of work. Each breath he took punctuated the sharp pain on the right side of his rib cage. That coupled with one good night's sleep out of the last five left him running on empty.

And then there were his emotions, like a field of land mines he didn't have the wherewithal to inspect. The mere thought of Cat set off internal explosions. The image of her tears last night spilling from those honey-colored eyes wouldn't leave. No one had ever cried over him like that before; no one had grieved over his pain, forgiven him so freely, accepted him for who he was, unafraid.

Engstrom nudged him. Dominick peered through the fence. An unmarked white van was backing down the service drive.

He tried to snap his mind to attention, slam shut the doors to all other thoughts and feelings that did not pertain to this moment. None of the old tricks worked. He knew he was in dangerous territory. Somebody could get hurt.

Dear God, I'm at the end of myself. Isn't this where You do Your best work?

Engstrom began videotaping through a tiny knothole. The exchange would be recorded. Later, somewhere down the freeway, the driver would be stopped by CHP officers for an imaginary broken taillight. And then they would read him his rights.

In the meantime, Dominick and Engstrom would monitor those involved at the Castillo. They knew the coke would be stashed in the turrets —

He heard off-key humming. His heart skipped a beat.

He touched Engstrom, silently motioned his intentions, then slid from behind the bushes.

He couldn't see her. Slipping from shadow to shadow beneath the trees, he hurried toward the sound.

What was she doing here?

Reaching the maintenance garage, he saw Cat strolling toward it, undoubtedly heading around it on her way toward the fence at the end of the service drive. The reverse of her usual route and two hours beyond it, she was about to walk into —

They would hurt her.

Unless they were expecting her.

He rushed to her.

A large shadowy figure came into Cat's view, just a few yards away. No sooner had she halted than she knew intuitively it was Dominick. Before she could react, he was beside her.

"Dom—"

He pressed his fingers against her lips, gently but firmly.

She got the hint to be quiet, but when his other arm grasped her around the waist, she wriggled. He squeezed her to his side and nudged her along the sidewalk. She stumbled. He lifted her, and her feet skimmed the concrete, then slipped through the sand as he urged her toward the boulders. When they reached the far side of them, he released her.

"Cat!" It was a hiss. "What are you doing here?"

"Oh!" She leaned toward him and hissed back, "Can't you just walk up to me like a normal person?"

"Answer me! What are you doing out here?"

"I don't have to answer you!"

"You're supposed to be gone by now." His voice was husky, almost threatening.

"So are you!" In a flash she realized that when he was pressed against her side, she had felt the gun beneath his jacket. "I'm dealing drugs, Dominick!" Her voice rose in anger. "What do you think?"

"Cat!"

"That's what you think! That's what you've always thought!"

He sucked in his breath. "Talk to me."

The light was too dim to read his eyes, but she could discern the ice in them. She couldn't communicate with that, wouldn't even try. "No." She spun on her heel, but he grabbed her wrist and twisted her back around. "Dominick!"

"Talk to me," he repeated.

"Not when you sound like that."

"I'm working, Cat; this is how I sound when I'm working. Now for the record, talk to me. Why are you here?"

"You're hurting my wrist." She yanked it away. "Why do you think I'm here? I work here! I live here! I care about this place. It's my castle, my home! You know all that. Why are you like this?"

He leaned back against a rock and pulled her to himself, held her head against his neck.

She resisted, but he didn't let go. His chest heaved, and she realized that he still hurt, physically and emotionally. She stopped struggling. Unsure where to hold him between injured ribs and a gun, she just nestled her face against him, laid her hands on his shoulders. They stood, silent except for his labored breathing.

"Oh, Cat. I'm sorry. I feel like I'm losing my mind. I can't remember you're not one of them."

"Not one of who? What's happening?"

"*It's* happening. The exchange. Right now, right outside the kitchen, right where you were headed. Drugs and money."

She jerked her head up. "Go! Make it stop!"

"Shh." He stroked her hair. "We're taking care of it. My partner's there. I saw you coming and — Oh, dear God, help. I can't think straight. How could I imagine . . . ?" He closed his eyes.

"Is everybody safe? Is everybody okay?"

"Shh, yes. Nothing's going down yet. We're just watching tonight. Please, please don't worry."

"But when — ?" She leaned her forehead against his chest. "Why is all this happening?"

"That's an easy one." He clasped his hands behind her neck. "So I could meet you. *Mi gatita,*" he whispered, his lips brushing her temple, "I keep hoping you're contagious."

"What?"

"Your goodness," he mumbled. "I need your goodness, Cat."

And then he was kissing her, and she was the one who couldn't think straight. It didn't matter who he was or where he had come from or where he was going. It only mattered that when the real Dominick breathed through the ice, he was the very essence of hope and safety.

"Mmm, I'm sorry," he murmured, his forehead against hers. "I wasn't going to do that. You are just so good, Catherine St. Clair, just so good and real and solid. Jill-of-all-trades. Wheaties box material —"

"Wheaties box?"

"Wholesome. Athletic."

She giggled. "You're so weird."

"At least you know that much."

She lifted her head to peer at him in the dim light. She touched his face. She loved his face with its cragginess and scars and angular nose, all untold tales of a life spent fighting evil. "I know more than that, Dominick. I don't know where you live or what you like for breakfast or who your favorite author is or where you went to school or what size shirt you wear or if you like boats, but I know you."

He kissed her forehead. "Just off Balboa Avenue, near the 5."

She heard the grin in his voice.

"Less than ten minutes from you when the traffic is right. One-bedroom apartment. University of Wisconsin. Frank Peretti. Extra-extra large. Speedboats yes, sailboats no. And Wheaties. Definitely Wheaties."

She smiled. "And I know you're very tired."

"Mm-hmm. I saw Carver with you today, out in the courtyard. It's easy to tell he's still crazy about you, huh?"

"So?" she teased.

He kissed her more intensely this time, totally scattering all traces of anger and castles and Trenton Carver.

"Cat?"

"Hmm?"

"Remember at the beach Monday morning, you said I was a stranger to you?"

"Mm-hmm."

"Now can we fix it?"

"Mmm." Words seemed to be slow in forming.

"Can we spend some time together?"

She swallowed. "Of course."

"We'll talk." He sounded weary.

"Okay. You should go home. Will you go home now?"

"Yes. I can take you home first."

"No, I'm okay." That was easy to say as she stood in the circle of his arms. "What about tomorrow?"

"What about it?"

"Do we have to do this again?"

He combed his fingers through her hair. "I got the impression you liked kissing me."

She laughed softly. "You know what I mean. Are you coming here?"

"Yes, just like today. We have to do this again. It'll be over soon though. I promise."

"Okay." She took a step backwards. He gave her hand a squeeze and let it drop. "I — I guess I'll go. Aren't you coming?"

"Not with you. You go ahead first. Wait at the end of the drive if you want me to follow you home."

"Which way should I walk now?"

"Uh, any way. No, on second thought, go on the far side of the restaurant. I'm sure nothing is going on now, but that would be better, from that direction."

She walked a few steps, then turned back. "Dominick, promise me you'll sleep?"

"I promise. Soon."

Nineteen

Late Sunday morning Cat drove by rote to her parents' home, her mind freed to ruminate over the last couple of days.

It had first been on Thursday that she awakened to a morning without the heavy nightmare fear. After that night's hushed conversation with Dominick at the edge of the property, she had slept well again, this time cocooned in the warm memory of his arms holding her, his voice whispering, his kisses. With the dawn, she again awakened to comfort.

Today she was greeted with her cool, practical nature racing in high gear. She was eager to get on with things. In spite of the ugly drug situation still looming, hope had replaced the fear. As if she had shed a jacket made of concrete and now her whole being felt light enough to fly.

It was an old and yet new outlook. Her relationship with God had been solidified. She was still herself, but with a new understanding of what it meant to be His. As far as the future was concerned, her calendar was empty, waiting for Him to fill it in whenever it was time, with whatever He thought best. As far as each day was concerned, she prayed she would know how to give Him the controls.

Then there was Dominick. Since that night she hadn't seen much of him, for which she was grateful because her obvious feeling of attraction to him was . . . unnerving. She had never felt this with Trent. Trent filled all the nuances she had in mind for a husband. He looked nice. He smelled nice. He played a nice game of tennis. His condo was nice. His family was an established part of nice society. He was predictable. He followed her lead, agreed with her decisions, wanted the same three children and lifestyle. He believed in God, attended church regularly.

Dominick, on the other hand, carried a gun.

And he talked to God with his eyes wide open in the middle of her office, grimacing with the pain of cracked ribs.

What he had done to her eight months ago at the mall was despicable. Under normal circumstances she should never speak to him again, except through lawyers while in the process of suing him. But she and Dominick weren't under normal circumstances. They were under God's shadow. It was possible to forgive him, even actually incredibly easy to forgive him, because she knew of two obvious life-changing results of his despicable behavior. First of all, he had been drawn to Christ. And second, she had been rescued from the major mistake of marrying for the wrong reasons.

The other matter of his not revealing his identity seemed a necessary part of his job. She couldn't hold it against him, but neither could she wholly trust him. An inner voice nagged that he lied, that she did not know him. It only quieted when he kissed her.

Which reminded her she truly was at a vulnerable time in her life. She had just defensively rebounded the ball, so to speak; she was still under the other team's basket. Dribbling down the court would take time. Setting things up for a shot would take time. She could hear the coach yelling to her to slow things up, while her heart was pumping and the irresistible urge was to plow ahead for the fast break. Falling for Dominick could happen in a minuscule amount of time.

But then again, maybe it would take a lot of time. Practically speaking, she did not have a clue as to what Dominick D'Angelo was all about. On top of that, how in the world could a DEA agent ever settle down into a regular relationship, let alone marriage?

Oops . . . Was that assumption stepping ahead of God?

But really, Lord! I mean, he works all hours of the day and night. It's extremely important work, horrifically dangerous work. He pretends to be someone he's not.

Cat shook her head, steered the car onto her parents' driveway, and parked. Figuring out this relationship was too difficult.

They would always have a special friendship because of what had happened. Perhaps that's all they would ever have in common. One thing was for certain — the kissing business would have to stop. She couldn't think straight otherwise.

At the Castillo yesterday he had met her in the parking lot when she pulled in. She had immediately jumped from her car.

"What's wrong?"

He frowned. "Calm down."

"This *is* calm."

"Cat . . ." He exhaled. "Listen, I'll do what I can to warn you before it goes down, okay? Please don't worry."

She noticed the dark circles around his eyes. He looked like she felt — exhausted and anxious. She bit her lip. "I'm sorry."

"I know this is tough for you. Can we take some time off tomorrow?"

"I plan to. It *is* Sunday."

"How about church?"

She hesitated. "Dominick, I'm still a little overwhelmed since last Sunday and — and everything. I need some time . . . And I have to tell my parents that I'm doing better. It is all right if I tell them that much, isn't it? That we went to the mall?"

"Of course. Cat, I'm not good at dancing."

"Huh?"

That corner of his mouth tucked inward. "Around the bush. The question is, *when* will you see me?"

He wasn't giving up. She liked that in a man. "Three o'clock tomorrow." She returned his smile.

"I'll pick you up at your place."

That was about three hours from now. She climbed from her car and walked toward the front door, eager to put her parents' minds at ease after all these months. Hopefully that wouldn't require too much dancing around the truth of why exactly it was that Dominick could erase the nightmare.

When Cat opened her apartment door to him, Dominick sensed the world was fading away behind him. That had been happening a lot lately, but it still caught him by surprise. Nothing mattered except that this gentle, honey-eyed woman shared this moment in time with him.

"Come in." Her low voice sounded distracted. The small smile on her mouth didn't crease the left cheek.

He resisted the urge to touch her face, to coax the dimple from its hiding place. If he didn't slow down, he might as well make it a good-bye kiss. In spite of all they'd been through, she was just this side of a rough eight months and probably still coming to terms with who he was.

She shut the door behind him.

"What?" he asked.

"What what?" She frowned at him. "Don't do that."

"Don't do what?"

"Tilt your head that way." She placed a hand on his cheek and pushed upward. "It's too *tender.*"

He laughed. "What's wrong with tender? I thought women liked tender and sensitive."

"It's — it's unnerving." She strode over to an armchair and sat down.

He followed her and settled into the couch. *What's wrong with unnerving?* Evidently his suspicions about her emotional state were on target. "Want me to try macho?"

Her forehead was still furrowed.

"You've got five seconds to tell me what's bugging you, Catherine St. Clair, or I'm out of here! One, two —"

Tears welled in her eyes.

He jumped up.

"Sit down, Dominick!" She stuck out her arm and pointed. "Stay over there. I'm fine. I am fine." She sniffed.

"Guess macho doesn't work either."

A smile tugged at her mouth.

"How'd it go with your parents?"

"Okay. Fine. They're so happy. And they didn't ask anything about why you did it. I told them you let me go alone, and I talked to God, and then you hugged me. What did you have in mind for today?"

It took him a moment to catch up with her. "Uh, just hanging together. We could walk around Balboa Park, eat downtown . . ."

"I have Twenty Questions in mind."

"I see." This was it. This was what was bugging her. "All right. Here? Now?"

"What do you know about me?"

"Talk about not dancing around the bush!" He smiled, slipped his right ankle atop his left knee, and tapped his foot on the carpet. "You get straight to the point better than I can."

"Maybe I could interrogate suspects for you."

He stopped smiling. This one question could make them or break them. He doubted she was going to like his answer, and he wouldn't even consider sugarcoating it. Lying was totally out of bounds.

"Dominick, I've prayed about —" She took a long, deep breath and exhaled. "About us. I have to start here, at the beginning. Well, not counting the mall beginning."

Prayed about us? Dear Father, help us. Help her understand.

"I mean, before you came to the Castillo, what did you know about me? After all, I was one of your suspects, right?"

He uncrossed his legs, leaned forward to rest his elbows on his knees, and laced his fingers together. "Before I came I didn't know anything except that my immediate superior was the assistant manager who sounded like a feminine jack-of-all-trades. It was a last-minute assignment. I didn't have time to do much homework."

"Why did you come?"

"I can't tell you that just yet. When I met you, of course I recognized you right off the bat. That threw me for a major loop. I figured my cover was blown. Part of me wanted it to be, so I'd have to tell you everything. When you didn't recognize me, I had a choice. No, truthfully only one option — to presume you were a suspect."

She watched him, waiting, her face for once revealing nothing. "Don't you investigate your suspects?"

"Uh, yeah. The homework I mentioned. It's mostly public record kind of stuff." He swallowed.

"Like middle name?"

"Like middle name. Address. And previous address since you had moved within the past six months. Parents' name and occupations. Siblings. Date of birth." He smiled. "They missed the adoption record. Somebody got sloppy. Umm, education. High school and college attended. Just the basics. Rent. Salary."

"You know how much I make?"

He nodded slightly. "Income tax. School loan. Car loans. Of which you have none. Priors. Nothing there either, not even a speeding ticket. We're interested in the monetary side of your life, not what videos you rent."

"That makes me feel . . . violated."

"I know. I'm sorry."

"Do you know all that about everyone on the staff?"

Again he nodded slightly.

"So basically you knew things before I told you and then some."

"Except that you were adopted. Or engaged. Cissy told me you and Carver were engaged. Umm . . ." He hesitated. Better to lay it all out on the table right now. "I had you followed into Tecate. That night I sat outside your apartment for about an hour, until someone took over for me. So I knew where you lived before I gave you a ride home. The day I took your car to wash it, I had it searched." *Torn apart.* "Taken totally apart and searched because you brought something out of the orphanage and across the border."

"*Buñeulos?!*" Her face crumpled, and her breathing was shaky, but she didn't cry. "What about here? Did you search in here?"

"No. I went through your office, but no one came into your home." Dominick forced himself to sit very still while his heart pounded violently in his chest. She had to work through this on her own.

She hugged herself and shut her eyes tightly. "It's so *ugly!*"

"It is, Cat. I work in ugliness. I've been immersed in it for years. When I met you, it took me a long time to comprehend your genuine goodness. Can I hold you?"

"No," she whispered.

"I'm sorry," he repeated.

She leaned her head back against the stuffed chair and stared at the ceiling.

He waited.

It was a few minutes before her breathing steadied. She sat up, arms still crossed against her midsection, and met his eyes. "Have you —" She bit her lip. "Have you ever killed anyone?"

"No."

Her body noticeably relaxed.

"Not that I haven't tried, like when I was sixteen."

"The guy who sold the drugs to your friend?"

He smiled in surprise. "Now who knows things?"

She broke their eye contact and stared out the window, apparently mulling over what she had just learned.

He twiddled his thumbs, waiting, preparing his response for when she told him to get lost. Of course she wouldn't say it in so many words. She would not be offensive. She would be . . . gracious. That was the word. Gracious. He had never personally known a gracious woman before, let alone fallen for one.

"Dominick . . ." Her hand covered his, halting the thumbs in mid-twiddle. "That's enough."

Here it comes. He looked up at her.

"Thank you." There was a hint of the dimple in her cheek. A trace of sunlight danced in her eyes. "Come on, let's go hang together. Can we start with your place?"

It was like a sunrise or sunset, another gift from his Father.

Cat had asked Dominick the unsettling questions, listened to his straightforward answers, and sifted through their details until they fell diffused and weakened, unable to shock anymore. As he drove her toward his apartment, she figured the worst was over.

And then he parked the truck on an unfamiliar street.

A new shock wave rolled through her. She knew the rock-solid feel of his arms around her. She knew the sweetness of his lips on hers. She knew he had awakened something deep within her that had caused her to turn again toward God.

But she didn't even know where the man lived!

"Cat?"

"Huh?"

He stood beside her open door. "Shall we go inside?"

She slid from the truck.

"Are you okay? Do these bother you?" He slipped off his sunglasses. "I should have asked sooner."

"No." She followed him from the street and then along a narrow sidewalk. She sensed the usual array of flowering bushes.

He smiled over his shoulder at her. "No, you're not okay, or no, they don't bother you?"

"They don't bother me." The nightmare of the stranger who wore those sunglasses had lost its power. She should leap for joy at that. Instead, she felt ill at ease.

Seldom in her life had she felt ill at ease. With everyone from teachers to coaches — even a few bully coaches — to obnoxious guests, she was secure in who she was, just Cat St. Clair, a take-charge, practical type. That was what had attracted Trent. It was what diminished after the mall incident.

Dominick stopped outside a door and selected a key from his key ring. "Is there something else you want clarified? Something else to ask?" He looked at her. "It's totally understandable, Cat."

His gray eyes were warm. There was no hint of that familiar Secret Service hardness. Actually there was no hint of anything familiar about him whatsoever. She wasn't even sure what street they were on. "No, it's not that. It's . . ." She pressed her lips together and ran her fingers through her hair.

He grinned at her loss of words. "You are just so — just so incredibly *delightful.*" He leaned toward her.

Cat jumped back like a startled jackrabbit. "Oh, please! Don't kiss me."

"Okay, okay! I won't." He tilted his head, raised his eyebrows, and held out his arms. *Hug?*

"No." Her voice was almost a whimper.

"Hmm." His forehead creased in a look of puzzlement. "Guess you need a little space, huh?"

She wanted to fall into his embrace. "Oh, Dominick! It's just so weird. All of a sudden you're a whole different person. You're not my temp employee, this drifter guy who caught my attention on the rebound." She gestured with her arms. "You're not this Secret Service type, DEA whatever, a government goon who loves God and made sense out of my nightmare. You're — you're — I don't know! You kiss me, and I'm off in la-la land like we're smack-dab in the middle of a relationship that never even had a *beginning.*"

He scratched his head.

"It's like we've got to work backwards."

He crossed his arms and shifted his weight to the other foot. "Like this is our first date?"

Cat thought about that for a moment, then frowned. "I don't know if I'd go on a first date with you."

He blinked. "Now I'm lost."

"Wellll . . ." She shrugged. "When you first came, everyone thought you were, as they say, hot. Everyone, uh, else."

"Ahh. Except you." He lifted a shoulder and raised his eyebrows, not in the least offended. "Hmm. Not your type. I take it Carver is?"

She thought of Trent and his nice appearance, so unlike this solid presence before her who seemed oblivious to what others thought of him. "Was."

He smiled. "Would you consider a blind date with a not-so-hot government employee?"

"Depends who set it up."

"How about God?"

In spite of herself, Cat burst into laughter. "Okay, mister, you got me in the door."

Twenty

When Cat saw Dominick's surfboard propped in the corner of his living room, her uneasiness began to lessen. This, at last, was familiar. It was what she had imagined of him.

His place reminded her more of a tiny, old-fashioned house than an apartment. It was at the end of an L-shaped row of connected bungalows, a simple square with one room across the front that served as living room and dining area, kitchen in the back left corner, hall space in the center, bathroom off of that, and bedroom in the back right. All four sides had windows, making it a bright home. Off the living room was a small, enclosed patio.

It was clean and organized. Given the sparse furnishings and bare walls, it wouldn't take much to keep it neat. The main area contained a couch, a recliner, a desk and computer, a television, a stereo, bookshelves, a table and chairs. And a surfboard.

It was nothing like Trent's elegant condominium. She liked it immensely.

As the hot late afternoon softened into summer evening, she delved into the private world of Dominick D'Angelo. The rough edges of their awkward situation softened.

He played his jazz CDs for her, music that was foreign to her ears. They discussed what she found on his bookshelves. He had all sorts of U.S. city maps, many books on the Christian faith, all of Frank Peretti's novels, two Bible translations, some spy novels, and drug reference books. He showed her a photo album full of pictures sent by his sister-in-law of his brother's family and his mother.

He was beginning to seem almost normal.

He offered to fix dinner for them. "I made bolognese this morning."

"Bolo what?"

He taught her how to say the word with the proper Italian accent.

"So are you fluent in that too?"

"Sort of."

Things like that crept into their conversation, little reminders that he had shaded the truth on earlier occasions. Their eyes would meet, he would tilt his head in that way of his, asking for understanding, and she would try to readjust her thinking. Sometimes when he moved she saw him wince, and she knew his ribs still hurt. It was a subtle reference to the dangers of his work, and it unsettled her.

Admitting they were both tired, they decided to stay in and eat his pasta. She followed him into the kitchen and teased him about the decidedly feminine shampoo she'd noticed in the bathroom.

His head was in the refrigerator, and he mumbled something about it being on sale.

It was then that Cat realized there was another side to Dominick she didn't know a thing about. "Maybe it's not yours?"

"What?" He set a large pot on a burner and flicked it on, glancing at her before turning his attention back to the stove. He stirred the ingredients with a wooden spoon. "Remember Cissy's somewhat forward question when we first met?"

Cat thought back to that day in her office. Cissy had entered and in her typically unabashed manner asked him if he was married, engaged, or otherwise involved. "Yes, I remember."

"I answered truthfully."

"You said no, no, and no."

He turned to her. "I haven't been with anyone for a long time."

"Okay." She decided to let it drop. "That smells great. What's in it?" She walked over to him and peered around his arm.

"Ground beef, ground pork, crushed tomatoes, a little olive oil, and butter. The trick is letting it simmer for hours, which I already did. It'll be ready soon." He gently tapped the spoon on the edge of the pot, set it down, and stepped over to the refrigerator. "Why don't you go sit outside and read the newspaper or something."

"Let me help."

"No. Thanks." He pulled out a bottle of S. Pellegrino sparkling water. "It won't be long. I just have to cook the pasta and dump the salad out of a bag, stick garlic bread in the oven." He poured the water into a glass and added a twist of lemon. As he handed it to her, his fingers brushed hers. "And besides, I can't seem to concentrate when you stand this close."

"Oh." *Maybe we should have gone out,* she thought.

"Either that or I'm hungry." He grinned.

His humor took the edge off. Cat was still in the get-acquainted mode. Despite the fact that she was liking what she was seeing, she wasn't ready to enter into the tension of romance. She found the newspaper and wandered onto the patio with her water.

A while later she found that Dominick's simple meal was delicious. His plates didn't match and were chipped, but he lit candles and smiled across the table at her before thanking God for the food.

"Is this okay?" He pointed to his hair that he had pulled back into a ponytail.

"It's okay." She smiled. "No problem. Go ahead and put the bandanna on too."

He grinned. "I save that for the major grunge look. This is just my normal look. Not exactly the yuppie, executive type. What?"

She was studying his "normal" look, the strong features and tiny scars and the ever-present 5 o'clock shadow and the thick black lashes over gray eyes. She wondered again about his nose. "Uhh, nothing."

"Come on, Cat. We're trying not to avoid stuff tonight, right? Just say what you're thinking."

She tore apart a piece of garlic bread. "I was thinking that yuppie, executive looks don't have any character." She picked up her fork again. "This bolognese is absolutely great."

He corrected her pronunciation.

She laughed and repeated it. "Did you add Parmesan?"

He nodded. "Fresh. Not that canned stuff. What do you mean by character?"

"Oh, I guess it comes down to, why do you do what you do? I mean, your life is written all over your face."

He thought for a moment. "Like scars and a broken nose?"

"Yeah. And there's that look about your eyes."

"The Secret Service one?"

"I know it's more than that. It's an intensity for what you do. So why do you do what you do?"

"It goes back to what Adam and Meg told you about my friend. His name was Mike. We were a lot alike. Our dads were gone. Our moms worked hard, mended our clothes, kept food on the table. We drove them crazy, and they smacked us when we let them down. We knew they loved us, but it wasn't enough.

"We didn't fit in at school. It was just easier on the streets. Fighting, dealing, smoking a little weed, popping a few pills. I found I could con my way in and out of almost any situation. By the time we were sixteen, I had developed a major business, and Mike had developed a major habit. He was hooked on heroin. He OD'd on stuff I gave him.

"I went after the guy who sold it to me. He spent a long time in intensive care. The judge sent me to a reform school, and there the story gets better." He gave her a small smile. "I figured out I had ruined a lot of lives, not just Mike's and his family's. I had to make up for it somehow, so I went into law enforcement. It was perfect. A blank check to keep on fighting and conning, only with the purpose of bringing in the bad guys."

Cat pushed aside her empty plate and rested her elbows on the table. "It sounds noble and exhausting."

"I don't know about noble. I think I've done some good, made a small difference. But that ugliness we talked about ate away at my soul. I hadn't realized how far gone I was until I met Adam."

"How old are you?"

"Thirty-five."

"Are you tired of fighting?"

He nodded. "Some days. It might be time for a change. I just can't see myself sitting behind a desk yet."

The phone rang. He reached for it on the desk behind him. A few seconds after his hello, he said an address and stood. "On my way." He hung up, found a pen and pad, and scribbled something. "Cat, I've got to leave for an hour. Two max. Somebody needs backup. No big deal, but nobody else is available. I don't have time to take you home."

"I'll do the dishes."

He handed her the pad. "If you don't want to wait for me, call this number. A man named Toby will answer." He walked toward the bedroom. "Just tell him you're at D'Angelo's and need a ride. He'll take care of you. The Parkers are out of town."

"Elli can come get me —"

"No." He stopped and turned. "You'd have to explain why I left you here. Not just yet, Cat. Do you understand?"

"All right. Yes." She began clearing the table. "I'll just clean up and watch television."

A moment later he stepped into the kitchen where she stood, running water into the sink. He had put on a denim jacket and had a gun in his hand. "I'll be back as quick as I can." He was doing something with the gun, not looking at her. There was a clicking noise. A snap. "Lock the door behind me."

And then he was gone.

Cat stood still, her hands and wrists immersed in the warm sudsy water. When the tears spilled over, she let them fall onto the bubbles. When the sob burst from her chest into her throat, she found a towel and held it to her face. When another sob escaped, she went and sat on the couch.

It was the sight of the gun that exploded

reality into the kitchen. Their worlds were light-years apart. He had asked her about the sunglasses and ponytail, asked if those fragments of her nightmare disturbed her. They were insignificant details on their own, simple mannerisms. He had not asked about the gun. And yet it was the gun that was his identity, what he had carried day in and day out for years like an extension of his arm.

Was it the same one he had pointed in her face?

Violent television shows and movies had always disturbed her. She took great care to avoid them, often staying at home even as a teenager rather than going with friends. She filtered news, shutting off her attention to much of it. She had wondered if events surrounding the first few months of her life could have subconsciously affected her. There had to have been violence in that place. The deaths were by overdose, but . . .

She looked around at the un-homey home that held such few traces of the man Dominick D'Angelo. What was she doing here? He had gotten up and left the table. What if they had still been eating? It wouldn't have mattered. It wasn't that he was just a night owl. Time meant nothing to him. His world was chasing criminals. His lifestyle was totally, completely beyond her comprehension.

She couldn't even call her sister because she couldn't confide in her who Dominick was. Come to think of it, she couldn't even call a taxi. She didn't know the address, she hadn't really paid attention to how they got here, and his number was unlisted, so he wouldn't be in the phone book. She wasn't about to wander out in the dark in search of a street name or knock on a neighbor's door. She wasn't about to call some stranger named Toby either. She'd just stay put, hopefully not all night. Hopefully he'd come home . . . and in one piece.

Cat felt just as confused as she had when this blind first date had gotten underway.

Dominick slipped his key into the door and was surprised to find it hadn't been locked.

He stepped inside. The lights and television were on. Cat was asleep on the couch, curled under a blanket. *She must be back to her pre-nightmare, naive days to not lock a door, then fall asleep beside it.*

He checked out the kitchen. Everything was put away. The room appeared brighter than he'd ever seen it. What'd she do? Maybe it was only her personality filling the place. No, the sink was a shiny white.

Back out in the living room he sat on the edge of the couch. "Cat," he called softly.

She didn't respond. Her breathing was deep and even.

He was pumped. He wanted to wake her and tell her about tonight. He couldn't, of course. The Castillo business should have been finished by now, but his partner Engstrom had stuck with the bread man and convinced them to hold off. The kid hung in there — like Dominick would have a few years ago — and found the bread delivery was clean, but the trash collection wasn't. Tonight they got the proof that this was a bigger piece of the action than he had thought.

The waste disposal service owned a warehouse that was a major collection point for cocaine carried across the border in small loads, in nondescript vehicles of all shapes and sizes. From there it was distributed to places like the Castillo, points from which dealers would be supplied. From there it hit the streets and found its way into the heart of America.

By Tuesday they could knock down the first domino and watch a long row of them fall one by one. They couldn't follow the trail back across the border and give Smitty everything he wanted, but they would effectively dry up one giant route. For a while anyway.

Dominick watched Cat sleep, wishing he could hold her like he had that night when she had the migraine. She was such a bundle of goodness. Who wouldn't want to wrap her in his arms and take her home? Even in his exhausted state just a few nights ago he had been serious when he kissed her and expressed the hope that she was contagious.

Tonight she had seemed almost shy with him, as if she were in the apartment of some stranger. In truth, he was a stranger to her. He knew that, but he didn't want to admit it.

He had almost been glad for the phone call. It interrupted his difficulty in dealing with those compassionate eyes and gentle words as he told his story. He didn't know what to do with the emotions she set rumbling in him. The only expression he had for them was to hold her. And she had made it clear that physical contact was off-limits. She was at the beginning of a relationship, an unacceptable place for hugs and kisses and la-la land.

He brushed her hair from her cheek now. This was off-limits too, but — "Cat."

Her eyes opened partially. "Dominick?" She smiled and reached for his hand. She held it between hers, under her chin.

"You're all right." She yawned. "I couldn't stay awake. What time is it?"

"Almost 2. I'm sorry. I'll take you home. Unless you just want to stay right where you are?" He would make her coffee in the morning. And an omelette. They'd sit on the patio in the morning sun —

"No, I'd better go." She squeezed his hand and closed her eyes for a moment, then sat up.

He noticed her rumpled, short-sleeved shirt. "Do you have a jacket?"

She shook her head and reached for her shoes beside the couch.

"I'll get something for you. It's cold outside." He went into his room and found a sweatshirt with a zipper for her. When he came out she was laying back down, half asleep. He pulled her to her feet and helped her into the sweatshirt. "Hey, thanks for cleaning up the kitchen."

"Mm-hmm."

It was a quiet, quick trip to her place. He walked her upstairs to her door. She mumbled good night and slipped inside.

He hadn't found the words to ask her if she would go out on a second, not-so-blind date. No, not words; rather nerve. He knew he would not be able to breathe if she said no.

Twenty-One

The next day Cat buried herself in life's everyday details. Laundry, cleaning, and grocery shopping filled the hours. It helped her not think about Dominick. By the time she headed to Elli's for dinner, the truth about him was buried in enough layers that she thought she could successfully avoid the emotional subject for one evening, even with her sister.

On Tuesday he didn't show up for work. Cissy informed her he had called to say he'd be in later. She lingered in the office doorway. "So, Cat, I hear he's crazy about you."

"Where'd you hear that?"

"From him." She studied her nails. "You know he's gone with me to a few parties. I invited him to a Sunday bash, and he said he had a date with you."

"That's it? That's crazy about me?" She chuckled. "Cissy, you have such a talent for filling in details."

"Well, it was his tone. I mean it's so *obvious*. And he said something along the lines of me being a wonderful *girl*, and he was a little on the old side. What'd you do on your date?"

"Oh, we, uhh, had dinner. We're just sort of friends."

"Nice restaurant?"

"His place. Ever been there?"

Cissy shook her head. "Nope. Didn't get to first base with the guy. He's sure a lot friendlier than Trent. You never know — maybe he'll change his drifter ways and stick around awhile. I better get back out front." Her heels clicked away.

Cat heard the hurt in the desk clerk's voice. The young woman knew Dominick was different. Despite his looks and his temporary role and seeming participation at her parties, she must know he had a depth about him. And he had chosen Cat over her.

Under the circumstances she didn't feel flattered. They weren't in a contest, though Cissy would see it as another put-down like she did when Trent had ignored her flirtations and chose Cat. Maybe when Dominick left, Cat could hire someone who fit Cissy's personality. Would the temp service think it discriminatory if she requested a certain age, physique, marital status, and future plans?

A feeling of anxiety for Dominick filled her. It was almost becoming familiar, this uncomfortable nagging at the fringes of her thoughts. The nightmare's stranglehold had been loosened, and she was praying more, trying to let God have more space in her life. However, at times it was impossible to fend off the anxiety concerning this man's safety. Not to mention the unsettled drug situation at the Castillo!

Isn't this what life would be like with him? She hugged herself.

Where was he now? Last week he had hinted that things at the Castillo were almost finished. What did *that* mean? Maybe he was off arresting people who used the motel. Maybe it was that man who delivered pool chemicals. His eyes were set close together. Maybe that new cook was involved. He hadn't warmed to her yet. Maybe —

The phone rang. "Hello?"

"Catherine!" It was her mother. "What's wrong?"

What was wrong? What *wasn't* wrong? "Huh?"

"You never answer 'hello.' It's always, 'This is Cat St. Clair,' your voice all confident and professional. What's wrong? Did you have an argument with Dominick?"

"Oh, Mother, there's just a lot going on. This weekend is the big end-of-summer celebration. I've still got a million things to do for that."

"Are you having the clowns again?"

"Yes, and all the competitions — golf and swimming and volleyball. And basketball."

"With prizes?"

"Mm-hmm."

"That sounds like so much fun. You know, I'm very proud of your work there. Well, did you have an argument with Dominick?"

"No!"

"We really liked him. Well, I guess you're just anxious then."

"I guess."

"You don't have to be."

"I know. 'Be anxious for nothing.' "

" 'But in everything,' " her mother continued the verse, " 'by prayer and supplication with thanksgiving let your requests be made known to God.' "

"I know!" Cat heard the screech and lowered her voice to a whine. "I'm sorry. I know. I really do."

"It's never easy. I'll pray for you. Now, there was a reason I called. What was it?"

She noticed the light for the other line on her phone was lit. "Mother, I think I have another call —"

"Oh, now I remember. Are you going to Tecate on Monday?"

"No, I'm running down Friday morning instead, to buy piñatas for the party. Why?"

She kept her eye on the light. Was it Dominick? Cissy would talk to him until she was off. Would he call her if he was hurt? What if it were bad enough —

"We're doing a collection for you on Sunday. But it'll keep. I'll get it to you the next time."

"I have to go, Mother! Thank you." The light blinked off.

"You're welcome, sweetie. Good-bye!"

She called Cissy at the front desk. "Did I have another call?"

"No."

"Thanks." Confused but having too much on her mind to deal with it, Cat went back to her work.

To her relief, about 8 o'clock Dominick came into her office. "Take a walk?"

She followed him into the parking lot. She noticed he didn't wear a jacket. No gun then . . .

On the edge of the lot, behind his truck, he stopped. "You okay?" he asked, his voice barely above a whisper.

"Sort of."

In the lamplight she saw his grin. "Listen, I want you to know that it's almost over."

"You've said that."

"I know, but now I can tell you it'll be by the end of the week."

"Dominick! The festival is Saturday!"

He sighed loudly. "Get in the truck." He walked around it, yanked open the driver's door, jumped inside, and slammed it shut.

"Oh!" She followed suit on the passenger side.

"When things go down, it won't interfere." His voice was no longer just above a whisper. "I promise. You don't have to worry."

"I've seen you after an arrest, with broken ribs. You couldn't breathe —"

"That was different than this will be."

"I've seen you point a gun at me —"

"Cat, get a grip!" His exasperation was obvious, and his words ran together. "You won't even know it's happening. Just a few quiet arrests. Oh, why am I even telling you this?"

"It would be worse if I didn't know *anything!*"

"No, this is too much of a responsibility. Look, I'm sorry. I forget you can't understand this from my point of view. I was trying to make it easier for you. Can you just do your best to act normal for a couple more days?"

"Well, I've made it this far."

"Mandi and Kevin have things under control for the festival. Take some time off."

He sounded angry.

"And I think you can't understand *my* job from *my* point of view! I'll probably put in ten hours tomorrow."

"Fine! Just keep busy. And don't worry."

"Will you tell me later exactly when it'll happen?"

"If I get a chance."

"Are you still our temp—"

"Cat!" His voice rose. "Nothing's changed as far as you're concerned, okay?"

She didn't reply.

"Please, just trust me?"

"I trust you, Dominick. But this situation — it's like my castle is falling apart, and I can't fix it no matter how hard I work. It's headed for disaster, and there's nothing I can do about it!"

It took him a fraction of a second to scoot across the bench seat and wrap his arms around her, cutting off her words.

She twisted, but he didn't let go.

"Sorry, Cat. You're overdue for a hug, and no one else seems to be available at the moment."

She closed her eyes.

"Now stop whining and listen to me," he soothed. "I will fix it for you, and it's not going to be a disaster."

He held her tightly for a few minutes until

at last she felt her muscles relax. *How did he know this would work?*

"Hey," his voice was muffled in her hair, "maybe la-la land would help."

That broke the final tension. She giggled, remembering what she had told him about her feelings when he kissed her. "No, it would not!"

"All right. If you're sure?" She nodded as vehemently as she could manage against his shoulder. He laughed softly. "I'm teasing. You're much too good to get messed up with the likes of me. Well, we're both going to be busy for a while. I'll, umm . . . We'll, umm, touch base next week, okay? When it's all over."

She nodded again, wishing they could sit like this until it was all over.

Cat drummed her fingers on the steering wheel in time with music from the car radio. She sat in Tecate traffic, at least three blocks south of the border. The backed-up line stretched behind her around a corner, out of sight. It looked as if half of the city must be crossing into the States. The noon sun reflected in a glare from the car that sat just inches in front of hers. As usual, the top of her Tracker was off, but she turned on the air conditioning anyway. It might help alleviate the pungent exhaust fumes as well as the intense heat that beat through her sunglasses, straw hat, white oversized cotton shirt, and long, full skirt.

She groaned. Friday was whittling itself down to the bare minimum number of hours needed for festival preparations. It started at 6 A.M. with sleeping through what was supposed to be the jump-start alarm buzz. No, it had started last night, by not getting to bed until 2.

No, it really started before that, with Dominick D'Angelo complicating her life in so many ways. In the three days since he had hugged her in the parking lot she had wrestled with the facts that this man filled her heart and that every other aspect of her life was quickly fading into insignificant details. She didn't like his carrying a gun and dealing with violence and ugliness, but the fact was, they were a part of who he was. And who he was captivated her thoughts day and night.

That arrests had to be made at her Castillo would be undoubtedly the biggest difficulty she had ever tackled in her career. There was no getting around that, but it would not be catastrophic.

Dominick had kept an eye on her these past few days. He popped into the office, found her outside, smiled often, motioned thumbs-up signs at the oddest times, brought flowers from the garden or cookies from the kitchen, wrote down his pager number for her. She could call him anytime. There were no more hugs; evidently he respected her thoughts on that subject. Although those thoughts were changing . . .

Much of this had spilled out at the orphanage today, which was why she had stayed an hour beyond what she had planned, which of course put her even further behind schedule. But she reminded herself that emotionally unloading on Rosa was a relief. If she hadn't taken the time to do so and in return receive her *abuelita*'s gift of showing her God's love, her fingers would be strangling the steering wheel instead of tapping out a tune.

While they had sat under the shade tree, each rocking a baby to sleep while the other children were inside cleaning up after lunch, Rosa studied her. "Catalina, I think you mourn your wedding day."

Cat could often sidestep her mother, but never her *abuelita*. Gently, she laid the baby on a nearby blanket in the grass, then did likewise with the one Rosa held. She sat on the ground and rested her head in her grandma's lap. The woman stroked her hair.

Months ago Cat had shared with Rosa that there had been a police problem at the mall that frightened her, that Trent was unsupportive and subsequently they had canceled their wedding.

"Do you know for sure that the *señor* is no longer in your heart?" She had always referred to Trent as the *señor*. Somehow it fit his demeanor.

"*Sí.*"

"Still, it hurts." It was a statement.

Through the years her *abuelita*'s statements had a way of shooing away clouds of confusion. There was understanding in them, acceptance, and often a nudge in the right direction.

Cat couldn't remember her grandparents and had no way of knowing her biological ones. When at the age of fifteen she met Rosa at the orphanage, she knew instantly that here was a grandma she would adopt in her heart. Cultural and language differences never interfered, and their friendship deepened.

"It is all right to mourn it, my child. Are you reading God's Word, to know how to mourn it?"

Cat nodded. "Now I am. Oh, *Abuelita*, I stayed away from Him for a long time. I was so angry, and now I'm so sorry."

"When you feel anger toward Him, you simply acknowledge that God is God. He could have prevented it, but He had to show you something. He wants you to see life as He sees it."

"But I'm not sure I want to trust Him again."

"Did you trust Him before?" Rosa laid her hand on Cat's fist. "I know you. You want Him to do things for you, but some-times only the things you choose."

She nodded.

"Do you have someone better to trust than our heavenly Father?"

"No."

"No, of course not. So, you cry over the loss. It will ease. And what of the other man, the big one? The one who made you laugh?"

"Dominick." Cat smiled at the memory of him with the children. "Oh, he's —" She swallowed. "His job might move him away."

"Ahh. Then we will let God take care of it." She chuckled. "He knows I want to dance at your wedding. He can't wait too much longer, not at my age!"

The blast of a horn yanked Cat's attention back to the present. She inched her car forward and reminded herself that the weekend festival details really were falling into place. She had picked up three piñatas.

One brightly colored donkey sat in the seat beside her; a fish and a rooster were in the back. She easily could have purchased them in San Diego, but these were made especially for her by an orphanage worker's cousin. It was important to her to offer support wherever she could, even in a small way like this.

Now she would drive straight to the Castillo, stuff the piñatas with candy, then ask Kevin to hang them in the courtyard. Mentally she reviewed the checklist of preparation details and prioritized them.

At last she approached the white overhang of the border station. There were two lanes, but as usual only one was open. Guards stood on the left, waving drivers through after momentary stops.

"Ma'am, please pull over to the side."

Cat smiled. The guard's face was familiar. He probably knew she often parked at the border as she proceeded to do now. Alberto, the Mexican guard on the other side checking traffic going into his country, was on duty today and was expecting his *buñuelo* treat that Rosa often sent with her for him.

Quickly she jumped from the car, brown paper bag in hand, and bounded across the single lane and onto the median strip. "Alberto!" She checked for approaching traffic from her right. There was none, and she stepped into the lane, startled to see Alberto running toward her.

"*Parar!*" His gun was drawn.

Only then was she aware of the pounding footsteps behind her, shouting voices.

"Stop!"

"Freeze, lady!"

Safety catches clicked as they were released.

Guards surrounded her, a wall of blue shirts.

It was as if an invisible hand punched her chest, squeezing air from her lungs, pushing the heartbeat into her throat, gorging her with nausea. *No, God, no!* An image of another gun pointed at her flashed through her mind. That had been a mistake. That had just been Dominick. Just Dominick.

Air rushed back into her lungs, and she gasped.

"Hand over the bag." A guard grabbed it from her outstretched hand.

"It's for Alberto! It's just *buñuelos!*"

Someone pulled her arms behind her back.

She cried out.

"Right. And what do you call the stuff inside the piñatas? Extra sugar to sprinkle on the *buñuelos?*" Cold steel circled her wrists.

The officer grasped her elbow at an awkward angle and guided her back across the street.

On her other side a female guard appeared. "Ma'am, you're under arrest for transporting a controlled substance across the international border. You have the right to remain silent —"

"What!"

A huge police dog on a leash was sniffing around her car. The piñatas lay on the ground, split open.

The concrete rose up to meet the bright blue sky, swirling before her in liquid waves of afternoon heat, flushing shame and panic through her.

Dear God, help me!

He finally had her undivided attention.

Twenty-Two

They let her make a phone call from inside the border station.

She wanted to call Dominick, but she didn't even know his phone number. It was in a file, in her office — maybe. Besides, he wouldn't be home anyway.

The pager number! But no, she'd have to punch in the number here, and he'd have to call her back whenever he could.

When she hesitated, the woman suggested a lawyer would be a good idea. They left her alone in a small room at a table with a phone and telephone directory, handcuffs off. Dominick's home number was unlisted. Was the DEA listed? But she wasn't even supposed to know he did drug enforcement work.

Well, she knew one lawyer's number by heart.

She called Jacobs, Pemberly, Carver and Carver. When the youngest Carver finally got on the line, all she could say was "Trent" before she started crying. She blubbered through the story, ending with, "Tell them I didn't do it!"

For a few moments he said nothing. "Trent!"

He let out his breath. "Tell me again — they found cocaine in your car?"

She heard the frustration in his voice. Again she felt cold steel, but this time it was an inner sensation clicking something shut, damming up the tears. "In the piñatas."

"For crying out loud, why don't you buy those things in town?"

There was a brief knock on the door, and the female officer appeared. "Ms. St. Clair, we're taking you to the DEA office in San Diego. You can tell your attorney to meet us there."

Cat stared at her. "DEA?"

The woman nodded. "Does he know where it is?"

Cat stared at her while Trent's voice bellowed in her ear, "DEA?"

"I can tell him," the officer volunteered.

She handed her the phone.

"Sir, do you know — Yes . . . No . . . It's the division office on Viewridge, just off 274, close to the 15. It's a large building, tan colors, not marked, across the street from Channel 9. Yes, sir . . . I'll put her back on." The officer raised her brows as if in bewilderment at the conversation. "Two minutes, Miss St. Clair." She left.

"Trent —"

"DEA!" he exclaimed again.

"Can you come? You have to help me. I have to have a lawyer fix —"

"Catherine, let me think. You're at the border now? That gives me about an hour. All right, I'll cancel my 3 o'clock."

"Will you call my dad?"

"Cat —"

"Please, Trent! He has to know immediately." The door opened again. "I have to go." She hung up the phone.

Ninety minutes later Cat again sat alone, at a rectangular wood table in a small, beige, windowless room. Hugging herself. Trying to take deep breaths in the airless atmosphere. Trying not to shake. Trying to sort her jumbled thoughts.

The ride had been a short, quick one in the back of a Border Patrol cruiser. Still, Daddy had had time to get here. He should have been here by now. Somebody always knew where he could be found. He was always available. Trent must not have called him right away. Had he called him at all?

Oh, Father! Help me!

Her prayers were simple, but they kept her from plunging over the edge. Absolutely none of this made sense. She wouldn't have knowingly bought drugs, transported cocaine. Anyone could see that about her, especially anyone who knew her. Then why did she feel guilty?

Because that poison was in her car.

And because Trent didn't believe her.

Oh, Lord.

Cold air began blowing from a wall register up near the ceiling. Her teeth chattered, and she scraped the chair along the floor, moving it from under the breezy path. She glanced around. Six chairs surrounded the table. The walls were bare except for one shelf that held a stack of Styrofoam cups. Where was the two-way mirror? An interrogation room would have a two-way mirror, wouldn't it? The door had been locked from the outside.

She shivered. At least the handcuffs were off again. Except for the fact that they put those on her, everyone had been polite enough. Even the mean-looking man named Smith had been gruffly polite. Not that they made small talk with her. Not that anything was normal —

Help me!

Dominick would come. This was his place. She couldn't tell anyone she knew that, but Dominick knew all about this stuff. He would come. He would believe her . . .

He had doubted once, though, that late

night near the boulders.

But then he kissed her and called her good and wanted her goodness to be — what did he say? Contagious. That was it. Contagious.

The door opened, and she jumped. The man named Smith stepped aside to let Trent walk in, then shut and locked it again.

He stared at her across the table.

The look on his face was like a do-not-touch sign. His eyes were narrowed slits. His lips were undefined, they were so tightly pressed together. She didn't go to him.

"Cat, they're going to book you."

"Did you call my dad?"

His voice rose; there was an edge to it. "I left a message with his secretary. I said they're going to book you."

"What does that mean?"

"Fingerprints —"

"I mean, the message with his secretary. What did you say? Where was he?"

"I said you were being held at the DEA office, and it was urgent he come ASAP. She said he was on a site up in Rancho California, but she should be able to reach him." He pulled out a chair and sat down heavily, hands in his lap. "Do you understand, Cat, that there is enough evidence to arrest you and put you in jail?"

She blinked. "But I didn't buy any drugs!"

"Maybe not, but you transported twenty kilograms of cocaine across the border."

"Maybe not? Maybe —"

"In the piñatas."

"They were empty when I picked them up!"

"Under the seat."

"Trent, somebody put it there. I didn't do it. Why would I do it?"

"Who would put it there?"

"I don't know! That's your job!"

They stared at each other. Trent's mouth was white with tension, and she knew he was very angry. She also knew she was red-faced and angrier than he was.

"Catherine, you need a criminal attorney."

She flew to her feet, the chair flipped over, and she leaned across the table. "I need a friend who trusts me and knows the law."

He stood. "You know I only do corporate stuff, but I'll see what I can do about bail." He glanced at his watch. "Hopefully it'll all come together so you won't have to spend the night behind bars."

If there had been anything at all less cumbersome than the chair to pick up, Cat would have thrown it at him. Instead she screamed, "Get out! Get out!"

The door opened, and her father walked through. In the blink of an eye he was around the table, and his arms were around her.

Bear squeeze time.

"Nice set of lungs," Smitty remarked as he sat back down at his desk. "She should have used them at the mall. I guarantee, somebody would have tackled you."

The corner of Dominick's mouth lifted. He was in the SAC's office, down the hall and out of sight but close enough to have heard Cat's dismissal of Carver.

"D'Angelo, run this by me one more time. That was her ex-fiancé?"

"Yeah. Evidently her ex-lawyer too."

Smitty chewed his gum for a few moments, studying Dominick's face. "She was caught red-handed."

"Yes, I know." He met the other man's gaze.

"She's a good-looking chick. Exactly how involved are you?"

Dominick crossed his arms and leaned back, tilting the chair on its legs. "Not that way."

"Engstrom saw you kissing her at the motel."

"Yeah. But that's all. And that's only because I was too tired to think straight." He shook his head. "She's an honest-to-goodness angel, Smitty, way outa my league. When this is over, I seriously doubt I'll see her again."

He grunted. "If that spineless lawyer friend is in her league, I think you got your minors and majors confused."

"Whatever. Anyway, we can let her go, but not back to the Castillo just yet."

"I can hold her until you're finished there."

"No way." He stood and glanced at his watch. "I've put her through enough as it is. You saw her dad?"

"Big fella."

"Mm-hmm. He'll take care of her. I just hope he doesn't kill me in the process."

They went down the hall. Dominick knocked on the closed door while Smitty unlocked it. He heard a gruff "Yeah."

Cat and her father looked up at him from where they sat at the table, their hands clasped. Her eyes were dry, but puffy from crying, her wide mouth pinched, unsmiling. Her dark hair was disheveled, the white short-sleeved shirt wrinkled.

His heart melted at the pure, innocent sight of her.

He set her purse, straw hat, and sunglasses on the table.

With a cry, she ran to him.

"Umpf."

"Sorry."

"It's okay." His words were muffled in her hair as he held her tightly, ignoring the pain in his side. He glanced over at Stan St. Clair and gave him a little wave.

Cat looked up at him. "You believe me, don't you?"

"Of course." He ached at the nearness of her mouth, then thought of the nearness of her father.

She pulled his head toward her and kissed him soundly.

So much for his indecision.

"Oh, I knew it." She smiled. "I saw it in your eyes. Thank you, Dominick. I have to get to the Castillo right away."

"Uh, it's a little more complicated than that. First, sit down. Hello, Mr. St. Clair." He shook the burly hand and forced himself to make eye contact.

The older man looked like a bear awakened too early from a long winter's nap. "You have evidence to hold her." It was a statement. He understood the facts.

"Yes, sir, we do." He sat with them. "But I know it's a setup. Did Cat tell you who I am?"

"She did. And I have to say that if you weren't wearing that gun, I'd seriously consider carrying out my threat. That mall business was despicable."

"Yes. I—" Dominick cleared his throat. "I respect your threat and can't tell you how sorry I am to have hurt your daughter."

"Apology accepted. Now her mother, on the other hand, probably *will* kill you. She kind of liked that fancy-schmantzy lawyer."

Silently Dominick gave thanks. "Would flowers help?"

"They might."

Cat clutched her arms across her waist, laid her head on the table. "Why did they stop me at the border?"

"They had a phone call, a tip describing you and your orange car, saying you would be carrying piñatas filled with coke. Who would be that angry with you? Is there some former employee maybe? Someone you fired?"

"I don't have a clue. And it's tangerine, not orange."

"Tell me what happened."

She straightened. "I went to Tecate this morning, stopped at a cousin of Maria's — she works at the orphanage — because she made piñatas for me. *Empty* piñatas. Then I visited the orphanage for about an hour and a half. Then I sat in traffic, drove across the border, parked like I always do so I could give *buñuelos* to Alberto, the Mexican guard, like I always do. And that's the last coherent thought I have."

He squeezed her hand on the table. "Monday's your usual day to visit Tecate, right?"

"Yes."

"Why today? Why Friday? For the piñatas for the festival?"

She nodded.

"Everyone knows your routine. Who knew you changed it?"

Her eyes widened. "I only told Ron and Trent last week. I mentioned it in our meeting."

He thought a moment, then shook his head. "Ron Hunter called us three months ago. He and Trent Carver suspected something was going on, something drug-related."

Now her jaw dropped. "They knew who you were?"

Dominick nodded. "Though I only met Hunter beforehand."

"Why didn't they tell me?"

"It was absolutely imperative no one else knew. Were there others at your meeting?"

"No."

"Your mother knew," St. Clair suggested.

352

"You told her when she called to tell you she would have some things for you to take to the orphanage. She thought you were going next Monday."

"Cat, where were you when she called?"

"In my office."

"When?"

"Umm, Tuesday. Not late."

"Your mother and I were having dinner, around 6," her father added.

"Were you alone, Cat?" Dominick asked.

She nodded. "With the door shut."

"Someone could listen in on the line."

"From the front desk or Ron's office. But why —"

He squeezed her hand again. "Don't ask that just yet. It won't make sense. Who was out front that night?"

She hesitated. "The usual. Cissy. Amber. Paul."

"You're sure you told no one else?"

"I'm sure. I was so busy this week with the festival, I didn't make plans to see anyone. I saw Elli and Jim Monday night, but we just talked baby plans."

"All right." He placed his arm around the back of Cat's chair but made eye contact with her dad over her head. "You can go now, but I have to release you to your father's custody."

"Fine," she said.

"Cat, you're not allowed out of his sight." He saw St. Clair nod slightly. "I can't have you at the Castillo."

She clenched her jaw. "Well, that's exactly where I'm going."

"No, you're not. When Kevin unloads the cocaine stuffed in the turret above your desk and I arrest him, you'll go ballistic."

Her face crumpled. "Kevin?"

Anticipating her sobs, Dominick pressed her face against his chest as tightly as he could. "I'm sorry, I'm sorry. I promise it will be all right, but please stay away until to-morrow. Please." He kissed the top of her head and let go. "Stan . . ."

Her father took his place and held her. "Shh. It's okay, Kit-Cat."

"Please, sir, promise me you'll take her home with you, to Poway." His stomach was knotting.

"There's nowhere else she's going." His voice rose above Cat's cries. "You have my word, son. Now, do what you need to do to clean that place up." He stuck out his hand to shake Dominick's. "And take care of yourself. My wife will be expecting flowers. She's partial to anything chocolate too."

Cat felt like a little girl again.

By the time she and her dad reached the house, her mother was home. Unaware of what had transpired, she simply took one look at her daughter and hugged her. Without a word she drew a bubble bath, found sweats for her to change into, and left to make chicken noodle soup. While Cat soaked in the tub and let the tears flow, she knew Daddy would be explaining things. Not to have to do that was a relief.

They hovered, and she loved them for it. Snuggled against pillows on the couch in the family room, she ate the soup and tried not to think of anything except this comfort.

"Do you think I'll ever grow up and leave you two alone?" She bit her lip to hold back the tears that still bubbled just below the surface.

"Oh, sweetie." Mother laughed and hugged her. "You're grown-up. You just hit a bump in the road. Albeit a rather large bump. We'd make chicken soup for any family member who got arrested."

In spite of herself, Cat giggled.

Her dad chimed in, "I'm just glad we didn't have to put the business into hock to post bail."

"But, Stanley, dear, we would have."

"Well, sure, for Kit-Cat."

Her mother kissed her forehead and col-

lected the empty dishes. "Do you want anything else?"

"Piñatas."

She smiled. "Will the Party Shop ones
do?"

Cat nodded. "Three. Thanks."

Her dad settled into his recliner and
reached for the television remote. "Want to
see what's on ESPN?"

"Okay. What do you think is happening at
the Castillo?"

"Well, my guess is that things are pretty
normal. While you were in the ladies' room
at Dominick's office, he told me that Ron
would be there to cover for you. He guessed
about six people would be arrested. They'll
have unmarked cars pick them up in the
back parking lot, without a lot of fuss." He
paused. "I like him, Kit-Cat."

"You're just saying that because he drives
a pickup."

"Yep. That says a lot for him. But the important thing is he cares about you."

"I don't know him, Daddy."

"Hmm," he grunted. "A mystery man.
Reminds me of our mystery baby."

Cat rearranged the pillows and squiggled
deeper into the soft cushions, pulling an
afghan up around her shoulders. She hadn't
heard a mystery baby story in a long time.

356

They seldom varied, but she always listened, enraptured. It was only about five years ago that she realized she was searching for clues to her real identity. Who was her mother? Who was her father? Were they Los Angeles natives? Or maybe from another state? Maybe another country. Maybe her mother had been a budding movie actress who fell in love with a visiting prince who left before he knew a baby was on the way, and he couldn't be contacted afterward.

The stories, of course, never offered any more clues, but each time she did find what she was looking for. In her dad's twinkling blue eyes she saw an unconditional love that had plucked her from a cesspool and given her the life of a princess in a castle. Their home was simply comfortable, not a mansion full of rich furnishings, but she knew the emotional wealth was priceless and a thing to be cherished.

"You know, Kit-Cat, we didn't know anything about you. How old were you? Were you addicted to cocaine? Would your hair ever grow? Were you allergic to milk? For a long time we didn't know if you would even smile. But what we did know was that you needed somebody to love you. We knew we could love you and that God would give us enough love to love you through anything.

Do you understand what I'm saying?"

"I think so." Dominick was an unknown in the details, but he needed somebody to love him. And her family might be the ones to do that.

"There's something I never told you." He stopped, his lips pressed together.

Fear tightened her throat. Her dad never ever hesitated, even if he was wrong about something. What was this? She could only raise her eyebrows in question.

"I prayed that God would break you and Trent up."

She stared at him. "You didn't."

"I stayed up all Christmas night." He studied the remote in his hand. "He wasn't right for you, Kit-Cat. I couldn't trust him to take care of you. He wasn't big enough on the outside or the inside. When that mall business happened and Trent turned goosey, I thanked God for whoever that man was."

"I remember you prayed for that man." That man . . . Dominick D'Angelo . . . her angel in disguise.

"Yeah, I did that too. I couldn't endure how he hurt you. I had to forgive him."

She hadn't told him everything yet, just that Dominick was that man and what he was doing at the Castillo. "Daddy . . ." He

looked at her. "That's when Dominick became a Christian. Right after. He felt so terrible about what he had done. His friend
Adam had been telling him about Jesus. All
of a sudden it made sense to him."

"Well." He grinned. "Hallelujah. Pickup
truck and a believer. And he's kind of macho
too, like me."

She burst into laughter.

"Seriously, Kit-Cat, I could trust him to
take care of you. If that guy makes a vow,
you know he'll die before breaking it."

She thought of the vow he'd made as a
teen, to avenge his friend's death, how he
had spent his life fighting drug crime. "You
got that right."

"So bring him to Sunday dinner again."

"Daddy, I have to get to know him better
first. I mean, what if he bites his toenails?"

"Yeah, you wanna check that out. Or what
if he never watches baseball?"

"Or leaves wet towels all over?"

"You should talk."

"Hey, I cleaned my place three weeks ago.
What if he leaves the cap off the toothpaste?"

"Or belches at the table?"

In between their jokes and her dad's
channel surfing for a baseball game, Cat
drifted to sleep, still smiling, praying in her
heart for Dominick and her castle.

Twenty-Three

The chaos started first thing the next morning.

Cat was thankful that she had slept so long — all evening on the couch, then in her old bedroom through the night. She awoke at 6 A.M. rested and alert. The mathematical side of her brain snapped immediately to attention. The twenty kilos of cocaine found in her car had to be worth an unbelievable amount of money. What was the point in forfeiting that? Just to have her arrested? And why didn't it work? How did they let her go when, technically speaking, she *was* guilty?

She swung her feet to the floor and reached for the telephone. This line of thinking would go nowhere, and she had work to do. She dialed the Castillo and, as she guessed, reached Ron there.

"Cat! Thank goodness. Where are you? How soon can you get here?"

"An hour. Is everything okay?"

"Well, the place is still standing, and only two guests checked out. So far. Cissy'll be here by 9. I need you to work with the temp agency as soon as they open. We're going to need help in the restaurant and kitchen and — Never mind. I'll fill you in when you get here. Maintenance is covered because I knew Dom — Oh, don't say anything yet about — you know. Hurry." The line went dead.

Cat stared at the phone in her hand. Restaurant. Kitchen. Who in those areas would . . . ?

This was going to be difficult. Insanely difficult. They were all her friends. Weren't they?

She sighed and got ready. Her mom had anticipated her wardrobe needs so she wouldn't have to go home first this morning. Last night Mother had gone to her sister's. Although shorter, Annie was similar in size and had sent two outfits that would be long enough. Cat chose the casual red dress over the black business suit. She wanted to look more festive today to counteract the somber events that had taken place yesterday.

In the meantime, her dad made phone calls. He learned that her car had been impounded.

"I don't want it anyway," she announced. "I couldn't drive it again, not after —" She shuddered. "Between that stuff and

361

Trenton Carver — Oh! I'll buy one myself."

Mother offered to drive her. Daddy offered to car shop and bring her one to try out for a few days.

Forty-five minutes later they sped down the freeway with three new piñatas in the backseat, already stuffed with candy by her elementary school teacher mom who loved this sort of thing. By 8 o'clock Cat had slipped into her Jill-of-all-trades mode, doing everything except festival coordinating. She hired her mother on the spot as she stood in the courtyard directing a gardener in the hanging of the piñatas.

"Catherine, don't be silly." She attached a walkie-talkie to her belt, then accepted the clipboard with its list of activities. Her short blonde hair shone in the early morning sunlight, and her eyes crinkled as she smiled. "I could pay you for letting me do this. Oh, it's going to be a gorgeous, wonderful day. Now, where do I start?"

Back at her desk, telephone tucked between ear and shoulder, Cat studied another list while on hold with the temp agency. Ron had briefly filled her in on what happened yesterday. Twelve people had been arrested, most from her shift, along with the night security guard. Ron had written their names. She wished he had just written their jobs, not their names.

Kevin . . .

Terry . . .

Jacey . . .

Pedro . . .

Deanne . . .

Reed . . .

"Cat!"

She looked up to see Ron walk in.

"Don't analyze it." His eyes were dark sockets in his somber face. "Just fill the vacancies."

"But . . . why?" She pulled another tissue from the box in front of her. "And how?"

"I don't know." He propped his hands on his hips and shook his head. "I don't know. I do know they're not all hard-core. They just found an easy way to make more than minimum wage."

"You look awful, Ron. Have you been here all night?"

"No, just until they hauled off our trusted security guard about 1 A.M. With him gone and a few DEA guys still hanging around, I figured it was safe. Are you on hold with the agency?"

She nodded. "She's going through some files. I think we can get the kitchen and security covered. And I have Mandi rounding up her dorm friends to wait tables. Miguel's coming in early."

He leaned over her desk and squeezed her shoulder. "That's my girl. We'll get through this. Just keep your guests in mind. We'll sort out the other later."

She gave him a small smile, then shifted her attention as the woman on the other end of the line began discussing business.

A short time later Cissy walked past her open door, then doubled back. "Hey, you're here! I didn't see your tangerine gumdrop in the parking lot."

"It got stuck at the border yesterday."

She laughed loudly. "You get a flat tire or were you running drugs?"

Cat winced at her choice of words. "Oh, it's a long story. I'll tell you later. Did you get along all right last night?"

"Yeah, but it was one weird shift. Kevin disappeared. Then Deanne left Housekeeping without a word to Ginger. We figured Kevin and Deanne are seeing each other and couldn't wait until quitting time. Two families checked out, said they didn't like the looks of a cop car in the back lot even though I explained they sometimes cruise by. Now today Ron calls me before 6 A.M., says he needs me because first shift is short and he'd pay me double time since it's my day off."

Cat thought things must have gone smoothly last night if the front desk clerk didn't know any more than this. "We appreciate you, Cissy. All your extra efforts. Well, we've got a couple of temps coming in for kitchen duty. With the festival we need —"

"Good morning, ladies." Dominick stood in the doorway.

Cissy grinned. "Hey, handsome. You're kind of dressed up for maintenance, aren't you?"

Cat barely noticed his sportcoat. What held her attention was the grim line of his mouth, the icy look in his eyes. *Oh, dear Lord.* Things weren't finished yet.

"I'm just stopping by. Actually, to talk to you, Cissy, privately. Why don't we go outside? Excuse us, Cat."

She watched them go through her door, then out the other door that led to the employee parking lot. Disbelief rooted her to the chair.

No! This had to be a mistake. Another major mistake.

She rushed around her desk and into the hallway, then shot through the exterior door, crashing it against the outside wall as she went. In the far corner of the lot, Dominick held Cissy's arm. His other hand was atop her head, guiding it as she slid into the back of a police car.

Before he shut the door, Cat was beside him, clutching his arm, speechless.

"Cat, this doesn't concern you."

"Yes, it does! She's my friend! Cissy!"

The twisted face turned toward her was almost unrecognizable. Cissy's hands were in her lap, the handcuffs shiny bracelets on her wrists.

Dominick started to close the door, but Cat stepped in front of it. "What is going on?"

"Get out of the way."

"Dominick!"

"Tell her," Cissy snarled. "Go ahead and burst her bubble. It'll do her good. She's just a spoiled brat!"

As if the words were physical blows, Cat backed away.

Cissy's eyes narrowed. "St. Clair, you've always had everything handed to you on a silver platter. You don't have a clue. You're just a stupid —"

Dominick slammed the door shut, then brushed past Cat. Through the glass she saw Cissy turn her head toward the wire mesh divider that separated her from the front. A uniformed policeman in the driver's seat started the engine. Across the top of the car, she met Dominick's gaze.

"Just go back to work," he ordered.

"Tell me. I'm okay. Just tell me." She bit her lower lip.

For a moment the ice melted. "Cat," he said softly, "she called the Border Patrol yesterday."

Cat blinked. She tasted blood from her lip. Cissy had set her up.

"*Mi gatita,* there are 200 guests who need your special touch. Right now." He opened his door and quickly climbed in. Before he shut it, the car had sped halfway across the lot.

Cat stood alone on the pavement under a brilliant blue sky, wearing her sister's red dress, listening to the wail of a distant siren, staring at her mother's station wagon parked in her spot, hoping ten strangers would show up to help run her castle. Cissy, her right-hand coworker, was gone. Trent, still her backup until his unsupportive response yesterday, was gone. Dominick, the mystery man who had tenderly breathed life into her dead emotions, was gone.

It was an upside-down world.

Dear Father, please be my right hand, my backup, my healer.

After the police car whisked away Dominick and Cissy, and Cat flung her desperate prayer heavenward, she stumbled back to her office as if in a state of shock. The urgency of hotel management details soon swamped her. A kind of numbing fog crept in, swallowing all other thoughts and feelings, enabling her to function.

She pitched in at the front desk, in Housekeeping, in the kitchen. Later, as temporary employees sporadically arrived, she helped train them in each area. In between she checked on her mother and the staff who were running the special swimming, miniature golf, basketball, and volleyball contests. She smoothed guests' ruffled feathers and answered their questions. She waited on tables at lunchtime. She accepted unfamiliar car keys from her dad and sent her mother with him; they had evening plans. She smiled.

Until 4:30. "Ron," she yelled, "I am *not* going home!"

He walked around the desk and shut his office door, then returned to his chair. "Sit down. Did you eat yet?"

"No. Did you?"

He ignored the question and rubbed his bloodshot eyes. "Sit down. We can't both keep this up —"

"Then *you* go home! This is my festival, and you look awful. I'm fifteen years younger, and I slept last night."

"Sit down and talk to me."

Cat took a deep breath and sat down. "We're in good shape. At least okay shape anyway." She counted on her fingers as she talked. "The caterers have the hog roast under control, so the restaurant tonight is not a problem. Mandi's filling in at the front desk; she's helped there before. No problem. I'll handle the new security guard; he's coming at 9. No problem. So go home, Ron. I am not going to miss the breaking of the piñatas or the fencing demonstration."

In the end he agreed.

She stayed until after midnight, then drove to her apartment in the nondescript white car her dad said would be an excellent buy. In the dark she shook her head at his choice, too tired to know if she was amused or put out that he thought she would like it.

As her head sank into the pillow, thoughts of Dominick came to mind. Within a few moments, though, exhaustion took over, and it was easy to push him aside, letting the internal fog engulf him once again. She knew it was a self-defense mechanism, one she planned on clinging to for a long time.

Sunday and Monday were sixteen-hour days for her and Ron, filled with one crisis after another. Cat felt as if she were treading water. It wasn't until Tuesday afternoon that her feet touched bottom and she breathed easily. The last of the temps and applicants had either left or had been interviewed and hired. All the vacancies were filled. Tentatively anyway. She and Ron were in the process of setting up their own police record checks and drug testing.

"It seems a crummy thing to have to learn," she observed as she tore open a bag of spicy tortilla chips. Wedging toe against heel, she pushed off her flats, scrunched down in a chair opposite the manager's desk, propped her stocking feet on another chair, and bit into a chip.

"What's crummy to learn?" Ron pulled a candy bar from his drawer.

"To be wary. To not take people at face value. To open all their closets looking for a skeleton."

"Welcome to the real world, Cinderella." He bit into his chocolate.

"Why didn't we do all this before?"

"All right, so I had one foot in fairy-tale land too." He shrugged. "I thought we had it covered. At least we'll be more efficient now."

"You never told me. What made you suspicious?" She crunched into another chip.

"It was just an undercurrent, really. Whispered conversations that stopped when I came by. Things like that. A couple of fancy cars that didn't jive with income or family. I heard Deanne lock your door once when she went in to clean. When she came out, the trash bag appeared too heavy for your junk, even if it would have been combined with the whole building's."

Cat thought a moment. A question needed to be asked. The numbing fog that had kept emotions at arm's length these past few days now propelled her ahead. Since feelings didn't matter at this point, it didn't matter what she might learn. "Ron, did you ever suspect me?"

"Of course not!" he barked out of the corner of his mouth. He finished chewing the candy, then swallowed. "Cat, you're a thoroughbred. I know one when I see her. You've proven yourself over the years. Trent Carver's an idiot, but we won't go down that road. I didn't want you getting hurt if I could help it. It seemed best you didn't know. For the record, I didn't even tell my wife."

Not sure what to say, she simply stared at him.

There was a loud rap on the door, and Ron called out, "Come in!"

371

Dominick opened the door.

Before the hello was out of his mouth, Cat's numbing fog had dissipated, leaving an onslaught of emotions in its wake.

"Hey . . ." Ron dropped his candy bar and stepped around his desk to clasp Dominick's hand. "There's my man." He slapped him on the shoulder, grinning. "I haven't thanked you properly yet. We've been a little preoccupied."

"Same here." He lowered his large frame into the chair from which Cat had just removed her feet. "I see you're both enjoying a nutritious late lunch." He eyed the chips in her lap.

She lifted a shoulder, her throat too dry for words, then bent forward to guide her feet into the shoes. The plastic tortilla chip bag crackled loudly.

Ron answered, "Lunch, dinner, and breakfast, I think. Dominick, I can't tell you how much we appreciate you keeping the Castillo out of the newspaper."

"No problem. How are you doing?"

"Hanging in there. We're devising new hiring policies. Can you tell us what was going on, give us an idea of where we were so dense?"

"Oh, it's not that you were dense. You did notice some things, which is why you called us. As far as not catching on, I think it has to do with not looking at life in a particular way. It's not wired into your everyday world to suspect that drugs are being sold right under your nose."

Cat watched his profile as he explained things to them. He wore a white shirt, unbuttoned at the neck, black slacks, and a gray tweed sport coat. She wondered if he also wore the gun shoulder holster. His thick black hair was brushed back. His 3 o'clock shadow jaw was relaxed, the smile genuine with its right corner tucking itself upward. And yet in his deep voice she heard . . . what?

"The thing is," he continued, "it's important to notice things. If you hadn't called and we'd learned about the trafficking through another source, you could have been held responsible. It's called 'tacit consent,' and we could have shut you down. I'm glad that didn't happen." He smiled. "I'm kind of partial to this place. Particularly the paint job."

Ron laughed.

"Anyway, we're grateful. Your phone call set in motion an investigation that ultimately led to a trafficker we didn't know about."

She thought his tone was professional. It

373

lacked that unemotional ice he was capable of, but . . . it also lacked the essence of the man who had held her hand in church, who had kissed her while whispering about her goodness being contagious.

That was it. Dominick D'Angelo was a different man, one she didn't know, hadn't even met. If he cared for her, cared to continue the relationship, he would have called by now. He would have, at the least, greeted her as he used to — warmly. There was an obvious standoffish air about him.

Intuitively she avoided eye contact. Whatever had happened between the two of them had not happened between herself and this guy. She knew if she looked at him now, it would somehow erase everything they had shared. When he glanced in her direction, she averted her gaze.

"Cat," Ron was addressing her, "add that to our list. New waste disposal service." He shook his head in disbelief. "So you're saying they delivered the cocaine on Saturday mornings?"

Dominick nodded. "Around 3 A.M., usually once a month. They had a key to the kitchen. While one of them collected garbage, the other collected money and stashed twenty to thirty kilos behind the stockpots. Cat, do you want to hear this? You look a little pale."

"I —" She sighed. "I'd better hear it."

He took a deep breath. "You know the trash bag you sometimes found left in the kitchen and then would carry out to the dumpster?"

She remembered, of course. She had had to reprimand the busboy about leaving garbage in the kitchen. She also remembered that night Dominick frightened her; he said he saw her placing the trash in the bin when he was coming from the maintenance garage. She had wondered how he could have seen her from there with the fence in the way. He couldn't have! Obviously he had been watching her.

"Well," he said, "there was probably about half a million dollars in it. I guess they were changing their routine. You okay?"

"What?"

"Are you okay?"

"Oh, I'm just great!" She tossed the chip bag onto the desk. "Not only do I transport drugs, I move the money around too. And half the people I manage know more about what goes on around here than I do. Talk about dense!" She frowned.

Ron gave her a small smile. "Formerly managed. And for the record, it wasn't quite half your staff. Finished?"

She nodded.

He turned back to the agent. "Okay, Dominick, what happened after the stuff was delivered?"

"Westin, the night guard, would take over. He stashed most of the coke in the two turrets — in the restaurant and above Cat's desk. The biggest chunk he sold to middle-of-the-night visitors. Over the next few days Kevin and Deanne distributed the remainder of it and —"

Cat winced.

"And collected money. They kept the money in the turrets too. It was all just another part of a route that starts in Colombia. We were able to stop these small-time peddlers and trace the system back to your waste disposal service. That was a big break. It turns out they're a good-sized front for money laundering. By the way, someone will be contacting you. We'll need to look at your invoices from them."

"But where did they get the cocaine?" Ron asked.

"We traced only one small shipment to their site from the border. The trail goes cold beyond that. More than likely the Arellano-Felix Organization is behind it, also referred to as the Tijuana Cartel. They organize every aspect of the drug trade, even into our country. We're not allowed to work in Mexico. It's too dangerous because of widespread corruption; too many officials are on their payroll. The best we can do is what we did here — stop as much trafficking as we can. By shutting down the waste disposal business, we effectively shut down, for a while anyway, everyone who delivered to them."

"And," Ron added, "all the little guys like our employees who sold on the streets for them. I take it the Castillo wasn't the only drop-off point?"

"Exactly. It's mind-boggling to think of all the lives affected. Just imagine one scenario, like your busboy, and multiply that by hundreds. He takes his weekly eight-ounce bag, gets nine grand on the street for —"

"Nine grand!" Ron exclaimed. "Exactly how much money are we talking?"

"Well, that's street value. Twenty kilos are worth almost 900,000 dollars."

Cat swallowed. Hadn't Trent said there were twenty kilos in her car? Worth how much? "Why would anyone throw away almost a million dollars to set me up?"

"Good question," Dominick replied. "It turns out only the donkey piñata had the real stuff, and not very good stuff at that. So she probably forked over only five to six grand for you."

"She? Cissy paid for it?" Had she hurt Cissy that much?

"She could afford it. She ran things from the inside here and, umm, kept a close eye on you, Cat. She always knew where you were so she could tell the others when the coast was clear. And she was smart. She had bank accounts that took us a long time to uncover. When she called the Border Patrol, she described you and your tangerine car in about ten seconds flat. They couldn't trace the call. We suspected her and got her home phone records. So we also know who she called in Tecate to plant the stuff in your car, but that's in the hands of the Mexican authorities." He shrugged.

"Is that why they let me go, because it was such a small amount?"

"No. We just learned that tidbit yesterday. You still could have faced ten years in prison and a huge fine. It was because none of us work alone. When Border Patrol punched in your name, the computer red-flagged it. They knew the DEA was investigating you. So they called. My boss knew I was . . ." His voice trailed off, and he cleared his throat. "Uhh, well, that I knew your name in connection with what we were doing here. He had them bring you to the office, then called me in. From the information we'd gathered, it was almost a foregone conclusion that it was a setup."

"What if she had done it two months ago?" she wondered aloud.

They sat silently for a few moments. There was no simple answer. If she had been "caught" before Dominick knew her —

Cat shuddered, overcome with the magnitude of the sadness and all the confused lives enmeshed in the situation. "Why did she do it?"

"I think," Ron offered, "she wanted your job. Once in a while she'd come in early, flirt with me, point out your mistakes. She really got her hopes up when you were going through that time of migraines and so on and so forth. I mean, she had legitimate complaints then."

"She was jealous of you," Dominick added. "It's not your fault. You grew up in a nice house with a loving family, and she didn't. If she didn't know the circumstances of your adoption —"

"You're adopted?" Ron asked. The phone rang at his elbow, and he turned to answer it.

Cat laced her fingers together. She could have shared more of herself with Cissy. She could have taken her under her wing, not been so preoccupied with being a manager, so engrossed with Trent —

"Cat, it's your mother."

She stood and took the phone. "Mother?"

"Catherine! The baby's coming! Elli's at the hospital. Jim's flying in from San Francisco. He can't get here until 6."

"I'm on my way. Bye." She handed the phone to Ron and hurried to the door. "I gotta go. Elli's in labor. Her husband's out of town. I'm her stand-in breathing coach. Oh, man, this is three weeks early."

"Go! I'll cover for you. Call me."

"Thanks, Ron." Her hand on the door-knob, she looked over her shoulder at Ron, then finally at Dominick.

His eyes held hers for a long moment. Without another word, she left.

Less than ten minutes later she eased her car into freeway traffic, glad she hadn't been stopped for going sixty on her way to the on-ramp . . . thinking this little nondescript white car wasn't so bad . . . hoping the baby wouldn't come until her brother-in-law got here . . . ignoring the fact that Dominick D'Angelo had just told her good-bye.

Twenty-Four

The tight-fitting, dolphin-like skin of the wet suit supported Dominick's rib cage, making the sharp pain bearable as he paddled facedown on his board toward the horizon. His exposed forearms, legs, and face tingled from the cold, salty water. The early morning sun, still too low in the sky to offer any warmth, beat on the back of his wet hair. The ever-present wind and the rhythmic whoosh of distant waves crushing against the shore filled his ears.

Adam had warned him that surfing could aggravate his injuries, even push the crack into a full-fledged break that could puncture something. If he fell, as he always did, hard enough, just right — But Dominick had tuned him out. He needed the shock of cold water drenching him inside and out, cleansing him in a way, reminding him he was still alive despite that feeling of deadness he couldn't shake.

The board lifted slightly as a wave rolled beneath him. The Pacific was more calm than wild this morning, a glassy surface that he skimmed easily, racing alongside a low-flying seagull. Only a handful of surfers lingered in the distance, in that promised land where the "big ones" ascended from the ocean's depths, offering to those crazy enough to trust, the chance to walk on water.

A wall of water began to build there now. He didn't have time to reach it and so lay prone, watching its ominous approach until it towered over him. He saw the first curl of its snarling descent and for a split second he wondered what he was doing here, then dove toward the murky tranquillity beneath the crashing beast. A moment later he emerged into the foamy white aftermath, spitting out the salt that coated his throat and mouth.

At last he made it to the waiting area and straddled the sticky fiberglass, his legs dangling in the water. He gazed at the navy-blue horizon. Waiting. Watching. A dull pain shot through his right side, but not enough. He had hoped for continuous, violent waves, for the chance to push himself to the limit, to see how much physical pain he could endure.

He didn't know how else to endure the other pain.

Maybe this leave of absence wasn't such a good idea. He should be working. Not that his opinion counted. Smitty and Adam didn't know each other, but between the two of them he had a SAC-ordered and a doctor-ordered vacation. There wasn't any getting around that.

In reality there wasn't any getting around his exhaustion either. He knew he couldn't function in any realm, except maybe the spiritual. It wasn't like last December when he had hit bottom. That bottom was flat line. There was no way to survive without accepting a new life in Christ. This bottom was different. In a sense it was more terrible though. Now he had a beating heart, and it was breaking in two.

Cat was precious in every way. Her athletic, healthy good looks attracted him. Seared in his memory were the honey-colored eyes shedding tears over him, the taste of her mouth. Her practical, easygoing mannerisms always made him feel welcome, even when he was deceiving her. If she were spoiled, it was only because her needs had been met by a loving family. She knew what she had come from and appreciated the gift given to her. She cared for the less fortunate in a Tecate orphanage, worked hard creating castles for others. She was imperfect but real. And she was precious.

He had pointed a gun in her face and

brought her world tumbling down. She called him an angel in disguise, landed with her feet on the ground pointed away from Carver, accepted the friendship he offered. Then again he had pulled the rug out from under her when he told her what he really did for a living. While she attempted to get to know him, he was chasing down dealers, not fulfilling his maintenance responsibilities at her Castillo, grabbing her in the dark, and suspecting her once again of dealing. When they finally got together and began in earnest a totally honest dialogue, he had raced off, leaving her alone to clean up his kitchen and reach her own conclusions.

To top it off, he had known all along that Cissy despised her and could easily betray her. True, he hadn't realized the weapons available to the young woman, but he could have warned Cat not to trust in that friendship.

And yet, what right did he have to talk about not trusting? He had encouraged Cissy just enough to keep her talking to him. On that last Thursday night she invited him out, he turned her down and foolishly let her know that he cared for Cat. That, of course, had been Cissy's last straw. The next day she set about removing Cat from the scene.

Even without being aware of all the details, it was no wonder Cat was leery of him in Hunter's office. He carried with him all the world's ugliness, and he spread it wherever he went. There was no place for it in her life. He would protect her from it. As he had told Smitty, she was out of his league.

Water lapped gently under his longboard. No hint of a real wave. The ocean was flat.

He had two weeks to begin working Cat out of his system, let scar tissue grow around that wound that felt like death. At least he knew he was not alone, knew that God loved him, knew He had a path for him and was available to show him.

He needed to get to know Him better.

Adam had given him a standing invitation to attend a men's Bible study downtown on Saturday mornings. He had balked at the thought of mingling with politically correct businessmen. Adam agreed some of the group were that but said the leaders were different. One guy worked part-time as a government consultant, coached Little League, and hung out with disabled vets. The other one was a rock-climbing high school teacher. And then, he thought, there was Adam himself, who chose to do middle-of-the-night surgeries on the dregs of society so he could pray for them.

Maybe he should give the group a try.

The sun was warming his back now. On the horizon the sky separated from the blue-black ocean into a brilliant aquamarine.

Maybe it was a good day to be alive after all.

A bell jangled above the door as Cat opened it and stepped inside. She clutched a shopping bag at her side and looked around.

It was a big, old house. The small entryway was bright with morning sunshine pouring through a tall, yellow-paned window alongside the front door. The worn linoleum floor was clean. Dark wood framed an opening that led to what looked like a hall.

"Cat?" Megan Parker's voice called. "Is that you?" She appeared then, smiling as usual, brown curls bobbing every which way.

"Hi, Megan." She returned her new friend's hug and glanced down at her own clay-splattered jeans and sweatshirt. "Excuse my appearance. How are you?"

"Fine, fine. Welcome to my home away from home! Come on in."

She followed her into the hall. Voices and clanging dishes could be heard from the back of the house. The scent of cooking food wafted through. It was a welcoming first impression, an obvious haven for homeless women and children.

They entered a tiny office where a woman stood beside the desk, stuffing crayons and coloring books into an attaché case. Two small children sat on folding chairs, suckers in their mouths, legs swinging.

"Cat, meet Tori Steed. She's been interviewing me about the shelter, for a weekly newspaper."

"Hello." Tori smiled and offered her hand. She was attractive with sparkling eyes and short black hair tucked behind her ears.

Cat shook her hand. "And who is this?" She smiled toward the identically dark-haired, round-cheeked twosome who had the biggest blue eyes she'd ever seen. "They must be twins?"

"Hard to tell, huh?" the reporter teased. "This is Sara and Philip, and they're three and ready to skedaddle, aren't you, kiddos? I'm sorry, I didn't catch your name."

"Cat St. Clair."

"She's originally from your neck of the woods," Megan added.

"North County?" Tori asked.

Cat nodded.

"St. Clair. That sounds — You're not related to Betty and Stan, are you?"

"They're my parents. Do you know them?"

"We're acquainted from church. Oh, and your mother teaches with a friend of mine who goes there too — Kendall Zukowski."

"Adam," Megan explained, "is in a Bible study with their husbands, which is how I happened to get to be interviewed, for which I'm very grateful."

"It's been delightful." Tori hugged her, then hoisted the bag onto her shoulder and held her hands toward the children. "Let's go. It's time to pick up Daddy. Megan, the article should be in next week's issue. I'm sure it will draw attention to your work here."

"And funds, I hope."

"We'll pray that way. It's a good work." The twins chattered and pulled on her arms. "Good-bye. Nice meeting you, Cat." They made their noisy way out the door.

Megan sat behind the cluttered desk. "Have a seat, Cat. I'm so glad you called. How are you?"

"Well, okay. It's been a full week. Just when all that business was taken care of at the Castillo, my sister had a baby. This was my first morning to get to the pot shop in a long time. And I thought since you were

388

close by, I'd bring this bowl . . ." She pointed to the bag she had placed on the floor. ". . . to you so you could pass it on to . . ." Her voice trailed away.

Megan's face softened.

Cat imagined what a saint she must appear to the homeless women and children who made their way here. "I don't know his phone number or his address." She hoped they wouldn't be offered. She hoped just to get this bowl, this reminder of a special moment between them, out of her sight. "Anyway, I don't think we'll see each other again, so . . ." She shrugged.

"I think he's at that Bible study right now with Adam and those other guys."

"Oh, that's nice."

"Adam made him take some time off. I guess his boss did too." She smiled. "His other boss."

"That's good. I'm sure he could use a break. Well, I should go. I have to stop and see my new nephew before work."

"Why won't you be seeing each other again?" Megan clapped a hand over her mouth. "I'm sorry — it's not my business."

"No, that's okay." She stared at the desktop for a moment without seeing it. "I think we had a relationship for a particular situation, and that situation is over now. I mean, I never got to know him really. And what he does for a living, well, it's just a different lifestyle than what I'm accustomed to. And vice versa, I'm sure. So it's for the best that we, uhh — You know, he probably doesn't want this bowl either. Just use it here." She stood. "Well, I'm glad I met you, Megan."

"Same here, Cat. Will you promise to keep in touch?" She came around the desk.

"Sure." They hugged each other. "Goodbye!"

Cat made her way quickly out the door before the tears in Megan's eyes spilled over. The woman really was too emotional.

During the next few weeks Cat devoted much of her spare time to cuddling her new nephew while studying the apartment-to-rent classifieds. She avoided working overtime and made a conscious effort to get reacquainted with old friends. Many of those friends lived nearer the neighborhood she had moved from. She met them now in familiar cafes and in the church that was within walking distance of her old home.

Strolling through the familiar blocks, she recalled how frightening the area had become right after the mall incident. What she had referred to as intriguing turned threatening. The eclectic array of peoples and stores wreaked of potential for crime. The church that opened its doors all week long to the homeless then left her feeling insecure. The late-night busy sidewalks had made her frantic for a quiet castle in the desert, one with high walls, a moat, and Trent. When it became clear he wasn't of the same mind-set, she moved to a bland, safety-conscious place with double bolts on three sets of doors.

Now, with Trent long gone and castles too distant to imagine, she began to pray for an apartment to become available in the old neighborhood.

When the new front desk manager fell in love with the new second shift maintenance man, Cat drove to Cissy's apartment near the beach. She wasn't sure why she was doing this or if Cissy would be there, though she assumed she was probably out on bail. She had never been there before but found it easily with a street guide map. As she had both hoped and feared, Cissy opened the door.

"Hi," Cat said.

The young woman stared at her. She didn't look well. Her skin was blotchy, her long blonde hair uncombed. A loose sweatshirt hung over her shorts.

"Can we talk?"

Cissy twisted her mouth, then shrugged. "This place is too crowded. Let's go down to the boardwalk." She shut the door behind herself and led the way down the rickety wooden, outdoor stairway. She was barefoot, a common sight so near the beach.

"Want some breakfast?" Cat asked.

Cissy lifted her hands, palms up.

"My treat."

"Sure."

They walked silently the few blocks to a café that offered outside seating. Cissy did not bother with small talk, nor did Cat. She had a purpose in mind for this visit. There was no reason to smother it with fluffy chit-chat. They spoke first to the waiter and gave their orders.

"So, Cat, how's Dominick? Or is that even his real name?"

"It's his real name. I don't know how he is. I haven't seen him in a few weeks. He's a DEA agent, and I work at a motel, and I want a husband at home every night with me and the kids." She smiled.

"Like I've said before, you are one naive girl."

"I know. And I know that's why it was so easy for you to run your side business and put the Castillo in danger and set me up. But I forgive you. Is there anything I can do for you? Do you need a job?"

Cissy almost dropped her coffee cup. "Ouch!" She grabbed a napkin to wipe away the hot liquid that had spilled on her hand. "You can't be serious."

"I am. We worked well together. But you don't know me, Cissy." And then she began to tell the former employee all about herself, all the vulnerable details she had never bothered to share before. She began with her birth and finished with Dominick's gun in her face at the mall. Somewhere in the middle the waiter served the food.

She concluded, "I apologize for coming off like a snob to you. I'm no different, no better than you. I'm just a few years older and have parents who can more or less give me whatever I need. But if I didn't trust that God loves me, I'd hate you and I'd hate Dominick and I'd hate Trent. I'd be a basket case and angry and one lousy assistant manager."

"You hate me," Cissy scoffed. "You're just classy enough to hide it."

"I don't hate you. I'm offering you a job."

"How can you not hate me?"

"Jesus."

"You're crazy."

"No, it's supernatural but real."

"I don't want to hear it."

"Yeah, well, He loves you. Now tell me if you need a job."

Cissy stared at her.

"Are you addicted to any drugs?"

She shook her head. "I was in it for the big bucks. You can't deal if you're addicted."

"Are you going to jail?"

She shrugged. "It might work out I'll just get probation and one humongous fine that'll put me in debt for the rest of my life."

"Then you need a job. I'll give you one."

Cissy bit her lip and looked away.

"There's a catch though."

"Figured there would be."

"You have to go to a Bible study. Once a week."

She blinked. "That's it?"

"For now. We might have to throw in church too. You obviously need a new set of friends. What do you say?"

"I'll think about it." She stood. "Hey, thanks for breakfast."

"Wait." Cat reached into her purse for a pen and paper. She wrote her phone number and handed it to her. "I'm moving in two weeks. Call me."

"I'll think about it."

"All right. I'll call you. Bye, Cissy. Take care of yourself."

Twenty-Five

It was a Saturday, the last one in September. A Santa Ana wind had been blowing for a few days, its fine desert dust irritating throats and tempers.

It would have been a horrible day for an outdoor wedding reception.

Tucked away in the low-lying dry creek bed, in the shade of the footbridge, Cat hid from the wind. She also hid from the hustle and bustle in her parents' house. It was one of those, as her mother called it, bustling in-and-out days. Every family member stopped by for one reason or another at least once during the day. Food was fixed, spontaneous plans made, projects shared. And of course today everyone tended to hang out longer because Elli and the baby were camped in the cool family room for the afternoon.

She hid, too, from work. Ron was the one who insisted she take the day off, but she didn't argue. He blamed her cheerless attitude on recent events, exhaustion, and the Santa Ana. Had he realized it, he would have also blamed it on this being her canceled wedding day.

Cat didn't know what to blame her attitude on. All she knew was that the magic had gone out of the Castillo. Why? She had moved into another apartment in her old neighborhood. Fears and migraines were long gone. Trent never stopped in during her shift. Business was good. What more could she ask for?

While she hid for a while this afternoon from family, work, and wind, she recognized that she wasn't hiding from God anymore. That was a significant development during the past month. She had gone twice now to the church she found years ago when she first moved out on her own but had not set foot in since the nightmare. She redeveloped the habit of reading the Bible and praying. Her thoughts were often a monologue with God, as now.

Father, please help me figure this out. My life is full. You put me at the Castillo, and it's everything I ever wanted in a job. You've given me a wonderful family and good friends who don't fuss at me for ignoring them for months . . . quiet times making pottery . . . an outlet for giving at the orphanage. Why is it all so empty now? Why is it —

All right, she would say it, say the words she had been hiding from for four weeks.

Why is it I can't stop thinking about Dominick?

She leaned back against the earthen bank and gazed up at the iridescent blue sky. A hawk, its wings spread, soared gracefully overhead, silent. Just like God.

In frustration she kicked a grouping of small rocks, scattering them in every direction, smashing what had been one of her imaginary castles. She had arranged this one just before the nightmare. It represented not only a floor plan but the future husband and children who would occupy it with her, enjoying a lifestyle she was convinced best suited her.

She stared at the disarray.

You want that too?

In the silence she understood the answer, covered her eyes with her hands, and took a deep breath.

Okay. The castle dreams are Yours. No more opinionated, cast-in-concrete plans for marriage, a big North County house, three or four kids, the Castillo work forever. You decide. I'll let You decide.

She opened her eyes.

Help me let You decide.

She fiddled with the stones, stacking them, rearranging them.

And what about Dominick? It's pointless to

think about him! There is no future in that relationship. Not that there is a relationship. He hasn't even bothered to call. Even an acquaintance would call after such an ordeal. His lack of interest is rather obvious.

Besides, he told me I was too good to get messed up with him. Not to mention there's no way on earth I could live with his lifestyle. Besides, he's probably been transferred from the area. Or will be soon, and that one really is not negotiable, Lord. I won't leave here.

She took a deep breath.

I'm sorry. I know that You don't negotiate. I know You know what's best.

But will You just take him from my thoughts? I'm tired of seeing him at every turn, his strong face, his laughing with the Tecate kids, his playing basketball with me, his Italian at the restaurant . . . that red tie and black suit with his black hair.

She sighed.

His saving me from getting arrested. He is not what I want in a man! He just is not. He doesn't fit my mold. He's unpredictable, mysterious, and too . . . too intensely alive with his muscular arms and shoulders and focused eyes and unwavering commitment to fight drug dealers, figuratively and literally. He's —

There was a noise on the dry hillside above her. Someone was slipping and sliding, out of sight behind scrub trees, boulders, and sagebrush. Probably a niece or nephew come to fetch her. With the heel of her hand, she wiped away a stray tear. A long jeans-covered leg came into sight.

A very long jeans-covered leg.

It was Dominick.

He wore loafers, jeans, a pale yellow polo shirt. His sunglasses were pushed atop his head. His black hair glistened in the sunlight. He jumped down into the creek bed and sat on the ground facing her. "I want to give it another shot." Just like that. No preamble, no hello, no how-have-you-been?

She stared at him.

The corner of his mouth tucked inward. His gray eyes were soft and warm. "I did all my dancing around the bush getting down here."

Her thoughts tried to leap from his disinterest at their last meeting to her convoluted reasoning that she wasn't interested to his impact right now on her ability to breathe. "I don't get it."

"The point is, I haven't been able to stop thinking about you. Can we just start over and get to know each other?" He held out his right hand and smiled. "Hi. I'm Dominick D'Angelo."

His genuine smile cleared her head. She

took a breath and accepted his handshake. "Hello. I'm Cat St. Clair."

"We've met once. I'm a special agent for the Drug Enforcement Administration, and I mistakenly tried to arrest you in a shopping mall."

"Oh! *You're* my angel in disguise!"

He grinned. "And I've been trying to find you for about nine months now, to apologize, to ask your forgiveness."

"I forgive you. As a matter of fact, I *thank* you. You changed my life. Really."

"For the better, I hope?"

She hesitated. "I — I don't know yet."

"Cat." He took both of her hands in his. "You are so beautiful, so precious. And I love you. I don't have much else to offer. My faith is new, but it's strong. I've done a lot of despicable things in my life, things too horrible to tell you about. There are scars, wounds that may never heal. Do you understand what I'm saying?"

She nodded.

"I don't fit into nice society. I don't know how to be a husband or a dad. I'm not the least bit interested in a house and all the American dream frills. May I keep going?"

She tilted her head in a sort of half nod. This was hard. He was laying it all on the line and in the process was crushing those dreams she had just been trying to gently let go of. He was also leaving himself totally vulnerable.

"I'm getting out of the DEA."

"What! Why?"

"It's time. When my friend died, I promised I'd go after all of them, all the dealers. I'm not done, but I want to do it in a different way now. There's a new task force being organized, working with the kids on the street." He lifted a shoulder. "Besides, if the DEA transferred me to Timbuktu, how would you get to know me?"

"Dominick —"

"Wait, please." He gently squeezed her hands. "I'm not done yet. I've been going to a men's Bible study. Now besides Adam hounding me to grow, I've got these two other guys, Jade and Erik. And I need a date for tomorrow night. They're all taking their wives to dinner and they think — Well, will you go with me? That would be a good way to start, wouldn't it, to get to know each other? Did I say too much?"

She bit her lip. She had never heard him say so much, and it was almost too much to process.

"They think I didn't give us a chance. Cat, I promise to go slow. I won't say I love you until and unless you're ready. I won't even kiss you. I'll give you all the time and space you need. And by the way, I've already cleared this with your dad. No way was I going around his back. And I gave your mother flowers and chocolate." He squeezed her hands once more, then released them. "Now I'm done. If you say it's a no go, I understand and I'm out of here."

"Oh, Dominick." No other words would take shape. She became aware of her heart beating in her throat, in her head. An emotional tumult broke loose. A part of her laughed, a part cried, a part shook with fear. Sitting there on the ground, he filled her vision, and she knew intuitively that he could fill every nook and cranny of her heart, castle or no castle. "Dominick . . ." She breathed his name, her voice tentative.

He stood. "That's okay. I just thought I'd —"

"Sit down!" she squealed.

He did so.

"Dominick . . ." Her voice faltered. "Five minutes ago I was praying that God would take you out of my thoughts."

"I was in your thoughts?"

"Well, yeah, and I was tired of you being there!"

"Hmm." His eyes widened as the significance of the answered prayer sank in. He grinned. "Guess He told you no, huh?"

Loud and clear! She took a deep breath. "I feel like I'm on a roller coaster ride."

"I do too. Isn't it great?"

The only choice seemed to be to either struggle against that ride . . . or to fly with it. She groaned. "Will you wear your black suit? With the red tie?"

His laughter echoed through the valley.

She lowered her eyes to the rocks — her future — scattered under the footbridge. "I, umm, was just throwing out some American dream frills here. I think it's time to re-arrange my castle floor plan. Want to help?"

In reply he picked up a stone and moved it aside.

She knew he felt as she did. It was time to let God move aside old visions and replace them with His own. It was time for them both to dream again.

The employees of Thorndike Press hope you have enjoyed this Large Print book. All our Large Print titles are designed for easy reading, and all our books are made to last. Other Thorndike Press Large Print books are available at your library, through selected bookstores, or directly from us.

For information about titles, please call:

(800) 223-1244
(800) 223-6121

To share your comments, please write:

Publisher
Thorndike Press
295 Kennedy Memorial Drive
Waterville, ME 04901